I0543572

Valiant Lady

Praise for *Courageous Lady* and *Intrepid Lady*,

Books #1 and #2 of the "Lady" Series

"A very good look at Native Americas and their spiritual beliefs . . . I could feel that I was in Alaska with Leigh, and her interaction with other people and especially the animals of Alaska. Highly recommended."

—Shirley A. Sampier, "Coyote Woman"
Dexter, Michigan

". . . It combines romance, adventure, and intrigue all at once. A must read for romance readers and historians!"

—LeAnne G. Wilson
Alexandria, Virginia

"I recommend this book to any lovers of Jim Harrison's 'Northridge' novels, since this has a similarly sympathetic ear to Native American concerns."

—T. Parker Flanagan
Clayton, Missouri

"I now believe that my life can change if I simply have the courage to act. A great read, it demonstrates a spiritual depth lacking in the modern world. BRAVO."

—Hellmut Oskar Klensch
Salt Lake City, Utah

"Mark Allen North not only takes the reader through the wilds of Alaska, but on a journey through the wilderness of one's own heart, reminding us all with his eloquent writing that if we believe in ourselves, we can achieve anything."

—Robert Tiran
Carson City, Michigan

"I am your biggest fan in San Diego. You write such wonderful, spiritual books; you have to have an interesting life to say the least. I am anxiously awaiting your next book."

—Rhonda Mason
Escondido, California

Valiant Lady: Novel #3

A woman's Alaskan quest for Native
American spirituality

Mark Allen North

Fresh Ink Group
Roanoke

Valiant Lady: Novel #3
A woman's Alaskan quest for Native American spirituality

Copyright © 2016
by Mark Allen North
All rights reserved

Fresh Ink Group
An Imprint of:
The Fresh Ink Group, LLC
PO Box 525
Roanoke, TX 76262
Email: info@FreshInkGroup.com
www.FreshInkGroup.com

Edition 1.0	2010
Edition 2.0	2013
Edition 3.0	2016

Book design by Ann E. Stewart

Cover design by Stephen Geez/Fresh Ink Group

Inspired by the artwork of Frank Minnick

Except as permitted under the U.S. Copyright Act of 1976, no part of this publication may be reproduced, distributed, or transmitted in any form or by any means, or stored in a database or retrieval system, without prior written permission of the publisher.

Cataloging-in-Publication Recommendations: General Fiction; Multi-cultural (Fiction); Contemporary Women (Fiction); Cultural Heritage (Fiction); Action & Adventure (Fiction); Mythology (Fiction); Alaska; Alaskan Wilderness; Tlingit Culture; Native American; Wilderness Survival; Women's Fiction

Library of Congress Control Number: 2013948599

ISBN-13: 978-1-936442-14-0

For my family:

My children, LeAnne Gail, Gay Lynn, and Ronald Milton,

And their mother, Shirley Ann Sampier

Acknowledgements

Writing *Courageous Lady*, *Intrepid Lady*, and the last installment, *Valiant Lady*, would not have been possible without a great deal of help. Leigh's experiences could not have reached this form without the contributions of many people. In many ways, both obvious and obscure, it is a collaborative work.

I want to express my gratitude to the people who helped develop the "Lady Series" along the way: Dave and Becky Halverstadt, Shirley Sampier, Gay Lynn Redick-Cookson, Tom Redick, Denium Roman, Anne Arnold, Betsy and Bill Ince, Carol and Chuck Jennings, Dave and Kay Wagner, Chuck and Non Rycenga, Pam and Bill Gnodtke, Glenn Bongard, Lyman Jones, Janet Curio, Ian Lamb, Robert Tiran, Scott Detloff, and Henry Phillips. Whether through financial or literary support, they all saved me from the more obvious forms of embarrassment when I used words to express my thoughts.

I am particularly thankful to Leonard Gasco (full-blooded Odawa Indian elder) for his counsel on Native American customs and traditions.

For her inspiration, I thank Madeline Kiser.

Thanks to George Parker for his faithful support.

Many thanks to Francis S. Minnick, whose artwork inspired the covers for all three books.

For his contribution of many storyline ideas, scientific insight, financial support, marketing ideas, and counsel, I thank Big Brother Milton Duane Redick. He's my best friend and supporter.

Heartfelt thanks go to Ann Stewart and Stephen Geez of Fresh Ink Group for the file creation, book design, and cover design.

Ultra-thanks go to my agent and ever-present advocate, LeAnne Redick-Wilson, who managed and coordinated publication with Fresh Ink Group—I couldn't do this without her help.

Of special note, I acknowledge my friend, David Duyst, Sr., whose constructive criticism was always welcome and whose creative ideas enhanced the story throughout.

Finally, thanks to my confidant and teacher, Stephen Geez, for his invaluable editorial opinions. He's a mentor, author, and patient artisan of words who contributed immeasurably to the book's readability.

I beg readers' forgiveness for any errors in the text, and for omitting any helpful people I have overlooked.

Author's Note

It has been an extremely rewarding endeavor writing *Valiant Lady*, the third book in the trilogy that followed *Intrepid Lady*, released in 2008, and *Courageous Lady*, released in 2006.

The "Lady" series chronicles Leigh West's many and varied adventures in Alaska. Its penning served as a release of love lost, a finding of new consciousness, a restored life. As a result of this cleansing, personal feelings are interwoven in the design of the story.

Native Americans tell many tales about the relationship between animals and human beings; these stories are found in various tribes and languages throughout the North. The versions expressed may differ from others collected by scholars and folklorists. The seed that grew into a secondary story of animals interacting with humans developed from a combination of many traditions involving ravens, owls, wolves, bears, and, yes, even mice. Many are coastal legends from Southeastern Alaska, and the others come from the northern interior. This novel is not meant to displace or contradict any of the scholarly work that has been done by authors prior to my efforts. However, rest assured, characters and events of the episodes are products of my imagination. Captivating Alaska, of course, remains very real.

The cities of Juneau, Skagway, Yakutat, Haines, and Sitka; the Lynn Canal, Sitka Sound; and the majestic Tongass National Forest are easily found on a map. The proud and distinguished Tlingit Tribe, around which much of the storyline revolves, is present in Southeastern Alaska, as are their neighbors, the Haida and Tsimshian Tribes. Native American beliefs about the Natural World and its Creator, their god, Manitou, "the hero with a thousand faces," strengthen their commitment to preserve Earth Mother and Father Sky as the backbone of tribal unions to deter white man's intrusion into their land, including his "taking" policies. Native beliefs were constantly challenged by this intrusion which led to many bloody wars.

Finally the White man and Indian learned that the notions of "god" and "divinity" should be used sparingly in life decisions, since these are *human constructs* that may "limit" as well as "enhance" our understanding of life's ultimate source and meaning.

Although typical, the landscape in and around Leigh's hut on the clearing is fictional.

Prologue

Satellite images of Alaska on the far reaches of the North American continent show the southwest portion of the state like a skinny irregular tail dangling from a large kite, an afterthought of the mapmakers. They certainly didn't arbitrarily intend to take this sliver of land from the Canadians; it must have been based on political logic. Indeed that appears to have been the case in 1728 as the Russians sailed south from the hostile Bering Strait to the more temperate south. They established fishing and fur trading posts at Juneau at the northernmost part of the archipelago, Sitka, centrally located on the Pacific, and Ketchikan, the most southerly at its terminus.

After 139 years of overharvesting fur-bearing animals, lumber, and fish, plus declining profits and increased native Tlingit hostilities, the Czar saw the colony as a burden. In 1867 he sold Alaska (alayeksa, Great Land named by the Aluets) to the United States for $72 million. Considering it a foolish investment at the time the doubters soon changed their tune. Three years later, gold was discovered in the Yukon, and America's frontier expanded in Alaska.

Between the 1900s and post-war time, ownership of the Tongass National Forest was altered by congress by whim ignoring Native rights. Despite protests from all three tribal groups along the coast—the Tlingits, Haida, and Tsimshian—their treaty violations were ignored. Their traditional subsistence hunting and fishing practices were ravaged by the wanton taking policies of contract industries from the lower forty-eight. This constant abuse of the land and its people was finally resolved in 1971 by the Alaska Native Claims Settlement Act, giving the Natives a role in the state's economic future.

The first book in the Lady Series, *Courageous Lady*, chronicled Leigh West's spiritual odyssey living in Alaska's wilderness. Surviving the terrors of man, beast, and nature, she gained a new perspective on life while writing about her experiences.

She achieved contentment through romantic relationships, first with a local bush-pilot, then with a Native American Tlingit shaman. She loses both. She faltered emotionally, but steeled herself, determined to survive. Bolstered by beliefs learned from the Tlingits, she welcomed the comforting presence of Manitou, the Natives' deity.

Her most striking mystic encounters involved witnessing the personification of ravens, owls, wolves, and others; and at times she found herself unable to distinguish between the animate and inanimate. She adopted an abandoned wolf cub, they returned to camp and discovered an intruder, the brother of her late Tlingit lover. They bonded in their grief, but tragedy shattered her life again.

A rogue white wolf befriended her, presented Leigh with her cub, and a fatherly British DNR officer came to her assistance. Undaunted, she found comfort with the three wolves. They led her to a Tlingit Chief, Chi Mukwa "Big Bear," who invited her to stay with the tribe's Raven Clan where she became an adopted member and was given her own spiritual name, "Runs with Wolves." She and Chi Mukwa decided to live together when the clan chose to abandon the subsistence lifestyle and move to local towns for work. As winter's snow threatened the landscape, her soul still felt naked, and she wondered if she would be able to write her story while sharing her life with a man.

The second book, *Intrepid Lady*, follows the relationship of Leigh and Bear, two independent souls with thorns in their romantic bed of roses. As a Conservation Officer with the Alaskan DNR in Glacier Bay National Park, Big Bear reports to his friend, British subject Joe Bloom, and juggles the rivalries of the "three-legged-stool" of fishery, lumber, and tourism industries. Bear loves working in the forest and along the wave-maulded beaches, developing his knowledge of and appreciation for nature's role in the web of life.

Big Bear learns to fly fixed-winged aircraft, allowing for more aggressive interdiction options and for monitoring animal habitat among calving glaciers, budding flora and birthing fauna. Leigh often travels with him, leaving Wind Spirit, the orphan boy, in charge of the camp.

With permission from the Raven Clan, Leigh and Big Bear recite their nuptial vows and adopt Wind Spirit and Raven Maiden in a moving, spiritual ceremony by starlit night. Many of the tribal members join them on the meadow to sanctify the event. With a heartfelt emotional plea to the clan, Leigh urges the resplendent assemblage to drop by their hut at any time to enjoy the beauty or the Tongass. Wind Spirit becomes a DNR intern working with Joe and Bear. He also becomes romantically attracted to Raven Maiden.

The new family explores the far reaches of Manitou's Kin(g)dom and the beauty of the national park with the excitement that two 16-year-olds add to their exploits. They also invite Chinodin "Big Wind," Big Bear's son in Skagway, to visit the forest and share in his extended family.

The third book in the Lady Series, *Valiant Lady*, continues the adventures of Leigh West (Runs with Wolves) as she and her spiritual mate, Big Bear (Chi Mukwa), explore the mysteries of the Alaskan wilderness and coastal waters. With their friends, the French Canadian ex-Mountie Josie St. Pierre and Brit Joe Bloom, they share many experiences with the young men at the DNR's Delta

Station on Sitka Sound where Josie is supervisor. The University of Michigan PhD candidates at Delta Station—Matthew, Mark, and John, with, their beagle Luke—call themselves the Gospel Boys, or Wolvies (short for Wolverines, the school's mascot), depending on their needs. They think on a different wavelength, converse in French, and speak in a jargon rarely heard in Sitka.

Due to the Delta Station being several hundred miles south of Skagway and the park where Leigh, Wind Spirit, and Raven Maiden live and work, they must fly helicopters delivering housing units to Delta station, rescuing a downed chopper, fighting fires in the park, flying back and forth to Sitka Field and flying to Juneau from all three.

Leigh's life finally returns to normal as DNR Director Geez decides to establish a Regional Training Center RTC at the clearing and dedicate it to her. The Center will train new and existing employees in several environmental areas in an attempt to preserve the habitat of the Tongass and the ecology of the sea. All of them share their hard-fought wisdom, including Bear, Josie, Joe, Windy, and Raven. Its purpose and impact on the environment is heartwarming to Leigh.

As the original, core group grows older, environmental patrons can't help but think that Leigh has lain a foundation for Wind Spirit and Raven Maiden to continue the work of Runs with Wolves, the Queen of the clearing . . . Leigh West.

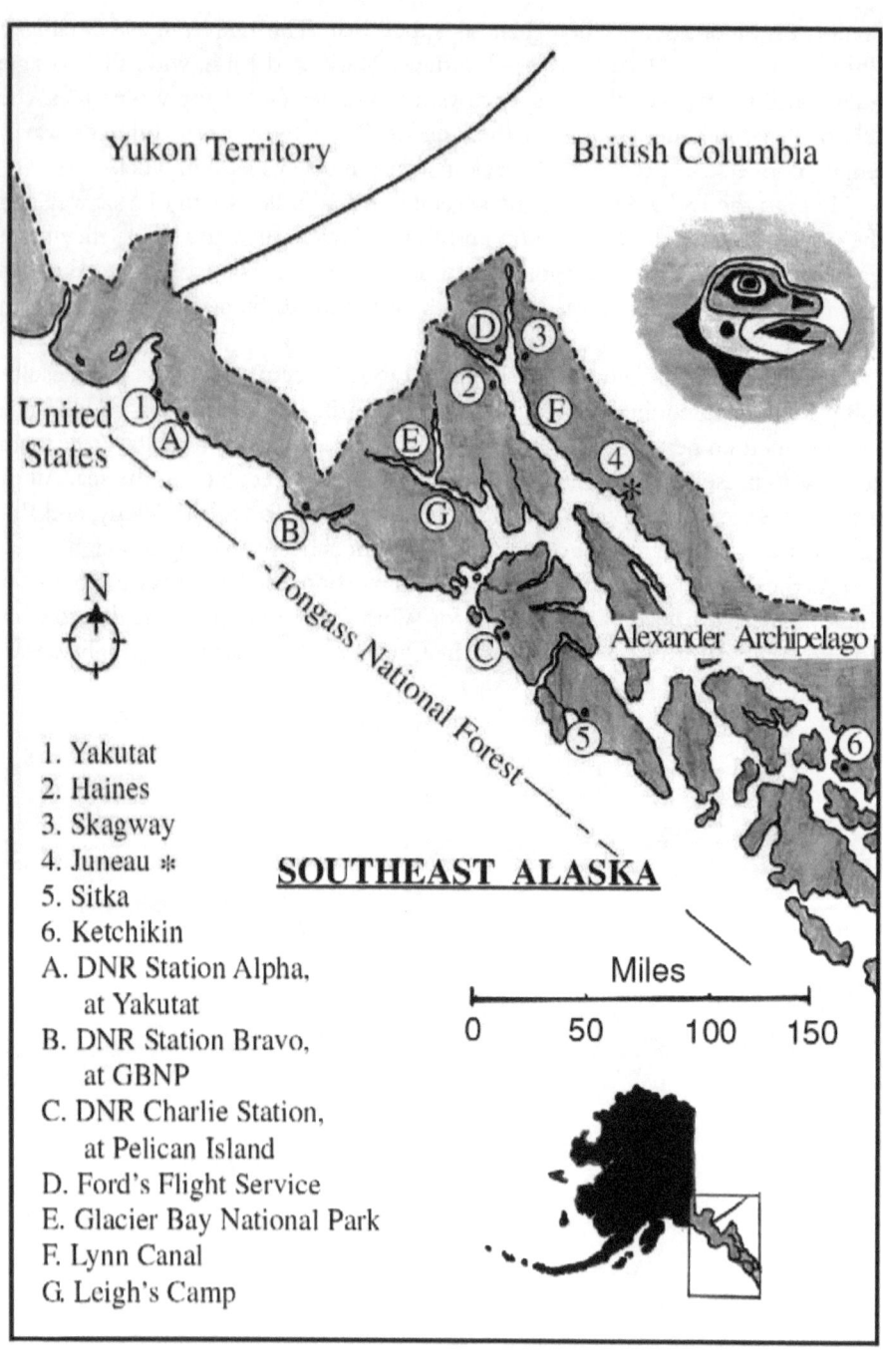

Yukon Territory

British Columbia

United States

N

1. Yakutat
2. Haines
3. Skagway
4. Juneau *
5. Sitka
6. Ketchikin
A. DNR Station Alpha,
   at Yakutat
B. DNR Station Bravo,
   at GBNP
C. DNR Charlie Station,
   at Pelican Island
D. Ford's Flight Service
E. Glacier Bay National Park
F. Lynn Canal
G. Leigh's Camp

Tongass National Forest

Alexander Archipelago

SOUTHEAST ALASKA

Miles

0   50   100   150

Chapter 1

Five miles west of Sitka in the Gulf of Alaska, two kayaks paddling together fought late evening waves in the bitter-cold water and wind.

Shouting over the sound of crashing waves, Leigh yelled, "Bear, I'm not sure we'll reach Sitka before nightfall, much less ahead of the storm! Something's brewing in the southwest. I can feel it in my bones."

"I can, too. I figure we're about an hour north of Sitka, and that storm is an hour south of us, headed our way. It looks like we, and the storm, may be entering the harbor at the same time."

Leigh answered, "Well, let's give 'er hell and beat it—and the sunset, too. It's no fun paddling these plastic tubes in rough water, much less in following seas."

"At least Joe will be on station to greet us," Bear said, "with a warm fire and a drink or two. Once we pass the harbor lighthouse, I feel we'll be out of this 'chop' and into the relative calm of the harbor. How you holdin' up?"

"Fine," Leigh answered. "But, as usual, the last couple of miles are going to be the hardest. I can't wait for the turn by the lighthouse."

"Hang on, dear. I'm certain old Joe and the Delta station crew will have a warm Irish coffee awaiting you, plus a hug from Joe's big arms, and a warm smack for your wet, cold lips. With any luck, we'll share a late Pacific sunset with Joe on the shores of historic Sitka . . . the first home of the proud Tlingit Nation."

"Okay, pal, I'll make it. But I'm damn tired of the salt spray stinging my eyes as waves break into the wind. I'd give ten bucks to rinse my eyes in fresh water," Leigh complained. "My arms are about to give up."

Bear yelled, "Hold on, gal. We'll be at the Lighthouse Point just as the sun sets; then you'll see 'da boys on shore!"

*   *   *

Joe Bloom, DNR Regional Chief for the Tongass National Forest stood by the fire on the windswept shore of Sitka Sound, talking to the newly hired conservation officer from Canada, a middle-aged woman boasting fiery red hair. As the new Delta Station Manager, the former Royal Canadian Mounted Police officer from Calgary would be establishing a fourth DNR Station at Sitka. This station would be the southernmost of the four which created a southeasterly arc that started at Alpha Sta. at Yakutat, Bravo Sta. at Glacier Bay National Park, Charlie Sta. at Pelican Island, and finally Delta Sta. at Sitka Sound. Located 50 miles apart, each station would be manned by a small team to perform scientific, biological, and other maritime tasks for the DNR and The University of Michigan.

Both pairs of eyes kept shifting their gazes from the fire to the mouth of the harbor as they anxiously waited for their friends to appear around Lighthouse Point. Big Bear (Chi Mukwa) and Leigh (Runs with Wolves) had left the DNR's Charlie Station 50 miles to the north at noon, in their new composite hulled kayaks. A normal trip in calm seas would take about six hours in their speedy new boats. They could have continued their trip by float plane, but chose the more adventurous route—the sea.

Earlier in the day, Joe and the Delta crew continued their flight from Charlie Sta. in the Ford Flight Services (FFS) supercharged Beaver 300 float plane. The FFS pilot, Milt, had voiced displeasure in flying from Skagway to Charlie Sta. on Pelican Island with two kayaks lashed precariously to the top of the plane's pontoons, but was delighted to shed them so he could fly unhindered by their aerodynamic drag on his last leg to Sitka. Milt was long gone on his way back to Skagway as the crew waited by the fire on the beach. Joe figured he would probably buzz the kayakers as he headed north along the Pacific Coast.

*   *   *

As Bear and Leigh rounded Lighthouse Point, the seas calmed and the wind subsided. They both relaxed for the first time since paddling from Pelican Bay.

"Bear, look, isn't it lovely?" Leigh sighed. "It's as if we've entered another world of calm, of quiet, of solace—a peacefulness."

"You're right, my dear: it's not only the Sound that's lovely—you are too, even while soaking wet," Bear said as he rested with his double-bladed paddle finally idle.

"Keep it up, love. A woman can't get enough flattery from the one she loves."

"You've earned it, babe. You've proven this afternoon that you're the best on land, and now in the water, too."

"Why . . . thank you, my dear. If I've any strength left tonight, I'll see if this body can say thanks. Somehow . . . some way, I'll find a way."

"I'll be there," Bear replied.

"I'm not pooped enough to let this beautiful day escape my memory. It's been glorious, clear, embracing, and just a lot of fun. Look at the trees in the evening sunset. They beam with vivid fall colors; the light through their leaves possess a theatrical quality. Look to the east. The smoke from a fire on the beach mixes very well with the pungent aroma of the sea. I've never felt so emotionally whole."

Bear responded, in a puzzled fashion, "I can't figure you out. Our butts are wet, the salt is stinging our eyes, our arms are about to fall off, and you feel emotionally whole. You're right, my dear, but I'd feel much better with a dry butt, clear eyes, and relaxed arm muscles. Let's head for shore."

"Oh, Bear, you know what I mean—I feel fulfilled."

*   *   *

On shore, Joe stood alone with the new manager; he had told the three crew members that they could take the afternoon off. He would stay by the fire and wait for Bear and Leigh to arrive. He busied himself throwing driftwood on the fire as an aiming point and a source of warmth while chatting about the harbor's beauty.

The new Delta Station manager, Josephine St. Pierre, finally spoke. "As someone who has stood alone on the darkest nights, I remember the quiet solitude that draws me to this kind of work. Whether the Canadian wilderness or the Tongass Forest here in Alaska . . . I love it. I've always found comfort and, yes, inspiration at night, particularly in the night sky. It is from basking in the splendor of the stars that we truly understand the majesty of creation and bear witness to the certain hand of the Great Spirit, Gitchee Manitou.

Josephine stood tall and solidly built, her features sharp and handsome. Her red hair was highlighted by the fire's glow. She was no Playboy #10 but a damn good nine. Her clothes seemed to hide a figure that would turn many a man's head. Her eyes were gray and captivating . . . focused as if looking through one's soul. She certainly was a welcome diversion to Joe. He decided, at their first meeting that, just maybe, he was not through with women.

Joe looked skyward, too. It was indeed a dazzling sight of twinkling stars in clusters tied to bunches, tied to other star systems within the infinite ether of the clearness found in Alaska's latitudes. Before he could speak . . .

"Plus cafe?" Josephine asked, meaning "More Coffee?"

Joe thought, *Oh no, here we go. She's always switching back to French.*

"S'il vous plaît," Joe answered.

"Voil'a, monsieur," she responded. Here it is.

"Thanks, h-m-m-m-m, this is good coffee," Joe said. "Hey, can I call you, Josie?"

"Sure can. You can call me just about anything that fits."

"Good. Do me a small favor; until we give the boys a few French lessons, we'd best speak in English. Is that okay?"

"Sure is; I'm just used to talking to you in French since I know your background. Remember, we've been together before . . . yep, no problem, man."

With a smile, Joe snickered. "Now you sound like an islander."

"Whatever." She giggled. "Josie will be fine, except when we're standing together. We'll have to decide who it is: Joe or Josie. We'll figure it out."

Joe smiled. "I can tell this is going to be a positive but complex relationship."

"I think so, too, and you know very well you do not like a passive woman. You've always liked a woman with a little pluck. Well, my dear, that's me. What didn't 'click' in Canada ten years ago now may. We both know that our clocks are running out of clicks, and I'm no longer a chick. Yes, dear, this will be an adventure."

Joe thought, *This is goin' to be interesting. She's got a firm hold of her tiller . . . and her bow is headed in my direction.*

*   *   *

With renewed vigor, the pair of kayaks headed for shore. The fire's bright beacon guaranteed them warmth and rest from the Pacific's chilly grip. They had been on the water for about eight hours, and their physical stamina was pretty much depleted. They were tired, but not discouraged, for as any athlete in a similar state would agree, exhaustion was sometimes stimulating, especially after hitting the wall and still maintaining the pace to the eventual goal: finishing the task.

Through on-shore conditioning, Bear and Leigh had trained for this trip. They had drilled extensively. Many repetitions of push-ups, sit-ups, and leg exercises to strengthen their abs had been beneficial. Bear had constantly reminded her, "No pain, no gain" as they wrung the softness out of their muscles. However, his focus had a tendency to drift when they finished doing push-ups together. Frequently, he rolled her over to the supine (face up) position from prone to satisfy his unquenchable lust. She resisted very little in his rough-and-tumble approach to love-making. She knew very well to save her words—"We do have a bed, dear"— since he was not listening. Mother Earth had always been his bedstead. At times she didn't know whether to punch, fight, run, or hug and kiss. Generally, it was the latter. Why fight it . . . she had said several times, for she had chased him down a few times herself; plus he was intractable in more ways than one.

They had made it. Nevertheless, they knew their next, and maybe most difficult, task awaited . . . surviving the surf's lethal forces as they approached the beach.

Leigh's mind wandered as they slowly paddled with the tide toward the fire on shore. She felt good in her new relationship with Bear. The trauma of failed love in Ann Arbor rarely crossed her mind now. She felt whole again—fulfilled— for the first time in years. Yes, she reminded herself, there had been others— Ford, Walkswithwater, and Walkswithwind—all taken from her early in their relationships. Bear just seemed so right for her. She took a deep breath as she enjoyed the moment. Moments like this rarely repeat in one's life. She embraced all aspects of her life: Alaska's wilderness, Bear's free spirit, their marriage, and their adopted kids, Wind Spirit and Raven Maiden. She reflected, *Who would think that in just one year my life would be turned upside down from a solitary task of writing a book about Alaska's beautiful Tongass National Forest, and the Tlingit Indian Nation . . . to marrying one of them and adopting two children.*

She looked up. "There they are! Look, Bear! Two figures by the fire. Whoopie! We've made it!" Leigh shouted to Bear over the roar of the surf.

"Sure enough, Gal, there's Joe, busy as always, telling stories. 'Da boys must have turned in for the night. Look at his arms waving and his body motion; it must be some tale."

"True, with his English accent and her French accent, no doubt their dialogue is entertaining. Now, my dear, do treat him kindly when we're by the fire. You know very well he'll be on his best behavior for Josephine. From what I've been told, they had 'a relationship' ten years ago. With her new assignment here, the two have been showing all the amorous signals only a blind person would miss. In short—behave. Don't ask the obvious. Don't say, 'Are you two an item again?' You know . . . be indirect."

Bear replied, "Geez, just like a woman to soft-peddle the obvious. You sound like a mother preaching to her daughter on her first prom night. Dang, woman, I'll be good. Trust me."

"I'm not so sure. I've seen you two together."

Their boats pitched, rolled, and ran with the crest of the breaking waves as they were thrown shoreward. The round-bottom crafts lurched and danced like corks as they were thrust toward the shoreline. They spent every ounce of energy to avoid turning over. Soaking wet, they fought to stay upright as the last wave threw them toward the rock strung beach. The last wave turned Leigh sideways. She rolled over and submerged in the billowing foam and seaweed.

*   *   *

Klunk!

An outcrop thrust the craft back to the surface. It righted itself as Leigh's muffled gagging cleared seawater from her throat.

"Leigh! Leigh! Are you okay?" Bear yelled as he struggled to keep upright.

No sooner had he yelled and thought he heard an answer—she went over again as the kayak hit a piece of driftwood on the shoreline. As quick as a wink, she turned full-circle and spilled onto the rocky shore.

"Leigh! Are you okay?"

"Hell, no! I'm soaking wet, bruised, and have sand in every part of my body. Yes, my crotch, too. Damn, that was a dunking. Thankfully, the helmet you *forced* me to wear may have saved me from a real head clunker. I'm just going to sit here a minute."

Bear fought through the surf and landed next to her.

"Wow! That was some show," he said, shedding the craft and moving to get her out of her boat.

"I'm glad you enjoyed it, dear. I can imagine what it looked like seeing me go 'ass over teakettle' by dunking and righting a few times. Give me a hand getting my wet butt out of this boat."

"Sure will, dear. Here's a little warm-up kiss, too."

"Why, thank you, my dear. I needed that. You know, you had warned me that getting through the surf at night, and high tide was going to be rough, but I never imagined it would be life threatening. Ahhh, that feels good," Leigh said as he gave her a big hug after getting out of the kayak's boot.

"Hey, look who's coming! Our shore party is approaching," said Bear.

"Hi, Joe. Come on over and get a look at a wet rat covered in seaweed!" Leigh jokingly shouted over the roar of the surf.

*   *   *

Joe and Josie moved from the fire to the kayaks' landing area. The pair had been tossed unceremoniously about 100 feet to the north of the fire.

Josie said, "It looks like they've survived, Joe. Then again, it appears as though Leigh may need some help."

"True. Would you believe it? She looks like a mermaid shrouded in a babushka of seaweed and small critters," Joe laughed. "I'll be darned. She's just removed a crab from her hair and thrown it back in the surf. We could use her for crab bait!"

"Joe, now don't tease her; she might be upset. On the other hand, I might as well save my breath; you two have been picking on each other, they tell me, for years."

Josie had taken a blanket from the fire when she saw Leigh go ass-over-tea-kettle. She ran to Leigh with the blanket open to wrap her up until she had a chance to get out of her clothes and get near the warmth of the fire.

"Hi! Thanks, Josie. I needed that!" Leigh said as Josie's arms encircled her and escorted her back to the fire.

Leigh yelled, "The kayaks!"

Josie replied without missing a step, "Bear and Joe will take care of the boats. Don't worry; we've got to get you cleaned up and warmed up by the fire."

"Hey, mermaid, where're you goin'?" Joe barked at Leigh as she walked toward the fire.

Josie cringed. "Men! I might as well save my breath. Leigh, I asked him not to tease you."

Leigh answered, "You were right—save your breath!"

Joe and Bear beached the kayaks, checked for damage, drained the hulls, and strapped the paddles to the decks with bungee cord. They hoisted the hulls to their shoulders and followed the girls as they walked to the fire.

In a crescent shape, on the windward side of the fire, all four finally sat in two pairs as Leigh warmed her chilled body with the help of the fire and Joe's grog, a combination of heated rum, lemon juice, and sugar. Leigh was uncertain which one was warming her more, the grog or the fire. Bear was warm for other reasons. His cojones were going through a pleasant twitch. He knew that Leigh had shed all her clothes and was sitting next to him naked as a Jay Bird under the blanket, her clothes drying on several logs by the fire. If alone, he and Leigh would definitely be having a BNR (bare naked roll-around) by the fire.

Under the clear, cool, starlit sky, the foursome chatted about their day. Of interest was whether the DNR was welcome. They were.

Previously, Bear and Josie had met with the city fathers of Sitka to discuss establishing the last of the four DNR Stations on the Pacific Coastline by Sitka. Delta would complete the plans for coverage along the coast in excess of 200 miles. Several University of Michigan graduate students would set up and operate the scientific aspects of its mission.

After reviewing the day's events, Bear looked at Josie and asked, "Do you know the background of Sitka and the conflict with my people, The Tlingits? Its establishment in 1799 and the Battles of 1802 and 1804?"

"Vaguely," she answered, "but I sure would like to hear the whole story personally from an authentic Tlingit, rather than a history book."

"Listen up, my dear," Bear said, with a grin on his face.

"Even after two centuries, the Battles of Sitka of 1802 and 1804 were fought between the Russians and the Tlingits, they remain intensely significant to the identity of my people, the Tlingits of Sitka," Bear explained.

Chapter 2

Bear proudly continued relating the fascinating history of his people, the Tlingits of Sitka Sound. "Sitka is one of the oldest cities on the western coast of North America. It is our privilege tonight to be sitting on the same beach by a similar driftwood fire on a comparable night as my brothers did many thousand years ago.

"We're located on the southern tip of Kruzof Island, on a prominence jutting into the Sound. Mount Edgecumbe, at eight thousand feet, towers over us to the north. We've asked for this exact location for our Delta Station. The town of Sitka lies to the northeast, across the Sound from this site. It is on the western side of Baranof Island. The town was built in 1804 on the same spot of the original Russian Fort and the Tlingit village. Before that the stockade was burned to the ground in 1802."

Josie interrupted, "Burned? For what possible reason? Why the apparent violence?"

Bear answered, "I'm not surprised that you asked, especially since the Natives of the area were peaceful and self-sufficient. Yes, there were tribal clashes between the Tlingit, Hiada, and Tsimshiam tribes . . . but they were infrequent and minor.

"The problems started in 1741 when Russian fur traders crossed the Bering Strait. The first thing they did was enslave Aleutian and Tlingit Natives on the Aleutian Islands, primarily to gain dominance in strangling the sea of fur-bearing animals. The otter and beaver pelts were in great demand for European fashions. After ravaging the Natives' villages and the way of life on the Aleutians, they moved to the east to Prince William Sound and Yakutat on the Pacific Coast. With the power of their guns, metal tools, and broadcloth—they continued the same destructive ways to the local Natives and animal populations on the Gulf.

"Alexander Baranof, one of the major Russian traders, moved southerly along the coast until arriving at this sheltered inlet in about 1792. He called the area Novo Arkhangelsk—New Archangel—now known as Sitka Sound. He made it his headquarters for Russian/American fur-gathering enterprises, and used the local Natives as his slaves. Well, that's not totally correct; he did exchange goods for their services, but in the bartering for iron, guns, and cloth, the Natives' compensation was niggardly.

"Therein lies the problem, my friends: enslavement. They not only pillaged the sea; they brought disease to the shores, raped the Native women, and broke their promises to this peaceful tribe of Tlingits.

"As I mentioned, by 1802, the Tlingits had had enough; the Russian fort was burned, and the Natives moved inland, to establish their new village fifty miles to the east on Peril Strait. Then they stopped all collection of sea otters. As an additional measure to keep all furs from the Russians, they blocked trade by all other tribes to New Archangel. After many lean years of fur harvest, the traders became frustrated, so they departed and stability returned to the coastal cities. Furthermore, the Czar of Russia was broke from fighting wars in Europe, and his traders were not getting the number of furs he wanted from Alaska, through depletion and lack of Native support, so he sold Alaska to the United States in 1867. Alaska became a District of the U.S. in 1900, and finally the 49th state in 1959.

"Now, I've talked enough for one night. Later, around a similar fire with matching beer, likeness in the food, and kindred souls like you, I'll tell you all the details of the night the Tlingits drove the Russians from their fort and burned it to ground. The chiefs made some very tough decisions that night, one being to kill all their dogs so they would not reveal their movements. There were other deceptive deeds that night . . . many that would try men's souls. As I said, later, another night, under another sky."

Leigh asked, "Before you wrap up, was that the extent of Russian's exploration along the coast?"

"No, they went as far south as what is now California. There still remains a beautiful Russian Orthodox church called Fort Ross built in 1812 on Point Reyes, located on the Pacific coast north of San Francisco. I've been there; it's a beautiful church with typical Russian onion-shaped domes, gilded with gold to honor their god. It has never ceased to amaze me that over the course of religious history some of the most wicked and violent persons are the most religious. Unfortunately, many clerics strive for power, dominance, and money, which frequently outweigh the positive principles of their well-meaning dogma . . . benefits of their faith."

"How true," Josie commented. "For reasons I'll never be able to understand, some beliefs, due to archaic myths/dogma, feel, as in the case of the Tlingits, that it was in the Natives' best interests to change their worship/beliefs, which were actually, for the environment in which they lived, more sound than their own biblical myths. Oh well, some things never change. We're fighting each other around the world, as I speak, over religious beliefs, many which fail the 'reasonable test.' It's too bad we can't reign in all this liturgy that says 'I'm the only one with a true route to God.' It's embarrassing to me, to think that some think their myth is better than another's."

Bear agreed, and said, "On a lighter note, let's get Leigh out of that blanket. She'll be dry by now. I'll help her get dressed. I'm trained for such tasks. Then I'd like to walk down to the shoreline and show you some of the other items in the Sound."

Leigh quickly responded, "Right on one thing, wrong on the other. I'll get dressed with *Josie's* assistance. Now, get! I'm anxious to take your little tour."

"Damn women, Joe. I bet my Tlingit ancestor would just grab his woman and take off."

Leigh reminded him, "Probably, but this ain't 1802, and we girls have a few more rights now. So, get!"

"Come on, Bear, let's grab a few beers and drift toward the shoreline while these uppity women primp for our nightly stroll. Yes, we're a beaten lot in the 21st century. Let's bugger off."

"Poor babies," the girls chimed in harmony, like the Andrew Sisters of old.

Bear and Joe fed the fire to provide more light for the gals, then strolled to the shoreline.

Bear spoke first, "Joe, those gals get strength in numbers, and brazen in a crowd. Alone, on any other night, she'd had let me dress her. I guess a little modesty is okay; I'll have a chance to be frisky later."

"True," Joe said, "I'm reminded of the poet Rilke, who said:
'When the wine is bitter, become the wine.'"

"Ha! Good point. I'll survive. I'll be darned, here they come. Let's drain these beers before they get here."

The surf crashed on shore as the four walked out to the Point so Bear could show them the features of the inner harbor, including the islands nearby.

The stars were so bright they made the sky look effervescent, almost daylike, as the four walked along the shoreline. Bear teased Joe about his newfound gal, Josephine, reminding him, as only a good friend would, that he had mentioned many times having sworn off women. Over the roar of the surf, Joe, of course, had a series of reasons, some reasonable, others completely illogical, why Josie was good for him—and him for her. After hearing all the mumbo jumbo about advancing age, health issues, and approaching retirement, Bear stopped, turned to Joe, looked him in the eye, and said, "Joe, enough. All these namby-pamby reasons lead to one conclusion: you're incapable of saying, 'I'm in love.' Go ahead and say it. Don't give me any more drivel about living expenses, geriatrics, and so on. Admit it, you old dauntless, love-struck, cuddly Irish lover."

"Okay! You bloody bugger. I like her a lot. Okay?" Joe called out loudly.

"No! Not enough. You old guys think it's a weakness to say 'I love you.' Well, my friend, it's not."

"Okay, I love her . . . I think. Bear, I'm just not certain—yet. You'll be the second to know. I promise. It's just that I've been buggered to death by lost love. It's never worked for me, so I've decided, with caution, to give it one more try."

"Okay, my man. That's good enough for me . . . Romeo."

That did it. Joe hauled off and slapped Bear on the shoulder, causing him to lose his footing.

Further down the beach, birds scattered as the girls danced along the shore, avoiding the foaming waves.

They both looked up as they approached the men. "Hey, Joe," Leigh yelled, "why are you beating up on my man?"

"Because he's a pain in the arse at times, and this is one of those times," Joe answered. "I've got to straighten out these Indians around here now and then. In my craw, he's been getting. I've just emphasized with a little hands-on friendliness—to bugger off."

"Ha!" Bear shouted, "I got you to say it—didn't I?"

Josie wondered, "Say what, Joe?"

Staring at Bear, Joe said, "Nothing. Nothing important. Let's have this local Indian tour guide tell us about his brethren from New Archangel."

"Boys, will you try to get along?" Leigh playfully pleaded as she grabbed Bear's arm and continued down the beach.

Josie snuggled up to Joe and followed the Tlingit pair to Lookout Point at the Sound's entrance.

As they approached the rocky edge of the Point, several otters dove into the surf. As soon as the otters reached a safe distance from the intruders, they rolled to their backs and gazed at the human forms.

"There goes the number-one reason for the Russians dropping anchor in this beautiful sound: furs. Whether sea otter in the ocean or beaver in the inland fresh water streams, to the Russians, they were hats and coats for the imperial fashions of Europe—yep, furs collected by the local Indians in trade for 'guns and butter.' I use the metaphor casually, yes, but you're all quite aware of how traders bartered axes, guns, and food for furs.

"Look to the northeast; Sitka's lights are visible at thirty miles on the western edge of Baranof Island as they shine on the lower clouds. Katlian Bay is to the right. Halleck and Krestof Islands are to the left. Both are barren, with only a few fishing shacks located on the safe harbors. Tomorrow, when all the work is done, we'll take the motor launch and tour the islands. Then you'll get a sense of the island chain leading north to Partofshikof and Chichagof Islands. Being on this promontory jutting into the Sound on Kruzof, our plans call for logistical and management support directly to Juneau a hundred miles the north north/west."

Josie interrupted. "Look, Bear, there go a couple of cats racing in the moonlight."

"Cats?" Leigh asked as she strained to see the colorful, dancing sails dart across the water.

"Hobie Cats," Josie said. "Catamarans. The crew from the DNR sailed their cats down from Charlie Station. They're out for an evening sail."

"It sure is an impressive sight," Joe said, "as the moonlight glints off the sprinting nylon sails; together they look like a rhythmical sea serpent."

Josie echoed, "Yep, the boys from The University of Michigan have been helping me lay out the camp right behind us. Wanna see where we're tenting tonight?"

"Tenting!" Leigh sighed.

"Yes, my dear," Josie replied. "Ford Flight Service (FFS) is airlifting three yurts from Skagway tomorrow. The crew have cleared the area, set the foundations, and made ready for dropping the three units in place. One is for me, which I'll use for an office and living quarters; the second for the crew's living/sleeping; and the larger unit for laboratory work, data analysis, and overall station operations."

They all walked back to the fire and beyond to the preliminary layout of Delta Station. While Josie and Joe were showing the layout's footprint, three Hobies *slammed* onto shore with hulls flying in the air. One, two, three . . . they slid ashore and quickly skidded to a halt. The jib and mainsail sheets were released to dump the wind. The sailors quickly scrambled across their tramps to release the halyards. The colorful sails of maize, blue, and maroon blew momentarily in the wind as the sailors hauled in the dancing nylon mains.

The 16-foot cats came ashore on one of the few areas along the rocky coast that had a sandy beach. This one was only 30 feet wide and, as such, was one of the major reasons for the location of Delta Station. The station needed beach for several reasons: access for seaside delivery; docking for pontoon aircraft; and docking for the station's launch, rowboats, and canoes. There was no other access to Sitka Sound. In fact, there were only ten miles of roadway on Baranof Island. There were *no* roadways on Kruzof Island where Delta Station was located.

As the boys pulled the cats higher on the beach and secured their sails, Josie continued the brief tour of her new assignment. Meanwhile, the three sailors quickly headed to the temporary kitchen with groceries, and a Native blanket of some sort they had bought in town.

"The crew is in the large 9-foot Pop Tent, we are in these two 4-person mountain tents, and, yes, I'm allowing Joe to stay with me, not sleep with me."

"Ha," Bear whispered to Leigh.

"I'll ignore that. You and Leigh are in the other one. The chemical toilet is up that path behind that old haggard spruce. You'd better look twice at dawn when I'm up there tinkling—I, too, look like a haggard old being in the morning. We ladies need a moment or two to put our faces on."

Joe chimed in, "Come on, Leigh, let's go meet the boys. They're all from the

U of M, but one is a native of Canada—me kinfolk. I'm just a little partial to me boy. Come on."

The four wandered down to the fire by the beach that had been invigorated with new driftwood by the boys. The partially-wet wood was steaming hot, as knots began to swell and pop in a staccato noise as they approached.

The boys were drinking local "Gold Rush" beer and roasting large links of sausage. Their earlier sail to Sitka was exciting on two fronts: it was a nice long sail with reaching winds from the south, and it was their first visit to town. Josie had told them, earlier to have a blast and get whatever they wanted before the standard DNR supplies arrived via FFS tomorrow.

Josie approached the three Michigan hunks doing just what most level-headed young men would do after a busy day pushing earth around for the camp and sailing their beloved cats in excess of sixty miles—they were eating anything palatable and drinking anything with a buzz in it. "Well, boys, it looks as though you've found something to fill those hollow legs. What's cooking?" she asked.

They all glanced at each other as if not knowing quite what to say. One spoke up. "Well, Josie, we have kielbasa to eat and an interesting tale to tell." She stepped closer to the fire. Large sausages simmered on freshly cut sticks. He continued, "We originally bought ten pounds of hot dogs, but a wave from hell attacked my cat and tore the box overboard. My tie downs failed."

"So what did you do?"

"Well, we all went back to the butcher with our sad story and the owner, Louis of Borbley's Market, was there and gave us the only meat he had left—a 20-pound box of his home made kielbasa."

Another boy spoke up amid the accompanying laughter. "Would you like a roasted one? We've got a lot: I believe enough for a week . . . or more."

Bear spoke up. "'Tis true, it sounds like a lot, but guess what? By the time the fly-boys from FFS arrive and unload the yurts, they'll make a big dent in that 20-pound box. Believe me, those boys will eat anything but the kitchen sink—and that, too, if cooked long enough."

The last boy spoke up apologetically. "Josie, we're at fault. We'll pay for the dogs that washed over the tramp and into Davy Jones's Locker. By now the otters, fish, and whales have had a good late-evening snack. Sorry."

"Sorry? Hell's bells, at two bucks a pound, I can write that off as chumming the fish so we could get a better bio sample of fish density in the Sound. Anyway, that twenty bucks is cheaper than the dehydrated fish guts the DNR sends us. See, boys, it's not a problem."

Josie looked at Bear and gave him a wink.

Joe commented, "Matter of fact, since I approve of all station expenses, the hot dog chumming will be approved."

All the boys raised their beers to the crowd and passed a couple to Joe and Josie, plus Bear and Leigh. All seven then held their bottles high and toasted the day, the station, the Great Spirit, His Kin(g)dom, and the day's happy outcome. The camp had been set up to receive the yurts, Bear and Leigh had made their hazardous trip with only minor mishaps, and the hot dog incident had been resolved. Life was good.

While all seven were drinking and chowing down, Josie said, "Boys, my disciples less one, why don't you introduce yourselves to Bear and Leigh."

Leigh interrupted. "Disciples?"

"Just listen, my dear; then you'll have the answer. Even though one's a Unitarian, the other an agnostic, and the last one a Buddhist. Go ahead, my men of the cloth."

Josie paused, giggled, and said, "Yep, Ann Arbor is a melting pot of humanity. You can find just about every nationality and religion represented."

The Canadian, Matthew, spoke first. "I'm Matthew, the skinny one over there roasting his weenie is Mark, and the bearded one soaking weenies in beer is John. There was no Luke—until today."

"Say what!" Josie exclaimed.

Matthew glanced around the fire, then focused on the new blanket by their tent, then the boys, back to the fire, and to Josie.

"Well . . ." Matthew stammered and stalled, "Louie, the butcher at Borbley's Market in Sitka, made us a deal today."

"A deal?" Bear asked.

"A-h-h-h, it's like this. A little beagle, apparently without a home, maybe a drop-off, had been hanging around his market for weeks, making a nuisance of himself," Matthew explained, "and he had to go. Louie was going to take him to the pound."

Mark interrupted, "We couldn't let that happen."

John exclaimed, "We needed a DNR mascot, a symbolic figure to bring us good luck, something to keep Josie company. She told us Leigh has wolves. Isn't that right, Leigh?"

"Well, yes," said Leigh.

"You see, women love animals."

Matthew chimed in, "Louie says the dog knows several commands: sit, stay, and come."

John spoke again. "And we thought the disciples would be complete if we named the dog Luke. We'd be the gospels with paws and tennis shoes versus sandals and togas."

Matthew started to speak—

"Boys! Enough! I do believe you have a proposal for me," Josie said.

Bear read her body language, tone of voice, and facial expression, all of which indicated she was not going to reject their find.

In unison, they implored, "Can we keep him?"

"Well, first I've got to see this little fella. I'm not agreeing until I'm eye to eye, even if I have to get down on my knees."

"Well, no sooner said than done. The little fella's sleeping in that Indian blanket over by the tent. I had to buy something to keep him wrapped up and safe on the cat. I'm afraid he may be a little seasick. There's only one way to find out; I'll get him."

"Okay, boys. Let's put a stop to this charade. Bring him to me. You didn't have to hide him; I'm not the Wicked Witch of the West. Your story sounds reasonable. Hop to it, you scally wags, you deceptive Wolverines."

Joe laughed, "All that, Josie?"

"You bet. I can see I'll have to keep my eye on these boys; hard telling what other ideas they've got up their sleeves. They've still got a lot of skullduggery left in their bones from their wild times in Ann Arbor," Josie said with a smile.

Sure enough, the loud voices and a good rest found the little fella sticking his nose out from under the blanket as Matthew brought it to Josie.

Once in her arms, out popped his muzzle, a pair of eyes, two ears, and finally the head of the hound.

Josie sat on the edge of the blanket as Luke looked around at the crowd. At first shy, he soon identified humans as fun and sources of food. He started licking Josie's fingers for the sausage flavor.

"Look at the little fella; he's hungry. Matt, get what's left of my sausage and let's feed this little boy. He's about to devour my hand—one finger at a time."

Bear leaned over to Joe and said, "It looks to me like you've got some competition."

"I heard that, you knucklehead."

By now, the entire group had formed a circle around the station's new mascot. Everyone had their fingers licked for whatever they offered to the little boy. Matt finally brought a dish of cut-up meat and bread for the little fella. Periodically he'd stop, give a little 'yap,' and return to his feast.

After finishing his bowl, Josie held the pup, who seemed more calm after his meal. She said, "Our boy seems a little thin. We're going to have to put some flesh on him—won't we, boy?" She snuggled his nuzzle.

"Josie, did I hear you say, *our boy*?" Joe commented.

"Josie, is that right?" Leigh asked.

"Well, I can't see any other option, can you?"

"Hell no," the crew said in concert.

Matt announced, "This is cause for a celebration. Another round of beer for all. In the Michigan tradition, it's time to sing our fight song. The boys stood and sang "Hail to the Victors."

Luke howled.

Spent, the mosaic of humanity drifted to bed.

The supervisor's tent had three occupants now, two two-legged and one four-legged.

At 0300 hours, all was quiet except for Josie and Luke. "Luke, you wanted to come out. You pee; it's chilly. Come on, do your thing. Ah, finally. Now let's get back to bed. Get back here, you rascal. You're a little like your friends, the disciples. They're slippery, too."

At 0400 hours, the temporary tent camp was quiet again. The only subtle sounds were the winds beating the sailboat's loose halyards against their masts, and the wash of waves. Quietly, a raven perched near camp as if a sentinel. It had been an interesting day for all.

*   *   *

Three hundred miles to the north in Skagway, it was 0500 hours. Milt and Dave were readying the helicopters and the yurts for the three-hour trip to Sitka Sound.

Chapter 3

Milt donned his flight suit, grabbed a cup of coffee, and walked to the flight line, enjoying a beautiful Indian Summer morning. The sky was clear and the weather crisp—just as he liked it. It was going to be a perfect day to fly.

As DNR contracts grew over the last year, Ford Flight Service (FFS) had doubled in size. Additionally, the number of downstate hunting, fishing, and sightseeing clients grew by leaps and bounds. Staffing had doubled, and administrative costs increased.

To handle the increased needs for construction and logging activities, a supercharged de Havilland MDHC-Otter prop-jet float plane was added to the fleet of fixed-wing aircraft. A used Sikorsky S-70 twin-turbine Black Hawk was also added for heavy lifting needs. It also had pontoons for increased rescue capabilities. The existing smaller single turbine Sikorsky S-70B Sea Hawk was rigged with skids. The skids offered less aerodynamic drag than pontoons, allowing the Sea Hawk to be more agile and fly much faster. The flight school was also busy: more than ten students this year had qualified for their Recreational or Private Pilots Licenses. Their ASEL (Aircraft Single Engine Land) certificate generally had endorsements to allow for flying: tail draggers (versus tricycle), winter skis, and pontoons (versus wheels).

As a natural course of events with Janet Curo, Milt's girl, and Morning Star, Dave's girl, becoming very close, the brothers made an easy but difficult decision and hired the girls to help at FFS; they needed good help to keep up with the added business complex because they knew it would be complicated to separate their romantic interests from their business operations. Their relationships were getting very serious. Many a night the girls stayed over in the sleeping rooms behind flight ops; but the girls did not sleep alone on those nights. None of the personnel at FFS said a word about the amorous activities unfolding under their eyes since it added to the intrigue of working with one eye on the lovebirds.

The staff enjoyed watching the old-fashioned, out-of-date fly boys make out on the sly in and around flight ops. Frequently at night the four would order in pizza, uncork a good wine and watch a movie or sporting event on TV. More often than not, they would pair off at midnight when the second shift arrived at ops, not bothering to drive home in four different vehicles to four different homes—to four lonely bedrooms. It seemed so "green" as watchdogs of energy conversation. It was environmentally germane. After all, the governor of Alaska had asked everyone to save energy; they were just following orders. Milt and Janet laughed many times about the staff watching them and Dave and Star.

While dressing and breakfasting they talked briefly about FFS business and the flight to Sitka; then he headed out to the flight line. Such was the case on the previous night prior to the crew's flight to Sitka Sound. Dave most likely had a similar chat with Star before he joined the crew at flight ops. The girls would join them later. Walking toward the choppers, Milt reflected on the risks involved with new copilots Rob and Ann joining him and Dave on this flight.

*   *   *

Rob was the number-three man at FFS and primary crew chief, and his new lady friend, Ann, would arrive on horseback from their ranch, in the valley, *The Lazy-R*. They, too, had developed quite a flourishing business of trail rides and packing trips into the interior. Many hunters could not care less if they shot a trophy animal; what they really enjoyed was the ride through the beautiful Tongass National Forest—and Ann's cooking along the way. They had a nice string of horses and mules that were hired frequently for rescue missions and surveying for local government. A stable had been built next to the airport and a couple of young men helped R & A Enterprises manage the operation.

Hearing a pounding sound, Milt turned and looked to the stables; it was as he thought, a couple horses racing to the barn. Sure enough, it was Rob and Ann galloping up the trail probably to see who was the fastest. Their summer help, Tom, Mike and Don, met them and led the horses away as Rob and Ann walked to flight ops. As a pilot, taking on the livery kept Rob a very busy man. He needed Ann in more ways than one. He loved her and her multiple roles she played in his life at the ranch and FFS. She was also a pilot.

Tall, clean cut and muscular, Rob enjoyed representing FFS when the owners were gone, but welcomed their taking a more active role in the business. Typically he'd rather install a part in one of the planes as to ordering the part from the manufacturer. Clerking was not his favorite assignment. He was shy by nature and rather be out-and-about than on the "blasted phone." His good looks were framed by a pony tail, wranglers, and boots. No one had ever seen him in a suit. Admired by all, nevertheless the girls said, when alone, one-on-one, he talked about as much as a fish. Many said he'd preferred to be with horses and airplanes, than people, the latter being less reliable. He'd always said that as soon as his finances improved, he'd return to college, get his degree, and manage the ranch. The folks at FFS were, in fact, shocked when he fell "head over heels" for Ann. Women were not in his earlier plans, a brood mare for raising horses, yes, but his own two-legged filly—no. Time would tell.

Ann had met Rob at school, in Juneau, during the previous winter term prior to coming to Skagway. Several suspected that it was no accident when she showed up at FFS the following spring looking for a job. They were like two peas in a pod now. Both at twenty-two and in the prime of life, they shared the excitement of living on the edge. Whether flying or on a risky pack trip—they embraced the challenge. As with many modern youths, they lived together for several reasons: to save money and to test their relationship. They had plans to tie the knot when the time was right, but both were very cautious in affairs of the heart. Each had been hurt in previous relationships causing them to think hard before kneeling at the altar. Rob's emotional damage had deep subcutaneous feelings that still lingered . . . his first girl's infidelity did not go away easily.

Ann was built like a ballerina with long legs and flowing arms and a walk filled with grace; she seemed to flow into a room like a billowing cloud. Yet, she was full of energy and could work side-by-side with all the FFS employees, male or female, and hold her own. Her long dark brown hair tumbled down to the center of her back, and deep blue eyes gave her a starlet's appearance that changed to a beautiful woman when she spoke. A Phi Beta Kappa, from the University of Alaska, she did not suffer fools gladly—all those who worked with her knew very quickly that she was a sophisticated woman of substance. A woman of contrasts, she was sensitive and beautiful, but would also play poker with the boys and drink the same straight Wild Turkey doubles while taking the whole pot with a bluffed hand of three tens. Yep, she liked living on the edge . . . with Rob.

*   *   *

Dave joined Milt and the FFS crew on the flight line with a cup of coffee. As the team prepared for the prolonged flight with the three KD (knocked down) yurts to the DNR Station at Sitka Sound, excitement filled the air. It was the first time both choppers would be flying together in formation for an extended period of time. In the back of Milt's mind were thoughts of the extensive variables for the flight. Three hours out, with the load, at half speed, the drop, landing, and the shorter unencumbered flight back to base.

After deciding the sling should have at least a 40-foot line, with a bungee cord loop, to the chopper, he was still concerned how flight velocity and wind conditions would affect the pendulous nature of the load. He wondered if it would hold steady, as expected, or rotate in a circular fashion—or worse yet swing sideways or fore and aft . . . time would tell. He could make some adjustments to ensure dead-hang below the chopper, but was still worried.

He was also concerned about the sometimes treacherous winds coming off the Pacific as they lowered the units at the Delta site.

Then there were the crew personnel issues: many were new. For the first time in years, Milt and Dave were in different aircraft with new copilots, Rob with Milt and Ann with Dave. They both were certified and talented, but they had never flown together on an assignment—only in training. However, as Pilot-in-Command, both felt comfortable, but cautious.

Since the girls wanted to see the gang at Delta Station, Milt and Dave had agreed to have Janet and Morning Star serve as crew chief and be responsible for releasing the sling attached to the chopper at the proper time. Disconnecting the load at the right time required good vision at the site and the proper communication to the pilot. Both pilots were certain that they could handle the task. Morning Star would fly with Dave, Janet with Milt. Each would be responsible for releasing the sling/line from the chopper at the exact time. They would be restrained, but also leaning out the side door at the site. Good communications and vision were essential for a safe drop. Milt made her aware of the chopper's vertical leap into the air as the load was released. The sudden rise was manageable from the cockpit—if—the pilot knew exactly when the load dropped.

Milt knew and Dave was also aware that for a successful drop, and return, rookies were not always a negative. Milt mentioned the real variable would be the same problem all Alaskan flyers face: bad weather. At Skagway it was a beautiful day; he hoped it was the same at the Sound in three hours. Milt was well aware that any flight plan was not cast in concrete and may change at a moment's notice as weather conditions dictate.

The ground crew finished all preflight tasks on both choppers, and both PIC's checked the slings around the KD yurts. The two smaller yurts were lashed together as one, the larger similarly tied. The big bird would take the heavier double package. At sixty feet apart on the runway, the loads were ready for hook up and flight.

Janet and Morning Star joined the group with some supplies and treats for the Delta team, and stowed them onboard. The briefing was short and to the point, for they had all rehearsed their tasks earlier. Milt repeated, the keys to a successful drop were timely and accurate communications from the crew chief to the PIC and to Josie on the ground. The crews separated and rendezvoused at their choppers, Milt, Rob, and Janet at the big Black Hawk; Dave, Ann and Star at the Sea Hawk. They checked out the commo links and their plans one last time. One of the wranglers, Mike, joined them; he would be hooking up the sling with its forty foot tie line. As in a team break, they raised and joined hands, and hollered: "Let's go!"

After the crew was in place, Milt powered up, and announced over the radio, "FFS control, Alpha number One, and Alpha number Two, using A-1 and A-2 for commo brevity, we are ready for liftoff; how do you read me, A-2, how do you read me? Over."

"This A-2, we read you loud and clear, how me? Over."

"Five by five A-1. Break. Break. FFS control, how do you read us? Over."

Tom, at ops, answered, "FFS Control, I hear both of you loud and clear. Per our plan, I'll monitor this frequency for the entire flight signing off only when you land or call. Roger?"

"Roger, wilco, yes, I'll make contact upon arrival—and departure. Nothing further, out."

"Roger that, we'll keep the home fires burning, out."

"A-2, this A-1. Over."

"This is A-2. Over."

"Hey, Dave, we're about to launch this bird; are you guys ready? Over."

"Sure enough. Ann and I have just finished checking commo; we too are ready to launch. By the way, tell your copilot, Rob, that it looks like I've got the better deal on *looks* for a copilot. Ann's charm radiates to the cabin compared to that dull 'old Rob' you've got sitting on your left . . . I'll let you know when I'm airborne. Over."

"Enough, my man; enough of your repartee. Let me know when you're airborne."

"Roger that. Have a good flight."

*   *   *

The crew on A-2 watched as the Black Hawk's twin turbines screamed to full power, lifted, hovered, then slowly descended for sling engagement, then rose slowly until the sling was taut, then continued lifting until the pair of yurts were clear of the ground and moved slowly in a southerly direction.

The sling hook up team of Mike and Don ran over to the Sea Hawk and gave the high sign when they were ready and repeated the same sequence with the sling. Upon completion of the attachment the Sea Hawk hovered and moved toward the runway. The ground crew looked up and gave a handholding "Go Blue," and within minutes the two hovered together for their long flight.

When Alpha Two was in formation, Dave informed Milt and the pair of choppers flew in tandem while climbing to cruise height, at an azimuth of 165 degrees south by south/west. Flight separation distance was one mile, elevation 1,000 feet, airspeed was 60 knots (69 mph) which kept the load's deflection aft on the sling line at about 30 degrees from vertical. To reduce drag and deflection, the ground crew had wrapped the yurts in heat-shrunk white plastic. Milt and Dave chose to ignore some of the salacious sayings the crew had written to Joe and Bear . . .

Boys will be boys.

*   *   *

As the flight cleared Skagway and headed over Lynn Canal, Mike and Don returned to ops and monitored the flight with Tom who was working on station.

Tom greeted the boys as they entered. "It looks like we've got ourselves a mission, boys; I think it's kinda exciting. I sure wish them Godspeed and a safe return. How 'bout giving me a break? I'll take a nap. Remember, we'll need to monitor their mission 24/7 for the next two or three days. See ya."

Don took over the FFS network while reading Courageous Lady, a novel about Alaska's majestic and mysterious Tongass National Forest and Native American spirituality.

*   *   *

Milt and Ann flew south over the Lynn Canal in accordance with the flight plan. If they had *any* problems, the shoreline would provide a clear area to touch down. The rotor blades needed a minimum of 150 feet of horizontal clearance for the bird to land safely. Conversely, the Tongass did not provide any emergency landing sites . . . especially if the tail rotor jammed and the bird was auto-gyrotating uncontrollably to the ground.

Milt reviewed their route ahead along the west side of Admiralty Island, over the Chatham Strait to the island's tip where they would turn west by southwest at an azimuth of 190 degrees over Baranof Island. The 25 miles over Baranof would be the most risky since there would be no emergency landing site. As with most of the Alexander Archipelago, the landscape was a combination of tall timber, lava outcrops, and wet sink holes.

Upon reaching Sitka on the east side of the Sound, they should have visual contact with the DNR station on a promontory jutting out from Kruzof Island. An additional aiming point would be Mount Edgecumbe, rising 8,000-feet directly behind the station to the north. If weathered in, it appeared that there would be several visual references around the station.

*   *   *

An hour into the flight, Milt rotated his Intercom (IC) select switch to on. "How are you doing, Janet, my fearless crew chief?"

"I thought you'd never ask. Darn good, actually. Well, I was a little airsick at first. The vibration and elevation kinda got to me, but when I looked out the window, to get a reference point, I felt better. The scenery is beautiful. I feel a lot better," she replied. "How are things up on the flight deck?"

"Fine. However, Rob is checking on some, troubling weather conditions developing on the Pacific Coast. It appears that a low-pressure cell is moving to the east in the direction of our flight path. With any luck, we'll be there before it arrives at Sitka. I know it's hard on you to fly slow, but I dare not go over 60 knots, and right now the various parts of the craft are not vibrating at the optimum cycles per second. In other words, like the vibration of guitar strings . . . they are not at harmonic resonance. Our bird is either 'flat' or 'sharp' in musical terms. On the way back I'll show you, this old bird sounds 'sweet' when flying at 80 to 90 knots. Then she starts humming . . . why she'll sound even sweeter than my Sigma Tau Gamma brothers, singing 'Red Sails in the Sunset.' Real sweet."

"That's a deal," Janet replied. "However, I've never heard any of you men sound . . . real sweet."

"That hurt. What do you say, Rob? Don't you and your frat boys sound sweet?"

"No comment," Rob replied. "If all the brothers sang to her, after being 'pinned' while under a moonlit sky, with candle light . . . I know she'd swoon.

"By the way, the FAA has just issued a storm warning to all aircraft flying north of Prince Wales to Yakutat. It sounds like it is dumping a lot of rain and wind. The warning is also on the automated FSS (Flight Service station). I'll keep monitoring the broadcasts."

Having heard Rob, Janet asked, "Is there a problem? Have you talked to Dave?"

"Actually . . . no. We're both monitoring the same channels, and touch base periodically, but having submitted a flight plan to FAA in Juneau, as a commercial cargo flight, we are under FAA security rules. We transmit only for official needs, meaning minimum personal chatter. They are monitoring our transmissions during the entire flight from several locations until we return to Skagway. Kinda nice, isn't it? FFS, FAA, FSS, and Josie at Delta Station are all listening in."

Janet responded, "Damn, it sounds like you fly boys don't take any chances."

"That's one way to look at it, but consider this: you are in a heavier-than-air helicopter whose motor has to *operate flawlessly* for us to stay airborne, and everything that man makes *sooner or later* fails. Besides that, you're about to fly into a storm front. What say you about that? Just kidding, Janet. We'll be okay."

Janet continued on the IC with a little nervousness in her voice, "That's almost too much information, but thanks . . . I think. You sounded like my 90 year-old aunt who is constantly describing her aches and pains . . . her lumbago, or whatever. She always gave me *too* much information. No sweat, I'll be okay, thanks . . . I think."

Janet fastened her seat belt and reflected on the risks associated with this flight. *I hadn't thought about the variables facing a cargo flight. I've flown a lot with Milt and Dave, but that has always been for pleasure without the schedule constraints or concern for hazardous weather conditions. This is entirely different. Thank goodness FFS has good equipment and the best personnel. Jan, don't worry, so much . . . they will make it. Nevertheless, I would like to talk to Morning Star, but that's apparently not going to happen.*

Then from the IC, "Jan, better fasten your seatbelt. There's some thermals below causing a little bump now and then. Roger that?"

"Roger. My butt is now secure."

*   *   *

Dave's chopper, Alpha Two, followed Milt at about a half-mile separation, close enough to observe, yet far enough back to escape turbulence. Dave and Ann had been monitoring Milt's and Rob's transmissions so they, too, were aware of the low-pressure cell moving into the Sitka area.

"Say, Ann, let's check on our crew chief. I have a feeling Star's unaware of the intercom. Go ahead, give her a call," Dave urged.

Ann reached to the control panel, threw the IC switch, and said, "Hello there! Anybody home? We were wondering up here if you're doin' okay."

Star responded, "Oh . . . ah . . . let's see, yes, I'm doing fine. I've been looking out the window and enjoying the scenery below. I've never had a chance to appreciate the archipelago at this lower altitude and slower speed. Most of the time Dave flies over the area, we're at a higher elevation and faster speed. This is wonderful . . . I love it! Are we on schedule?"

Ann answered, "Yep, right on time. We'll be leaving the southern portion of the Lynn Canal soon and passing over the northern tip or Admiralty Island at the confluence of Peril Strait."

"Great! How's that fly guy in the right seat doin'? Is he in control of this flight?" Star teased.

"Why don't you ask him? We're all on the same IC."

"Oh . . . I'm glad I didn't talk about him. I thought it was just us girls on the line."

"Ha, so I almost heard what you *really* think about me?" Dave interrupted. "How are you doing?"

"Fine. I have noticed a little more vibration with you flying slow. You've always told me that each aircraft has its own frequency or harmonic where everything vibrates in sync. That we ain't . . . right now."

"True, dear. Well if it's of any help to you, we're a third of the way there now, and it won't be much longer. On the way home, we'll be bookin' and find the, harmonic of all this sheetmetal."

"Good, Dave. Thanks for checking on me. Maybe we can talk again when we make our turn at Baranof Island."

"Deal. Talk to you later."

*   *   *

At 75 miles inland, the radar on the flight deck of Alpha One showed the storm front moving across the Pacific to the west at 20 mph and shifting to the northwest. Juneau ATC (Air Traffic Control) had alerted all aircraft in the storm's path. As the pair flew south along the west edge of Admiralty Island, it became very clear that based on the speed of both the storm and the choppers, there would be a competitive race for the aircraft to land before the storm slammed into the coast.

Milt and Dave discussed the ATC notice and the changing conditions at the landing site, then considered three options.

One would be to abort the flight when it appeared too hazardous to land.

Another would be to land at their alternate site on Admiralty Island.

The final option would be to continue the flight and hope that winds were less than 25 mph, fog did not restrict vision, and the rain was not blinding. Josie had a strobe light for just such occasions, and both choppers had radar.

Milt decided to initiate a conference call and see how the whole group felt about their options.

"Alpha Two, this is Milt. Let's all six of us talk about our options. Over."

"This is Alpha Two. Roger your request. I've switched the IC on so we can all participate. Over."

"Roger, likewise here. These are our options, folks."

Milt went over the three options as they flew southward without any change in the flight plan. They all gave their opinions and debated the risk factors of continuing to fly aided by radar versus significantly reduced vision; an abort versus increased winds over 25 mph; and Josie's support with her landing light and radio versus extreme vision problems at Sitka.

They did develop a logical fourth option: drop the yurts and return to base or land at an alternate site near Sitka until the storm cleared.

Finally, Milt took over the discussion and said, "This discourse was well worth our time; you guys have come up with a winner. I'm in favor of option four. I know both of us can drop our loads, which by the way is the primary reason for this flight, and we can find a landing site in the area until we're able to land at Delta Station. Good show, folks. I'll contact Josie with our plan so she'll be prepared. However, remember this: we are still going to drop our loads and land per our primary mission—unless on site conditions say otherwise. It sounds like we've got a consensus. Any objections? Let me know as I call your name. Rob?"

"No."

"Ann?"

"No."

"Janet?"

"No."

"Star?"

"No."

"How's that for being democratic? Since we have no objections, we'll continue on our original flight plan. If you wonder why I didn't ask Dave, he already voted, and was aligned with all of you."

Confident they had made the correct decision, the choppers moved along Admiralty Island with an anxious-yet-determined crew.

Were they not similar to the Tlingit warriors who followed Chief K'alyaan as he led his people toward the Russian Fort at New Archangel in 1802? No, not in this case to destroy the evil traders. Nevertheless, this crew was just as determined to achieve their goal.

Chapter 4

After her last walk with Luke, Josie had a feeling from the increased winds blowing off the ocean that a storm was brewing out in the Pacific. A southern breeze generally indicated that a low pressure cell, with its CCW rotation, was headed their way. She suppressed her thoughts of a damaging storm, thinking she was overreaching. It was most likely due to her reflection of the FFS crews departing Skagway in the morning and due at Sitka about noon.

Vision was limited at camp at this time in the early morning. This period called astronomical twilight (AT) masked details of the environment. The sun at AT was still about 18 degrees below the horizon where the sun does not contribute to earthly vision, only to sky illumination. Josie had to keep Luke close by. In fact, without his white muzzle and stockings, Luke would be almost invisible.

"Get over here, boy. Don't be sniffing and peeing on every rock. Come along; get some exercise," Josie hollered.

With the wind picking up speed, and Luke trailing along, she checked the tie-downs on the tents, supplies, and tarps covering the temporary kitchen.

As she worked the ropes on the kitchen fly, several rodents scattered about the rocks and sparse weeds. As the furry creatures, tailless voles, mice or whatever scattered, Luke gave chase to one . . . then another . . . and then another in a futile effort as the warring mouser. The rodents had the advantage of twilight, their home territory, and Luke's less-than-focused attack. He wanted them all, but had to settle for none. Wildlife were scarce on this rocky island, but as nearly everywhere in the world, even on this lava outcrop, rodents found a way to survive. They must have had a very limited diet with only a few plants emerging to the surface not to mention during the harsh winter at subzero temperatures. Josie had seen fox scat, circling raptors, and the normal complement of soaring shore birds, while setting up camp with the boys, but for other living things, zilch.

Caw—Caw—Caw.

Josie suddenly stopped and turned to the direction of the call. Luke dropped to his belly, looked around, and shook.

Josie's eyes scanned the faint tree line and finally located the solitary ebony bird perched at the edge of a nearby willow copse on a tall, gnarled spruce sticking up like a tower.

Caw—Caw—Caw.

"Well, hello, my raven friend. Did we disturb your nightly rest, or your hunt? I've a feeling you're always on the hunt, whether perched on a limb, or soaring in the ether of Father Sky while searching the mantle of Mother Earth. In any event, Hi! How be you? Hey."

Caw—Caw—Caw.

Luke hugged the ground tighter.

"Well, you sound alarmed. Is it the dog? Maybe it's the crew and me tramping all over your hunting grounds. Or is it something else?"

Caw—Caw—Caw.

Luke finally raised his head and looked around, then looked toward the sound in the tree. He slowly rose to his feet, turned to face away from the tree, sat, and slowly looked over his shoulder. He still shivered . . . likely of the unknown.

Nearby, a tent flap opened, and Bear emerged in his long underwear, with untied shoes and a flashlight. He, too, had apparently heard the bird's croak.

He looked around and finally noticed Josie and Luke in the limited starlight standing near the kitchen fly.

As he came her way, Josie commented, "If you—if we—are not a sight for sore eyes. Look at you in your long johns and me in my pink flannel night shirt. I hope we're not discovered by the local police patrol; we might be arrested for indecent exposure or old-timer hanky panky."

Bear snickered, "Ha! I'm more concerned about Joe or Leigh or the boys seeing us."

"You're right!"

"Tell me, what's going on out here that has our raven friend causing such a ruckus?"

"Not sure what's alarming the bird, but from what you and the Natives have told me, it could be that we're on its hunting grounds or, more importantly, its appearance could be as a messenger. The local Natives believe that the Great Spirit, Manitou, sends the raven with good and bad news—kinda like an alert, a warning, a caution sign, or an announcement of an important event. The local tribal leaders pay close attention to its presence . . . its call . . . its appearance."

Bear commented, "You have learned well from the natives, my dear. It is true. On several occasions Manitou has even shaped-shifted to a raven or wolf. Let's linger awhile and see what develops. He may reveal Himself. Gather your frightened dog, and let's wait here for a moment. He may have a message of importance to all of us."

*   *   *

Bear was patient. He was not sure if the raven had a message for them or was on a mission for Manitou. He had convinced Josie that they should build up the smoldering fire in anticipation of a spiritual contact. While enjoying the growing sea breeze, she shared her thoughts about her involvement with Joe by telling several stories of her work with him in Canada. She reminisced to Bear about her somewhat difficult relationships with men and how Joe changed her feelings about men. He was a winner; however, he was not interested in her. Although he hadn't gone into detail, his former squeeze was not faithful. That did it for the time being. He bought a dog, saying the obvious "She loves me no matter what." Nevertheless, with her joining Delta Station with him as her supervisor in the DNR, she noted that she now fit into his game plan. Time cures most wounds, she said. "Of course," she remarked, "he's also close to retirement and just may not want to live alone."

She also confessed that she was no longer a spring chicken, being more like an old hen, but with him around she felt like a pullet. Joe had turned back the pages of time to renew her youth. He had already given her a keepsake that was his mother's . . . now that's serious.

She swooned and looked at Bear. "Enough about me, Bear; how are you doing? Was your choice with Leigh as difficult? Or, as with me, was it like pulling teeth to get a commitment? I'm afraid, in my case, that I'm head-over-heels in love. Plus, he's a provider. At my age, that's critical."

"Damn, that's all good news," Bear answered. "We all look for someone to be with in retirement. You've not only found a new lease on life—a future—you've found a mate to share your life . . . and remember, you're a provider, also."

"So true," Josie said in a melodic voice.

Bear nodded and looked across the Sound at the lights of Sitka shining on the lower clouds. Then his eyes scanned the treetops in search of the raven. There it was, as if an ebony jewel, a jet black onyx frozen in place . . . waiting. Waiting for a storm? The flight from Skagway? What?

Restless, Bear decided it was unlikely the raven had any more indication of what was to happen, so he resolved to move a little to get the juices flowing. "Hey, woman, I've an idea. Do you think that old Irishman would mind if I showed you something of interest near the beach?"

"By all means, but let's make it quick. It's the boys that I'm concerned about, not Joe; he's sawing logs. If the boys saw us together dressed—or dressed like this—hard telling what story they'd dream up, You know, academia teaches creativity, and they're very good at imaginative stories . . . you ought to hear some of the stories they tell. I don't believe all of them. Some are told just to get me excited . . . the buggers. I see their wink and a nod . . . they think they're so clever. Yep, let's make it quick; they all get up early to jog the beach."

As they stealthily moved past the boys' tent, both giggled at the appearance of drying underwear, t-shirts, pants, shirts, other clothing and life-jackets. They were strewn on, over, and around the tent, clinging to little trees and lying on beach chairs. Part of their chuckle was the reaction to how ratty the shorts, shirts, and shoes looked. Their clothes were torn, ripped, and patched to the point of throwing them in the rag bin. It became obvious that the boys' daily sailing required two sets of clothes—one on and one set drying . . . wherever.

While they moved along the primitive path to the shoreline, dawn was breaking over the landscape to the east enveloping the area in nautical twilight. The sun was at approximately 12 degrees over the horizon. It was starting to illuminate the ether at 0400 hours. The landscape to the east revealed the Earth's skyline versus the infinity of pitch black darkness. Additional illumination on the crashing surf and fluorescence of the sea seemed to add another dimension of measure in the semi-darkness.

"Let's stop here," Bear whispered.

"Okay. Why are you whispering?"

"You'll see. Look toward the Sound, to the south where the waves are plunging over each other. Do you see the transformation in our little inlet?"

Josie answered, "Not sure . . . Oh . . . it's hard to focus . . . Oh, I see it now. The tide is out."

"Yep. Now look a little closer. Step over here away from those rocks. Do you see any movement on the flats? Over to the right—see 'em?"

"I'll be darned. Are those otters?"

"Sure enough. They're foraging for their breakfast of clams, crayfish, abalone, and other edible sea mollusks."

"Well, this is neat; there is indeed a much different world in the twilight with the fluctuation of the water's surface. Who would have known what's going on unless a person was 'up' with her peeing dog—and her friend—in their pajamas . . . ugh!"

"Woof!"

"Sush, Luke," Josie whispered.

"Oh, oh, Luke has picked up their scent. He's straining to see them. It's not going to happen down at his level. You'd better pick him up, Josie, before he takes off after them."

While Josie attended to Luke, Bear reflected on the location, the time of night, and to the past.

"Here we are, Josie. Just think, the Tlingit Indians stood at this point a mere two-hundred years ago. Living a subsistent lifestyle, they made food a central part of their culture. They had to; without wise farming of the sea, they would perish. They literally competed with the otters for sustenance . . . for survival. They had to win this battle.

"By the way, pass to the boys that the 'T' is generally dropped in Tlingit, and is pronounced as Lingit. One of the boys was a little tongue-tied on whether or not to use the 'T.' They may even know, since the 'T' in Russian words is seldom written or pronounced anymore. Like the ruler, 'the tsar' is now spelled and pronounced czar.

"Just look at the activity out there," he continued. "You see, the land covered by the sea is like a plantation, a cornucopia of seafood delights, an abundant provider. There's an old saying along the seacoast: 'When the tide goes out, the table is set.' This refers to the richness of intertidal life found on the beaches of the Pacific. Many an Indian chief has told his people, 'In tribal life along the shore, you'd have to be an idiot to starve.'"

"I've an idea, Bear. When we're dressed properly, let's get the crew together and dig some clams, harvest some abalone, and have some of my homemade seafood chowder. In fact, you guys dig 'em, and I'll cook 'em with my special recipe. Deal?"

"Right on, gal. Is there any doubt?"

Time was running out on their early-morning excursion, so they collected Luke and headed back to the campsite.

"Come on, little fella," Josie urged as she gathered the wet-footed canine. "There will be another time, a better time, in the daylight to chase crabs and trapped minnows."

*   *   *

Bear had gone ahead while Josie dried off Luke's paws.

From an unknown location, in darkness ahead, Bear yelled out, "Say, gal, would you step over here a minute? I just found a neat set of petroglyphs etched into this big boulder. I'm over here, behind the willows to your right of the path. Do you hear me?"

"I do now. You had me concerned for a minute when you disappeared. It gets pretty lonely—quickly—at this time of morning."

"Over here, I've pulled aside several branches of this small copse of willows. See me?"

"Yep, I'm coming."

"Follow the flashlight's beam."

She moved into the willow thicket toward Bear's flashlight. Luke growled as they approached in the close quarters near the covered boulder.

"It's okay, Luke. It's Bear. Easy now, fella."

"Step a little closer to where the light is pointing. Do you see them?"

"Sure do; it looks like two people, two people of importance with elaborate headdresses and feathers and decorations."

"You're right on. I think it's an etching of a chief and his bride. The detail is impressive, don't you think?"

"Bear, they're beautiful."

"Now look closer. Do you notice anything unusual about the woman's face in the side profile?"

"Ah . . . no. Wait, let me get a little closer. Here, take Luke. Hand me the light." Josie stooped a little lower and shined the light on the woman's face. "Yes. There is something different. Her lower lip appears to be extended and stretched outward. Ugh, how terrifying! Furthermore, it appears to have a disc of some sort holding the lip in an extended position. Am I right?"

"Sadly, you are, my dear. Years ago, women of nobility practiced lower lip piercing and insertion of a small bone or seashell as a symbol of beauty. Thankfully, it's not practiced anymore. When the Russians discovered the tribes along the coast in the 1800s, they noticed this practice and called the natives Koloshi. This is the Russian term for lower-lip piercing. Another 'beauty' mark, decorative scarring of the skin luckily does not show up on this etching.

"Look over here. This is one of the many symbols of their representatives of the Great Spirit, the raven who, by the way, is probably still maintaining its vigil back at camp. Isn't it unique?"

Josie answered while still staring at the etching, "It certainly is. It's beautiful. It's very simple, but leaves no doubt that it is a bird, a bird of importance . . . of praise. Then again, I still can't get over the lip piercing and scarring as symbols of beauty or nobility. Their zeitgeist, the moral/cultural state of their culture in the 1800s, was indeed unique—to a fault, if you ask me. At least their society was transparent; they wore their beliefs on their skin. Fortunately, they've changed as time alters most of us. I feel sorry for the women of the past who had to suffer from the archaic practices that were forced on them by chieftains who were too long in the tooth for reforms."

Bear commented, "One thing is certain: they were artisanal people, regardless of their unique beliefs."

Bear continued, "Yes, dear, as with most religious myths, whether Christian, Islamic, Judaic, Hinduism, Native Indian or other Asian beliefs, none of them satisfy the *objective* reasonableness test. All these beliefs require *extreme* leaps of faith.

"As we mentioned earlier, when the raven flew into camp this afternoon crying, hooting, and croaking, it may well have been a messenger from the Great Spirit . . . if you 'believe' it is so. On the other hand, without the N.A.I. belief, the poor bird could have been just bawling us out for taking over its hunting grounds. As in all human beliefs, it depends on what historic doctrine you believe—as to what you see.

"I've a feeling the raven may be a messenger, but also believe it is barking and croaking at us because we're camped in its camp. Let's go and get a little shut-eye before the gang gets up."

"Deal," she agreed. "Thanks so much for the background info and nighttime exploration into the present . . . and past."

As they walked along the path, Josie chatted about her beliefs. "I was introduced to several faiths along life's path here and in Canada, and found the various texts so bizarre, especially the book of Genesis, that I quickly realized that organized religious myths were not for me."

"True, some of the Native Indians beliefs are really far-out, too. Simply put: the raven creating earth . . . that's a stretch. Nevertheless, belief in something helps to explain their part in the universe," Bear explained.

"I agree, others can believe what they wish, no matter how eerie or mysterious, that's fine, but by the time I moved on to explore all their creation stories, I was annoyed. Many appeared to be a piece of patriarchal propaganda. Natives believing the raven created earth is as intolerable as Genesis . . . so I follow the golden rule that is in every belief and try to love as the prophet Jesus loved when he walked this earth. As a Deist I believe that God exists in some form and remain curious about the spiritual forces in the universe. I just do not want to be a cafeteria believer in an organized religion and pretend to believe the unbelievable, like so many of my friends who selectively pick and choose their beliefs. Enough of my thoughts."

Bear walked ahead, leading the way to camp, and said, "Good, because the next time we're out-and-about, in the daytime, I'll show you the bat cave just around the bend, and all its petroglyphics. Some are spiritual, others of animals from the period."

He said with a little chuckle, "Wanna see them now?"

"Oh, you're funny. No! You know better than to ask . . . you 'stinker,' let's get back to camp."

After they wound their way back camp, she gave Bear a brotherly kiss on the cheek in appreciation for their little sojourn from the station. They went to their separate tents as the wind blew down from Mount Edgecumbe and lenticular clouds once white turned to billowing darkened cumulus. The vast tweed of feathery grasses, red bearberries, and seeping willows leaned in the wind as its velocity waxed.

*   *   *

The wind-blown raven prevailed and struggled to remain on its perch. Was the bird's presence that of a spiritual messenger warning DNR personnel of the impending peril . . . or an angry hunter having no intention of giving up its hunting grounds?

Time would tell.

*   *   *

Bear opened the tent flap, crawled in, buttoned up, and gave Leigh a little 'accidental' bump.

"Aren't you cold?" Leigh asked drowsily. "What took you so long?"

"Well, I ran into Josie, who was also checking out the raven's cry. We chatted a bit while she walked Luke."

"How's she doing with that new guy?"

"Fine, I guess, but he had to pee twice during the night."

"Not Luke! How's she doing with *Joe?*"

"Oh, she's head over heels in love."

"Great! Now get to bed; we've only a few hours 'til our wake-up call."

"You're right. How 'bout letting me crawl into your sack and warm up these bonhomie bones?"

"Not a chance. Good night, my love."

Before she rolled over for a couple more hours of sleep, he kissed her on the neck and grabbed some flesh through the sleeping bag.

"Hold off on that, babe. Try again tomorrow night. You'll have a willing partner."

"Deal."

Silence.

Then Leigh asked, "By the way, if you were in your long underwear, what did Josie have on?"

"Oh, she was well dressed."

Bear crossed his fingers, hoping she wouldn't ask what *well dressed* meant. Luckily, silence followed—but for the howling wind.

*   *   *

Josie crawled into the tent with Luke who, like her after the extended nightly walk, was ready to drop off to sleep.

Joe was snorting and snoring like the noisy raven perched outside the tent.

He had roused when Josie left to check out the noise and take Luke to pee . . . again, but showed little interest in her return. In competition with his sleep, she lost.

As the two settled down for the night, she was well aware of the impending storm knocking on their door. There was no sense in worrying about its intensity or time arriving at the station. The FFS boys would have plans to carry out their assignment, with a contingency plan if necessary.

Josie looked at her newfound love and kissed his cheek. He snorted as she whispered, "Night, love."

*   *   *

A second later, one of the disciples was next to stir. Matthew had heard the agitation of the wind on the tent and the clothing hanging outside. One of the life-jackets had slammed into the side of the tent with quite an impact. Looking outside, he saw some of their clothes blowing away, so he scrambled around camp in the twilight, retrieving everybody's garments. He stuffed everything in a bag and threw it in the tent. He quickly double-checked the tie-downs on the Hobies and quietly approached the adult tents to see if they were secure. He paused . . . then stopped cold when he heard voices. He thought, *What the heck are they doing up at this late hour? Maybe those two old birds are trying the old trick of sharing a sleeping bag to get warm. Oh well, they're consenting adults.*

Matthew moved on with a wry grin on his face, crawled into the tent, slipped into his bag, and fell asleep as the wind howled.

*   *   *

A hundred miles to the west, storm clouds swelled endlessly in changing patterns up to five miles high and thirty miles wide, their build-up of moisture simmering and hissing.

As early morning nautical twilight broke over the horizon, only the raven maintained a silent vigil over the camp.

Chapter 5

The choppers headed south over the channel between Admiralty and Baranof Islands. In a minute they would be near the turning point and headed southeast to Sitka Sound.

Milt said, "Now there's something unique, Rob. Look to the right and compare the western to the eastern horizon on the left. Tell me, isn't that the most contrasting view you've ever seen?"

Rob leaned forward and looked. "You're right; now that's a contrasting set of horizons. The bright yellow sunrise was a welcome sight compared to the dark gray to black storm front to the west. Yep, and here we are smack dab on the edge of dawn's downfall. That storm's goin' to eat up the sun's charm. Trouble is, we're about to turn to the west and head directly into that destructive debacle of rain in those windy downdrafts. These choppers are not going to fair well in those water-driven winds."

Milt nodded his head in agreement, saying, "Rob, I figure we're about five miles from our westerly turn, and then about fifty miles from Delta Station. Let's give Josie a call to let her know we'll soon be on our last leg and headed for her station."

"Roger, I'll give her a call," Rob replied. "Delta Station, this is Alpha One. Over."

Static . . . more electromagnetic noise . . . a buzzing sound . . . a pause, then silence.

"Delta Station, this is Alpha One, do you read me? Over."

Static, followed by atmospheric disturbances.

"What do you think, Milt? The storm on the coast line is over the station now, but they should be able to receive and transmit easterly in our direction."

"Yes, I'm concerned. We're only fifty miles to the east, so at one-thousand feet our signal should be very strong and easily received. Now, their transmitting power is less, but that shouldn't be a problem. Also, the storm's electromagnetic interference is not between us. Let's try again."

Rob double-checked the frequency setting on the transceiver. It was correct at 121.5 MHz. He depressed the transmit button on the handheld microphone and looked at the needle on the power output. It registered 100 watts. It was working as prescribed.

"Delta Station, this is Alpha One. Over."

Silence.

"Delta Station, this is Rob on Alpha One. Josie . . . Bear, do you hear me?"
Silence.

"Milt, I'm concerned. Our signal strength is at full power, and I've just contacted Alpha Two without any problems. They hear us and have tried to contact Delta station, too, without any luck. I'm a little frustrated."

Milt answered, "I understand. Let's keep trying. Say, we're at the turning point; let's contact Dave and let him know we're on a new heading of two-hundred forty degrees southwest and descending to an altitude of five-hundred feet."

"Roger, Milt; I'll give 'em a call."

The energy of the wind's force on the starboard side of the chopper shifted to straight on as the aircraft turned SW from a southerly direction.

"Alpha One, this is Alpha Two; we've just made the turn, too, and are following you at one-mile separation at the same azimuth and elevation. Are you picking up the same head-on buffeting wind and rain? I'm sure you are; these wipers are just barely handling the volume. It looks like the wind and rain may even get worse; that big, black billowing cloud ain't gettin' smaller. It's huge!"

Milt answered, "Right you are. We're getting more buffeting, too. Dang, the rain is coming at us in sheets. Without more speed to blow away the rain, the wipers can barely keep the wind screen clear."

Dave answered, "I've had no luck raising Josie, either. We might as well give up for now. She either has a problem with equipment or location, or very unusual interference from the storm."

"Roger that," Milt answered. "Let's give 'em another try when we're closer. With any luck there may be a calm in the center of the storm. Rob's trying again. Any luck, Rob?"

"No luck, I think we'd better consider our fourth option, our drop without landing at the site. What do you think?"

The chopper lurched sideways as the wind's direction suddenly shifted from offshore to the south and increasing velocity to at least 25 miles per hour. Along with the shift, it brought a sheeting torrent of rain to the port side of the chopper.

As Rob struggled with the controls, Milt said, "Okay, Rob, we'll certainly be unable to land in this weather. Let's call Sitka Field and let them know we may have to land there soon with or without our load. Nevertheless, let's continue our flight to the station and try to drop the yurts. However, unless by some miracle the storm passes the site in the next thirty minutes, we will not be landing. In fact, we may not be able to find the drop zone and deliver these yurts. In this wind they start swinging like grandma's chest while on a carnival ride. They become a liability in keeping us airborne, so we may have to drop them in the sea. They would quickly become very expensive otter housing."

The winds shifted again, this time to the east as the front moved over the

Sound, and the choppers flew over the town of Sitka.

Rob called, "Milt, I just let Sitka Field know that depending on the storm's impact at the site, we'll be landing at their field with or without the load. Bill, the airport manager, offered ground crew assistance and hanger space if necessary. He has been monitoring our frequency. He wishes us good luck."

Milt answered, "Thanks, Rob. Let's check to ensure Dave and Ann agree."

Dave answered before being contacted, "We've been monitoring your call, and we concur. We'll have a hard enough time finding the drop zone with this limited vision, much less dropping the load and flying clear. This yurt is swinging like the pendulum on a grandfather's clock."

Ann interrupted. "Milt, did you notice your brother had a much more appropriate analogy—than using grandma's chest? Shape up, my man."

"Oops, sorry 'bout that, babe. I'll work at being more proper."

"Forget it," Ann replied. "You're too old to fit into the twenty-first century."

"Meow," Milt responded. "Dave, did someone say cat fight?"

"Bashful, she's not," said Dave.

"True," Rob said as he joined in the conversation.

Ann answered, "You stay out of this!"

"Well, now that we've lifted the tension of the flight off our chest. Oops. Grandpa's chest. Let's get down to the business at hand," said Milt.

By the time Ann had checked Milt on his analogy, they had flown to the center of the Sound and were feeling more pressure on the flight controls. The choppers were not easy to handle with a load, and now they had added the dynamics of the wind's increasing velocity on the aircraft and the yurts.

Milt continued discussing the flight plan. "As I see it, we'll still approach the station from the northwest as planned with only our radar's profile of the promontory. In the absence of Josie's strobe light, it's going to be tough to find the drop zone in the center of the clearing. But we do know it's at the base of Mount Edgecumbe, and that will be easy to see on radar. Our challenge is to not fly into its side. Now, listen up, the clearing is a circle about two-hundred feet wide and has a wide clear-cut leading up to it from the beach, so its shape is like a banana squash. I may or may not fly right up the neck to the clearing or drop down into it. It depends on the wind velocity, direction, and resolution of the radar images. On our approach, we must be prepared to drop our load and abort without concern for the yurts; personnel and aircraft safety come first. Remember, we practiced this flight in reduced visibility with a strobe light, but it appears that will not be available today. Dave, do you agree with the plan?"

Dave responded, "Sure do. In fact, even though I can see the point now, it is getting less defined as we fly closer. Its clarity is diminishing with a blanket of electromagnetic snow."

"Roger that, Dave. My screen is starting to lose detail, too. It looks like we're about twenty-five miles from shore, so we'll be over the shore in thirty minutes. Any last comments? Speak now or—"

BANG!

Static on the radio.

Silence.

Milt hollered, "What the hell?"

As the flight gauges returned to normal and the radio squawked back to life, Milt said to Dave, "Well, my friend, we just got blasted by a lightning strike. Do you read?"

"I do. We saw it, way back here. You lit up like a Christmas tree. We were expecting the same back here. Are you guys okay?"

"I think so. The flight deck has come back to life. The radar is still working even though it's full of snow. We're descending to three-hundred feet on our final approach. I've decided to fly to the opening of the clearing by shore and hover a moment before heading in."

"Roger that. I'll stand-off about three-hundred feet and also hover until you decide what to do."

"Roger . . . standby."

Silence.

"Dave, the inconvenient truth is that this drop is at the margins. I'm at the shoreline and having a hell of a hard time holding this bird steady. The radar shows the shoreline through the snow, but it is very vague. It will be less than a fifty/fifty chance to see the clearing, much less descend and drop the load. Damn, I wish Josie was here with the strobe light; that would clarify some of the unknowns. What the hell, here we go. I'll give you a call when I've dropped the load . . . or aborted and headed for Sitka Field."

"Roger, I'm hovering—"

*　　*　　*

BANG!

Static.

Silence.

"Damn it!" Ann shouted. "We've been hit by lightning, too. Dang, this is not fun. This is not going to work. Dave, let's abort. Let's get out of here."

"Not quite yet, my dear . . ."

"Don't call me 'dear'!"

"Okay, I understand your feeling, Ann, but our gauges are back to normal, this old ship is holding together, and we'll complete our mission in the next few minutes—drop or not—so let's try."

"You're right. Sorry about the outburst. Wait, did you see that?"

"What?"

"A series of flashes inland. It could be lightning bouncing off the mountain or my eyes playing tricks on me. Look inland about three-hundred feet."

"All I can see is A-1's running lights and the flash of lightning on the mountain. Wait, Milt is moving inland. Do you imagine he, too, has seen a winking strobe light? This latest deluge of rain is obscuring my vision."

Ann cried into the mic, "Please, Manitou, let the light be someone, maybe Josie . . . anyone signaling Milt from the drop zone. Please. Go Milt, our thoughts are with you. Sorry I was so catty. Rob, take care of yourselves."

Dave consoled, "Ann, they'll make it; they're the best, they'll not take any unnecessary chances. They believe in the old adage: There are a lot of old pilots, but few old and bold pilots. Relax."

"Oh, Dave, I'm so worried about them. Will they be careful?"

"My dear, Rob will be okay; Milt will make sure of that . . . for you and him."

*   *   *

The sun was two fingers above the horizon to the east as the wicked storm continued to plow wind-driven water against the shore. Delta Station personnel were about to stir.

Josie nudged Joe. "Joe . . . Joe! We've got to do something. The wind and rain is so fierce, it's about to blow the tent over on us. Joe!"

Joe roused from his sack and quickly tuned in to Josie's concerns. The tent was leaning over at about 45 degrees and from best estimates—about to break loose from its moorings.

"Damnit. Woman, you're right, let's get out of here. We've got to alert the rest and head for cover; this storm is a villain," Joe exclaimed. "I've got Luke."

Josie grabbed her shoulder bag with its flashlight, TX radio, and strobe light.

"Good thinking, dear. I'm glad you remembered your tools; the FFS boys will be calling us soon to help them land . . . or maybe not. It's a maelstrom of wind out here."

"Yeah, I got up at five and tried to raise the boys on the radio, but didn't have any luck. There was too much static due to the storm."

They quickly roused Bear and Leigh, sleeping in the same bag, who were about to have the tent collapse on them. They got up, zipped up the tent, found some rocks to lay on it, and moved to the boys' tent. As they dashed through the rain they found the boys laying rocks on their tent, too.

All seven ran to the kitchen area, salvaged what was not blown away, then dropped the tarp over the coolers and stove. They formed a huddle much like in football and discussed the quandary in which they found themselves.

"Are we going to seek shelter in the woods?" Leigh asked.

"No . . ." Bear paused. "No, we're going into the cave by the shore, the bat cave. Follow me."

"What?" Mark said in a skeptical voice.

Several older trees fell on the edge of the clearing, while small branches sprayed the group. One large branch knocked Matthew off his feet. He quickly recovered and looked at Mark, saying, "We better get in the cave."

Bear yelled, "There's no time to explain—follow me. Josie also knows the way. All of you, hold hands like you did in the kindergarten, and don't unlink until I tell you to do so. If you stumble or fall, do not let go. Come on, time's a-wastin'."

They trotted to the shoreline, dodging limbs, leaves, grass, and sand while trying to maintain their footing.

Bear hooked a left just before the crashing surf at high tide and followed a rudimentary path along the boulders next to the tumbling, toppling, tumult of waves. Due to the high tide, they trudged through the knee-deep salt water and turned by a willow copse.

She noticed that Leigh had let go of Bear's grasp.

"Stop!"

Leigh had slipped on a bed of kelp seaweed that had washed ashore. She thrashed to regain her footing as Joe, holding her other hand, jumped on her so she would not be carried out to sea in the rip current.

Bear jumped in, too, and held tight to any part of her body he could grab. "Gotcha, gal. Grab hold; I'll help you get up," Bear hollered over the surf's roar.

"I've got her, also," Joe yelled. "We've got you mate—'tis no mermaid to-night for you, my love. Up we go."

Between the two burly gents, Joe and Bear, the group continued on their way.

Bear separated the willow branches hugging the boulder's edge and pulled them away from the rocky wall of cooled lava. "This way!"

They slowly moved along the slippery edge for about 30 feet while willow branches lashed them like a cat-of-nine-tails. They stumbled onto an opening about the size of double doors at a church, wide and pointed at the top.

"Here it is! Follow me! Don't mind if a few bats are darting around your head. After all, this is their home—we're their guests."

Mark spoke out again, "Ugh , . . bats, I hate the little buggers."

Bear responded quickly. "Would you rather hang around the clearing until the storm clears?"

"Point," Mark answered with a little humility.

"I guess we can unlink now if we have seven noses and seven butts, and finally relax without limbs whacking us. This will be our safe harbor for an hour or two until the storm passes. Your night vision will kick-in after ten or fifteen minutes. Leigh, are you okay?"

"Yep, I just left my pride on the kelp-strewn rocks. And—thank you, Joe for having a grip on me. Hard telling where I'd be now if you had not been holding on as I thrashed about."

Josie took Luke from Joe and caressed the whining pup who had survived a pretty rough ride while tucked into Joe's shirt. Still shaking from the dark womb of Joe's clothes, Josie stroked the little fella until the boys took over. She had other tasks to keep her occupied. "Joe, I'm going to stand by the entrance to the cave and see if the TX radio can pick up the FSS boys. They're in the air now, and most likely heading south along Admiralty Island."

Joe answered, "Lots of luck. I don't think a hundred-watt transmitter could get through to them, much less your twenty-five. Nevertheless, I know you too well; you've got to try."

Josie stood at the cave's entrance trying to make contact with the airborne choppers. Sadly, she returned without any luck.

Mark grumbled, "Look at the cave's ceiling. Do you guys know your butts are sitting on years of bat guano? There must be hundreds of bats up there."

Bear laughed. "True. Would you like to leave?"

"Okay, I'll hush up. But I still think this is a creepy place—surviving the storm or not."

Matthew looked at John and said, "You're still a wuss; you always will be. Take a nap; then we'll not have to hear you."

Josie called everyone together in the dark cave and presented the situation as well as she could possibly predict what would develop. There were a few questions about the storm's duration, the arrival time of the FFS boys, and the contingency plan if the choppers arrived while they remained protected in the cave.

She answered them as best she could, then suggested they use the next few hours to take a nap. If they could not help the choppers land in the storm, and they were on their own, she assured them that the FFS boys would find a way—including an abort of the mission until the weather cleared.

Being up most of the night, Josie, too, leaned against Joe and caught a wink or two.

*   *   *

About an hour and a half later, Josie heard an additional roar besides the crashing surf; it was the noise generated by screaming turbines of an aircraft. A chopper was hovering at the edge of the shoreline.

She bolted up from her fretful sleep, looked around at the slumbering group, grabbed her bag, and ran out of the cave into the driving sheets of rain and noisy surf to see if she could assist in landing the choppers.

At the cave's opening she saw the hovering giant so close to shore that she could almost touch its load on the umbilical. The load was oscillating in the storm, so much, she knew, the pilots would, have to drop the load very soon, no matter where. She decided to fight her way to the clearing and activate the strobe light. She strapped the bag over her shoulder so it would not slip off.

She looked back and wondered if she should tell Joe that she was leaving, but decided not to awaken him.

As she turned on the ledge to break through the willow branches, she slipped on a bed of kelp and fell into the dashing surf.

Sadly, no one knew of her peril as she screamed for help against the roar of the breaking waves.

Chapter 6

Matthew was not resting well during the night. Part of the reason for his unsettling sleep was Luke's tossing, turning, and wiggling while scratching his belly with the pup's sharp little claws.

"Help!"

Dozing again between little whines and licks, he heard what sounded like a voice yelling outside the cave's opening. He wondered if it was a bunch of bats returning from their nightly hunt for bugs.

"Help!"

No, it wasn't a bat's shrill cry . . . it was a woman's scream.

He bolted upright and looked around the cave. Leigh was lying near Bear, Josie must be so close to Joe that he couldn't see her. He leaned over to get a better view.

"Dang!" Matt cried.

He noticed that she no longer snuggled in Joe's arms.

"Help!"

Terror filled his thoughts as he jumped up and ran over to the boys.

"Quick! I think Josie is in trouble outside! Come quickly; I heard her scream!"

Matt dropped Luke on Joe's coat, and the three boys dashed out of the cave's opening into the roaring wind and mauling surf.

"Help!"

"There she is," Matt yelled to the boys, "over to the left of that rock."

"Over here!" Josie cried.

"Quick, she's slowly being dragged out by the waves. Here, hold hands, as Bear had us do, and jump in. We'll snag her before she's washed out too far."

They all jumped in and kicked their legs like Olympians in a lane.

Several times as they got closer a wave would draw her away; then they'd approach her again, but again without getting close enough to grab her.

Her floatation skills seemed to be at the breaking point as she started to falter. Her words were now garbled with a seawater mixture.

"You're getting close . . . boys . . . keep . . . trying!" she pleaded.

Finally a big wave carried her up and down on the boys in a crash. Finally, they collided and joined hands in a happy saltwater reunion. The four bodies now kicked to shore in unison like a Mississippi Paddle-wheeler.

"Blub . . . thank goodness . . . blub . . . you guys heard me."

"This way . . . over here!" Matt yelled. "Come this way, my feet are touching bottom; I'll carry you in the rest of the way."

Matt aggressively grabbed her and made certain she was on shore above the wave action before letting her go.

As the four caught their breath on the rocky shore, Josie told them what happened. "Thankfully, I was in the water no more than thirty seconds when you guys arrived." She hugged each one of them and gave them a kiss on the cheek. "Now for our immediate problem. The first chopper has moved inland to the clearing, and we've got to get there quickly with the strobe light. They'll never drop the yurts unless they know they're over the clearing. Dropping our yurts in the trees is not an option. Let's go."

Making sure everything was in her shoulder bag, she ran ahead at breakneck speed with the boys struggling behind. She quickly arrived at the center of the clearing.

Matt yelled, "There he is! The chopper is hovering at the edge of the treeline. I'll bet he's wondering where he is. Damn, he seems to be moving away."

Josie yelled, "No, Milt . . . Milt, no!" She quickly turned the blinking strobe toward the chopper.

Anxiety filled the air as the chopper seemed to be leaving the area. Then, a smile washed over Josie's face.

Mark yelled, "He's stopped! He's swinging around to the center of the clearing. He's seen your light, Josie."

John cried out, "He's seen us. He's descending. By god, he's going to drop our house. Go, Miltie, go! No more tent or cave for us. Yahoo!"

With the chopper's screaming turbines, the wop-wop-wop of the rotor blades, and the whine of the tail rotor, the noise prohibited anyone from hearing what was said. Matt read Josie's lips: *He's going to drop the load—I know he is.*

The hovering continued as the bird lurched and turned in the wind. Tension mounted as the winds battered the chopper's stability.

Thump!

Before they knew it, the yurt and sling dropped the last few feet to Mother Earth. The chopper exploded into the air and headed to the northwest.

"John, get my bag, be quick about it. We've got time to contact Milt or Dave on the radio. Hurry before Milt gets out of range. Be brisk about it."

John searched the water-soaked bag, retrieved the almost-dry radio, and gave it to her—quickly.

"Thanks. Now go help Matt and Mark with the yurts; we'll also need a damage assessment ASAP."

When she turned on the radio, the red light glowed like a thousand suns. It was working! She transmitted quickly. "Alpha One, this is Delta Station. Over."

Static.

"Alpha One, this is Delta Station. Milt, do you hear me?"

Static.

"Delta Station, this is your favorite pilot. Thanks so much for the strobe light. It did the trick. We were about to leave. Love you, babe. Tell Joe it's a professional love."

"You're welcome, my dear. I was afraid you could not receive me with this little radio in the storm."

"No problem. We heard your first call, too, but we were pretty busy keeping this bird under control from the downdrafts of good old Mount Edgecumbe to the north. Its winds played havoc on our control surfaces. We almost spun around once when the tail rotor could not overpower the side-loading winds from the north. As for the delay, you'll soon learn the rule of priority from a pilot's perspective: it's *Aviate, Navigate, and Communicate,* in that order. Anyway, babe, thanks again; we're on our way to Sitka Field. We'll call when we land. If the storm blocks our signal, we'll try again later. As I see it now, we'll stay there overnight and return to your little station in the morning. We've got the rest of the supplies lashed down and still secure for an early-morning delivery. See you. Bye. This is Alpha One. Out."

"See you then . . . whoops, here comes Dave. Back to work. See you."

Alpha Two followed the strobe light to the center of the clearing, hovered, and slowly descended to a safe stand-off altitude.

The boys took a break from the first yurt set up and encircled the drop zone. While waiting for Dave to drop his package, Mark came up with one of his off-the-wall ideas. Always saying the unexpected, Mark mentioned, "I've come up with a new name for our group: 'Caster's Cutthroats.'" No one asked him why he felt the boys were like Colonel Caster's soldiers who, with Aleut Natives, drove the Japanese off Attu and Amchitka Islands in 1942. Mark had been given Pearson's book a few days ago, and understood his point. Apparently Mark was the only one.

Matthew spoke up. "Mark, it's true, the U.S. Army drove the Japs from the Aleutians in '42, and yes, it was primarily due to the freezing weather conditions, but this is sixty-five years later. There is no war, and our island, and our Kruzof is in the panhandle, not next to Russia. And the only war we have is with the weather—a battle that man has been fighting since the dawn of life. Now, a better name for us guys might be: 'Josie's Enlightened Wolverines.'"

John spoke up. "Hell, no! Did you think of the acronym? JEW boys. Well, no."

Matt responded, "You're right; we'll keep working on it."

"Josie's Cutthroats?" Mark said sheepishly.

Josie snickered, and said to herself, *He's not going to give up.*

The turbine's screaming suddenly abated.

THUMP.

The second load was dropped. Alpha Two powered up, lurched into the air, and immediately headed to the northwest and Sitka Field.

Josie made a brief call to Dave and Ann. She quickly responded with many thanks to Josie for the strobe light, adding, "Babe, we couldn't have dropped this little house without your courage. Get some rest; I heard you've been up most of the night . . . and took a swim, too. This is Alpha Two. Out."

*   *   *

A whining dog, a hovering chopper, and a missing woman startled Joe. "Hey, Bear . . . Hey, Leigh . . . Josie's gone. The boys are gone, too. Let's see what's up. Follow me."

Joe tucked Luke in his shirt again, and the three remaining cave dwellers hustled out of the cave, across the walkway, through the willows, along the rock wall, and up the cleared route to the site. As they arrived at the clearing, one of the choppers was descending with the second yurt.

There she was. Josie was holding the strobe light while the boys were checking for damage on the yurts.

The boys looked up. "Hey, look who the cat dragged in. Welcome, Joe, Bear, and Leigh."

"'Tis a fine lot you are in leaving us in the cave, but it looks as if you've been busy."

"Hi, babe. Indeed, we've had quite a harrowing experience. Thankfully both choppers have dropped their load, and are headed to Sitka Field for the duration of the storm. They'll most likely return tomorrow with the rest of the supplies—assuming it's clear by then."

"'Tis glad, I am, to see you've helped 'em land. Sorry I did not hear the first bird arrive. Better yet, you got some work out of those wolverines."

Josie replied, "More than you'll ever believe. By the way, I promised Milt and Dave we'd have both yurts set up by late morning."

"'Tis a hug then, I need, my dear. You've had a strenuous morning."

"You're right on that. I'm so fortunate to have you, the boys, and those two over there, Leigh and Bear. You're all part of Delta Station."

Joe gave Josie a big suck-face kiss, came up for air, rung out his wet cap, and freed Luke from his warm womb-like sanctuary. As he poked his little head out, the rain pelted his nose first, then his eyes, and finally his tongue, which he stuck out for a drink. They all giggled as Luke reacted to his first big downpour. Joe put him down to wallow in the water and get a good drink from the puddles.

"Hey," Bear yelled, "we've got the big yurt, the office unit, set up. Come over and get out of the rain. Come on."

They all trotted over to the six-sided yurt with its wooden bottom, sides, and nylon fabric stretched over an aluminum framework. The door was in place, and the plastic windows were letting in what light was available in the storm.

Josie said, "Well, I'll be darned. Maybe we can finally get out of the rain—and the bat guano—and catch some shut-eye. Let's do it."

They all crashed on the floor of the yurt, exchanged stories about the last twelve hours, and hugged each other in celebration of their personal survival . . . and of the safety of the flight crew on their return flight to Sitka. The success of the first aspect of their mission seemed to glue together their relationships, their care for each other, and their forgiveness for their idiosyncrasies . . . Yes, even for Mark.

Mark asked Josie for permission to give thanks for their survival. "Of course," she said, wondering what he would say.

Mark spoke, "Our recent plight was realistically assessed by one of my favorite men in history. His name is Montaigne, a 16th century French philosopher, whose writings apply very well to our predicament today.

> "Whenever your life ends, it is all there. The advantage of living is not measured by length, but by use; some have lived long, and lived little; attend to it while you are in it. It lies in you, in your will, not in the number of years, for you to have lived enough."

"That was beautiful, Mark. Thank you very much," Josie said while giving him a hug.

After all had settled in the dry yurt, and the stories of each of their experiences had been retold, Joe asked the boys to go out one more time to see if they could recoup a cold meal from the damaged kitchen.

Halfway to the damaged kitchen area, Joe stopped.

"What's up, Joe?" Matthew asked. "Did you change your mind—not hungry?"

"Ha! No, that's not it. I want to take a private moment with you characters, you free-thinking knuckleheads from Ann Arbor and its prestigious University of Michigan, and thank you from the bottom of my heart for saving Josie. You'll never know how much your heroic actions mean to me. I'll remember your bravery, your courage, for the rest of my life. She will, too. I know, you'll say a man will risk his life for his own flesh and blood, and to me you have done that. You risked your life for her as if she was just that, your own flesh and blood."

He moved to each boy and gave an individual hug of thanks.

"Okay, you blokes, enough of this emotional drivel. Let's get some grub."

*   *   *

Much later, while resting in the yurt, Josie reflected on her past, and her recent experiences with the boys.

I know today was not a typical or routine day for me and my men as part of the bouillabaisse of humanity at the DNR's Delta Site. However, the university team had settled into a pattern of expectation that concerned me. Each member of the team was very different. I wonder if the contrast of their academic rigors to the rollicking times of 'live today—for tomorrow we die' will bother me. I wonder if they'd rather sail their Hobies, eat pizza, drink beer, and read the latest bestseller than perform the requisite science at the site. Nevertheless, that aspect of their job has not been tested yet; so quit your worrying, girl. They saved your life at their own peril.

It appears that Matthew is the leader, the spokesman, and the one with a more rounded personality; Mark is the timid girl-boy and the most finicky, but also the most dependable, so say, his professors; John is the quiet one who seldom speaks unless spoken to. What a gang. Actually I'm anxious to work with them, learn from them, and make Delta Station the very best along the coast.

"There you are, Luke. Come to mama. What do you think of our boys? I know you like 'em, for they sure love you. You know, Luke, supervising the U of M team is going to be a real challenge. But guess what? I've had similar assignments with the Mounties in Canada, so I know the tricks men use when being supervised by a woman. These young whippersnappers with triple-digit IQs may present a few different problems, but none I can't handle.

"One thing is certain, Luke: I love 'em as if they were my own; besides, they saved my life.

"One may ask where would I rather be. Nowhere else but here."

*   *   *

Two choppers in a maelstorm of wind, rain, and hail were approaching Sitka Field at 100 knots from the southwest.

"Sitka Field, this is Alpha One from Ford Flight Service. We've just dropped our load at Delta Station. We're one mile to the southwest at five-hundred feet; request landing instructions. Over."

"Alpha One, this is Sitka Field, Bill here. I'm glad you guys were successful; it's not a good day to fly. In fact, FAA has just grounded all flights in this sector of the panhandle. You're up there alone. How's that make you feel? Just kidding. Land on runway nine-zero and proceed to hanger Bravo One. We'll meet you on the apron and open the doors when you arrive."

"Roger that. Are there any overnight accommodations at the airport? There's six of us, three male."

"Affirmative. We've several rooms with a combination of single and double beds. Who sleeps with who is up to you."

"Bill, you must write lyrical verse as well as manage an airport."

"I do—glad you noticed. Seriously, you can stay here; it's no problem."

"Affirmative. Say, can I buy you dinner? We're so hungry the crew is about to eat the pages out of my flight charts."

"Negative. The Chief of the Tlingit Tribal Council, Golden Bear, has heard of your operation in Skagway and your relationship with the DNR. He wishes for you and your crew to join him for dinner at the tribal dining commons. I'll let him know when you land."

"No need to defer. We'll be there with bells on. We're on our final approach, Bill. See you on the apron soon if I can land this thing in a blinding rain. Break— Break, Alpha Two, do you concur with our dinner date?"

"This is Alpha Two, is the Pope Catholic" Wouldn't miss it. I'll see you on the apron soon if I can land this thing right-side up."

"Roger that. Say, remind me to call Josie when we're on the ground. We may not get through in this storm, but we'll try. Also, let's call our base and let FFS know we've completed the first portion of our mission."

"Roger that. Ann said she'll make both calls."

"Roger. Out."

Bill and his crew stood in flight ops waiting for the choppers to arrive in the persistent storm passing through Sitka Sound. The landing would not be easy, as wind gusts of 25 miles-per-hour, and more, had been playing havoc with other aircraft all day.

"There they are," Bill exclaimed as the two choppers appeared on the radar screen. "Bring 'em in, boys. Be careful, that last leg has experienced a lot of wind shear when clearing the coastline. Easy does it."

Silence.

The silence was suddenly broken.

Bill yelled, "Look, one chopper is losing altitude—it's the second one! Damn, it may be going down. I'll call."

"Alpha Two, this is Sitka Base, are you in trouble? Over."

Silence.

Alpha One gave a call, too. "Alpha Two, this is Alpha One. Are you okay, Dave? Dave, do you read?"

Silence.

The only sound in ops was the radio's low frequency hum. It droned on as the wind's fury continued to blow violently across the runway.

Chapter 7

Twang! Crunch!

The vibration increased, and the aircraft's sheet metal started shaking violently.

"Christ!" Dave shouted.

"Damn," Ann cried, "It sounds like the turbine is shutting down . . . I think we may have ingested something in the intake, damnit!"

Dave looked at the flight-deck instruments. "Do you see what I see?"

"Yep, we're losing RPMs."

"Babe, we're about to fall. Disengage the transmission, kill the power, and let's get this bird down as quickly as possible. Luckily we're at only three-hundred feet and should pancake easily in the water with our pontoons absorbing part of the impact."

Ann yelled, "No, we've just cleared the breakers at low tide; we'll make the flats. They're below us now."

"Good."

Dave flipped the IC switch. "Star, I can't explain right now, but we're going to make a landing in the tidal flats without power—buckle up."

"Dang. Will do. Geez-O-Pete," she responded in a shrill voice.

"Ready, Ann? I'm disengaging the shaft and setting the rotor blades flat to capture as much air as possible. We'll be on auto-gyro soon. Hold on!"

The chopper's silence was numbing as the slower *Wop - Wop - Wop* of the unpowered rotor blades fought against the rain-drenched air. The air's density helped the blades lower the craft at about three feet per second, three times the normal rate. It was going to be a hard landing, even with the soft mud flats and large footprint of the huge pontoons.

"Ann, call Bill and tell him we'll need Milt to haul us out of here as soon as possible. His chopper is powerful enough to lift us with the cable he has aboard. I don't want to be here when the tide comes in. We've got less than one hour. I don't want to be rolled over in the surf."

"Roger that."

Compared to a dead-stick landing on a fixed-winged aircraft, when the pilot has a fairly long glide-path, Dave's dead-stick landing in the chopper would depend on the free-wheeling rotors turning with sufficient RPMs to let them land softly enough to prevent major damage to the undercarriage and rotor blades. Thin air in hot weather would prohibit this type of landing, but luckily Dave was flying in air dense enough to capture the needed resistance. He had performed this procedure as part of his training/certification, though not in the limited vision of driving rain and on a mud flat covered with kelp.

How different it now seemed when the test wasn't for a score, but to protect the precious lives of Ann and Star. Now this was what thousands of hours came down to, a single moment, live or die. Just as he believed in Ann, had faith and trust in her, would count on her if she had the stick; right then he found confidence in knowing she had that kind of faith in him bringing them down.

Wop - Wop - Wop.

*   *   *

"Emergency-emergency, Alpha One, this is Sitka Field. Alpha Two is going down due to a power loss. They are in need of help. Over."

Milt responded, "Yes, I heard Ann's call."

Bill answered, "It appears, with turbine loss, they're attempting to land in the flats just short of the runway. Dave has requested your assistance in lifting them out. Do you follow? Over."

"Roger, I'm about to touch down. After landing, Rob will get the lifting cable out of our locker and we'll have Janet exit. Then Rob can hook up the cable, and we can get over there quickly. Over."

"Roger. I'll relay to Alpha Two since I imagine they're pretty busy right now," said Bill.

*   *   *

Wop - Wop - Wop was the only sound Alpha Two heard from their bird.

As Dave' chopper descended toward the runway, it yawed, tilted, and awkwardly tipped to and fro as it dropped out of the sky to the crustacean-laced tidewater muck.

Dave spoke to the crew in a calm voice to ease their concern. "I'll be a son of a biscuit. I think we're going to make it . . . maybe even right-side up. You're doing fine, Ann. I couldn't do this without your help. Star, when we're down, please exit quickly and lock the door in the open position. Be careful as you wade to the shoreline; Ann, follow her and standby on the shore."

Ann quickly responded, "No. Absolutely not! I'm staying with you during the hookup."

"Okay then, here's my plan. I'll crawl up to the top of this bird as soon as we land, and wait there for Milt to arrive. When the lifting cable is lowered, I'll grab the hook and attach it to the lifting ring . . . and roll or jump off. Does that sound workable?"

Ann answered, "Affirmative. Our options are kinda limited. Can I help in the hookup?"

"Negative. There's not much room up there. Luckily, a lifting ring at the bird's center of gravity is easily accessed. It was designed for this and other times when the bird had to be hauled by air."

Star said, "Do be careful; it will be slippery up there. It's windy and the rain is turning to hail; it will be like walking on little balls of ice."

"I will."

Wop - Wop - Wop.

So far the rotors were turning in an optimum manner, and the chopper's body was falling in a fairly stable fashion. Nevertheless, tension filled the air as the flats seemed to rise to meet them any second.

Then it happened!

Dave yelled, "We're about to rotate . . . we're going to spin . . . hold on . . . we're going to hit hard . . . we might topple . . . hold on!"

Splat-crunch, slip, pause, slide, sink—stop—pop.

"Damn," Ann cried. "A downdraft must have caught us just before we hit!"

"Star, are you okay?" Dave yelled.

*   *   *

Wop-Wop-Wop.

Milt's landing was routine, considering the conditions. They taxied through the torrent of rain toward the hangar bathed with lights, and idled down slightly. The *Wop-Wop-Wop* of the slowly rotating blades and the soft scream of the turbines fought to block communications between each other.

Bill met Rob as he escorted Janet out of the bird and without a word walked with her to the dryness of base ops. Rob returned to the chopper, retrieved the lifting cable, fastened it to the undercarriage ring, and jumped back in his seat for take off.

Milt powered up the chopper and ascended into the sheeting rain and hail. As the bird gained altitude, Milt asked Rob, "How's the cable hanging? Is the weight, by the hook, heavy enough to keep the cable fully extended in this maelstrom?"

Rob answered, "Just barely. It's oscillating like a pendulum. It will be difficult for Dave to snag it, but once we're hovering over his fallen bird the cable may settle down and stabilize versus sway."

Milt answered, "For his sake, I hope so. One thing is certain: we've no other choice but to get over that downed bird and hope Dave can attach the lifting hook—wind, hail, and rain be damned. Why don't you give 'em a call and tell them we're on the way. I think Ann has a hand-held radio, too."

"Roger that. Break. Break, Alpha Two mobile, this is Alpha One. Do you read?"

Silence.

Rob repeated the call.

Static.

*   *   *

"This is Alpha Two mobile, Ann here. I hear you weak but readable. Dave's just crawling up to the top. We've left all our landing and running lights on so you can see us better in this storm. Where are you now?"

Rob answered, "We're coming to the end of runway nine-zero so we'll spot you very soon. Wait, there you are straight ahead."

Milt responded, "Good. Ann, Rob, and I will use you as the relay in directing our flight to direct the cable to Dave. Roger that?"

Wop-Wop-Wop.

"Affirmative. I hear and see you now, and the weight above the hook. It also helps to have your landing lights shining on the weight. We're going to do it, Milt. You and Dave are the best. It's going to happen."

Milt answered, "That's the spirit. Now, for your directions to either Rob or me. Just assume you're here on the flight deck and tell us to go either of the four directions and up and down from our position. Got it?"

"Affirmative. You're already in excellent position, but move to the right about four feet, and down about ten."

"Do you see Dave?" asked Ann.

Rob answered, "Yes. One of our running lights reflects off his face while blinking. The landing lights are pointed too far ahead to do much good. Do you see him, Milt?"

"Yep, off and on in the blinking, like you. His perch up there is quite a challenge in this weather, and it appears the slight angle is a result of one of the pontoons's structure collapsing. Is that true?"

"Affirmative. At the last moment, a couple feet off the deck, we lost autogyro and hit hard on the port side. Everything else seems to be okay, except for the turbine. It's full of feathers. Darn geese. Why the hell would they be flying on a night like this?"

Milt chuckled. "They might ask you the same question."

"Touché. Now, about four feet down and two feet to the left."

On the top of the inclined bird, with the alternating silhouette, Dave appeared white, green, and red-faced in the running lights' reflection. The flash dancing image belied the danger of trying to stay atop the bird, while also trying to grab the swinging cable—with very limited vision. One thing was certain, he was not only on a precarious perch—the weighted hook could easily knock him off with the force of a Civil War cannonball. Add the turbulence of the prop wash driving down on him with the combined vortices of wind driven rain.

Ann and Star stood on the shoal no more than twenty feet from the downed chopper, shouting encouragement to Dave. All three were affected by the elements under the prop wash—plus the salt water spray stinging their eyes.

Ann continued to shout her complex directions to the rescue chopper.

After an unsuccessful pass, Dave sat on the rotor blades' armature for stability and rested his weary legs.

After several failed attempts, Dave motioned to Ann to signal the boys to approach from another vector. She signaled her understanding, from Dave, with a wave of hand and arms, and got back on the radio.

*   *   *

"Good move. That's a better approach, down now, a little more—about two feet—good . . . the hook is swinging toward him, hold . . . steady . . . hold . . . here it comes, Dave's about to grab it . . . hold—he's got it!" Ann yelled.

Dave quickly bent down to engage the hook as she watched amid the blinking lights. Then, all of a sudden, a strong gust of wind came from a new direction, as if sent by Satan, and for reasons known only to him, Dave held on.

Worse yet, the same hellish gust of wind caused the chopper to rise.

Ann yelled, "Let go! Dave, let go!"

With Dave directly under the chopper now, Milt had no idea what was happening below.

Ann, in a panic, got on the radio. "Milt! Dave's still holding on to the hook! He's dangling below! Move away from the chopper and drop down—he'll soon fall thirty feet—he can't hold on much longer! Milt, do something!"

"I'm dropping down."

"No!" Ann cried.

Dave fell about twenty feet to the side of the downed chopper. Star, by impulse, disregarding her safety, ran to him.

"Milt, he's fallen. I'll get back to you in a minute."

Ann ran over to Star and Dave. He had survived the fall, but looked like a mud puppy covered from head to toe with tide-water muck, silt, and kelp. Star was removing his right shoe when Ann arrived.

"Is he okay?" Ann asked.

Wop-Wop-Wop the chopper continued to hover above the trio.

Dave answered, "Yes and no. That was a dumb trick holding on, but I was getting frustrated. I'll get the dumbbell award for that move. And, yes, I survived for some reason, but I think I have a sprained ankle. I can already feel the swelling. I'll be damned; I've screwed up this rescue. We're in trouble now."

Ann gave him the hand-held and said, "Not so; I'm going to give it a try. Give 'em a call. I'll be on top in less than one minute. Bye."

"No, Ann. This old bird will probably float to shore as the tide comes in."

Star spoke up, "Save your breath; she's committed. I can tell. She'll not come back; she's determined to rescue that bird. Come on, let's go. Here, I'll help you walk."

"You're right," Dave agreed. "I'll get on the radio."

As Star helped Dave move to higher ground, Ann climbed up the side of the chopper.

*   *   *

"Milt, this is Dave. I'm okay, just a twisted ankle. We're not through yet. Ann is climbing up the side of the chopper now. Sorry, Rob. I couldn't stop Ann."

"Roger that, I understand. That woman . . . I doubt if I could have, either."

"Milt, she's in place. Drop down ten feet and move over to the right five feet . . . very slowly so the cable doesn't start swinging . . . that's it, slowly."

"Better now?" Milt asked.

"Yeah . . . good, just like that."

Ann looked like a flash dancer too as the blinking lights illuminated her on the top of the armature.

Dave continued, "Roger. Now descend another four feet. That's it. Hold . . . good, she's got the hook. No, it slipped out or her hand. The ball is swinging back. Yes, she's got it. Hold . . . hold; I think it's hooked. Yes, the cable is taut."

Milt answered, "Great. Tell her to slide off now! I'm giving this old bird some power. Your bird is stuck in the mud. Quick, tell her to jump if necessary, but get her off!"

Ann was sliding down the side of the chopper on the door side when the lifting chopper suddenly lurched into the sky. She fell down into the open door as Milt powered up and lifted the downed bird airborne.

*   *   *

Ann screamed as she tumbled down the side of the chopper and into the open door.

"A-h-h-h . . . Damnit . . . What the Hell?"

She hit the floor and slid into the dark cabin's interior.

"I've got to hold on to something . . . anything. Ah, here's a seat leg!"

The chopper suddenly lurched to the side.

"What the hell. Can't hold on . . . Christ!"

She lost her grip, and fell hard against the opposite side.

"O-h-h . . ."

Blackness.
Silence.

*   *   *

Dave yelled in the radio, "Ann's still aboard. She's still onboard!"

Rob came on the radio with a message she could not hear. "Jump! Jump now! Too late: Hold on, gal; you can do it, hold on! We'll get you out of there."

Now in the cabin area, unconscious, Ann did not hear Rob's plea.

Dave yelled, "What are you going to do, Milt? She may fall out!"

*   *   *

Milt answered calmly, "Nothing. She'll be banged up a little—but safe. I'm going to fly toward the hanger at full power and dare not stop. It's only a three-minute flight."

Rob, concerned for his gal, against commo rules, argued on air. "Damnit, Milt, we've got to set down now; she may be hurt. You know she'll be banged up. We're clear of the tidal water. Milt, we've got to go down. Milt!"

Milt answered calmly. "Rob, you may be right; she may be hurt; she may be knocked unconscious, but a few more minutes will get us nearer first aid at the hangar."

"Damn you, Milt, you're the PIC. I yield, but you're wrong. That's my future in that disabled chopper. She's my reason to live . . ."

"I understand. I love her too, but remember we're only a minute or two from the hangar. She'll make it."

Silence.

Milt called flight ops and requested a vehicle drive to the end of the runway and pick up Dave and Star.

Bill answered in the affirmative. A vehicle was already on the way, and a doctor on his way from Sitka to treat Dave and Ann, if necessary.

"Feel better, Rob? Bill's on the ball. As you can tell, he's been monitoring our channel—as any good manager would."

Rob responded, "No, five minutes could mean the difference between life and death."

Milt, with a little disgust in his voice, said, "Rob, have you figured how much time it would have taken us to lower the damaged chopper, drop the cable, land, and let you run to Ann's side? Let me answer—more than five minutes. Now, get ready to land. There are the hangar lights. You'll be releasing the cable in thirty seconds, get ready."

Silence.

A shock . . .

"Alpha One, this is Alpha Two. It looks like we'll finally make it back to the cage with this broken bird. Thanks for the ride."

"Ann! Are you okay?" Rob exclaimed.

"Yes and no. I've a big goose egg on my head. I must have been knocked out a few minutes, but you guys gave me such a rough ride, I came to and crawled into my seat. By the way, thanks."

"This is Milt. Welcome, girl. You did a great job, but had us worried . . . especially one guy up here. We're about to drop you, gal. Do me a favor and get away from your broken bird as soon as possible since I'll be releasing the cable right away."

"Roger that; let's go down."

The lowering went well for such weather. Ann evacuated safely with her newly found bumps and bruises, and the cable fell harmlessly to the apron.

While Milt and Rob landed, a vehicle hustled Dave and Star into ops for an exam by the waiting physician.

Within one minute, Bill and George from the service area had a dolly under the broken bird's carriage and pulled it into the hangar. Milt and Rob landed without incident. A field crew moved their bird into the hangar. After dashing into the ops area, Rob asked to talk to Milt alone. They moved into the kitchen area for coffee.

"Milt, please accept my apologies for my actions tonight. I was not thinking clearly. I'm sorry."

"No problem; your heart was in the right place, and for a moment it bumped or 'pumped' logic aside. I expected as much; you're in love. Let's just chalk this one up as a learning experience. You, too, will be a PIC and have to make a decision based on the safest option versus emotion. Say, that gal of yours is a real winner. Remember, I love her, too. Don't let 'the one' slip away."

"I'll do my best. Thanks again, Milt."

Rob hugged Milt, much to Milt's discomfort. They returned to flight ops to tell their stories, and unfortunately fill in the requisite paperwork on the incident for the FAA. It had been a long, difficult, but rewarding day for all.

Chapter 8

Sitka Field personnel and FFS crew shared some of their stories of the rescue while celebrating in ops. Milt, sensing a little too much loquacity, requested Bill, the manager, to step into the hangar a moment. He asked him if he would keep a lid on the chopper incident. Being kinda quiet would be better for all personnel. Milt considered the ingestion of a goose—or two—a normal flight problem along the coastal flyways, and the incident routine. He would report it as such. Milt did not want any probing FAA lackeys or local reporters trying to get a juicy story with the accompanying hyperbole in local and state newspapers.

Bill understood. He also said he would sign off on the FAA report in the most liberal fashion to eliminate the incident as an accident with personnel injuries. Dave was not hurt that bad, and Ann's bumps and bruises were minor. Retrieving the downed chopper would also be reported as a minor without mention of the weather's impact. The crushed landing gear on the pontoons would be treated as a routine strengthening/maintenance. No falsehoods would be used, just low-key terms that would not trigger an investigation.

Milt was by no means minimizing the problems of flying in the mountains and hazardous weather of Alaska. FAA had good reason to investigate *serious* accidents. FFS was one of the 150 general aviation-type commercial aircraft operators which flew in the rugged Yukon, British Columbia, the U.S. coastal areas of southwest Alaska. The local FAA director had said many times that the CFIT (Controlled Flight Into Terrain) in restricted visibility and unpredictable weather were the killers in the mountains.

There were a total of 1,665 aviation accidents in Alaska for the 10-year period of 1990- 99, an average of one accident every other day, with a fatality every nine days, making aviation the most dangerous profession in Alaska; 11% of the pilots would die in accidents, compared with 2.5% average in the other 49 states combined.

Milt and Bill agreed that the FAA report would be rudimentary as follows: one Sea Hawk helicopter forced down due to a bird strike; landing with autogyro was effective; landing gear was slightly damaged; retrieval by second helicopter was routine; repairs were completed at Sitka Field by certified airframe mechanics; aircraft log book was updated and signed; no personnel injuries were reported; aircraft was returned to service within 24 hours; one set of photos were available in the log book annex; no further entries.

Milt also requested that there be no interviews to outside sources by either of the two crews involved in the rescue and repair.

"Sounds good to me," Bill said. "I'll personally repair the landing gear tonight with one of my crew here, and troubleshoot the turbine's bird ingestion. I'll treat it as routine, even though we'll probably be working all night—or maybe not. Who knows until we get our hands dirty . . . or feathered."

"Thanks, Bill. I'll never forget you and your team's positive attitude."

"I've a feeling you've been stung in the past by an overzealous press looking for a spectacular story or an FAA person looking for a reason to fly to Alaska and hang around to suck on their government per diem. I've had a few of them, also."

"Right you are, Bill. I'll share a few stories with you over a beer someday." Milt chuckled. "By the way, did you pass my regrets to the chief?"

"Sure did. He scheduled you for tomorrow, okay?"

"Yep, that will give me a chance to fly over and drop off these supplies, pick up the Delta crew, and be back for lunch. Good work, Bill."

Milt and Bill returned to ops for a moment. Bill addressed his crew on Milt's request. Ann reported that she'd called Josie at Delta Station and Tom at FFS as to their status; and everyone was anxious to press their bunks.

Bill mentioned the dinner with Golden Bear tomorrow for all personnel present and the Delta Station crew. Sitting with his ankle soaking in Epson's Salts solution, Dave briefed the crew on their departure plans.

As they started to leave ops, Morning Star asked Milt if she could give thanks to the Great Spirit for His guidance and protection.

He answered, "By all means. Morning Star . . ."

She asked the assemblage to form a circle, join hands, and reflect on the day's events and adversity, then to offer thanks to the Great Spirit.

After a minute or so, she moved to the center of the circle, retrieved her medicine bag, and cast tobacco to the four points of the compass; then she looked up, extended her hands and arms upward, and chanted a melodic message:

"We thank you, Great Spirit, for this day
That we are allowed to live upon
Our Mother Earth.
For us two-leggeds,
 You give us courage and endurance;
These strengths are now ours.
We are blessed
As we face tomorrow."

*   *   *

The group thanked each other for their part in the evening's fraternity and paired off for a good night's sleep.

Silence returned to ops as Chuck from Bill's crew took his turn at the control center. George, Bill's other technician, joined him, and they left for the hangar to start their repair job.

Bill lingered a minute longer in ops, saying, "I won. Pay up, you scoundrels. I *told* you who went with whom. I believe the bet was ten bucks. That'll teach you rascals to bet against the boss. Yep, Dave with Star; Rob with Ann; and Milt with Janet. I've an eye for that sort of thing."

The boys paid up, but accused him of insider information, which he rejected. Bill and George headed for the hangar, and Chuck stayed to man the ops center console. It would be quiet tonight, but there still might be someone out there needing a place to put down in the storm.

* * *

Moments later, Ann wandered back into ops and asked Chuck if she could use the radio to call Josie. Caught off guard in seeing what she was wearing, he had a little trouble answering quickly since he had not seen a beautiful woman in her night clothes—up close and personal—for months. "Of course you may use the radio. I'll set the frequency for you."

He fumbled with the dials. He wasn't used to a woman's wonderful smell fresh out of the shower. He was not only nervous; he was stimulated.

"There you go; I'll step back. Here, use my seat."

"Why, thank you, Chuck; you're so kind."

Her body rubbed against his as she squeezed into his chair. He was aroused to the point of embarrassment as he backed away. He mused, *Control yourself, Chuck. It's just a woman, unfortunately that's the problem . . . hold on boy.*

* * *

Josie's radio was strapped across her chest so she could work around her new yurt office and still hear incoming messages. Later on, when the crew had crashed for the night, she was in the process of slipping her boots on when Ann's call came in.

"Delta Station, this is Sitka Field. Do you hear me?"

Josie keyed the mic. "This is Delta Station, Josie here. How're you doing, Ann? I'm so glad you called. This whole crew is half asleep, wondering if the boys and you girls made it, over."

"Indeed they did. Here's the latest: Alpha Two is being repaired as we speak; Dave's ankle is getting some TLC by Star, and I'm bruised a little, but nothing to worry about. My cosmetics will cover my black eye, and well, the bruise on my butt will be covered from everyone . . . but Rob. He thinks it's the greatest symbol he's ever seen for falling—the truth being, he likes the contrast with the other cheek—men—I'll carry it for a couple days, no doubt. I can hardly wait for what he'll say when it turns to purple, to red, and to yellow . . . geez. Speaking of horny guys, how are your men doing?"

The two gals' frisky chat stimulated Chuck even more as he sat back acting disinterested.

Before signing off, Ann told her about Milt's plans to fly over in the morning with the supplies and pick up everyone to have dinner with the chief.

"Get this, Josie; the chief asked if you wouldn't mind bringing the beagle pup with you; he kinda got used to the little fella at the meat market and wondered where he had gone. It's a small world, eh?"

"Indeed. That sounds great, Ann; I'll pass on the info to the crew here. I'm certain they'll rest easier now. Thanks for calling. Nothing further. Out."

"Sitka Field, out."

*   *   *

Ann gave Chuck a warm smile as she offered his chair and returned to her quarters. Before opening the door to the sleeping units, she turned back.

"By the way, Chuck," she said in a casual manner. "What bet did you just pay to Bill? I'm just curious; I heard my name."

"'Twas nothing, just on what time you guys would arrive here at ops. It gets a little lonely here, so we gamble a little to pass the time. That's all."

Ann gave him a quick look, then a doubting grimace to question his veracity, a look that had a lot of doubt in it.

"Really . . . what?" Chuck said with a nervous grin.

I've heard you were a good technician, pilot, and jack of all trades. Now I can testify that you also have a little Svengali in your story line."

"Not true!"

Ann walked toward him in a slight swagger and said, "Fess up. I don't believe you." She stopped within inches of his sweating brow. Her fresh, womanly scent filled his nostrils.

He faltered. "Okay. Busted! Our innocent little game, or bet, after noting there were three guys and three gals, was: Who was with whom? and Who was closest to *Playboy*'s Ten. We're guilty—as charged. Anyway, Bill won both bets. He guessed you were the Ten. He must have had some inside info. Anyhow, you and Rob look like you're made for each other; I wish you two all the best. And know this: now that I've met you, you're a Ten in my book, too."

"No harm done. I'm glad you boys had a little fun with your mysterious visitors from Skagway. Good night." She surpised him again by turning back and giving him a little kiss on the cheek. "I like men with a little spunk. Thank the crew from me for working tonight."

*   *   *

Chuck was taken aback by Ann's aggressive style. It was refreshing to have her around. Ann sure lit-up a room; she's a winner.

"Night," Chuck said as he reflected on her winning ways. He returned to the ops console and checked for incoming messages while Bill and George worked on the broken bird in the hangar. One thing was certain, it would take all his skills to get Ann off his mind . . . and all Bill and George's skills in restoration and technical know how to get the Sea Hawk flying again by dawn.

*   *   *

Bill said, "George, let's look at the bird strike to the turbine inlet first; the aluminum struts supporting the pontoons will be the easiest to repair. We'll get to them later."

They rolled elevated work platforms to both sides of the chopper. George started pulling off the larger pieces of body parts that were impacted against the screen covering the air intake. After removing a few pairs of legs with webbed feet, a beak or two, and various primary feathers, he felt better about the damage assessment. "Bill, there's more than one bird splattered on the screen over the air intake; I've an idea that most of the larger parts did not go into the blades of the turbine—much less the combustion chamber—or the propulsion fins. The good news, I think, is that the turbine stopped due to air starvation; there could be no combustion without the turbo blower working. Whoever added this debris screen had probably lost a turbine once by tree leaves or bird strikes. That's expensive, especially if you cannot recover by autogyroing to the surface. I'll bet once we remove all these impacted parts, this old feller will cough and choke a little and spring back to life. Let's give it a try. Come on, I'll bet you ten bucks she'll turn and start the first or second time."

"You sound pretty certain, George. If you're right, the FFS boys will be happy."

George answered, "Okay, I'm just about finished vacuuming."

The hum of activity resonated about the hangar. It was music to Bill's ears. Good technical support personnel, like George or Chuck would rather be working on aircraft or flying than doing nothing.

George said in an excited voice, "I'm finished. Come up and take a look. I've got this bird looking cleaner than your jeep."

Bill took a look. He said, "You're wrong George; there are no feathers in my jeep . . . or dried blood. But it looks good. Let's do it?"

After getting down, Bill opened the hangar door slightly so the turbine would not suck all the air from inside the hangar. Meanwhile George climbed into the pilot's seat and said he would set the instrumentation for an automatic starting sequence. He reported that all systems checked out, and that the battery charge looked good. He was ready. "Bill, are you ready?"

"Yep, the door is open a bit, and it appears we're all set. Wait! I'm going to swing the bird around so the exhaust is pointing to the door. I don't think we want the inside of the hangar looking as if we'd had a pillow fight."

Bill rotated the dolly 90 degrees and stayed a little off center from the exhaust plume. "Go, George. I'm waiting here for some scrambled goose eggs."

Silence . . . but for the howling wind streaking under the door as George initiated the start sequence.

Then a low frequency grinding noise: *G-g-ggg-r-rrr*. The starting motor had engaged the flywheel.

Ka-tchoom!

Silence.

G-g-g-g-rrrrr.

W-o-m-p!

George yelled, "We've got ignition!"

P-o-p!

"Damn," he added. "We've lost it!"

Bill yelled, "Figures! Try it again!"

"Will do."

G-g-g-g-g-r-r-rrrr.

W-o-m-p.

"We've got it!" George yelled. "We're good here on the flight deck. What is it like out there?"

"Let's put it this way: I look like the lead dancer in the ballet 'Goose Lake,' minus the tutu. It looks like most of the debris has passed through. Run her up to one-thousand RPMs for a few seconds and shut her down; we can do a full test outside in the morning. Ugh, what a mess."

"Bill, I'd like to engage the rotors just to make sure they're okay. Stand by."

"Sure enough, good idea."

With pride in his eyes, Bill watched George working in the cockpit as he engaged the transmission to the blades. It was a good idea. He might have overlooked this point. That's why he trusted George with anything he owned; he was top notch.

"She's in good shape, boss. I'll rotate a few more times, change pitch, and call it a night on *this* part. Now for the landing gear repair."

As George was turning off the system, he announced, "Bill, we've got a visitor."

"What!"

"Try to behave yourself; Ann is here. Look over your shoulder."

"Why? What?"

Bill looked towards the ops door and, sure enough, there she was in her robe. Already titillated by her presence earlier in the day, he walked toward her—and immediately undressed her with his eyes. Her three-quarter length light blue robe, that matched her eyes, was of a thin material that hung on her body, leaving little to the imagination. Her red hair, no longer in a pony tail, hung down over her back on one side, and over her ample breast on the other.

"Hi!" she greeted him. "I was having a restless sleep and couldn't help but come out and congratulate you guys for getting the old Sea Hawk smoking again. Good work, men. Good karma must be with you tonight, or as Morning Star would say, 'Good Medicine.' I'm so glad I came out to see you guys; now I know we'll make it home tomorrow. After this incident, I'll never look at a goose in the same way. Why couldn't we have ingested a local migratory bird like the Bristle-thighed Curlew? They only weigh one pound versus the twenty-pound goose. Oh well; that's life. It's too bad any have to die along their migratory route, but who said life's fair? Believe me, it's not."

"No problem, Ann," Bill said as he moved closer. "That's our job—keep 'em flying."

George had closed the door and joined them as they chatted about strengthening and welding the crushed landing gear connected to the pontoons.

"Hi, George. Good show. I love the turbine sound. Lucky for us, it's back. I'll see you guys in the morning. I'm buying. Good night."

She started to walk away, but turned back and approached them again.

"You know, I shouldn't be handing out kisses in my robe at bedtime, but here's one for each of you. You both deserve a little thanks."

After she gave each a kiss on the cheek and walked away, one thing was on Bill's mind.

"Damn, George," Bill said, "from the action I see from here, I don't think there's anything between that gown and her."

"Me neither. There's no way. There's just too much action there."

She stopped, turned around quickly, and caught them wide-eyed, staring at her. She spoke in a calming way, "It's good to see you guys are normal. My butt isn't. Checking out my 'action' or altered walk with a bruised 'cheek' is flattering. Thank you fellas, and good night."

As she walked into ops and closed the door, they both looked at each other, and Bill said, "George, her visit was worth a lot to me. How 'bout you?"

"Damn."

"Hum, I've rarely heard you speechless. That's what I thought, too. Damn. Well, my man, we'd better get back to work. We've a full night ahead of us. One thing is certain, though; we've just received a little stimulus to do our job with gusto."

Bill mused, *She knew exactly what she was doing to us. She knew what we needed, even without the bruised cheek on her butt.*

"I'll get the welding equipment, George. You get the other tools. Let's make a crooked and crushed straight and strong."

Chapter 9

As the sun crested over the mountains to the east, Milt walked while Dave limped from ops across the apron to hangar B-1. They stopped halfway to give Dave's ankle a rest and looked across the field to runway 90, which had not been very visible last night.

The air was crisp and clear from the storm's cleansing effect. The freshness gave the land renewal in a deeper green and the sky in a clearer blue. Milt felt thankful for surviving the harrowing experiences the previous night. The darting and croaking seagulls had returned to scavenge the storm's debris.

A raven sat in a stoic manner on a large cedar near the hangar. Other storm-tossed branches were scattered across the apron and runways. Several youngsters were already picking up miscellaneous debris around the apron, runways, and taxi-ways. Someone was on the ball to have the kids hustling so early. Then again, maybe it was an automatic assignment for some nearby kids.

The kids suddenly swung their little tractor and trailer around and headed toward the men. A cute girl yelled, "Hey, mister, you want this torn windsock? We've already put a new one up the pole. We thought you'd like it as a souvenir of your difficult landing last night. By the way, mister, welcome to Sitka."

She gave Milt the flag; then the kids drove away and continued their cleanup. The talkative girl waved from the back of the trailer. As Milt and Dave waved back, Milt wished he could chat with the girl who understood that what to others would be a rag was to them a memento of their survival.

Milt held up the tattered, sun-bleached wind sock, squeezed the water out, and folded it neatly.

"You know, Dave, that girl's a winner. I'll ask Bill who she is. She was right that I do collect things like this."

Dave grimaced. "Collect! You've got so many 'collectibles' hanging on the walls at our flight ops—it looks like a little Smithsonian."

"You're just a little hard on me, don't you think? Your trouble is, you've missed out when the Great Spirit handed out emotions."

"You're a piece of work. I've got emotions—and the 'tidy' genes that you lack."

"Maybe so, but remind me to pay Bill for the replacement sock the kids just put up. It's the least we could do for their help, and let's make sure they charge us enough for the overnight, overtime repairs. The DNR will be sharing this bill, be assured of that."

"As to your inordinately collection—deranged mind, you'll probably want the damaged struts from the Sea Hawk, too."

"Hey, good idea."

"When will I learn to keep my big mouth shut around you 'string collectors'?"

"All kidding aside, isn't this a beautiful spot? The mountains, the bay, and the ocean so close. The Delta Station crew is really goin' to like it here. It's only about twenty-five miles to their site."

"Okay, my man, let's move on; my ankle is rested. I'll make the last trek to the hangar without a problem. I'm anxious to see how the boys did last night."

As they approached the partially-opened hangar door, Dave stopped and smelled the air. "Smell that? I swear that's the odor of drying paint. Gal dang it, I'll bet they're done rebuilding the struts and they've thrown a fresh coat of paint on, too. Damn, that's good news. Come on, let's open the door higher and have a look. You do it. I can't put much pressure on this ankle."

Milt leaned over to lift the huge hangar door, then paused.

Milt said, "You dummy, this door weighs a ton; it's probably raised with a chain-fall assist or a power opener—"

As the words left his lips, a motor's whine sounded as the door started moving in a slow, grinding motion and the leviathan inched upward. At eight feet, they could look in and see the Sikorsky Sea Hawk 70B sitting silently as if waiting to leap into the sky. Then again, it also had the looks of a large spider staring at its approaching victims as if hoping to entangle them in its lethal web. Dave and Milt looked at each other, smiled, and looked back into the hangar.

The grinding, lifting noise stopped as the massive door reached its full height and they heard footsteps inside.

*   *   *

"Good morning," Bill said in greeting the FFS boys. "Coffee is brewing, sweet rolls have just been delivered, and your chopper is ready for a test flight. I've entered the strengthening modification to the landing struts in the chopper's log book, plus entered routine maintenance to the turbine. Your ship's ready. It's signed, sealed, and delivered—FOB—Sitka Field. Isn't that right, George?"

"Absolutely. The routine maintenance you requested is complete," he responded with a grin. "I've entered my FAA authorized stamp in the book."

All four shook hands and moved toward the inviting smell of freshly brewed coffee and that wonderful aroma of sticky buns. Adding to the splendor of the magnificent machines housed in B-1 was the entry of the sun stealing across the floor.

As they encircled the Sea Hawk with coffee in hand, a noise just outside the doors caught their attention.

The clean-up crew had stopped outside, and a young girl yelled.

"Hey, Dad, we're done and on the way to the dumpster. Is there anything else you need?"

"No, that's fine, babe. Good job; I'll see you for lunch. Your mother is busy, and you're going to be my date with the chief. Remember, here at noon."

"I wouldn't miss it. Hi, Milt and Dave . . . and George, I know you're in there somewhere. Bye."

"Hi, Lynn. I'm in the Hawk. See you later. Bye."

"I should have guessed, your daughter. We met earlier. She's some gal; I bet you're proud."

"Yep, she's sixteen going on twenty. An academic, a pilot, an athlete, and my shooting star, she never slows down. In fact, she's giving ground school training to some new student pilots this afternoon. I'll make sure we sit near you and Janet so you can get to know her."

"Fine, I'll look forward to meeting her formally."

Bill mentioned that Milt's Black Hawk looked kinda lonely since the Sea Hawk was getting all the attention, but said that he had topped the tanks and cleaned her up, too.

The four reunited at the Sea Hawk, and George explained the repairs and replacement parts to the struts. Sure enough, Milt wanted the twisted and crunched tubular aluminum.

One word from Dave to Milt said it all: "Figures."

George asked, "What's that mean?"

Milt looked at Dave, then at George and said, "Nothing."

Bill chatted freely with a sense of pride. "The rain washed a lot of the footprints off the turbine housing and rotor's armature, but it took a good shot from the power washer to eliminate all those footprints. It looks as if you had a board meeting up there. Who was up there?"

Dave explained with a little humor in his voice the circumstances of his failed first attempt to attach the lifting cable, then Ann's success.

George interrupted. "Damn, I didn't realize how difficult it must have been. You're two lucky people, you with only a sprained ankle—was Ann hurt?"

Their attention shifted to the ops door.

Dave said, "Why don't you ask her? She and Rob are entering the hangar now."

George turned and looked toward the ops door. Sure enough, there she was—dressed—and said, "I've got to tell you, Dave, we saw some 'action' on that woman last night."

"What do you mean?"

"Well, she stopped by with a short thin robe on, and . . ."

Ann, with a fresh cup of coffee, yelled, "Hi, guys!"

George whispered, "Later, Dave. Let's just say she's hot, and she kinda strutted her stuff last night."

George and Dave attacked the 'bun' table.

Ann joined the group and shared her thoughts on her visit last night with Milt and Dave, which was to give them some emotional support.

Milt and Bill pulled the Black Hawk out while Ann and George pulled the refurbished Sea Hawk to the apron. Dave sat, resting his ankle.

Ann had a little private talk with Milt and, when they separated, she called George and Dave over to share a decision Milt had made.

Ann would be in charge of the Sea Hawk's flight test, the trip to Delta Station with supplies, and the return of the station personnel by noon. Rob would be in support. They would be PICs for both choppers. Milt and Dave would fly as copilots. The decision was partially triggered, Milt explained, to give Ann and Rob PIC experience, and Dave a lesser role due to his injury.

*   *   *

Ann asked everybody to stick around so they could get together for a quick meeting as soon as the girls arrived.

While having their last cup of coffee, George approached Ann cautiously. "Ann, I want to thank you for the visit last night. Ah . . . it made . . . ah, me feel good . . . kinda stimulated. Thanks."

"Well, thank you, George. I'll let you in on a little secret. I came in my robe because I couldn't find anything else to wear; my flight suit was in the wash. Anywho, after I heard that turbine, I felt so good, I would have come out there naked—well, maybe not, but I was excited and wanted to share the feeling with you guys. I hope I didn't throw a monkey wrench in your activities."

"Hell no! I mean . . . no way. Your visit gave us a 'mental lift,' or you might say, a reward, or a stimulant to give the impacted geese . . . a goose!"

"I'll say it again: even though I was partially dressed, it was a privilege to join in your success last night. Look at my proof of being here."

She turned around and displayed a goose feather in her curls.

"Bee—Yoo—Tiful," George said. "Your feathered tresses look much better than mine looked earlier. Just after I shut down the turbine, Bill said I looked like a gosling fresh out of the nest."

Ann chuckled, "Indeed you did. I remember well. In fact, much of the hangar was littered with feathers. Where'd they fly away to?"

"'Twasn't easy, but an air hose and vacuum did the trick."

"Right," Ann chimed in, "but you two looked like winners to me with your hair and body frocked with feathers or not." She giggled.

George let her know one more time how nice she looked last night. "Ann, you look great in your flight suit, but not as sexy as the outfit you had on last night."

"Thanks. Between you and me, and my butt, I'm still walking with a lot of action to minimize the pain."

They both giggled and started talking the business of the day—flying.

Bill and Milt joined the jocular pair as Dave and Ann traded stories about the harrowing flight last evening, and George teased them about flying into goose air space again today.

When Star and Janet entered the hangar, Ann announced their arrival. "There you are, girls. Welcome to this lighthearted crowd of merrymakers. Help yourselves to chow before these animals inhale the remains."

"Will do," Janet said, "but we both need some dessert first."

Ann gave them a puzzled look.

Without hesitation, both Janet and Star grabbed their men and gave them a big good morning smack. They kissed with such vigor that Ann felt a little envious. In short order, Ann laid one on Rob.

As the girls chowed down, Ann took the initiative to brief them about the overnight repairs, flight readiness, and Milt's plans for departure to Delta Station.

"Milt tells me that Dave and I are going to Delta Station in the Sea Hawk, too. It will be our test flight since it's only twenty-five miles, and Rob and Milt will be on our wing. It will also be less crowded flying back with the four Delta crew, Joe, Leigh and Bear, and yes, the beagle."

Rob joined in the briefing to give details of time of departure, stay time at Delta, and estimated arrival time back at Sitka Field.

Ann spoke up. "If you're wondering why Rob and I are doing the briefing today, it's because Milt and Dave have been generous in letting us fly as PICs. Don't worry, they'll remain as copilots. Any questions?"

If there were, none spoke up.

"Okay then, listen up. Everybody hit the latrine. We'll take off in thirty minutes. It's zero six hundred now. We depart at zero six-thirty."

As they paired off, Rob joined Ann, stealthily grabbed her butt, and said, "Good job, dear. I'm sorry I didn't get a chance to check out that butterfly on your cheek this morning."

"Butterfly!"

"Yes, indeed, Papillon!"

"What? What the hell are you talking about?"

"My Dear, papillon is 'butterfly' in French, and your bruise has taken that shape. Take a look tonight. You'll need a mirror. I can hardly wait until it turns from black, to purple, to red, and to yellow . . . and back to pink. Somewhere in that transition—you'll be a fluttering Monarch."

"You know, with all your balderdash, you should be a poet—in the underground press."

She motioned for him to come closer.

He moved to her side.

Smack was the sound as she hauled off and laid a fist to his abs. "Let me know if there's a bruise, and if it's in the shape of a butterfly, you bugger."

He giggled.

She grimaced. "Damn, that hurt, you ol' rock-belly."

"Good," he jokingly said as they headed their separate ways to the choppers.

Ann coordinated departure times with Chuck in ops, filed a brief flight plan, and asked him to contact Josie at Delta Station.

During loading, Bill asked to see Ann alone.

"What is it, Bill?"

"I've a special favor to ask you."

"Shoot."

"Lynn, who is so impressed with the FFS and Delta Station group, would like to fly with you today. As I can tell, she'd just like to be with you guys, and meet Josie and the boys from U of M. That may be a big reason. She's heard about them, saw them sail over here a few times, and I'll bet she's interested. What can I say?"

"Say no more. I'm sure she can come; we've got room, even with the beagle riding back to see the chief. In fact, I may ask her to fly as my copilot—if Dave approves. His ankle injury makes him a marginal pilot with the pedal controls anyway. You said earlier that she had been checked out in a chopper. Which one, what model?"

"The one over there in the corner, the Bell-10, two-seater, piston-powered bird."

"Do you think she'd like to be my copilot?"

"Is the Pope Catholic? Yes!"

Ann looked at the smaller B-10, then at Bill. She smiled and said, "If Dave and Milt agree, it's a done deal."

Ann asked Bill to stand by as she talked to Milt and Dave with their proposal. After huddling a few moments, they shared some serious concerns regarding her qualifications, FFS insurance coverage, and age. They glanced over at the father and daughter, then back at Ann. After some serious soul searching, especially in light of the recent incident, they agreed to take a chance. The only other person aboard would be Dave as back up, and they'd treat the flight as a training flight and checkout of the refurbishment.

Bill and Lynn waited as Ann, Dave, and Milt approached.

Ann thought, *I hope I'm doing the right thing. Why am I taking a chance in light of what happened last night? Manitou, be with me on this one. I'm going to need all the help I can get.*

The trio stopped and faced Bill and Lynn with serious expressions.

Ann spoke. "Lynn, Milt, and Dave have given tentative approval for you to fly as my copilot, but have deferred to me as the PIC for the final decision."

She shifted her eyes to Bill.

"Bill, I ask you, since Lynn is underage, do you approve?"

Lynn looked at her dad with all the emotion she could muster.

Bill looked at Lynn.

In a crisp, strong voice, Bill answered, "Affirmative!"

Lynn teared up, stepped to her dad, and hugged him so tight that, he, too, teared.

"Enough, you two. Come with me, Lynn; we've some work to do. Ann explained the flight plan as they walked to the bird.

"Here's the test-flight paperwork for the FAA. It will be your responsibility to fill it out correctly."

"Yes, sir."

"It's Ann. Let's get aboard and check this baby out."

Before boarding, Rob, the new PIC with Milt, stopped both of them. Rob spoke first, "Welcome, wingwomen. It will be a pleasure for us to be your wingmen on our flight today. One thing has to happen first . . ."

Ann warned her, "Look out, he's up to his old romantic flying tricks—from the past!"

Lynn said, "Ohmygod! What have I forgotten, Ann? What?"

"Nothing—look out!"

Rob gently grabbed Lynn. "We've got to give you the kiss of luck from an old hand at flying—it's tradition!"

Rob gave Lynn a little peck on the cheek, shook her hand, and wished her luck. While Ann was giggling on the sidelines, he quickly grabbed her and laid a big suck face on her. Rather than shake her hand, he grabbed her butt, and said, "How's my papillon?"

Lynn gave her dad a puzzled look.

Not to be outdone, assuming there was such a tradition, Dave, Milt, and Bill kissed the girls and shook their hands.

*   *   *

As Rob, Milt, Janet, and Star boarded the Black Hawk on the tarmac, Star said to Janet, "My, hasn't my Dave turned into a cavalier gentleman. I'm surprised he took the initiative to kiss Lynn."

Milt countered, "You're right, my dear. A couple months ago, he would not have done so—much less get that close to a woman. You've been good for him, Star. He's now a much more rounded man. Congratulations."

"I guess you're right."

As the pilots started their preflight checks, Star thought, *I hope he's not too well rounded, and forgets where his true love dwells.*

Star looked out the window of the chopper with a melancholy feeling as Ann, Lynn, and Dave boarded the Sea Hawk.

Suddenly the spell was broken as Rob spoke into the IC. "Strap 'em in; we're ready to rumble."

Star and Janet waved at the ground crew that watched as the turbines screamed with power while they lifted into the blue Alaskan sky.

Unsettled by all the activity, a raven retained its perch in a nearby tree.

Chapter 10

As the two helicopters lifted from the tarmac and flew to the southwest, a regal ebony raven followed as if the third wingman.

Ann was a little nervous being the first to fly the Sea Hawk after the bird strike and repairs. Nevertheless, she did not want to show her concerns to copilot Lynn, or Dave acting as crew chief. Yet, every different sound—a click, a change in RPM or a *pop* all of which were routine, triggered a concern, a worry, a thought that somehow a fan blade or rotor may have been damaged. In fact, she found herself straining over the *Wop-Wop-Wop* of the rotor blades to hear . . . to create a new, a strange, an unusual sound in the turbine's whine. She remembered so well that since the first flights of man leaving the earth's gravity, all pilots listen for the *unusual* sound, the change in pitch, the doubting of instruments . . . could they be in error? From Orville in 1903 in his plane at Kitty Hawk, to Neil in 1969 in the lunar lander Eagle on the moon's surface, pilots have listened to the *normal* sound . . . hoping not to hear the abnormal.

Fortunately, there seemed to be none. She had to admit or convince herself of the simplicity of the turbine design and its reliability over piston-powered engines. Early in her training, she had learned of the turbine's dependability, partially due to its fewer moving parts. Everything about the turbine was advantageous, except for the critical need for large quantities of air through its intake and the thermal problems associated with masses of hot gases escaping to the rear.

As the pair gained elevation to 500 feet, the splendor of Sitka Sound was expressed by the sparkling aquamarine water blending in with the green coniferous forest. In contrast, the mountains now free of snow looked forbidding. They were, as pilots had frequently avowed . . . demonic. They had claimed the lives of many a friend. Many had paid the final price for a shortcut over them, only to fly into them.

Ann called Rob with an idea that they might fly along the coastline to the south in a clockwise pattern over the old fort and the fishing villages, then approach Delta Station from the south.

Rob agreed, but with one condition: the shakedown flight had to be their number-one priority.

While the Sea Hawk flew over the old Sitka Fort with Lynn talking to Ann as if a tour guide, Ann had an idea.

"Alpha One, Lynn is giving Dave and me a real treat as she describes the historical and current aspects of Sitka and the area around the Sound. I'm going to switch to channel seven, frequency one-zero-two point one. Okay? Got it? Put on your IC, too. She says it will only take her about ten minutes. Over."

"Roger." Rob answered. "Channel seven for ten minutes." He told his crew what was planned and switched channels.

"Alpha Two, this is Alpha One on channel seven, send your traffic."

"Cool. Have at it, Lynn." Ann replied.

*   *   *

With a charming and magnetic voice, Lynn gave the background of the Russian fur traders and their brutal treatment of the Aluets and the Tlingets from the Aleutian Islands all the way to Sitka Sound. She described the defensive purpose of the elevated Russian fort on the island directly in front of the settlement. From 1799 to 1802, the town was called New Archangel, and the furtraders' relationship with the local natives was peaceful. The change in their relationship took place when the otter and seal population declined. Hostility followed when the settlement's rations were cut, and the Russians had to divert their attention to the British and American explorers who also prowled the area for furs in the early 1800s.

The local natives and Russians lived near each other during the fruitful days of harvesting the local otter and seal population. Over time, the abuse to the natives became unbearable, so they revolted.

With a little giggle in her voice, she explained that every cannon along the stockade wall was aimed out to hostile ships at the entrance to the Sound, but when the fort was attacked by local Indians in canoes and then on foot, the cannons were useless. Their trajectory could not be lowered enough to shoot canister rounds. The fort was burned to the ground, the island abandoned; and the Tlingits moved inland. The record shows, she added, that the artillery officer was hung.

The fort was rebuilt, but the fur trade declined, and without native help, the Russians left in 1818.

As the choppers swept around the southern shore, she pointed out the two major industrial buildings that hugged the shore. The one with the tall stacks billowing and numerous ships at dock was the cannery. The second was the pulp mill with its huge pile of logs on one end and a pyramid of wood chips and sawdust on the other.

As with most of Alaska's shorelines, there was very little beach, no gradual incline to the water, and the mountains seemed to terminate at the shore. This physical characteristic did not favor human habitation along the shore—bird rookeries, yes; people, no.

She pointed out the little island outcrops of lava where some of the fishermen processed fish and tended their nets.

As Ann turned to fly due north across the Sound's entrance, Lynn pointed out a pod of killer whales in pursuit of baby seals for lunch. She mentioned that Orcas frequented the Sound now and then to vary their diet from salmon to otters to seals. They rarely bothered humans. Lynn got the nod from Ann and relinquished the mic to her.

*   *   *

"Alpha One, this is Ann. Our chamber tour, so well done by Lynn, is over. Return to channel nine. Over."

Pause. Static.

"This is Alpha One. Roger. All of us here have enjoyed Lynn's briefing. We'll be better prepared now when we meet the chief. Thanks again; pass on our regards to Lynn."

"Roger that," Ann responded. "Break. Break, Delta Station; this is Alpha Two; do you read?"

Static.

Silence.

*   *   *

"Alpha Two, this in Josie, I hear you loud and clear. We be waiting for ye with bells-on, me god. Da boys have two landing pads marked of ye—one permanent, the other temporary. Come on in."

"Good. A-One is monitoring, but I'll pass the word. See you soon."

"Rob, did you hear that?"

"Roger, gal. We'll hold off out here as you might as well land first. Give us a call when you're down—right side up—I hope." He giggled.

"Listen, with this female crew . . . was there any doubt? Roger, we'll call when we're safely resting on sweet Mother Earth."

"Roger. By the way, how's that copilot of yours working out?"

"Mighty fine. Dave has been working with her as I fly. He indicates she just may be ready for a check flight in this bird. Like all us women, she, too, is a quick study. She'll soon be a leader of men, too."

"Geez," Rob whispered in the mic.

"Well, it's true!"

"Yes, dear. This is A-One on the side."

Josie chuckled at the frisky sexual interplay between Rob and Ann. At times, she felt weary of their banter back and forth about equality. But, being of a different age, she felt less inclined to verbalize her thoughts. She let her actions speak in the competitive world of tough women and rough men in Alaska's unforgiving environment. Ann had retained a bit of feminism hatched in the '60s and gave

Bear, Joe, and others that stare of "How could you say such a thing about women?" Of course, these old guys would never change. Women were women and men were men—the twain ne'er to be equal. Half the time her love, Joe, never even noticed Ann's stare when he made a sexist faux pas. There was never any harm done; neither of the old boys were obnoxious about it—for they never even knew of their error.

Ann had been paying her dues to equality. She'd mucked out the stalls with Rob, and ridden lead on trail rides. In fact, she'd taken the parties to the mountains by herself. She was a wrangler, a pilot, a college graduate; and still she maintained the air of a loving, dedicated wife.

*   *   *

As A-2 approached Delta Station on its final, Dave sat near Lynn.

"Here's what I want you to do," said Dave. "Put both hands on the controls and your feet lightly on the pedals. I'd like you to get the feel of the controls as Ann brings her to a final, hovers, and lands.

"Will do," Lynn answered in a nervous tone.

"Good idea," Ann said. "I'll tell her what I'm doing so she'll also know the why."

"True, good idea. Lynn, I'd also like you to take over the commo to the ground. Do you copy?" said Dave.

"Affirmative."

"Is that okay by you, Ann?"

"Affirmative."

*   *   *

At 500 feet, one mile due south of the station on the promontory, Lynn called Josie.

"Delta Station, this is Lynn in A-Two, we're on our final. Are the pads clear?"

"They are. 'Tis as clear as they will ever be, but remember, 'tis no concrete pad with a pretty white X marking the spot as you have at Sitka Field. 'Tis only a cleared circular area marked with rocks on the perimeter. This is not downtown—it's out-of-town."

"Roger that. It sounds good to me. With the record rain, we'll not likely stir up the terrain."

"'Tis true. As Bob Barker used to say, 'Come on down.'"

Dave moved closer to Lynn and watched her hands and feet as Ann started down to her final. "Do you feel the controls? Are they similar to the H-ten?"

"I do. As expected, they're heavier and stiffer than the little H-ten."

Within minutes, the A-Two was throttled back as they passed over the shoreline and Ann changed rotor pitch as well. The bird rocked upward in a tail-down mode and quickly righted as Ann gave the forward pitch control a little nudge forward.

The station's layout was triangular, like an arrowhead, with the larger operations yurt at its point and the two living yurts to the rear. The landing pads were at the southern edge of the clearing.

"Lynn, that motion is typical of most of these birds; they pitch and roll a little when you throttle down or change rotor pitch. It's nothing to be concerned about. Did you feel me nudge the pitch control to level us out?"

"I did."

"It will happen again when I swing the tail around when aligning to the pad for touchdown."

"Roger that."

The juryrigged pads were easy to find, as was the wind-sock, which those in the choppers didn't expect to see.

With a slight offshore breeze, Ann circled around to the east and landed into the gentle wind on the pad to the west. By doing so, Rob would not have to fly over their chopper.

The noisy activity must have triggered the raven's flight; it left its favorite perch to soar over the Sound.

*   *   *

"Thank you, Lynn. I'll take over now. Good job. I'd feel uncomfortable if I wasn't on the horn at touchdown."

"Josie, I'm about to crash your party. Are you prepared for this gang?"

"Ready, willing, and able, my dear. Bring her in."

"One question first: whose pantaloons did you alter to make that windsock?"

"There's no need to know. Da boys rarely wear anything but shorts anyway. Plus, if I was their mother, and I'm close to being so, I'd shut to the rag-bag half of their torn and patched trousers. By the way, da boys are sure interested in your copilot."

"Is that right? We'll see if the Wolverines can behave. 'Nuff said. Anyway, I think the sock is beautiful as long as the guys do not have to run around with their bare butts hanging out."

"Ha," Josie said. "Wait 'til you see the patches on their clothes."

"I'll be off the radio for a while, Josie. We're about to land."

Ann called Rob in A-One and let him know they were about to land and their landing site would be clear.

As they bounced the landing gear onto the pad, Ann said to Lynn, "Why don't you shut her down with Dave's help while I let Sitka Field know we've landed."

"Will do."

Lynn cut the turbine power, disengaged the rotors, and shut off the fuel supply. Dave watched with interest while she demonstrated a serious professional manner. After shutdown was complete, they joined Josie, Joe, Leigh, and Bear by the makeshift kitchen area. While sharing stories of the previous night's trauma, the boys joined them and added their two cents.

Seconds later, the boys had convinced Lynn to help them unload the chopper before A-One landed.

"Well," Josie said, "it didn't take them long to get her to 'volunteer.'"

Ann said, "They mean no harm; they know very well she's 'jail bait.' They're well aware that she's only sixteen. They're just anxious to talk to the new girl on the block."

No sooner were the supplies unloaded than the four headed toward the shoreline and a quick tour of the camp along the way.

Josie laughed. "I'd like to be a little mouse and hear all the stories those Wolvies are laying on her."

*   *   *

"Fellas, I feel so good, kinda buoyant—supercharged is more like it—yet still full of goose bumps from the FFS people letting me fly. I'm ecstatic. Please excuse my preoccupation with the honor they've extended. It will take me a moment to get my head out of the clouds and down to earth."

As they listened to Lynn's exciting story of flying the big bird, introductions occurred, and not surprisingly, Luke was the one of the four Gospels who got most of the attention.

"Come to me, baby; we've missed you. I hear the chief has, too," Lynn cooed.

Matthew gave her the puppy. She embraced and kissed the little fella. "Thank you—is it Matt?"

"Oui, Mademoiselle." *Yes, madam.*

"Parlez-vous français?" Lynn asked. *Do you speak French?*

"Je parle un peu français." *I speak a little French.*

"D'ou' venez-vous." *You speak very well.*

Matt mentioned that Josie had been giving lessons to the boys at night. She had teased them that the dog, Luke, was picking it up faster. She indicated that Luke already knew, venir—come, s'asseoir—sit, and talon—heel.

Lynn had to laugh at that comparison.

"Arreter!" Lynn said to the dog as she played with Luke. *Stop chewing!*

"Yeah," John spoke up, "so far Luke is learning French faster than all of us. Luke's certainly smarter than Mark."

With that, Mark gave John a quick smack. John immediately apologized to Lynn, and Mark did the same.

Lynn laughed. "No matter. I've a little brother who's always teasing me. In fact, he's always on a slippery slope. We punch on each other all the time."

"Touché," John barked. "It sounds like we've had enough of our dirty wash exposed to our guest."

"Conversely," she chuckled, "you guys appear normal to me."

"Come on," Matthew said, "Let's go check out the Hobies."

As they showed Lynn their Hobie Cats, Alpha One descended over them and headed for the landing pad.

*   *   *

"Thanks for the comeback, Josie; we'll be landing in a few minutes. The pad looks great. Thanks. By the way, we also appreciate the wind-sock. Whoever donated one leg of their pants is to be thanked. If you, I'm anxious to see you in a one-legged outfit. I'd even sing you a song: 'Josie's the Queen of the Burlesque Show.'"

"Funny you're not, Rob. I can see you've got some of the same ideas as these Wolverine boys. Anyway, the sock is not from my pantaloons."

"Okay then, you can cut the other leg off and wear them as 'hot pants' as in the '70s. That would look swell to us guys."

"Stop it, you scalawag. Milt, tell him to behave himself and hand that bird over to you."

Milt answered, "He's beyond help. However, I'll do the best I can and hold him while you punch him out in about one minute. We're descending now."

"Men! You're all alike. Wait, did you say you'd hold him? That's a deal."

Rob flew the Black Hawk over the clearing, turned, and flew into the wind, then gently set down on the improvised pad.

He immediately called Sitka Field and told Chuck they'd landed, and that both choppers were working well. He also asked Chuck to pass on congratulations to Bill and George for a job well done on both choppers. He mentioned that they'd be returning to Sitka in two hours for lunch with the chief, with an ETA of 1220 hours and plans to depart for Skagway at 1700 hours.

After a complete shutdown, Rob, Milt, and the girls—Janet and Star—joined the gang in the kitchen area. They all toasted each other with a cold one.

Rob and Milt were given a quick tour of the station's layout. As he walked by the Wolvies plus one, he overheard the following plans.

Matthew whispered, "Okay, it's settled then. Lynn, you ask if it's okay to sail back with us to Sitka. Tell 'em you know how to sail; you know the waters better than us, and it's only a one-hour sail. Okay?"

John agreed. "Yeah, you've a way with words. Act like it was your idea."

Mark added, "Yep, we've all got life-jackets, and we're all experienced."

Luke barked.

Rob moved on without saying a word.

*   *   *

Josie was first to notice the gang approaching from the Wolvies' yurt. By their dress, she kinda knew what to expect. They were all in cut-offs with life jackets over sweatshirts. Lynn was in the lead.

Josie thought, *I know they want to go for a sail before we fly to Sitka. It's just like those boys to try to wet a hull before we leave, and put Lynn up to ask. I'm anxious to hear her story. We've only a half hour 'til departure. Oh well, I'll wait to see what they want.*

Lynn spoke. "Josie, can we sail to Sitka and meet you guys there?"

"What!"

Lynn's story was convincing. Being a sailor herself and knowing the distinctive attributes of the Sound's currents, Josie reluctantly gave them permission to sail to town.

Josie walked with the crew to the shoreline. Along the way, she laid down the law to the boys on being careful and coming directly to the tribal meeting house from the municipal beach. As an additional measure of safety, she gave Mark her cellphone. She added, "Use it if you get into any trouble." She told them a chopper could be over them in minutes. In fact, they'd be in the air on the way to Sitka Field while they were in the Sound.

Although preoccupied with rigging the Hobie's sails and tying down a tag of dry clothes on the tramp, Josie continued her comments to each of the boys.

Matthew assigned the crew's placement on the tramp. With one quick push and a following gust of wind the Hobie slid into the water. The wind was at 15 knots from offshore, and the waves showed a slight chop as they sailed on a broad reach into the azure blue.

As the laughing, playful group disappeared into the chop, Lynn rose up and waved to Josie and yelled, "Thanks mom!" The boys had started calling her mom, also. Sensitive with age and embodying a heart filled with love for her fellow man, she teared up as she waved back and turned to rejoin the group. They, too, were getting ready to leave.

A shiny metallic gold item caught her eye on the footpath to camp. She picked up the necklace and read the pendant: *Go Girl. First Solo. We're proud of you. Mom and Dad.*

Although well aware she was out of sight, Josie yelled, "Lynn, I've got your necklace!"

As the waves crested and broke on shore, she watched while the red sail bobbed in the distance. Then, much to her dismay, she also saw the dorsal fins of a pod of Orcas between the shore and the Hobie, headed in their direction.

"Ohmgod! Manitou, please be with my sailors. Please be with my kids."

Chapter 11

"How high's the water, Mama? Three feet high and risin'," Mark sang as the 'cat's' hulls sliced through the oncoming waves.

With the heavier load, the 16-foot Hobie rode a little lower in the water. Designed for two or three adults, its performance characteristics were limited by a fourth. They *would not* be flying a hull today. Yet, Lynn probably weighed only 100 pounds or less, so she added very little weight. It was the third Wolvie's 200 pounds that altered the Hobie's performance. The added weight also lowered the trampoline's clearance to the water and caused it to be awash with eye-stinging salt water most of the time. Still having a woman aboard was worth it. With this weight, coming about, the wind at the bow, or jibbing, with the wind at the stern, could be tricky. The latter would be an absolute no-no with a heavy boat; submerging the bow was a real possibility.

Matthew's ears had started to 'twang' with all the Johnny Cash songs, so he yelled, "Mark, can't you sing something else? We're kinda overserved on JC."

"Yeah, no problemo, man," said Mark. He started singing "The Wichita Lineman" by Glenn Campbell. "I am a lineman for the county..."

"Oh, brother," John chimed in, "that does it. Come on boys, it's time to teach Lynn the Wolverine fight song."

In three-part harmony, they all sang to Lynn. She picked up the words on the second stanza, and they finished with the more melodic fourth part.

Undaunted by the criticism, Mark started singing another JC song: "I hear the train a comin . . ."

"Lynn, what would you like to hear?" Matt asked.

"Okay, I get the message," Marked whined, "I'll hum some Neil Diamond."

A pause followed by "Cracklin' Rosie makes me want to . . ."

Finally, a smooth melody accented the winds in their sails.

"Look!" Lynn yelled.

She was pointing to the wake at the stern of the cat.

"A fin!" Mark hollered.

Everyone's heart seemed to skip a beat as a huge killer whale breached alongside and dove under the cat with a splash.

Matthew spoke in a calm voice. "Okay, guys, hold on. Our toothy friend may be just playing . . . or irritated with us. We'll see. We're certainly no seal, otter, or salmon, but we could be a welcome change in its diet—like dessert. Lynn, is Luke secure?"

"Yep. He's in my bodice, snug as a bug in a rug."

Matthew thought, *Lucky dog.*

"Okay. Here's my plan. I'm going to tack to the northeast from this northwest heading. It's only slightly evasive, but we may be over the whale's fishing area."

John yelled, "There's the rest of the pod to the port side."

"Let's keep our cool. By now the pod's leader, a female, will have made a decision whether we're okay or not. The rest will follow her lead."

Lynn said, "The truth of the matter is, they've probably been following us for some time now, and surfaced to take a better look. They're a curious lot."

"Dammit!" Matthew yelled. "Part of the pod is dead ahead—holding fast—just hovering—just looking at us."

In a quick motion, Lynn rolled over toward the helm, grabbed the main sheet line from Matt, released it from the cleat, and let the sheet run out to dump air from the mainsail.

"What?" Matt shouted.

Lynn yelled, "We've got to slow our forward motion. I just dumped the main to slow down. If we can't stop, we'll surely capsize if we run over the pod's huge dorsal fins."

Her efforts failed. The flying jib carried them over the lounging pod.

"Too late," John yelled. "Hang on; we're going over."

As if in slow motion, the cat's starboard hull rose out of the water, and the port hull buried itself in the froth as the mast and sail slapped the mass of bubbles. Everyone slid down the tramp into the churning water.

Matthew yelled, "Hold on! Grab something! Don't leave the boat! Mark, you stay with Lynn; John, you and I are gonna climb up the tramp and righten the cat by standing on the hull and leaning back. Our combined weight will act as a counterweight, and we'll lift the cat out of the water while holding the sidestay wires. Hang on. Mark, maneuver the boat around so the sail is on the windward side of the tramp."

"Roger that."

"Come on, John, let's move. We've got to scramble to the top of the hull."

As Matt and John struggled up the elevated portion of the tramp to the airborne hull, Mark and Lynn pushed the hull around so the wind would help blow against the tramp and sail as it came out of the water. The wind was their friend indeed.

*   *   *

"Look at 'em," Lynn said. "The whales are hovering in the water as if we're the main attraction in today's performance."

"Yeah," Mark said. "I hope they know their interference caused us to capsize."

"No doubt," Lynn said. "They probably needed a little diversion . . . some unusual entertainment after a hard day chasing seals. We probably looked like some fun."

They finally had swung the hull around so the sail pointed windward.

Lynn gently said, "Don't be alarmed, Mark, but one of our mammalian friends is just about ten feet below you. I hope it's to get a better look at your legs, not eyeing you for dessert."

"Funny, you're not," Mark said as he looked down at the huge row of teeth on the leviathan below and groaned."

"Oh, no, what do we do now?"

"Nothing."

"What?"

"They're just curious. They would have attacked us by now if they were hungry."

Lynn thought, *Keep positive; this guy is scared out of his wits. Although also concerned, I know curiosity versus violence, and these mammals are well fed. They have a right to examine our intrusion into their domain. Capsizing gave them a little fun . . . at our expense. There you go again, Lynn, anthropomorphizing.*

*   *   *

Matt yelled, "Okay, here we go. Mark, you swim out to the top of the mast and hold it out of the water the best you can; Lynn, hold the mainsail boom out of the water as we're leaning back."

Mark swam to the end of the mast as the whale followed; while thrashing in the water, Lynn held up the boom to raise it as high as possible.

Luckily, a gust of wind caught the sail, it cleared the water, and the counterweight boys leaned backward at just the right time. The starboard hull slammed the boys into the water as the port hull exploded out of the water with a tremendous splash.

Submerged for a few seconds, Matt and John surfaced and climbed aboard before the cat tried to sail off on its own—unmanned. Matt grabbed the tiller, lowered the rudders, and turned the cat into the wind. The sails rested at a luff. They immediately threw a line to Mark. Holding on nearby, Lynn was helped aboard. Finally, Mark was pulled onto the tramp. They had made it. Then the boys asked if Luke was okay.

*   *   *

Lynn checked on Luke. Having slipped down a little on her chest, the dog was now snuggled comfortably between her breasts. He appeared to be okay. Wet and squirming, he looked out from her parka and licked his salty lips. "Wolvies, it appears that our little beagle is fine. He's going to be a survivor."

Lynn thought, *Look at them, they all want to change places with Luke. That would be okay by me . . . Behave, Lynn, you're too young for this kind of idea.*

As soon as Mark boarded, they all collapsed on the tramp to gain their composure. It had been a harrowing life-or-death experience for the boys—a terrifying experience for Lynn.

"Fellas, would you take a look at our companions of the deep" They're now lollygagging around the cat as if thanking us for the show. I'll swear they've a smile on their faces. Aren't the contrasting black-and-white markings beautiful?"

"Yeah," Mark said. "Their teeth are ivory white, too. Great for scrimshaw."

"Not funny, Mark," John retorted with a sigh.

Lynn replied, "Well, you must have noticed by now, our stinking-wet beagle has just about the same markings . . . and white teeth."

She held on fast while drying out the stinky pup in the sun.

*   *   *

After they caught their breath and checked for damage in the rigging, Matt arranged the crew's places on the tramp. He asked, "Are you guys ready for the final tack to shore?"

John spoke first. "How can we move? There must be a dozen orcas encircling the boat. Who knows what they'll do if we sail through the pod?"

Mark grumbled, "Well, we can't stay here all day. In fact, we're drifting out to sea now as the tide moves out."

In contrast, Lynn said, "Mark's right. I believe the whales will let us through and not block our exit. They've had their fun for the day."

Matt said, "I believe you're right. Plus, I'm having trouble keeping the bow to the wind, keeping the sails at luff; and the wind is picking up from the west. Right now we'd have a fast, broad reach to shore."

Without further discussion, Matt turned the boat to the north. The westerly wind billowed the sail, and the hulls started cutting through the chop. He trimmed the jib and leaned to the windward.

As predicted by Lynn, the orca's leader breached as if to signal the pod, and they suddenly raced toward the Sound's opening to the sea.

They all watched as the huge dorsal fins slowly vanished in the chop.

After the cheering subsided, they all heard the sound coming from the north, so they looked to the sky. Behind the choppers, a raven soared.

Sure enough, both choppers were headed their way, a mere 100 feet off the deck. They must have seen them and diverted from their direct flight to Sitka to do a fly-over and say hello.

"Well, well, I see the gang is going to pay us a little visit," Mark said.

Matt echoed his thoughts. "Yep, they'll certainly beat us to town now. By the time we reach shore, they'll be at the council meetinghouse. We'll have no shore party to meet us. So, let's give 'er hell, get the last knot out of this baby."

Both Matt and John rode high on the windward hull while Lynn and Mark inched up the tramp, too, as counterweight to the windward.

The Hobie sliced through the chop at a maximum hull speed of 12 knots. The taut rigging and sails sung the sound of beautiful speed.

Matt was the first to broach the subject. "Are we going to explain our late arrival . . . and what happened out here? What do you guys think?"

Before anyone had chance to speak, Lynn said, "I've an idea. It would be wiser to let this capsizing stay with the whales and us dunkers. Think about it. Josie, my parents, and god knows who else would overreact to this incident. Why? 'Cause the capsizing occurred over, or by, a pod of killer whales. As you are now aware, the orca is no killer. It's a misnomer of novice whale watchers. Yes, they feed aggressively on baby seals, otter, and fish, but generally not on humans.

"I'm sure you guys capsize all the time, especially when 'flying a hull' in a strong wind. True?"

Matt answered, "'Tis true. You have a good point. Let's put it to a vote. What do you say, you Sound-soaked sailors?"

Mark, a stickler for details, asked, "So, do I understand if asked, and only if asked, that we might admit to capsizing, but not over a pod of killer whales?"

"You've got it, Mark," Lynn said as the cat skimmed the surface at maximum hull speed in a 15-knot wind from the north. Then surprisingly, she looked at Matt and said, "Let's vote."

Seeing the anxious look in her eyes, Matt yelled, "All those who agree that what happened in the waters of Sitka Sound stays in Sitka Sound, indicate by saying 'aye.'"

The roaring affirmation of ayes startled Luke. He barked for the first time, then kissed Lynn.

Lynn gave a thumbs up to the soaked crew and lay back in total satisfaction that this adventure would not reach her parents. She whispered to Mark, "Do you realize what would happen if they knew I was with you guys when we capsized over a pod. I'd never be allowed to be with you again. I'm so happy that's not going to happen."

The wetness in her eyes was from more than the stinging saltwater.

*   *   *

"Look at 'em," Ann said to Rob in A-One. "They're still about thirty minutes from the beach. I'll bet they've been running all over the Sound or lollygagging at the luff. Yep, they should have been to shore by now. What do you think?"

"Oh, it's hard to tell, but I don't see a problem. We'll rendezvous at the councilhouse at about the same time. No sweat. It looks pretty peaceful down there. The Hobie's taut sails on a reach look not only beautiful, looks exciting. Lynn is in good hands. Right, Josie?"

On the IC, Josie responded, "Absolutely. The boys are excellent sailors, the chop is moderate, and the onshore winds are gentle. The only thing that could possibly happen, and that's remote, is a pod of orcas following them for a while. They're a curious lot."

Ann added, "Yeah, they seem to be okay. Look at 'em go . . . they're plowing through the Sound. Plus they look dry as a bone. Yep, they've had no trouble as I see it."

Dave said, "Let's give 'em a buzz and head for the field."

"Roger that," Milt said as he, too, flew by at 50 feet. The S-70 and S-70B dumped their down draft on the crew below, and waved to their gang as they dashed to shore at 80 knots.

*   *   *

Matt tacked one last time and headed for shore a quarter of a mile away.

As the hulls bottomed out on the gravelly beach, Matt pulled the rudders up with the tiller, and Lynn freed the mainsail sheet. John and Mark pulled the dagger boards up on each hull, and Lynn loosened the halyard for the mainsail. Mark unsheeted the jib. Having secured the rigging, and stepped ashore, Matt yelled, "We made it!"

Everyone yelled in one way or another. "Yeah, we've done it. We're on dry land." Lynn let Luke down to pee and run among the flotsam.

As they gathered together and hugged each other, Matt briefly stated, "Remember, for Lynn's sake, and ours, as the old saying goes, 'What happens in Vegas, stays in Vegas.' Got it?"

"You bet," John said.

"Absolutely," Mark said.

"Thanks." Lynn sighed.

Knowing they'd be sailing back in a couple hours, they temporarily secured the Hobie, retrieved their clothes bag, and headed for dinner with the chief, with Luke leading the way.

*   *   *

Golden Bear was second in the reception line at the council's meetinghouse. Bill, from Sitka Field, was first to make introductions for the chief. Josie was especially pleased that many Tlingit council members, local businessmen, had invited their families, too. All of them processed through the receiving line. She felt strongly that this gesture was a good example of respect in having them meet families as well as the local leaders.

Visitors included the DNR's Delta Station personnel, Ford Flight Service pilots and crew, Bear and Leigh, and finally, William Geez, the DNR's regional manager from Juneau.

Josie had expected that some VIP had arrived from out of town due to the shiny new Boeing H-10 chopper parked at the airport. It was Geez.

Joe, Bear, and Geez huddled with Milt and Dave at one table; Leigh, Ann, Janet, and Star at another. Josie was anxiously waiting at the door for her crew and Lynn. She couldn't imagine what was keeping them. They were only a half-hour behind. It was not stylish, here in Sitka, to keep the chief waiting.

*   *   *

In fact, Bill had asked Josie to replace him in the reception line, next to the chief, since her crew were the only ones yet to arrive.

Bill joined George, Chuck, and their families at another table. Lynn's mother seemed a little concerned at her daughter's late arrival. Bill had tried to console her earlier, knowing their Hobie was on the beach—in one piece. He explained that they were probably getting out of their wet clothes and into dry ones. Nevertheless, he was concerned, too: she was rarely late. Of course, she was not alone . . . at 16, she was with three high-strung 23-year-old Wolvies.

*   *   *

"Would you believe it? Look who's come to see you, chief. From what I see, he seems to know you pretty well," said Bill.

Luke ran into the room, looked around, found Josie, ran to her, then ran to the chief. The chief leaned over as if young again, and with a quick snatch said, "Come to Papa, you little ball of fur." Luke obliged him, and gave the automatic kisses before his eyes darted to the feathers and earrings that adorned the chief's regalia.

Luke started licking, then biting, the dangling earrings and feathers woven into his beautiful jacket.

Before Luke could destroy his jewelry, the chief lowered him into his arms where he started chewing on his coat's fringed buckskin trim. He said, "Don't you ever feed this dog? He acts as if he hasn't eaten since scrounging for scraps at the meat market downtown."

"Here," Josie said, "I'll take him to the kitchen and get him a good bone to chew on." As she turned with Luke in her arms, the Wolvies and Lynn entered the lobby. Josie thought, *They were surely smart, letting Luke in first to solve any irritation the chief may have had for their late arrival.*

"Hello, my fellow members of Delta Team!" Josie shouted.

Their well-planned entrance was by the numbers. Matthew led the group wearing his Michigan T-shirt. He chatted briefly with the chief, then turned and nodded to the doorway where Mark, John, and Lynn seemed to be waiting for Matt's cue.

Lynn's mother looked worried, but Bill appeared to be reassuring her. Bill consoled her again, saying, "Don't worry, she'll be okay."

There was a slight pause as the crowd turned and whispered to each other. Then, the entrance.

Lynn, in a Michigan T-shirt, was riding on a two-man hand-over-wrist carry seat by John and Mark, who had Michigan T-shirts, on too.

By plan, hers was maize with blue letters, theirs navy blue.

As if queen of her crew, she held her head up high in regal style, holding a present for the chief.

Matt stepped in front of the carried queen, assisted her down from her royal throne, and presented her to the chief.

Lynn spoke, "Hail to thee, Golden Bear, chief of the Tlingit Nation. Since you are a warrior and a winner amongst men, and since Michigan men have made me their spokesperson and mascot, we feel it's fitting and only proper to give you a symbol of our gratitude for your accomplishments. I am proud, as the Michigan mascot, to award you this Michigan T-shirt with all the rights and privileges we of Delta Station share."

The chief good naturedly played their game and nodded in thanks as he took the shirt from Lynn.

Still acting out her part, she genuflected to the chief.

Lynn backed away, as one would to royalty.

The boys and Lynn paused, then stepped forward with a grin and greeted the chief in a more traditional way. Lynn gave him a big kiss on the cheek and whispered, "Not bad, huh? Bet you didn't know I could act."

The chief, having seen many moons and many ceremonies, said, "I've always had an idea you had acting blood in your veins. Thanks, Lynn."

Josie thought, *This crew is certainly one of a kind. Little do they know that they were on a slippery slope between respect and humor. Luckily, it came off, and the chief seemed to love it.*

The chief unwrapped his shirt, showed it to the crowd with pride, and spoke. "My dear friends and family, I'm honored by your thoughts and the delivery of this special gift—for its association with your prestigious school, and for the fellowship of the Delta Station boys, with their new mascot. I look forward to a continued positive relationship in the future. Now, without any more speeches, let's eat."

After everyone had taken their places, the chief stood and asked for their attention one more time.

"As my father and his father would say, I say again to you today:

"You will always be welcome at my lodge to

share a meal and to warm your spirit by the fire."

Josie said her own personal thanks. *Manitou, bless us, for you have given me a wonderful opportunity to work with these fine young men.*

Chapter 12

As the council members enjoyed a dinner of poached Sockeye salmon, the conversation seemed to be positive towards to the Delta team. Their colorful entrance and introduction with Lynn and the gift seemed to provide an ice breaker to the formality expected by the chief. It was soon discovered that they were indeed proud Michigan men, but also highly-trained scientists. Their skills in the biological and, especially, marine disciplines were reflected in the casual conversations with council members. Very quickly they proved that they knew a lot about Sitka Sound. Little did they know that Lynn had given them a briefing of local history to supplement their knowledge of the marine environment.

Their actions while meeting the chief prompted him to ask for their presence at the head table. Surprisingly, they asked Lynn to join them.

Joe whispered to Josie, "It looks like the chief needed a little humor in his life. The salmon catch is down, and a recession is at his doorstep. The timing of this visit is perfect. Plus with Geez agreeing to speak to local and state issues, it should be a good night."

Josie leaned over. "You're right. Those boys are a tonic for all of us. Shhh, Geez is about to speak."

* * *

Geez startled the crowd with a real attention-getter. He quoted an estimate from the scientific community suggesting that if trends continue without abatement, half the world's species may disappear by the end of this century.

A buzz rose among the tables of local dignitaries and council members' families.

With a smile he regained their attention as he explained the mission of Alpha Station near Yakutat, Bravo Station near Glacier Bay National Park, and Charlie Station on Pelican Island along with their local Delta Station that covered in excess of 400 miles along the coast. He explained what kind of data they would be collecting and the type of equipment utilized. They would monitor the oceans: temperature variants, zooplankton and phytoplankton concentrations—the bottom of the food-chain—carbon dioxide levels and changes, and monitor seismic hydro phones along the numerous fault lines along the coast. Other aspects of local concern were also considered, especially when the coastal fisheries were affected.

That statement caused a murmur in the audience.

He stressed that one of their recent concerns was the climate's warming effects on the permafrost and the resulting release of methane gas. Its consequences to thinning the earth's shield from solar radiation would be devastating.

Sensing another uncomfortable feeling in the audience, he gave them some positive aspects of the economy and new industries growing in the Alaskan panhandle. On the educational front, he mentioned that Charlie Station on Pelican Island has a dozen or so high-school students interning with the staff there. "We're getting a toehold on future scientists who may plan to go on to school and get a college degree much like the Gospels that you've met tonight. We are encouraging Tlingit students to join us through scholarships and transportation to the island. So far, these young Native boys and girls have shown to be valuable assets to the class."

Following his prepared remarks, Geez took a few questions from the council members and their families as dessert was served.

*   *   *

Matthew leaned over to Lynn and asked, "What is this?"

"Baked Alaska. It's cake topped with ice cream, covered with meringue that's quickly browned in the oven."

"Damn, it sure tastes good. I've never had this before. Is it only served in Alaska?"

"No, silly man. Don't you ever get out and about town in Ann Arbor? I guarantee it's on the menu of a least a couple of restaurants in town."

"Listen, girl, we're not as sophisticated as you are here in Sitka. In fact, if the restaurant doesn't have cheap tap beer, we're elsewhere."

"Poor, baby."

Mark leaned into the conversation and said the same. "I've never had this, either!"

John added, while pilfering a spoonful from Mark, "Nor I. Dang, it's tasty."

Mark *smacked* John's hand with his spoon.

"Now, boys, behave," Lynn said, as she looked around. "Take me sailing again and I'll make you all some Baked Alaska . . . at the station."

"Deal," said Matthew.

"Right on," replied Mark.

"Okay!" said John.

*   *   *

At the next table, Joe leaned over to Josie and asked, "What are your boys organizing with Lynn?"

With a sigh, she said, "Hard telling. I can't keep up with their shenanigans. It will be legal, but I guarantee—devious. I'll see if I can wring it out of them later. They generally check things out with me . . . generally."

*   *   *

Geez tapped on a glass to get the crowd's attention for some additional remarks.

"I had a few questions from your chief about local fisheries that I'd like to share with you. We know the Pacific salmon harvest has diminished over the years. We know you *do not* like the restrictions the DNR has imposed on you along the coast. We know *no one* likes quotas."

The crowd groaned and sighed in agreement.

"What you may not know is that the *same* conditions are being experienced 1,500 miles to the west on the shores of the Kamchatka Peninsula, in Russia's Bering Sea."

The crowd was abuzz again.

"Our Cold-War enemies are now joining us in the same research we are conducting along the Pacific shore. They have several stations along the coast to help them determine why their catch is also down by 50%."

Geez then discussed his concerns over the sudden burst of volcanic activity and the plume of hot mantle rock that released enormous quantities of carbon dioxide. Over time, he emphasized, this release may have contributed to global warming, and to significant negative changes in ocean chemistry.

At risk, he shared a conversation he recently had with his wife, who said that she was upset that her skin was slipping and sliding with age, and the trouble he had gotten into when he said her skin was just like the earth's mantle . . . that's slipping, too. He noted that as soon as he said it . . . he was in trouble. The crowd chuckled. He quickly added that not only was he a little too scientific, but it also cost him dinner at a five-star restaurant . . . and flowers.

After a few catcalls from the women in the audience—"it served you right"— he further stunned the audience.

He started by saying, "Excessive CO2 is a biologist's nightmare. It can kill things directly by physiological effects, of which ocean acidification is the best known, and it can kill things by changing the climate. The old saying applies: If it gets warmer faster than you can migrate, you're in trouble.

"These young men you've met tonight, with their supervisor, Josie St. Pierre, will be assisting the DNR in determining causes of these life-threatening changes. In the end, the most deadly aspect of human activity may simply be the pace of it. We may not have the answers this year—or next. However, be aware that just in the last century, CO2 levels in the atmosphere have been changed by man—a hundred parts per million—as they normally do in a hundred-thousand years' glacial cycle. Meanwhile, the drop in the ocean pH levels that has occurred over the past fifty years may well exceed anything that happened in the seas during the previous fifty million."

Chief Golden Bear interrupted, "Geez, will you be sharing some of the data with us?"

"Certainly. In fact, I'd like you to consider the Sitka Sound, Delta Station—your station, too. Let me have Josie give you a little briefing about her concerns and plans. Josie?"

*   *   *

Josie stood and thanked Geez for coming to Sitka and the chief for his hospitality.

"Folks, you've all heard the media warn that melting ice threatens polar bears. That is true. However, we marine scientists are more concerned that the state's marine waters are turning acidic from absorbing greenhouse gases faster than tropical waters, potentially endangering Alaska's billion dollar fishing industry.

"The same things that make Alaska's marine waters among the most productive in the world—cold, shallow depths and abundant marine life—make them the most vulnerable to acidification. That is the primary focus of our data collection and analysis.

"As Geez mentioned, ocean acidification, the lowering of basicity and the increase of acidity of marine waters, is tied to increased carbon dioxide levels in the atmosphere.

"Here's a tragic story that we'll be analyzing. When carbon dioxide dissolves in sea water, it forms carbonic acid. That decreases the amount of calcium carbonate used by marine creatures to construct shells or skeletons. DNR's Alpha Station, north of here, has sampled waters in the Chukchi and Bering seas and found that concentrations of shell-building minerals were so low, that shellfish, including crab, were unable to build strong enough shells."

The crowd gasped.

"Acidification has also affected the tiny pteropod, also known as the sea butterfly or swimming snail. It is also threatened. At the base of the food chain, it makes up nearly half of the diet of pink salmon. A 10 percent decrease in pteropods could mean a 20 percent decrease in an adult salmon's body weight. This is a trend that is not good for Sitka fisheries . . . or me. I love salmon.

"You're all welcome to stop by the station, and we'll show you some of the samples that I have mentioned. Thank you."

The crowd's murmur continued.

"Thanks, Josie. Here's one last example of how fast our environment can

change with the aid of technology—some good—some bad. In a single afternoon, a contagious pathogen, like influenza, can move via any number of airlines
halfway around the world. Before man and his state-of-the-art technology entered
the picture, such a migration would have required hundreds, if not thousands, of
years—if, indeed, it could have been accomplished at all."

Seeing the crowd's negative reaction to some of Geez's and Josie's comments, Joe spoke up. "There are some positive aspects of new technology in the
DNR. It's making my job much easier in analyzing animal population trends and
changes."

"Your point."

"We no longer capture grizzly bears with inhumane snare traps—we merely
collect their hair with a 'rubbing pole' and analyze the DNA of a single hair to
determine identification, age, sex, and health."

Geez responded, "How true. Good point, Joe."

The crowd buzzed again.

Geez continued, "My point here today, along with Josie, with this most interesting crowd, is to alert you to some trends in our environment and help to
explain how Delta station will contribute. They've a tough job gathering data to
help us make decisions in Juneau and Washington. They may need your help. I'm
proud of Josie and her Gospel Men . . . including the dog. They will be supported
by Joe, Bear, and Leigh doing the inland work and helped by Wind Spirit, our
intern, and his new bride, Raven Maiden. I must also mention our support crew
out of Skagway. Ford Flight Services flies in all the supplies to our outposts along
the coast and inland. You've probably met Milt, Dave, Rob, and Ann by now.
Their lady friends are also with them tonight . . . Star and Janet. Would you all
stand and be recognized? Take a good look; I've a feeling you'll be seeing them
again."

A few hands clapped cautiously, and then all joined in with applause. A loud
whistle by Lynn got Luke barking.

"Thank you. We've indeed a good team. I leave you with one last thought.
Currently, a third of the reef-building corals, a quarter of all mammals, an eighth
of all birds, and one-half of the salmon species are classified as threatened with
extinction. You know as well as I that, in light of this reality, Sockeye salmon
breeding farms are flourishing along the coast. The United States is not alone in
this regard. The Soviet Union has hundreds of breeding pens along the Kamchatka Peninsula.

"Finally—I think I've said this before—ocean acidification could be the
cause; our teams will find out. Am I an alarmist? Yes, and no. I'm just pointing
out the stress on our environment, our fisheries, our livelihood.

"Today, it's not like we have stress and the stress is relieved and recovery starts. It gets bad, and then it keeps being bad, because the stress doesn't go away. Why? *Because the stress is us.* Thank you; you've been a wonderful audience.

A pause followed as the crowd grasped his final statement . . . *The stress is us.* Then they applauded, Lynn whistled, Luke barked, the old chief's eyes watered at the reality of the changing future for his tribe.

As the chatter and shuffling of the crowd diminished, the chief stood. Silence was immediate out of custom and respect.

Without direction, all his people rose, the crowd followed their lead, and everyone bowed their heads for the closing thanks to the Great Spirit. The chief spoke.

> O Great Spirit, whose voice I hear in the winds and whose
> breath gives life to all the world, hear me! I am small and weak;
> I need strength and wisdom.
> Let me walk in beauty, and make my eyes ever behold the red
> and purple sunset.
> Make my hands respect the things you have made and my ears
> sharp to hear your voice.
> Make me wise so that I may understand the things you have
> taught my people.
> Let me learn the lessons you have hidden in every leaf and
> rock.
> I seek strength, not to be greater than my brother, but to fight
> my greatest enemy—myself.
> Make me always ready to come to you with clean hands and
> straight eyes.
> So when life fades, as the fading sunset, my spirit may come to
> you without shame.
> Peace be with you.

*   *   *

The crowd filed out of the council chambers and headed to their jobs, homes, canoes, helicopters, and Hobie Cats. Geez had stirred the thinking of all those present.

*   *   *

As the DNR gang walked Geez to his chopper on the flight line at Sitka Field, he sensed a vibration indicating a call on his Blackberry.

"Excuse me, folks; I'll be with you in a minute. I've a message. It won't take long; Juneau is probably calling to see when I'll be back."

Geez took a moment to acknowledge the call, then quickly hustled to the cockpit of his H-10 where his laptop was located. He entered his code in the keyboard which displayed the message from DNR headquarters, Juneau. It read:

> Urgent Message for W. Geez—H-007-09 at Sitka Field:
> The Alaska Interagency Coordination Center, AICC, requests all available personnel in your sector to respond to wildfires in the interior of Glacier Bay National Park. Due to its central location and facilities, the ranch of DNR employee Big Bear and his wife, Leigh West, is to be used temporarily as our operations center. DNR Intern Wind Spirit, with the help of his wife, Raven Maiden, is already in receipt of some of DNR's fire-fighting equipment and protective clothing. More supplies will be air dropped later today.
> All personnel you select are to proceed immediately to the ops ctr, obtain the necessary clothing and equipment, and await orders for insertion by FFS choppers.
> After insertion of personnel, FFS choppers will be assigned water-drop flights with other tankers. Two water buckets have been dropped at FFS, one of 1,000 gallons for the S-70, a second of 750 gallons for the S-70B.
> Joe Bloom will be in charge of this operation and coordinate with me, as needed.
> Josie St. Pierre will supervise the Delta Station personnel.
> Big Bear and Leigh West will be in charge of coordinating the team's activities.
> FFS personnel, Milt and Dave including their copilots and crew chiefs, will be directed by flight ops out of Juneau.
> End of message. Please report ASAP
>
> > L. Gasco, Manager
> > SW DNR Director.

"What's up?" Joe asked, leaning over the shoulder of Geez. "That's an urgent message, isn't it?"

"How true. Let's all gather around for a moment. We've got ourselves an emergency assignment—portions of Glacier Bay National Park are ablaze."

Overhearing what Geez said, they all gathered around him.

"Listen up. Here's the deal. I'll hold up the screen of my laptop so you can see the message. I'll read it aloud, too."

Afterward, they all chatted about its impact on their next assignment. Geez heard Mark whisper that he'd never fought a brush fire, much less a forest fire.

"Joe, as you see, you're in charge with Josie's crew in support along with Wind Spirit and Raven Maiden working with you, too. FFS will report to the flight director in Juneau. Are there any questions?"

Josie said, "A dozen or so, but I'll wait until we get to the ops ctr."

"Likewise," Bear said.

"We've worked with the flight director from Juneau before, so it shouldn't be a problem," Milt said.

*   *   *

Joe said, "Good. I'd suggest, Bill, that we form the teams pretty much as you've described with a DNR employee in charge of each, and FFS reporting to Juneau. Let's form into three Fire Teams. Bear, you be number one, Josie, number two, and Wind Spirit number three. Your radio call signs will be the same . . . FT-1, -2, -3. Milt, your call sign will be Airborne Fire Team A, AFT-A; Dave yours is AFT-B. Any questions? If not let's vamoose, as the Wolvies would say.

Walking with Bill to the choppers, Joe said, "Bill, I'll jump in and out of Bear's team as the situation dictates. What do you think? If you approve, we'll be on our way."

Bill responded, "Good. I'll send a message to headquarters on your plans."

He paused by the boarding area. "Folks, I appreciate your service. Remember our number-one concern: safety. Do not take any unnecessary chances. Finally, follow the directions of your DNR leaders. They've been through all of this before. They can help you cope in a tight spot. That's all; I'll be in touch."

Everyone nodded to Bill in approval as they walked to the choppers.

Joe asked them all to gather around by the aircraft. "I know some of you are wondering what's involved in fighting a fire on a fireline in the forest. Be assured, when we get to the ranch, we'll provide you with the requisite instructions. For now, we've given Geez what he needed: personnel from his sector. That's us. We will perform well. We will do our jobs better than anyone else. We will put out this fire. We will succeed. Any questions?

Silence.

"Okay, let's board."

Matthew gave a quick look to Lynn on the sidelines. She ran to him. He gave her the necklace Josie had found, and then asked her to take care of Luke, and the Hobie using it if she wished. She hugged all three boys and left without turning around. Her eyes were moist . . . again.

Matt asked Josie, "Bear mentioned Big Wind will help, too. Who's he?"

"Bear's son. He lives in Juneau and decided to help out. You'll like him. He's an experienced fire fighter."

"I like him already."

Lynn's dad came out to wish them good-bye and good luck. Lynn, in tears, seemed embarrassed to come back for a final good-bye.

Without further chit-chat, the turbines wound up, the blades started their cyclical beat, and the choppers lurched into the air.

* * *

As they gained elevation, all personnel noticed the large white plume of smoke to the north.

Josie thought, *I know Bear and Leigh are wondering how close the fire is to their ranch. I applaud them for not mentioning it to the gang.*

* * *

Bear hugged Leigh as the chopper flew at full throttle to the north. He whispered, "Dear, be certain your children are looking after your home . . . our home. It's in good hands. The best. They are as tough as you are. Why? You've taught them well. Your ranch may be threatened. Yes. But not incinerated. No. That. Will. Not. Happen. Hold on, Babe."

* * *

After a quick stop to secure Delta Station, packing some personal items, an in-flight briefing by Josie, Matthew said to the members of his team, "Well, guys, professor Smith in Ann Arbor said nothing about fighting fires for the DNR, but if we're needed you can bet we will be the best. Go Blue."

* * *

As Milt powered up the chopper in an effort to rendezvous with Dave, a raven soared effortlessly to join them.

Chapter 13

A snappy *Wop-Wop-Wop* indicated that Milt was pushing the chopper at near full speed. Cruising at 80 to 90 mph at 500 feet, they'd be arriving at the ranch in about one hour. The atmosphere in the cockpit was tense. This was a no-nonsense flight with unknown consequences.

Silence also ruled the faces of the Gospels as they rode north to an assignment with varying unknowns . . . and certain danger. This was not what they had expected when they looked forward to their field work on their PhD program. All three looked worried.

Sensing the tenseness of her boys, Josie told an old joke that had been passed down over time among Alaskan Indians—once forbidden, now acceptable to modern man.

"Say, guys, did you hear the one about a young Indian chief?" Josie said with a wry look on her face.

The boys looked at her. They knew they had no choice . . . they were going to hear it. Then they looked at each other as if a shaggy-dog story was about to pierce their ears.

"Well?" she asked.

"Okay. It appears we're going to hear it anyway," Matt said as he looked around the cabin. "We've no parachutes."

"Not funny." Josie replied, "I just may withhold my humor, and you'll all be sorry."

"We wouldn't think of it. Why . . . you're our Kathy Griffin, but certainly on our A-List. We need your joke to round out our Native knowledge," Matt said.

"Oh, please, Jo, do tell us. We need your insight," John urged. "I'm all ears," Mark said, sighing.

"No. You're still speaking like scoundrels. I'll bet you tell all your prospective women that they're on your A-List—for your personal gain."

"Perish the thought. Now. Look at us. We're all ears," Matt replied.

"No."

Mark finally interjected, "Pay no attention to Matt; he's just nervous. The only fire he's had to put out was from a 'hot-foot' in the sixth grade. I'm nervous, too. The only fire I've had to dowse was from an overcharged volcano simulation in the tenth grade. I thought a double charge of saltpeter would impress the teacher. I almost burned a hole in the teacher's desk."

"Bite your tongue, Mark," Matt hollered.

"Okay, Josie," John said, "I want to hear your joke. So do they. They're just upset from the thought of swimming with killer whales—ah, no, in leaving camp."

"What!" Josie yelled. "Killer whales?"

John quickly replied, "It's nothing. We just saw some orcas while sailing from camp to Sitka."

"Oh. Yeah. I saw 'em, too. Well, if you Wolvies are ready, here goes."

"We're all ears," they said in unison.

"If you say that one more time, I'll scream."

"Josie, we've crossed the Rubicon and burned our boats. No more messing around," Mark said.

They looked at each other with wry smiles.

"Here goes. One autumn day, several Tlingit Indians got together and asked their new chief whether the winter would be cold or mild. Since the young chief never learned the ways of his ancestors, he told them to collect firewood. Then he went off and called the National Weather Service. 'Will the winter be bad?' he asked. 'Looks like it,' was the answer.

"So the chief told his people to gather more firewood. A week later, he called again. 'Are you positive the winter will be really cold?' 'Absolutely.'

"The chief told his people to gather even more firewood. Then he called the Weather Service again. 'Are you sure?' 'I'm telling you, it's going to be the coldest winter on record.' 'How do you know?'

"'Because the Indians are gathering firewood like crazy!'"

Silence reigned in the cabin as the rotor blades continued their crisp Wop-Wop-Wop.

The boys looked at each other, paused, and looked at Josie.

Matthew spoke first. "Now. That. Was. Funny."

Josie smiled and said, "Thank you."

The boys, apparently by prearrangement, echoed "You're good to go."

"However," Matt said, "a career in 'stand-up'—no."

"We'll continue to be your guinea pigs until you're ready for prime-time, babe," John said.

"I disagree," Mark said, "I believe Josie and Kathy G could share the stage. Yep, you'd pull her up to the A-List."

"Enough of your malarkey; I've a full time job keeping track of you rogues of the midwest. I'd like to put a bridle on each one of you."

Having had their fun, the three boys closed their eyes and rested. Before Josie also had a chance to do so, Star rotated her fingers at her temple—the ASL for goofy—and pointed to the boys. Josie acknowledged and gave her the sign for true, then closed her eyes to rest.

*   *   *

As Dave crossed Baranof Island in A-Two, heading north over Peril Strait, he called Milt in A-One to let them know their position.

"A-Two, this is A-One," Milt responded. "Thanks for the location update. I see you've caught up with us. I presume Delta Station is buttoned up, and Josie has had a chance to brief the boys on how to work the fireline?"

"Roger that. I've even heard her telling them some of her folksy jokes—to put them at ease for the task ahead, I suppose. As you know, they're not bashful. They speak their minds quickly and clearly. They'll fight the fire as well as anyone; however, it's clear they'd rather be sampling Mother Earth's oceans than dowsing her flaming mantle with her waters. Did you hear me? I'm even starting to talk like them. Save me!"

"No sweat, you've always needed a linguistic upgrade anyway," said Milt. "Knock it off!"

Rob broke in. "One thing's for sure: no matter how the PhDs enunciate, and its effect on Dave, they're a tight team, honest and loyal to each other and their beloved school. Josie is fortunate to have them, and we are, too."

Ann said, "From my point of view, all three of you could use a linguistic upgrade. Speaking with the correct words makes understanding each other a whole lot easier. Long-windedness is not an attractive trait—except maybe for a tribe's Holy Man. Don't get me wrong, I love the ethnic flavor of varied speech. Josie and Joe will always sound a little like French Canucks, Leigh a Midwesterner, and Bear half Tlingit and half Alaskan. Of course, I've a near perfect East Coast accent derived from the King's English, circa 1700—yes, I'm a blue-blood. Put that in your pipe and smoke it."

"Gee whiz!" Rob exclaimed. "Are you done? Excuse us? Are you finished?"

"Yes, but remember, I come by it naturally; my grandparents came over in wooden sailing ships. Ha! It was nice having fun with you men. Josie and I have to take our shots when the opportunity arises."

Dave chimed in with a laugh. "Now that she's got that off her chest, let's move on with our plan. We're about to clear Kurzof Island. We'll be on our final into the park in about fifteen minutes. What's your plan, Milt?"

*   *   *

The smoke jumper, Kicking Bird, from the Tlingit, Raven Clan, had flown in on the DeHaviln, Beaver from DNR Headquarters in Juneau. On the first pass over the ranch, three wooden crates of firefighting equipment were dropped. On the second, at a higher elevation, he parachuted into the clearing. He immediately secured his chute, doffed his coveralls and helmet, and found Wind Spirit and

Raven Maiden busily dragging the crates to the barn area.

Kicking Bird was three parts sublime to one grotesque. His face had a battered and bronzed look without being hard. His nose was prominent and buttressed a strong and high forehead; his eyes were high-vaulted and had an expression of sadness; his mouth and chin were too close together, his cheeks hollow. All in all, his appearance was not very attractive until one heard his voice, which possessed a variety of expression, earnestness, and shrewdness. All this framed a half-eaten and half-smoked cigar.

Without fanfare or idle talk, Kicking Bird said, "Hello. I guess you know who I am. Let's get these crates moved and unpacked; the choppers are on their final."

Just as they moved toward the barn, three deer bolted out of the east side of the clearing and ran toward the river. In seconds, they bounded over the river and continued westerly into the swamp.

"That will be happening for the next couple hours as the fire drives game out of their natural habitat," Kicking Bird said.

Earlier radio contact from Geez allowed Windy and Raven to get a jump on what was expected from them.

They lined up the individual crates in a row according to Bird's instructions. The first had personal protective clothing; the second, rucksacks with a radio, survival blanket, water bottles, medical kit, and emergency air canisters; the last crate had shovels, axes, rope, chainsaws, and signaling devices.

Windy wiped his brow and asked if there was anything else they could do. With a slight smile on his face, Bird said, "If you have any pull with Manitou, put in a request to protect us for the next day or two."

Two coyotes ran through the clearing, stopped, looked around, and continued into the swamp across the river.

"Come on," Bird said, "let's gas up these chain saws and get 'em running. Each team leader will carry one. Don't be alarmed, Raven, but I'd also like you to get two buckets, fill 'em in the river, and water down the area around the yurt and barn. Yes, the fire's miles away, but a glowing ember can be blown miles, too. If you do that, Windy and I will tackle these chain saws. Hop to it, the choppers are only ten minutes from landing. I want everything ready. We're going to suit up the teams and get them aboard in five minutes or less. I want them inserted into the proposed fireline within fifteen. We've no time to waste. The fire is moving this way. The only time we can relax, and then only a little when the fireline is established, and the backfire is burning vigorously. I want this bugger snuffed out by dawn. Let's jump to it."

*   *   *

Fortunately, the fire was east of the ranch, and the onshore wind carried the smoke in an easterly direction. Unfortunately, the fire was moving to the west at a rate of two to five miles per hour, depending on the type of fuel and wind velocity. Luckily, the landing approach would not be masked by smoke.

Milt, in A-One, called Dave as they crossed the Bitterroot River south of the ranch.

"Good news, Dave: it appears our landing area is clear, and the fire, although moving toward the ranch, is at least five miles away. I just talked to Wind Spirit. He told me Kicking Bird is definitely a take charge guy."

"Fine," replied Dave. "I'll pass the word to Josie and her crew."

"Good idea. Bear thinks Geez sent Kicking Bird since there is no need for a smoke jumper for this fire. He also said Big Wind will be there on the next tanker flight. He'll jump in. Kicking Bird has also asked us to hold the choppers at the clearing while the troops get dressed. That will allow us to insert them while on the way to Skagway to pick up our water bags."

"Damn, I don't think that's a good idea. We'll be delayed."

"I thought so, too, but he guaranteed to have the troops ready in five minutes—even if he has to dress the Wolvies himself."

"Oops. He knows about our rookies."

"Yep, but is not concerned. Similar students have worked out very well in the past. They're always in better shape than the rest of us old-timers."

"That's good to hear."

"Dave, Kicking Bird would like to talk with all of us, but especially the fire-team members. He's asked us to put his uplink on channel seven and our IC so he can give some additional instructions. It will save time when on the ground. Could you set that up on your chopper, too?"

Dave set it up and relayed the message to Milt. Kicking Bird was tied into both choppers as they approached the park boundary.

*   *   *

"My friends," Kicking Bird told the group," although we've never met, we will become very close over the next twenty-four hours. We have been assigned to halt the spread of 'Marge.' Yep, they name fires up here. Here are a few changes.

"I will direct strategy on the fireline with the teams, and also relay needs and progress to Big Wind, who will stay at the ranch and contact Juneau, as needed. More about that later. Joe will join Josie's team. Let's talk about what we'll be doing. Listen up, you're only five minutes from landing. This is it.

"It appears that from what we all can see, Marge is moving westerly at about two miles per hour. She is about five miles from Leigh's ranch. She has been burning for twenty-four hours. Our instructions are to halt Marge, and also protect the ranch. We will do both.

"Here's my plan: after landing—and relieving yourselves since the choppers have been shaking your bladders for an hour—you will don protective clothing, grab your tools, then board the waiting choppers. We will attack the fire fifteen minutes later.

"We will assault the front of the fire by establishing a fireline ahead of the fire's movement. The distance from its leading edge will be decided prior to insertion.

"There will be three teams led by DNR employees. Number One, Big Bear and Leigh; Number Two, Joe, with Josie, Matthew, Mark, and John, with me attached for accountability; Number Three, Wind Spirit and Raven Maiden. I'll be coming and going to all the teams, as required.

"Ah, good, Big Wind just flew in.

"The teams will be inserted based on the lay of the land. First you will knock down the larger coastal canopy with power saws. These trees are generally one-hundred feet tall or more. Be careful, trees do not care who they fall on. You'll find beautiful hemlock, fir, spruce, and cedar—nice to live in and view, but perilous for carrying flames. Don't get sentimental, saw 'em down. At the same time, some of you will be clearing the understory brush with axes. The rest of you will be chopping down the tall grasses, trimming deadfalls, and shoveling undergrowth into the dirt—if possible.

"Once we've provided a five- to ten-foot clear zone and the cuttings are moved to the rear, we lay our backfire, at my command. You've been provided accelerant.

"I'll decide how far ahead of the burn we build the fireline and subsequent back fire; don't worry about these details. Besides, all of us but the boys have worked a fireline. However, I know the Wolvies will do well. As always, safety is job one. Remember, in fighting fires, we use the buddy system. Never do anything—*alone*. Don't take any chances; you are too valuable to lose. We will put Marge to rest. We will succeed. She will die. We will win.

"Don't ask any questions until you're back on the chopper, ready to fight our enemy: Marge.

"There will be aerial flights bombarding the leading edge, both with retardant that produces CO_2 to rob the fire of O_2 and, of course, water. You'll see Milt and Dave and their crew dumping water, too.

"Wouldn't it be fine if their bombardment halted Marge's advancement? Yep, but we will make sure she has a short life. We will succeed.

"See you soon, I'm anxious to meet you all."

*   *   *

"A-2, this is A-1. I'm switching back to channel nine. I'll join you there in a moment," Milt announced when Kicking Bird was done.

Silence.

"A-1, this is A-2 on channel nine. Over."

"Roger that. I'm on my final to the ranch. I'll land in the clearing near the barn. You can follow me in. Remember, we only get a short time for a pee-break; then the teams have to don their protective clothing and get their tools. That's a real hustle; the women will have to squat in the bushes, so we'd better have them go north, and us, south from the choppers."

Ann broke in, "Been there, done that. No problem, man. Don't worry 'bout us women; we can do anything you can do—maybe better."

Off-mic, the women heard Ann's comment and yelled in the background, "No problem, man."

Milt whispered into the mic, "I hope the girls have bandages for scratches to the butts after hanging them out in the bushes in the clearing."

"I heard that," Ann yelled.

Dave replied, "Okay, we'll behave."

Milt announced, "We're about to land, so let's hop to it and kick *Marge* in the butt, and keep our women sweet."

"Milt, stop it," Ann said, sounding frustrated.

As the leaves and loose grass flew like a maelstrom from the downwash of the rotor blades, the choppers landed and the fire fighters all leaped from their crafts.

The women went north, the men, south—except the joker, Matt, who made a faux move to the north until Josie told him, "Get!"

When relieved the team members grabbed their gear and were ready to board when Big Wind held them for a quick chat.

*   *   *

"Listen up," Windy said, "as coordinator of the three teams and aircraft, it is essential that I am called every hour with a head count by name and approximate location. Got it? It's very important to do so. This means that you team leaders *must* maintain visual contact with your people at all times. This is especially important for Bear, who has the largest team. Again, if you have problems, Kicking Bird will be your contact on site. You'll notice he has realigned the teams so its members are more compatible. Now mount up and slay that dragon. Bye."

Without any idle chatter, they all ran to the choppers. Milt took team Two, the largest, and Dave took teams One and Three. Star and Janet, serving as crew chiefs, helped the teams load with their bulky coveralls, boots, and tools. They strapped in, and, before they knew it, the turbines turned full power, and the choppers leaped into the smoke-filled air. The fire was getting closer.

Without delay, Big Wind started performing one of his additional tasks. He hooked up Old Gal to an improvised plow and started making an earthen fireline around the clearing and next to the buildings. Luckily, on the east side of the ranch, the Bitterroot River formed a natural barrier for ground fires.

Six deer ran through the clearing, stopped, stomped, and fled as he urged Old Gal to pull hard through the sod-like surface. After the third pass around the clearing and buildings, he rested Old Gal while he threw several more buckets of water near and on the buildings.

As he hustled back to the clearing, a raven soared above, then slowly dropped to the clearing and perched on a majestic red cedar.

"Well, hello, my friend. I've wondered when you'd arrive. Welcome."

Just as he finished giving water to the horse, he received his first call from Kicking Bird. He said, "Fire team base, this is fire team Two. All teams have been inserted and are starting to clear a fireline. I have visual to all members of teams Three and One, so they will not be checking in now. It is 1600 hours; the next sked from all units will be at 1700. The choppers are on their way to Skagway. The Wolvies have further named the fire 'Marge's Mayhem,' after their not-so-favorite English professor, Marjorie Mourning.

"The fire is about a thousand feet to the east, moving faster now as the winds from the west subside. Nothing further. Out."

Big Wind thought, *Manitou, be with your people today. They'll need your guidance and protection as the setting sun robs daylight.*

Chapter 14

The choppers with their anxious fire teams flew easterly in a tight formation at 500 feet, side by side, moving toward the inferno. Many of the local Indians had a healthy respect for fire . . . more like a fear. Local legend held that the spirit of death lurked in the flames.

"A-Two, this is A-One," Milt called to Dave as they approached the leading edge of the fire. "Kicking Bird likes that clearing with the grass on your left flank, dead ahead about three-hundred yards. What do you think? Let's take a look. He feels it's important to land right now. We're close enough; any closer and we'd be at risk, so he says."

After viewing the fire's advance from the chopper's elevation, The Bird told Milt that he had modified his plan of attack. He determined that due to the narrow point of the advancing fire marching like an arrowhead, only one insertion would be required. Teams One and Three would still cover the flanks of the fire-line preparation, and the larger, team Two, would still be in the center.

He also told Milt that the fire-line would be no more than one mile long with teams one and three clearing 440 yards, and team two, 880 yards. The line would be at an azimuth of 350 degrees north or 170 degrees southerly back azimuth.

As they slowed and descended, The Bird asked Milt for a commo net to the IC of both choppers so he could present his plan in detail. Both pilots linked him with the teams, and he took less than two minutes to brief them on the latest plan.

To the crew's surprise, Mark exclaimed, "Good! I'm glad we're all in this closer to each other. I feel much safer now." The gang stared at him in disbelief. "Well, I admit it. I'm probably the 'skeerdest' of the lot of you. I've seldom been in big timber, much less, a blazing inferno."

With a wry smile, The Bird whispered under the roar of the turbines and Wop-Wop-Wop of the blades, "Stay close to Josie or me; you'll do just fine. The experience will look good on your resumé. From a marine biologist and fire fighter, we offer like a double major . . . kinda like a surf and turf."

The crew groaned at Bird's attempt at humor.

Team leaders Wind Spirit and Bear in A-Two called and acknowledged the new instructions and indicated they were ready to fight.

*   *   *

"Okay," answered Dave. "Let's do it! I'll go down first and check out the landing site in the grassy clearing. Stand by."

While the smoke billowed up, both choppers descended quickly near the small opening in the canopy of the forest.

"Milt," Dave said, "I'm not sure there's room for both of us; I'd better go down alone, unload, and clear before you come down."

"Roger that."

As Dave descended to ten feet off the deck, the tall grass bent over, leaves blew, and dead bushes tumbled away in the downwash. "What the hell . . . musk-rats, too."

The cabin odor quickly changed from the residual smell of jet fuel and exhaust fumes to barbecued wood. At this distance of approximately one-half mile, the smell was reasonably pleasant, only because the air contained a fraction of the contaminants of smoke from the burning pitch. Dense smoke was a whole different matter; it not only burned eyes; it could fry lungs. In more concentrated amounts over a short period of time, dense smoke could kill.

As Dave descended the last five feet into the tall grass, he was shocked; the tall grass concealed a small pond-like swale full of water. How deep was unknown. He carefully lowered the skids onto the grass. "Holy Christ!" he barked into the radio. "Sonabitch, we're in the backwaters of a damn lake. Abort!"

Ann helped as they applied full power before the water-soaked grass sucked the skids into a murky grave. The chopper leaped into the air . . . and hovered.

"Milt, we're in a little trouble. It's too wet to land here; however, maybe I can hover just above the water line and have the crew jump out."

"Roger that. But, what if the water is too deep? The crew could sink," Milt said.

"No problem. They'll float and get to the edge of the swale in seconds. Besides, we do not have time to find another site. We've got to commit."

"What does Wind Spirit think?"

"He's ready to go and has deferred to me; he's ready to swim."

"I thought so. Have at it. If your chopper sinks to its belly, I'll pull you out. I've done it before, and can do it again. Lots of luck."

"I hear you loud and clear. Thanks. I'm going back down and just kiss off the grass and hope for the best. The swale is only fifty feet wide; they'll get to its edge and solid ground quickly."

As Dave descended again in a slow deliberate manner he thought, *The crew is going to get soaking wet or mucked up to their waists. I hope the gals can maneuver with all the weight of protective clothing, rucksack, and tools. Manitou be with them; they'll need your help again today.*

Just as the chopper descended, a raven soared overhead.

In a slow *Wop—Wop—Wop*, Dave lowered the aircraft ever so slow. Big Bear slid the door open at twenty feet from the deck and readied the crew to jump. At the kiss-off point, Ann was to give them the call when to jump.

Ever so slowly, the chopper descended.

Wop—Wop—Wop.

Carefully, Dave touched off on the top tassels of the grass, pushed the stalks down with the skids, and flattened the stalks to the water.

"Now!" Ann yelled.

Wind Spirit hit the bent grass first and sank immediately to his knees. He quickly extracted himself, turned, and caught Raven Maiden as she leaped from the cabin. She hobbled to the edge of the swale's grass to an elevated rallying point.

Bear and Leigh jumped in a similar fashion. They joined Windy and Raven, checked their tools and equipment, and moved out to higher ground within sight of the swale.

Milt descended quickly as Dave's chopper moved out of the swale. He dropped in the same fashion as he had observed Dave. At the key moment, Rob called for the teams to jump in a prearranged order: Kicking Bird, Joe, Josie, Mark, John, and Matt. After the six exited the chopper safely, and cleared the quagmire of grass and muck successfully, they waded to the edge of the swale.

They all turned and waved as Milt powered up and leaped into the air to join Dave on their flight to Skagway. They hoped to see them again as they dowsed the fire by air.

They met the previous crew at the rallying point and exchanged a few quick comments on their altered plan of jumping out of the chopper. As expected, Mark was the most vocal complainer on being soaked to the bone. Josie gave him a little sympathy—the other boys, none. In fact, Matt chided him with "Poor baby."

Kicking Bird quickly checked all the equipment and asked if there were any injuries from the leap while seemingly looking at Mark. As expected, Mark complained of a little soreness in his crotch. Immediately, Josie told the other boys to "zip-it" before they took advantage of Mark's open-ended line.

Kicking Bird, while chewing on an unlit cigar, lined the teams up in order and in line with the azimuth of the fire-line. He directed Wind Spirit and Raven to head out to the compass direction and distance by pacing, one step to equal one yard. They were to go 1/2 mile or 880 yards and start their work. Likewise, Bear and Leigh the same but in the opposite direction. Bird asked for questions, and without any gave them a last-minute radio check and reminded them of the one-hour sked to Big Wind. Both teams moved out.

*   *   *

"Okay, babe," Bear said, "you pace off the 880, and I'll guide you in a straight line ... well, an approximate of straight. The good news is that the westerly breeze is keeping the fire in check and blowing most of the smoke away from us. By the way, you'll be dry by the time we get to our end of the fire-line."

Leigh sighed. "You're so accommodating with your sympathy of my wetness. I'd prefer my dryer back home. Do you realize that every step creates a squish in my boots? That ain't no frog croaking. Yeah, I'll be dry. It'll be from my own BTU's."

"Poor baby. Don't feel like the Lone Ranger; my sound is similar, more like a slosh."

"Okay, I'm complaining ... that's my right. In fact, I'd feel better if you weren't so hell-bent to get to our work zone. I need a hug. Jumping off the chopper was not a pleasant experience. I was scared, but was not going to show it in front of The Bird, or you for that matter.

Bear sensed her need, turned, grabbed her, and gave her a big hug. It was good for both of them—even though there was little contact through the protective gear, rucksack, and helmet.

Around an android like Kicking Bird, they had all acted a little tougher than they really were. They began the daunting task of clearing a fire-line as a pair when, in fact, in the past they had always been a part of a larger team of firefighters. Be that as it may, they'd do the best possible job with the ingenuity and experience they had gained from previous firefighting assignments.

"Hey, babe. I can't feel your butt, and hardly any of your exotic body, so what say we raise the shields on our helmets and lay one on?"

"Deal!"

After a little suck face, they continued over hillock, through swales, and around sink holes. They tied a yellow flag on a long stick and drove it into the ground at 440 yards as a marker between team One and Two. They arrived at their designated spot in approximately forty minutes. They immediately analyzed the tasks at the site and doffed their gear. Bear called both Big Wind and The Bird as to their arrival and gave an assessment of their clearing tasks.

"Bear," Leigh said, "let me talk to Big Wind before you sign-off."

Bear said, "Hold it a minute; your mom wants to say hello. Here, she's on."

"Hi. How are things at the ranch? Are you okay? Are the buildings protected yet? Are the animals okay? How are the wolves handling this excitement?"

Big Wind interrupted, "Leigh, I've completed an earthen barrier around the buildings, all the animals are fine, and you need not worry about anything. Your ranch is in good hands."

"Thank you so much. Sorry. I'm just concerned. Thanks."

"This is Bear. Thanks for caring for your mom; be talking to you again in one hour."

The pair returned to their task of felling trees and clearing brush. Bear sensed that Leigh worked with more vigor after the chat with her son. She appeared to have a little more peace of mind in knowing her ranch, her wolves, and, yes, her son were okay.

Bear thought, *I'm one lucky guy to have a family centered around that woman. Yep, one lucky guy.*

* * *

Joe asked team Two to gather around him. "Come on, let's go over our tasks one more time. Daylight's aburnin'."

Joe explained how the teams would be organized. Mark would support him while he felled trees with the power saw; John would support Matt with a power saw; Josie would be paired with Kicking Bird who would be in and out of the team since he'd also be checking on the other two teams, and coordinating the air tankers.

"Any questions?" Joe asked. "Being none, let's get to it before those flames start lickin' our lips."

Joe and Mark split, shot a compass heading of 350 degrees, picked out an aiming point, and started felling the taller timber to the north.

Matt and John shot a back azimuth of 170 degrees, picked out a large cedar as a reference, and headed south along the proposed fire-line. As Matt gnawed away on a large hemlock, John whacked the lower brush with his axe. Josie and Kicking Bird scurried around dragging bushes, limbs, and small trees.

The six firefighters moved along the fire-line. Three one way, three the other, in opposite directions. They bush-whacked a path, so the fire-line slowly developed into a real barrier to leaping flames.

With the roar of two power saws and bushes being cut, Kicking Bird approached Joe. "Joe, I'm going to check on team Three and head east to see what kind of terrain and fuel is in the path of the fire as it advances this way. I'll be better able to judge how long we've got to prepare our fire-line and set the back-fire. I'll keep in contact. See you later. Keep up the good work."

Joe cautioned, "Are you sure this is a wise move? It is dangerous to move towards a fire—alone. You're violating the buddy system. Can't the aircraft give you that kind of information?"

"No sweat. I'll keep in radio contact. In fact, I'll call every fifteen minutes. Bye."

"Be careful, and don't forget to call," Joe hollered as The Bird disappeared into the timber.

A moment later, Joe thought, *I have a feeling, no matter how good he is, I should have stopped him. No one should travel alone. Fire does not care what it consumes.*

*   *   *

On the back azimuth, team Three was getting organized. After checking their gear one last time, Raven Maiden took off to the south with determination.

"Raven," Windy said, how are you going to know when we've walked one-half mile?"

"Silly man. Many times I've hit the spot within yards."

"I'm not so sure; I'm going to count the 880 paces."

"Go ahead, but follow me with your pacing, and I'll bet when you think you're there, I'll be on the spot."

"Deal! I'll keep the count to myself."

The couple took off on their assigned azimuth from the rallying point. Raven shot the 170 degree angle only once, put the compass away, and headed out briskly with Windy pacing behind.

Windy never felt so proud of his new bride as he followed her through the thickets, over knolls, and around downed timber. She moved like a dancer with all the grace of a light-footed cat as she went over, up, around, and under obstructions in her path. It was as if she were keeping time to the music of a ballet.

He reflected on the last few weeks of splendor with her on the ranch. Sure, they'd had a few spats, but nothing major that disrupted their undivided caring, sharing, and loving.

He'd learned that she was more independent than he previously thought. Yes, they needed each other, but she could stand alone without a man if she chose to. Her Indian background taught her to be self-sufficient. Clan life was like that, for the men were gone much of the time. In fact, the clan was matriarchal. Women ran the camp; men provided for their subsistence. True, men held key ceremonial positions, but women managed the camp. She had learned her lessons well.

"I'm a lucky man," he murmured.

"What?" Raven asked as she stopped and turned to him.

"Oh, I just said we're almost at the halfway point."

"You're right; it's just over there at the base of that cedar."

"Dang, girl, you were right on; I've only ten paces to 880 yards."

"Good, let's doff these heavy rucksacks. I'll start clearing brush while you get the power saw ready."

"Right on, babe. Let's kick butt and show Kicking Bird and the team how good we are at fire-lines. I'll call Big Wind and The Bird and tell them we've arrived at our spot."

While working, he heard a noise, "Look out!" Windy yelled. "There's a herd of deer headed your way. To me their wild eyes look like they'd care less if they ran over you. The fire must have spooked them. Look at them, they're terrified—

and they have a right to be."

*Roar—putt—putt—*RRRRRR.

Windy started cutting down part of the timber reaching to the top of the canopy in an effort to stop the flames from leaping over the fire-line below.

Slash—crash—splash.

Raven attacked the brush and threw it to the rear of the line.

As they worked, Windy was certain he also heard aircraft dropping water on the leading edge of the advancing fire.

He thought, *I'm a little concerned; the activity seems to be only a few miles away—very close—closer than what Kicking Bird had said. I wonder where he is; he was to have stopped to check on us by now.*

*   *   *

About a half-hour later, Kicking Bird's pace slowed and fatigue attacked his well conditioned body. The air that reached his lungs was contaminated. Toxic gases from the fire had taken a large percentage of oxygen and replaced it with carbon dioxide and ash. Numerous windfalls, hillock, and swamps hampered his progress, but the major determinants were the huge out-cropping boulders, surrounded by a lot of cracks and wide crevasses. Some of the deep fissures were several feet in width and deep enough to swallow a careless animal or tired man.

As he moved toward the advancing fire, he determined that from the density of the smoke and crackling sound he was only one-half mile from the fire's leading edge.

Even at that distance, a less skittish wolf slinked pass him at a moderate lope. His attention was on the fire, not man. The former was more trouble to the wolf. Many denizens of the forest had already experienced fires over their lifetimes. Relocating due to fire, drought, game shifts, and man's intrusion into their hunting grounds were frequent events.

As he walked up and over the boulders, Bird murmured, "Oh, oh, I'd better get out of her way. As he hid behind a tree, a large black bear sow and her cubs scurried by. Then she caught his scent, stopped, raised up, barked, lowered her huge body, and continued on her way.

As he came from behind the tree, he said, "Thank you, Mrs. Bear. I'm glad I was not of interest to you today." He knew very well she had only survival on her mind, not a human intruder.

He noticed the accumulation of ash on his clothes, and said, "This is close enough." The billowing smoke and dense ash indicated that he was only a hundred yards or so from the leading edge of the fire.

He turned and looked at his return route, which would be the path of the fire, and noticed that the landscape of rock and boulders would probably slow down the fire's advance. Large boulders with small shrubs fighting through fissures and cracks do not make good fuel.

Feeling relieved that his survey had yielded good information for the teams, he turned to return to the team's activities. They would be elated to have enough time to finish the fire-line.

Bird climbed up a large boulder for a better look at his exit route.

"Ah, that's it, 220 degrees back azimuth to the line."

As he put away his compass, he grabbed his oxygen bottle; it was getting harder to breathe this close to the fire. He looked out to find an aiming point. While placing his booted foot on the rocky surface, and his eyes elsewhere, he noticed the wide crevasse too late.

"*O-o-oh-h-h-h!*" echoed across the boulder field as he slipped and fell into the cavernous crack. The oxygen bottle flew out of his hands as he grabbed for the edge of the fissure.

Kerplunk

"Christ!"

He had fallen too quickly to grab the edge of the hole. He'd been in a survival mode—hands over his face.

He immediately tried to extract himself, but much to his dismay found that his right foot was wedged in a secondary crack. More than that, he had a feeling it was sprained. He felt the pain of swelling as it tightened in the vise of rocks.

He looked around in the shadowy cavern. Fortunately, his rucksack fell with him, and it contained some key survival gear like a rope, food, and a medical kit. "Damn," he cried, "I've dropped the 0-2 bottle. Sonabitch."

Before opening the pack, he tried calling the gang on the fire-line with his AM/FM receiver. As expected, no luck with either channel seven or nine. FM being line-of-sight transmission, so there was no way the signal would get out of the hole. A bird or a plane, yes, but the beam would be narrow.

He tried the AM radio next. Its signal radiated through sky-wave propagation and just maybe would reach out enough to be heard. He dialed in the emergency frequency for aircraft at 122.9 MHz and called.

Silence.

"Damnit! Nothing. I'm just too deep into Mother Earth's breast to reach out. Damn. Damn. Damn. I must be at least ten feet down. Unless an aircraft flies directly overhead, I'll never be heard. I'd better get used to being on my own to extract myself from this earthen cavern."

He retrieved his med kit, swallowed some aspirin, then took his rope, made a loop on the end, and threw it up, hoping to latch on to a projection above the hole.

"Jesus Christ, that's not going to work; I can barely clear the opening."

Soaking wet with anxiety, totally fatigued, and now hyperventilating, he decided to relax for a moment . . . and think.

Ash started falling into the hole as the fire approached the boulder field. Without a doubt, the fire was going to pass over him—within minutes. His only hope for survival was the depth of his location, and the absence of fuel near the hole. Frustrated and depressed, he covered himself with his heat blanket.

He thought, *Manitou, if I've ever needed your help, it's right now. If I do not survive while this fire passes over me, this location, this vault will indeed be my sarcophagus. I pray it is not.*

Chapter 15

Waiting at the ranch, Big Wind was very concerned about Kicking Bird's unknown whereabouts.

Joe's team two, which The Bird was assigned to for accounting purposes, had not shown up in more than an hour. Joe indicated that he had left his team at least an hour ago to examine the terrain in front of the advancing fire. Also, The Bird had missed his planned visit to Windy and Raven in team three on the way back. That had not happened. Bear and Josie in team one had not seen him, either.

Big Wind examined the roughly drawn overlay on the Park's terrain map, which indicated where the fire had started, and that it was still moving in a westerly path. The fire could move neither to the south due to the huge Brady Icefield, nor to the east to the icy waters of Glacier Bay.

The crew's fire line would stop the fire's westerly trek before reaching the ranch on the foothills of the Fairweather Mountain Range. Also, several state and federal monitoring stations were located at elevation along the range.

This left the broad expanse of the northern forest butting against the Saint Elias Mountains that stretched at least 100 miles north. The fire could advance in that direction, but it was not likely; the water tankers had been creating a wet barrier there for several hours. Luckily, the fire's advance had been slowed due to the extensive boulder fields throughout that terrain. The field had very little fuel to feed it.

Big Wind decided that he may have to call FFS choppers working the northern line and request their help. They could look out for a lone firefighter exploring the earth below. They flew lower and slower than the fixed-wing tankers, and dropped close to 100 feet off the deck with their load. Only the choppers could make a few passes at hover to spot a human, and only then in an opening in the canopy.

Frustrated, he called The Bird again . . . but got no answer.

Big Wind thought, *Why the hell doesn't he answer his radio—or call out to us? Dammit, Bird, what's up?*

He switched to the air emergency frequency 122.9 and called the FFS pilots. "A-One or A-Two, this is Big Wind at fire base. Do you read? Over."

Static.

He repeated the call.

More static and background noise of other pilots talking to each other or their base operators.

He repeated the call again.

An audible tone, *ii—ee—oo—ee*, indicated someone was keying their mic to respond.

"Fire base, this is Milt in A-One. I read you loud and clear. Sorry for the delay. We were on a drop, and pretty busy. What's up? Over."

"Roger that. I need for you to look out for The Bird in the sector you're working."

"He went in alone? That violates all the DNR rules of maintaining the buddy system."

"I know. Roger that. You know him; The Bird thinks he's bigger than life . . . indestructible. It's not like him to ever be out of radio contact. Something must have happened to him—something serious."

"Damn. Okay. I'll pass the word to Dave and Ann. Rob and I will do our best. Damn. Alone. Christ! What was he thinking?"

"Roger that. Thanks. I knew I could count on you."

"Yep. By the way, we've contained the northern border with retardant and water. If your teams are ready with the fire break/line, from what I see up here, it's time to light the back fire."

"Roger that. I'll call Joe and see if they're ready. Your view from there is just what we needed. You know, that's what the Bird was trying to do from the ground. Damn, he didn't have to make that trip. Juneau Control was going to tell us when to start the fire. It was going to be based on pilot sightings anyway. Damn."

"We'll start looking. It's no problem. I'll be off the air awhile. We're dropping down to Glacier Bay for another load. A-One, out."

"Fire base, out. Break. Juneau Control, do you copy?"

Static . . . an aural tone . . . static.

"This is Juneau Control. Geez here. I monitored your transmissions, Big Wind. As to starting the back fire by Joe's crew, please give him permission to do so if he's ready. This directive is based on Milt's aerial view of the fire's advance. Any questions? Over."

"Negative. I'll take care of it," Big Wind replied.

"I, too, am concerned about The Bird. I'll see what other resources are available and also keep trying to raise him on the radio. Good luck. This is Juneau Control. Out."

"Fire team Two, this is Fire Base. Over."

Big Wind repeated the call three times before Joe responded.

"This is team Two. We were a little busy. We're about done here. We're down to dirt in most places. What's up?" Joe replied.

"Two things. One, we're starting an air search for The Bird; two, Geez, at Juneau Control, has given you the authority to start the back fire—when ready."

"Great. We're just about finished. Team one has linked up with us, as has team three. After a lot of hugging and kissing, they're all here drinking every bit of water I've got. I swear, Mark is ready to suck water from the swale . . . tadpoles and all. We're all tired, hungry, and proud.

"We'll hop to it. I'll have Bear run the line north with accelerant, and I'll run south. Are you sure you're ready? What about Bird? What if he's out there headed this way or hurt in the path of the back fire?" Joe said.

Silence.

"All your concerns are valid. Nevertheless, we have to start the back fire. It appears from aerial sightings that the fire's advance is only about 440 yards from the fire-line. You must start the back fire—now. The back fire must consume the fuel and rob it from the advancing fire."

"I roger. I'm just concerned about The Bird being trapped in the flames."

"So am I," said Big Wind.

Silence.

"Okay," Joe answered, "you're right. Bear has the wicks lit on both canisters. We're ready. Nothing further. Out."

Big Wind paused after talking with Joe. He lowered his head, dropped to his knees, looked to the sky for guidance from Manitou . . . and prayed.

He cast tobacco to the points of the compass.

> Greetings, all my relations,
> and the Great Spirit.
> Have pity on me; help me
> to walk the straight path here on earth.
> Be with Kicking Bird
> in his time of need.
> Many thanks.
> I am finished.

*   *   *

Kicking Bird reflected on his current lot in life.

As he thought of his actions that led to his entombment, he noticed that a companion had joined him in the crevasse. Most likely to escape the smoke and toxic air, a small field mouse had scurried down the side of the cavern to rest on a small ledge.

He looked up at the mouse, and said, "It looks as though we've got ourselves into a real predicament. There go our ideas of being indestructible. How 'bout you, Mighty Mouse?

"Yep, you're smart to have come in here . . . and me a fool to have done so.

"But, that's reality. I'll do the best I can to survive the next hour or two. By now the back fire is also roaring toward us from the west, and the original fire is advancing toward us from the east. It will just be our luck for the two to meet at the godforsaken boulder field where we're trapped.

"If that happens, you and I are goners. The roaring fire will rob the oxygen from the air . . . and we will be no more. What do you think of those marbles?

"How 'bout you, my friend? Do you think you can survive as the fire passes overhead? I'm guessing not. At least we can die together, thank goodness. Hate the thought of dying alone.

"Here's what I can do: I'll tape the transmit button down on the radio and set it up as high on the wall as possible; then the passing aircraft will be able to sense the carrier-wave of the signal. It will be a very narrow beam rising out of here, that's for sure. However, if a pilot flies directly overhead, the signal will be picked up. How's that Double-M? Yep, that's what we'll do."

The Bird taped the send button down on the radio, and mounted it on the side wall with tape. Unfortunately, the antenna was about three feet below the opening. While he set up the radio, the mouse ran out, but returned in one minute and sat on his little ledge.

"Hi there. Welcome back. Didn't you like the smoke and heat out there? I understand. You're kinda like the canary in the coal mine. You'd better hang out here with me. Does it look as bad as it sounds out there? The crackling and crashing don't sound good to me. The ash is falling in such volume now, you're covered and it's finding its way into our little cavern. You look more gray than black now. That's not a good sign."

The Bird decided to finally relax by lying back and waiting for the miracle that would save his life. As the air grew thin and the smoke grew thick, his respiration rate increased and coughing became more frequent. His eyelids started to feel heavy. He fought their closure by blinking again and again as the ash clouded his vision. He slumped over on his lap. A burning limb fell over the opening of the cavern. Glowing pine needles dropped on his head.

*   *   *

Wop—Wop—Wop echoed across the boulder field.

The distinctive sound aroused The Bird from his slumber.

"Wait. What's that? Yep, it's a chopper. It could be Milt or Dave looking for me. I hope they come this way."

He looked up at the radio to see if it was still there with the send button taped down. It was hanging down with half the tape released from the wall, but still there.

"Hey, little radio, you're my ticket to life. I hope you're sending a signal out to the living world. Let's hope that chopper flies directly over this soon-to-be mausoleum in the wilds.

"Oh! There you are. You've returned again. Welcome back Mighty Mouse. I missed you. It's nice of you to join me in this submerged smokestack. I say stack because I've noticed there is some movement of smoke and hot gases past us to an opening below. That's not good. That will guarantee a constant supply of le-thal, heated air.

Kicking Bird covered his eyes and mouth with the last bit of moist cloth and drank his last drop of water to sooth his irritated throat.

"You're on your own now, Mighty Mouse; I've got to keep my eyes and mouth covered—hold on, we'll make it—hold on. The fire will pass over us soon, and who knows, maybe the chopper will pick up our signal, land, and rescue us. Hold on."

He slumped into a contorted fetal position, covered his face, and moved the one usable leg over his trapped swollen and numb appendage. He awaited his fate with the thoughts of the good life he had had with family, friends, and his buddies in the Navy, his buddies who always wished him fair winds and following seas . . .

*   *   *

"Ann, did you hear that? There's a signal coming from that boulder field. It's just a carrier-wave. Let's get a little closer," Dave said as they searched for Kicking Bird where the fire had crossed over the boulder field below.

Ann said, "I agree, let's hover in the area awhile.

"No," Dave answered, "we'll suck in too much ash and particulate. When we're moving, the surface that's disturbed by the prop wash is behind us and no problem; hovering invites ingestion of turbine-killing ash. No, we can't hover, but we can fly a tic-tac-toe pattern in the area . . . a few times, say at 100 feet. What do you say to that?"

"Fine. We're at 500 feet now: let's go down and start our pattern. I'll fly, you look and listen. You've always been the eagle-eyed one up here."

Ann descended to 100 feet and flew the pattern in the area where they had barely heard the weak radio signal.

Dave reminded her of the full water bucket they still had hanging 50 feet below the chopper. Their flight's primary mission was to dowse hot-spots in the burned-out area, and look for Kicking Bird, too.

As their flight progressed over the pattern, Dave sensed that one of the passes seemed to pick up a faint radio signal. He turned up his receiver's volume as they passed over an area of large boulders and deep crevasses. He mentioned it to Ann, and she hovered over the site.

"This is surreal," Dave said. "I do hear something, but there's no one down there. At this height, we should see something. Maybe The Bird had dropped his radio with the send key depressed—but I doubt that."

"Not hardly," Ann said. "The transmit button is spring-loaded to not stay down . . . no way."

"So you explain it. By the way, get moving, you're kicking up a lot of ash and it's about to reach our turbine's inlet."

"Right you are; I'll get going. Before we leave, Dave, take a mental picture of where we were, where the signal is strongest; I've an idea," she said as the chopper gained altitude.

At altitude, they hovered and checked the terrain below for hot-spots. During this time, the airwaves were full of chatter from plane to plane, from plane to their base, all talking about their success in conquering Marge. They even heard Joe talking to Big Wind at the ranch. Dave noticed that Ann was very quiet, too quiet, and a little too reflective.

"What's up, Ann? You okay?" Dave asked.

"I'm okay, it's nothing."

Silence.

Dave had been around women long enough to know "nothing" in that tone of voice actually meant something.

"I've marked the location of the signal on my map here. Look," Dave said. "If it is Bird's radio, we can go back after we land back by our original position, then walk in and check it out. The boulder field is only a mile in from where the crew built the fire-line. In fact, I can call Joe and have them ready to go with us after we land. Does that sound like a good idea?"

Silence.

He thought, Oh no, I've got a problem on my hands; she's upset about something. I'd better see what it is.

They continued flying over the burned area looking for hot-spots.

Then she kinda exploded with a barrage of words. "Dave, I think Kicking Bird is in that boulder field. I think he's fallen and hurt himself—real bad. I think he may have fallen into one of those crevasses. I think he's the one holding the 'send' button down on his radio. I think he knows we're here and expects us to rescue him . . . now."

Silence.

"Dave, I've got a feeling I'm right. We've got to find a way. Dave, we've got to go back. Dave, as PIC you can do it. Dave!"

"Ann, you know better. If we land at the boulder field the ash and burned debris would be sucked up in our turbines and snuff them out. Think what you're asking me to do. We could lose two lives trying to save one—if he's even there . . . or even alive. I could lose my license if we're unable to fly out."

Silence.

"I know, but what if I'm right and he's there? If he's hurt, he may die before a ground rescue team is allowed in the area."

Silence.

Ann yelled, "I've got it! We go back over the boulder field, hover by the area where the signal's strongest, and dump our water over the area to turn all the ash to mud and the embers to harmless wet charcoal. Then we land, see if The Bird's trapped in one of the fissures, and rescue him. We've got rope, a flashlight, and a medical kit. We may be able to save his life. He's there, Dave, I know he is."

"Dang it, all that could be true, if it worked that way; have you considered the risks?"

"Yes, but it's worth it if he's alive, and just think if you were in his place: you'd want to be rescued—at all costs."

"Yes, but what if he's already dead and has fixed his radio so we could find his body?"

"Dead or alive, we've got to try, and we've got to think he's alive."

"You're telling me that we're supposed to make an emergency landing in a freshly burned-out part of the forest, in a small area, still smoldering, dowsed with water, in a million-dollar aircraft, to possibly rescue even a lifeless body?"

Silence.

Ann cried, "Yes. Why? Kicking Bird is my cousin. He's from the Raven Clan. He left years ago to make his mark working for the DNR in Juneau."

"Why didn't you tell me?"

"Because it makes no difference. He's alone. Don't you see, Dave . . . he's alone. No man should die alone. Or, if dead, we should retrieve his lifeless body as soon as possible. Do you understand? We've got to try."

Silence.

"Dave, please, I'll take all the responsibility."

"You can't . . . I'm the PIC."

"Dave, I beg you."

Silence.

"Girl, you're a pain in the butt, but you make a good point. As Manitou has said many times . . . 'we must take care of our people, they are special.' I'll see what I can do. Break. Break. Fire base, this is A-One. Over."

"A-One, this is Fire base. Big Wind here. What's up?"

"Thanks for the come back. We may have found Kicking Bird. We're going down to investigate. We'll check in when we leave the ground, whether we find him or not. Please relay this message to Geez at flight ops."

"Roger that. Lots of luck. There's a lot of people here hoping you find him. You may not know it, but he's a Tlingit from the Raven Clan. He's one of my brothers. He got his name from his dancing style; he could kick so high it was as if he could reach the birds."

"Yes, I know, I just found out. Nevertheless, we'll do our best."

"Dave, be careful; all it would take is one glowing ember near your fuel to blow you up. That would not be pretty."

"Roger, we'll be in touch."

Ann looked at Dave with tears in her eyes, an expression that spoke a thousand words—of gratitude. She mouthed the words, "I love you," and got down to the business of flying. "Dave, I'll fly again. You tell me exactly when we're over the signal, then I'll dump the water and get out of the area quickly when the dust and debris flies. Okay?"

"Roger that. Let's go; daylight is aburnin'."

Ann carefully descended and hovered over the boulder field. Dave listened for the signal, found it, and yelled, "Now!"

Seven-hundred and fifty gallons of water splashed over the boulders and into the various crevasses as Ann poured power to the chopper's turbines and the chopper sprang into the air. Below, a maelstrom of smoking ash, twigs, and debris got soaked.

Hovering at altitude for a minute or two, Dave commented, "Damn, that was effective, just like a cow peeing on a flat rock—you'd better move or you'll be wet. Good drop, gal; let's get on down there to that clear area that I told Big Wind had not seen the fire."

"Now, you know a little white lie never hurt anyone . . . especially in this case."

Ann carefully descended again in a perfect vertical fashion so as not to disturb the surrounding smoldering terrain. As soon as the bucket touched, she moved laterally 50 feet and sat down. The rotors were disengaged, and the turbines put to idle.

"Good landing, gal. I'll search the area; you'd better stay with the ship."

"Roger. Be careful. All that ash has turned to mud. It will be slippery."

Dave crept slowly across the slick boulders with a rope over his shoulder and flashlight in his hand. When he reached the first series of fissures he started yelling, "Bird! Kicking Bird! Hello!"

Several of the crevasses had been washed clear of ash and debris, while others were full of undergrowth. Some were open with water in the bottom, others washed as if the water had passed through and left a clean hole. After falling several times, he grabbed a sturdy branch to help him walk with more stability.

Unfortunately, the weak signal had disappeared, and there were only about two or three fissures left to explore. He crept up the side of an incline to a big one at the base of a huge boulder and grabbed the edge.

Holding the lip, he brought the flashlight to the edge and pointed it down the washed walls. The flashlight's beam traveled down the side. The hanging radio reflected in the beam. It had slid down with the antenna turned upside down and the tape only partially holding it in place.

He quickly pointed the beam to the bottom of the hole. The light revealed a crumpled mass of humanity in protective clothing, helmet, gloves—and a wet mouse sitting on The Bird.

The depressing scene took his breath away. He paused, caught his breath, and lay on his stomach to contain the shock. The mouse leaped off the body, then scrambled up the rough-hewn wall and out of the crevasse.

"Bird! Bird!" he yelled into the cavernous vault. After no response, he quickly tied a rope around a nearby rock, the other end to his waist, and lowered himself into the hole. Halfway down, he retrieved the radio, pocketed it, and continued on down. He removed Kicking Bird's helmet, checked his carotid artery . . .

And found no pulse.

He bowed his head and wept.

From the temperature of the body and its rigor, he estimated the time of death as when fire passed over an hour ago. The fire had robbed all oxygen from the air. When he tried to move the body, he also found, that Bird's foot was wedged in a vise-like hold.

Kicking Bird, Tlingit warrior of the Raven Clan and DNR smokejumping firefighter had lost his life.

Kicking Bird would dance for his people no more . . .

Chapter 16

After several futile attempts to remove Kicking Bird, Dave resolved that with the limited light and room in the crevasse, he could not move the body alone. Entrapment of his foot was only part of the problem. The dead weight of his body pushed Dave's strength to its limits.

"Old fella, I'm gonna need help getting you back to your people and a proper burial. Hold on, I'll be right back; I'm going to get one of your sisters to help—hold on. I know it sounds trite to you as if you're alive, but who knows, your spirit may still be with you until your chief gives you the rites of passage to another life. So please permit me the right to share some time with you . . . it helps me endure the pain of your loss."

He climbed out of the cavern with a hand-over-hand lift on the rope using his knees as feet.

Although she probably already knew, his walk to the idling chopper didn't give him enough time to properly prepare a sensitive comment to Ann about Kicking Bird's demise.

She leaned out of her copilot's seat with a look of anticipation, knowing but probably not wanting to hear the inevitable. "How is he?"

"Ann . . . he's dead."

"No!"

"Yes. From the mask of death with purple like owl eyes, and his skin color, I'd guess he had been dead for an hour or two. Unfortunately, that's about the time the two fires converged here. The timing of his fall and entrapment couldn't have been worse. I presume the air was so toxic and oxygen depleted, his asphyxiation was quick—very quick. I'll suggest an autopsy to confirm the cause of death. I'll bet when he realized his predicament, and before he lapsed into unconsciousness, he rigged the radio to keep transmitting—the rest we know. Dear, I'm so sorry for you and your people, I know your father was a Tlingit elder. Nevertheless, you did everything possible within the timeline we had. Do you recall our—correction—your conversation less than one-half hour ago?"

"I do," she said. "I'll always remember the risk you took in landing and trying to rescue him, against *all* FAA flight rules."

He asked her to help him remove the body.

*   *   *

"Okay, let me shut her down; I'll join you in a second. As you know, this is another FAA violation. Oh, well."

As Ann went through the shutdown procedure, she thought, *Dave is taking another chance in cutting power. If the turbines are partially fouled or the ignition ports are plugged with ash, there's no way for us to get out of here. He'd be in big trouble with the FAA as PIC. He's the kind of guy I'd want on my team.*

She hit the ground running and started to move ahead of Dave. He stopped her and acknowledged her tears. He grabbed her and gave her a big hug.

She wrapped her arms around him and bawled. He hugged her tighter. "Oh, Dave," she cried, "no matter how hard we tried, he died alone. He died without any of his friends to comfort him. I know, he lived on the edge, and an unusual death . . . a tragic death was expected. But, alone. After all, he was a parachutist with hundreds of jumps, a lot of them on the edge of fires. Being a smoke-jumper for the DNR is risky business. It bothers me that he died alone . . . his foot locked in a stone trap."

"If it's any solace to you, it appears that he did not die alone. He had a friend. A mouse."

"What?"

As they sadly walked toward the crevasse, he paused.

"The way I see it, Ann, in knowing his beliefs, the mouse I found with his body was probably his companion during his last minutes. He loved nature, as you know. Whether four-legged, finned, or winged, they were his joy. Some say he liked the four-leggeds of the forest more than the two-leggeds.

"The last time I dropped him into a forest ablaze, he confessed that the reason he never married was due to his choice of living on the edge; taking the most dangerous assignment was one of his goals. He did not want a wife or family to worry about him. In the U.S. Navy he was a demolition expert; now that is a risky business. Geez can tell you stories of him volunteering for many missions that he thought were not doable.

"Today his luck ran out. His exuberance today lacked the discipline for which he was known.

"Anyhow, babe, let's believe—between the two of us at least—that he died talking to the mouse, a mouse that is indeed one of Manitou's creatures, equal to the magnificent grizzly in His forest. Manitou may have even shape-shifted to the mouse to be with him during his perilous situation in the vault. The Great Spirit moves in mysterious ways.

"See that raven perched over there in the burned out pine? I happen to believe its presence is no accident. That bird has been sent to be with Kicking Bird at this time . . . and it's my guess that the Great Spirit was first to know of his demise."

"Dave, I never knew you were so aware of Indian beliefs—especially Tlingit beliefs."

"I may not be as knowledgeable or faithful as I appear. I do not have absolute certainty or trustworthiness of what the holy men teach, but I do accept and find comfort in the transcendent beliefs of the nature-centered spiritual life of the Indians. Our existence on the planet is based on the effects of physical and natural laws, not the pontification of mystics before the age of reason. As you know, many religious beliefs are very unreasonable and unbelievable.

"I choose to believe the spirit is within us; all we have to do is accept its presence in our hearts and do unto others as we would have them do unto you. Thankfully, many beliefs embrace this rule, a rule that the aborigines developed long before modern religions brought it from the middle-east."

"It's been nice talking to you on this level, Dave; I thought I knew you . . . I didn't. I like the Dave I've just met."

Silence.

"We're about to get dirty. Are you ready?"

"Yep, let's do it," she said.

As they approached the crevasse, Dave explained that he needed her to pull on the rope and lift Bird's body while maneuvered into a position to free his trapped foot. Once clear, he explained, he would climb out of the hole and they would pull his body out together. Getting traction on the slippery wet ash would be a slight problem. Once free, loading him in the chopper's cabin would be easy. They'd tie him down and call Geez on disposition of the body.

Within minutes the plan was complete, and Kicking Bird was carried back to the chopper and tied down.

"We did it, gal. In fact, I'm not sure I could have done it without a second pair of hands—and a strong back. Thanks. I know it was difficult for you."

"I wouldn't have it any other way."

"Okay, let's get out of here. You do the flying, and I'll hop on the radio to Geez.

Ten minutes later, Ann had successfully started the engines and leaped to the air as close to vertical as possible so as to not to disturb the dry ash.

Dave was on the horn. "Juneau Control, this is A-Two with the body of Kicking Bird. We await your instructions. Over."

Geez returned the call from Sitka where he had just purchased another heavy-lift chopper for the DNR. He informed Dave to fly to the ranch and rendezvous there with the other DNR personnel. He would join them later. Geez made a quick comment that he wanted to have all personnel pay their respects to The Bird, and also to thank all personnel for their fine work fighting the fire. His best guess was that tribal elders would stop there, too, and later he would take the body to wherever they wished. That's the least he could do for one of his most valued employees.

He added that several of the DNR's fixed-wing pilots had already landed by now and would want to join the group at the ranch. He would offer his personal Bell H-10 for them to fly to the ranch from Juneau. Those pilots had dropped The Bird hundreds of times on the edge of roaring fires to single-handedly organize firefighting teams. Sometimes those teams were the local Indians that had a vested interest in halting any fire that might ravage their land. Those Indians many times shared the 'ground truth' in helping to fight fires. No one knows the lay of the land better than those who live on its breast. He warned Leigh and Bear that there may be a few Indians coming to visit the people who worked with their brother. They may wish to meet those who worked with their fallen brother.

*   *   *

Milt, Rob, and Janet had returned to the fire-line, picked up the remaining crews, and flew to the ranch while Dave and Ann scoured the area looking for Kicking Bird.

After deboarding, Leigh greeted her son with a big hug, as did Bear, with less emotion. The ranch had escaped the fire's fury. The only effects of the fire's intrusion were a few circular spots in the meadow where glowing embers landed. The grass had apparently not provided enough fuel to expand beyond a small three-foot ring.

Under Big Wind's supervision, the firefighters doffed their clothing, then returned their helmets, boots, and tools to the original containers. Although a pall of sadness hung over the group's activities, a certain joviality was also present since they had won—they had bested the fire. They were glad that the fire had been contained, but sad about the loss of life. They knew that at any minute Dave and Ann would be arriving with the body.

Leigh recognized the conflicted emotions and hatched an idea.

"Folks, I've a plan. While Raven and Windy are getting dinner ready, why don't we clean up in the Bitterroot? It's time to wash the burned Tongass forest off our bodies. Come on. Bear and I have decided to go; join us. Don't be bashful. If you choose, it will be shorts for men, bras and panties for us girls. For the more modest fully clothed. As you see, Big Wind has a roaring fire in the pit, there's a stack of towels, and the heat of the fire to dry off. Come on. Bear and I will lead the way."

Janet looked at Milt for a signal on what to do.

Josie looked at Joe to see what he was going to do.

Big Wind stripped to his shorts, called the wolves, and jumped into the water. The wolves followed and playfully attacked him as usual.

Before the "lookers" could decide if—and in what—they would swim, Josie led the way by stripping to her underclothes. Joe followed, and carried her to the edge of the stream, and threw her in.

Milt and Rob grabbed Janet and Star, who chose to leave their slacks on, but doffed their shirts, and carried them to the water.

Star whispered to Leigh, "What will Dave say?"

Leigh answered, "Nothing, you're among friends. What do you think Ann will say when she finds out Rob carried a half-naked woman into the drink?"

"Oh, I didn't think of that. In this case, it's nothing. He's more like a brother."

As soon as chow preparation was complete, Windy and Raven came out of the yurt, saw what was happening, and jumped in with the rollicking throng—clothes and all.

Surprisingly, the youngest, the most liberal, and the least sensitive—the Wolvies—took the longest to doff their clothes and jump into the water.

Not a soul was left high and dry as the wolves wrestled with the boys and Windy wrestled with Raven. The older couples, more sedate, passed the soap around to wash up. The only frisky actions were revealed when washing each other's backs. Joe was slapped when he started washing Josie's cleavage.

"Damn," Joe hollered, "now I know what the slap of a beaver's tail means. It means get away from me. I wonder if they learned that from Josie?"

"Josie slapped him again. "Behave, you old goat. Take a rain check."

"Ah my dear, that's why I love you so—not now, you say—but later."

Matthew, as expected, tried to scare the wolves with his Sasquatch imperson-ation, but lacking body hair and towering height he fooled nary a one. The moth-erly white wolf ended his charade quickly as she jumped on his chest. Her claw marks her calling card.

As the suds flowed downstream and the activities slowed upstream, the group slowly emerged from the icy bath. As Leigh explained earlier, the stream was fed by ice melt from the Brady Glacier less than ten miles to the north.

The cleaned, cold, and hungry group huddled by the roaring fire for warmth and drying qualities. Many turned circles to dry all sides of their squeaky-clean bodies. The scene looked much like a chop-house grill with kabobs on a rotisserie.

A large pot of coffee and a bottle of booze were handy for the individuals who wanted to be warm on the inside, too.

An accomplished hostess, Leigh was in her element as she watched the boys dance by the fire, the guys holding their gals in blankets while all told stories of their day's rewards. She couldn't help but notice how the boys tended to embel-lish their stories . . . just a little. No lies, just a little too much bravado.

Their verbal skills were on display to the point where Star said, "What the hell did he say?"

Rob said, "Nothing that a two- versus a four-syllable word would apply. They still talk as if they're in class at Ann Arbor."

Star said, "You know, Rob, they are goofy in a way . . . but you've got to like 'em."

"True. We're fortunate to have them with the DNR this summer."

After numerous towel fights, cups of coffee laced with booze, and stories told and challenged, the cleaned and relaxed group was ready to eat.

Leigh thought, *There are a few more firefighters coming. Maybe we should wait to eat. Let's see, there's Geez, the tanker pilots from Juneau, and of course Dave and Ann with the body. We'd better wait for them.*

Leigh asked for the attention of the group. "Folks, we need to wait a few minutes; a few key people will be here shortly. While waiting, would you mind doing something that has been done in my family over the years?

"It is very simple. In a circle, we all tell a brief story or experience that you've had with Kicking Bird. Bear, let's start with you."

"Sure . . ."

No sooner had Bear started than from the edge of the clearing, a man appeared.

He was dressed in ceremonial regalia, and led a painted pony pulling a decorated travois. He halted at the edge of the fire.

Speaking to Leigh, he said, "I am Wind in Hair, the Raven Clan Holy Man. I have come to take the body of my brother Kicking Bird, to his people for the spiritual celebration of his life."

Leigh said, "It's a pleasure to see you again, Wind in Hair. I've had the pleasure in the past."

The group that was not aware of the Holy Man stood in silence at his presence. He stood ramrod straight at six feet or more. His eyes were a penetrating gray, his hair in braids, his looks and skin that of a septuagenarian warrior.

"Please join us. We, too, are celebrating The Bird's life with heartfelt stories of his relationships with each one of us."

As Wind in Hair joined the group, and Bear took his pony. Windy offered him a drink.

Having met him before, Raven put her arm around him and introduced him to the celebrants.

Wop-Wop-Wop

Leigh whispered to Raven, "Tell him Dave and Ann are landing with the body now."

Raven told him and, in the classical politeness of a man of wisdom and care for his fellow man, continued the introductions. His brother's body was in good hands and would soon be delivered to him.

"My dear," he replied to Raven, "thank you. I will meet with the pilot in the next few minutes."

Wop-Wop-Wop

Leigh looked across the clearing to see Geez's H-10 descending. It had the two DNR tanker pilots from Juneau to pay their respects. They knew The Bird very well.

Leigh and Bear met them. "Hi, guys," Bear said. "Glad you could come. Follow me to the fire for introductions, and some coffee."

As they chatted on the way to the fire, another sound echoed across the clearing.

Wop-Wop-Wop

A large Sikorsky H-70 hovered over the clearing and slowly descended. The fourth chopper's presence made the clearing look like an operational airfield in the center of the Park.

As Bear tended to the tanker pilots, Leigh went to greet Geez. After powering down and greeting Leigh with a big hug, he turned to help his passenger deboard. Much to Leigh's surprise, it was Lynn, Bill's daughter, from Sitka.

"Welcome, Lynn. I'm so glad both of you could come."

"Likewise," Geez replied.

The three walked toward the fire.

Geez said, "Knowing the Tlingit traditions and burial rites are performed as soon as possible after death, this is the only chance I have to show my respects."

"True," she said. "Lynn, it is so nice to see you again."

Geez responded, "I think you know the other reason why she's here. Having picked up this chopper in Sitka, and having to return tomorrow, she asked if she could come along as copilot and see the ranch, too. I couldn't refuse."

With a wry smile, Leigh asked, "Is that all she wanted to see?"

Lynn blushed, "Why, yes, of course. However, if the boys are still here, I could say hello."

"They certainly are. Why don't you slip away from your PIC here and trot over to the fire and surprise them."

"Permission, sir?"

"Permission granted."

Lynn gave Geez a peck on the cheek and took off at a dead run.

After reaching the fire, the boys turned toward the approaching girl, discovered who she was, and yelled in unison, "Hi, babe!"

She got three big hugs, three kisses on the cheek, and each tripped over their tongues telling of their prowess in fighting the fire.

Mark gave her an Irish coffee. She refused, saying, "Just black, I'm not sure when we'll be flying out."

Back at the chopper, Leigh said, "Isn't she a delightful gal?"

"She sure is, and the boys think so, too."

Geez asked, "What are your plans, Leigh? Are you going to have a ceremony here in the clearing for Kicking Bird?"

"We'll see; I had planned to say a prayer with the group after you turn the body over to his people. Their Holy Man, Wind in Hair, is here to take the body back to the village. I suppose it would be best to ask him if he would like a short ceremony here."

As they approached the group by the fire, they saw the Holy Man still chatting with the group.

"A ceremony here sounds good. I'll ask him what he would like to do, imply that it is his decision, and we'll provide whatever we can to help."

"Thanks, Geez; I appreciate your assistance. You're not so bad, even though you're always taking my man from me on DNR business."

Geez smiled, "Speaking of business, before I go, I've a proposition for you and Bear to consider. We'll talk about it later. It will be exciting."

"Oh, no!" she groaned. "I think I'm not going to like this."

"Yes, you will! Trust me."

"That will be the day!" she replied.

"Ha, you'll see what it is—soon enough. Come on, let's go honor our fellow man with a prayer to the Great Spirit. I'll tell you of my idea when we're together with Bear. Come on."

As she chatted with friends by the fire, she felt good about her enjoyable evening with the complex group assembled, yet a little puzzled at Geez's proposal and sad for the smoke jumper's life being cut short. Kicking Bird was a good man.

After it appeared that the Holy Man had run the gauntlet of introductions and conversations about the forest fire, the DNR, the glaciers in the park, and finally telling everyone about the Raven Clan's settlement, he sought out Geez.

*   *   *

Without any specific words from Geez, the Holy Man asked him to bring Kicking Bird's body to the fire. Then he asked the group to gather around and form a circle with The Bird's body inside.

He had decided that the kindred spirit formed by Leigh's friends and family would be a good group to attend a burial ceremony prior to the ritual at the Clan's settlement.

Geez had removed The Bird's protective clothing and laid him on the bear pelt on the travois.

Then the Holy Man said with strong conviction, "My friends of the forest, join me as we commit our brother's body to Manitou's care." The celebrants all stood and encircled the fire, holding hands as instructed.

While standing by The Birds body, the Holy Man looked to the late afternoon sun. He offered a silent prayer to Manitou as he cast tobacco to honor the spirit of Kicking Bird's life.

He asked for silence.

He then directed each of the celebrants to think of a good experience they had with their friend, The Bird.

As the group reflected on their individual thoughts, a raven croaked, flew into the clearing, and perched on one of the twin pines.

Wind in Hair prayed:

> Creator—Manitou
> our Protector,
> Hear my thanks and my plea.
> Bless Kicking Bird for his courage;
> Provide for his future and give him strength.
> We praise your role in our lives.
> Let the spirit of the raven watch over us, too.

*   *   *

The scene was elegant with the friends and family encircling the Holy Man, the fire flashing on and off his words, and Kicking Bird's pony standing rock-solid with its former rider resting on a beautiful black bear's pelt.

Leigh thought, *This is a poignant experience for everyone to see. Despite the sad reason, at least my family and friends had a chance to witness a part of Indian customs and traditions.*

Without another word, Wind in Hair motioned for Leigh to help in wrapping The Bird's body in a Chilkit blanket, tying it to the travois, and leading his pony from the circle. As he left, he bowed to the celebrants and to Leigh, his hostess. He led the pony across the clearing and into the big timber of the Park.

Several deer followed them as they disappeared in the shadows.

There were no dry eyes in the group as they sat down and quietly reflected on their day of conquest . . . and sorrow.

Chapter 17

Geez had to make the decision soon. The Sitka crowd wanted to stay overnight and party, which was okay, but he had to be in Juneau by noon tomorrow. Of course, the boys and Lynn were the gang behind the request to stay; it was up to him.

Geez approached the boisterous celebrants by the fire. "Okay. Here's the deal. If Leigh and Bear agree, we can stay overnight, but I need to be in Juneau tomorrow by 1300 hours. That will mean leaving here at about 0600. I have to drop off the Delta Station crew and Lynn and gas up. If you're early risers, it will work. I'm getting used to getting up early."

The boys and Lynn seemed to respond in unison, "No problem, man!"

Lynn added, "We'll be at the chopper at 0600—bright-eyed and bushy-tailed. I'll make sure the Wolvies are up."

While looking at Josie, Geez replied, "Good, if Josie agrees, we've got a deal."

The Sitka crew looked at her with their 'longing' eyes saying P-L-E-A-S-E. "As I've already said, it's okay with me. I love visiting with Leigh and Bear at the ranch."

"Deal," Geez said. "Now let's help our host and hostess prepare for this over-nighter."

*   *   *

The crew helped deploy a parachute between trees for cover, cut cedar boughs for natural mattresses, and brought blankets out to the area from the yurt.

Then, much to her surprise, Leigh was approached by Milt and Dave with a request to stay overnight, with their gals, too. She answered, "Gladly, join the gang."

Thinking the overnight crew was set, she was further startled when the laconic tanker pilots asked if they could stay, too.

As earlier, Leigh had one answer, "Gladly, the more the merrier."

With this last request, Leigh's blanket supply was stretched to its limits. She stood by the window of the yurt and relaxed for a moment. She looked across the clearing to the opposite side and was surprised to see yet one more visitor. Unbeknownst to the celebrants, a beautiful wapiti stood majestically while looking over his domain. The elk was an infrequent visitor, but must have been attracted by the commotion of the partygoers. A beautiful six by six, he soon turned and slowly walked into the big timber. In doing so, he displayed the large white rump which led to the Indians calling it wapiti: white rump.

Leigh was probably right in guessing why the elk came to the clearing. He was probably amazed at all the activity. There were frisbies flying, wolves wrestling and chasing, horsebackers riding, helicopters sparkling, and lots of people busily setting up camp.

She thought, *It's true what my mom always said: folks gather in large numbers for weddings and in this case, a wake.*

*   *   *

Bear walked up behind her and held her around the waist. He kissed her on the neck and said, "What's up, hon? Are you reviewing your kin?"

"Would you believe everyone stayed? Everyone. There's nineteen of us, Bear. I'm not sure I have enough blankets, food, towels, and booze for this size of a crowd. What if we run out?"

"My dear, Leigh, we've everything we need, and if we're short a few minor items, trust me, no one will care. They'll make do, they always seem to. Remember, they're here for each other . . . and you. Do you understand? Your ranch has become a meeting place for kindred souls. Need I remind you of why Wind Spirit and Raven Maiden came here? Big Wind? Joe Bloom? Dave and Milt? Everyone I've mentioned loves you. That's what really happened here today. Your friends came to you because they feel comfortable here."

"Bear . . . you're here, too."

"Yes, my dear, but I'm only a small part of the attraction of your ranch."

"Thank you, but I disagree; you're the backbone around here."

"Maybe, but you're the heart. Do you have any idea of what happened here today? You know, you're not even aware how you've been honored."

"What?"

"Who visited us today and stayed longer than expected?"

"Why, the Holy Man, Wind in Hair. He's such a lovely man."

"Have you ever heard of him leaving the tribal area, much less visiting Washichu, the white man's camp? No, you have not. He could have sent someone else to retrieve Kicking Bird's body. Have you any idea why he did not? No, you are totally unaware that you are one of the few respected women in the area."

"Well, if you say so. But remember, he mixed with all our friends whether student, pilot, wrangler, entrepreneur, or PhD. He enjoyed them all."

"True, but is that all he did?"

"Yes, I guess so . . . why?"

"Not true. What else did he do?"

"Yes, you're right, he did honor our guests with a celebration of Kicking Bird's passing. The celebration was quick, simple, and direct for the fallen warrior.

You're right. I never expected him to do that. I was impressed. I have never been part of an Indian burial ceremony."

"Leigh, that's my point. He felt at ease with you and our friends, comfortable enough to share—to share a short prayer with us in honor of his brother."

"Bear, you and Geez helped. Half of the people here were with the DNR, they're *our* friends."

"Yes, true. But they all felt totally relaxed coming here from miles away, at some expense. Look out there, how many wanted to stay overnight and enjoy the fellowship found at your ranch? How many? *All of them.* True, Josie helps; her feminine touch complements yours."

"Every one of those people out there love you, as I do."

"You so and so, thank you. If you keep this up the tears in my eyes will drop."

By the time she turned around, they had; the tears spread to his cheeks as they shared each other's lips.

She pulled away and said, "You're quite a man with words. I suppose that's one of the reasons I love you, and will show that to you tonight . . . if we can find a moment and a spot to be alone among the other seventeen.

* * *

"Uhmmmph, excuse me, you two love birds. May I have a word with you?" Geez asked as he entered the yurt.

"Oh, hi, Bill. Bear, from the look in his eyes, he has business on his mind. Had he mentioned an assignment possibility to you?"

"Yep, but he wanted to talk to us when together."

"Oh, good, what's up, Bill?"

"Excuse me," Geez said as he went back to the door and yelled, "Come on in; they've got their clothes back on."

Bear said, "Bill, give it up, you're not good at telling jokes."

"Okay, okay . . . I try."

Rob entered the hut with Ann and said, "That's quite a gang you've got out there, Leigh. I think we've got just about everything in order for the gang to have a good night's sleep, eat a quick breakfast, and be airborne in the morning. Let me know if there's anything else we can do."

"Thanks, I think we're all set now. The tougher task will be for Josie to corral the boys and Lynn and get them to bed before daybreak. I swear they never look at a clock."

"True," Geez added. "Now that I've got you all together, here's what I need."

"Uh oh," Ann said. "I can tell when he's in a bind of some sort and needs us to bail him out."

They all smiled a little—except Geez. He looked at Ann and said, "Precisely, and you can be the chief wrangler. You've done it before, and did a good job."

Rob looked at Ann, then at Bear and Leigh, and said, "I've a feeling we'll be hitting some leather soon. What's up, Bill?"

"Here's the deal. DEA agents have asked for our help in breaking up a drug ring that is operating north of Haines in Canada and crossing our border through the park to make deliveries.

"They're capitalizing on the remoteness of the park's glaciers and rocky out-crops to mask their movements by using pack animals on game trails and old two-tracks from lumbering and mining days. Yep, as in the Old West, on the ground with horses and mules. Apparently, the air and water routes have been thwarted. The Mounties have been very effective in halting these routes.

"Our task, if we choose, would be to act like trail riders/explorers on similar routes in the park and report any unusual activity by radio to the DEA after they cross the border. After you clear the area, they would move to apprehend the pack train.

"You might be wondering, why us? It has become very apparent that Ann and Rob have been crisscrossing this area with tourists and hunters for some time now. As such, your presence would not be noted as something unusual. Mark my words, if the Mounties know you've been in this area awhile, the crooks do, too. So, you would not be suspect. From what I hear, you've also taken several Cana-dian clients on hunts. Don't ask me how they know."

"Sonabitch," Ann barked. "Nosey cops."

"Now, Ann," Rob said in a consoling voice.

"I just do not like 'big brother' looking over my shoulder whenever they feel like it, and spying on my private business. Bastards.

"I don't like the smell of this plan. What say you, Rob?"

"I agree, Ann. But, remember, the real bastards are the crooks who start our youth on illegal drugs. There are a lot of easy targets. Many youngsters are alone, confused, and living lives of crime that are easy prey for the pushers. That activity must be stopped. Many of our youth face this perilous decision to find the strength to refuse this demonic and destructive track to destroy their life. Yep, I've seen the 'tracks' on their arms. I'd like to help that effort."

Ann replied, "You're right. It's just that when you work with the feds, they seem to cut corners on our individual rights. Then again, Big Wind tells me drugs are readily available on campus at the University of Alaska. I'd like to be part of an effort to reduce the availability of drugs there."

"Yes, Ann, the officers make mistakes. Don't we all? Their job is tough. The stress is unbearable at times. The western district has lost two officers this year. They don't wear bulletproof vests and carry Glocks as a fashion statement. Okay, to the point, will you help them?"

Ann looked at Rob with a blankness Geez had never seen before. Her stare was full of doubt, an expression of concern, but hard to read. She looked down. Then she looked out the window at her friends. Then she looked at Rob, and said, "If Rob agrees, we'll do it, but be aware, if the drug boys are on to us, we're gone. By the way, how are Leigh and Bear involved?"

Geez quickly added, "They're going to be your clients."

"Oh, that makes sense," Ann said.

"Plus I felt better knowing there are four of you, and Bear's also familiar with that section of the park. Get this, I also said they look like a wealthy couple."

"Please," Leigh groaned.

"Are you and Bear coming along?"

"Wouldn't miss it," Leigh said. "How 'bout you, hon?"

"Let's do it; I kinda think it's part of my civic duty."

"Good," Geez said with a smile. "We'll rendezvous at your ranch in Skagway at 1300 hours tomorrow. At that time I'll have a check for five-thousand dollars for the planned four-day trail ride through the Fairweather Mountains. Leigh and Bear will pose as wealthy business owners from Anchorage. The check will be drawn from a shell corporation.

"If it's not a problem, you'll leave on the trail ride tomorrow afternoon. That will give you a chance to be on the trail the next day.

"When I say we, I really mean my assistant, Carol. She's experienced and sharp as a tack. You'll like her. When she's finished with you, she'll be flying to Whitehorse. Keeping me at distance is important. The drug boys may know of me from previous encounters. They do not know Carol. Who knows where informants lurk? I don't want to take any chances.

"Now, today is Tuesday, right? The feds think a shipment is coming to Canada by pack train, through the area you'll be riding, on Thursday. With a little luck you may see them. I know it's a long shot, but let's give it a go.

"You'll have one AM/FM radio with a scrambler to contact agents in Whitehorse and DNR Station A in Yakutat. This will be the only aspect of your role that would reveal your true identity. Under no circumstances let this radio out of your possession.

"Ann, you've wrangled dozens of trips through this area, so take what you would generally need for four days on the trail. You're all being paid very well, so don't skimp. Arm yourselves as you normally would, but be sure that all four of you carry 8x20 binoculars, for obvious reasons.

"Now, if you accidentally meet the traffickers on the trail, do not engage them in any unusual way. Hello and goodbye is fine. If this does happen, wait awhile before you report their locations. A Garmin GPS will be provided for this report.

"Although Carol will cover this, for the record Leigh and Bear are Mr. and

Mrs. Prestel from Prestel Tool and Die in Anchorage. Ann, you and Rob are well-known in livery circles, so you'll play yourselves."

Rob complained, "That's gonna be tough. He's some guy."

Ann sighed. "Oh brother, you're something else."

"That's enough for now. We thank you for your support. Now let's go join our friends."

*   *   *

As they left the cabin, Ann whispered to Rob, "This sounds like a simple civic duty, but it could be our bête noire."

The gang finally settled in for the night, and as expected, Josie had to threaten the boys to get them away from Lynn, into bed, and calm thereafter. Although the boys looked to Lynn as the sister they never had, Josie made certain that Lynn slept next to her under the gleaming white parachute.

By two o'clock, Leigh and Bear, followed by Windy and Raven, headed for their beds in the cabin. Before entering, Leigh paused. "Bear, where are the wolves? They're normally here by the steps."

Bear replied with a smile, "My dear, you've been replaced—they're lying on, over, and between the boys beneath the parachute. I'm not sure between the two- and four-legged animals who is most bushed, the boys or the wolves."

"Did you check on the horses?" said Leigh.

"No, Windy did. Settle down, my dear. I know it's a little unusual to have fifteen guests sleeping on the edge of the clearing and four helicopters sitting like huge insects. But, my dear, relax. As I said earlier, your ranch is a comfortable way-point in life for many kindred souls."

"But shouldn't we add some more logs to the fire?"

Before she could say anything more, Bear picked her up, carried her into bed, and whispered, "I'll make one more round of the clearing for you, and now, do me a favor and get to sleep; I'll take a rain check on the romance you had planned for tonight. Maybe I'll collect tomorrow night . . . on the trail under the stars. Get some sleep, dear. Wake up time is in five hours. G'night."

Just as he was leaving her side, Leigh said, "I talked to Windy and Raven; they'll watch things here while we're on our trail ride. I told them that Geez wanted us to have some get-away time, and they'd be next to go."

"Fine, good night—or is there some other little comment?"

"No, you bugger, good night. Love you."

"Well, that's good to hear. Good night."

"Don't you love me?"

"Ugh, so I forgot to say it tonight. I love your butt, your bust, and your lust. Good night."

"Okay, that's more like it. I love your tight little ass, too."

"You'd better stop that kind of talk, or slide over there."

Silence.

*   *   *

At a small out-of-the-way town south of Whitehorse, Canada, the livery was busy on Thursday morning.

"These goddam mules are as stubborn as my first wife," Tom, the local wrangler, yelled as he threw a pack frame on a blanket over the mule's back, "plus this sonabitch thinks she knows everything, but knows not a damn thing worth a dime. Get your butt over, bitch."

Tom was chubby, with a face that resembled a worn catcher's mitt. He wore a heavy Mackinaw over a shoulder holster that held a Glock. He was no average wrangler who took tourists into the park to camp or hunt.

As one of the lesser wranglers of Double R (RR) livery, Tom had been hired to take several heavy packages across the border to a small town north of Haines, Alaska, USA. He had successfully delivered one load without detection two weeks ago so he had been hired again, feeling very confident that he could pull off the charade again. His cover was simple. They were on a hunting trip and, if apprehended, he'd say that they had accidentally wandered into the USA.

He would not be alone; a rogue Indian from the Haida Tribe would be joining him soon. The Indian knew the secondary routes better, and how to avoid other trail riders who were also exploring the beautiful park and forest.

"Get over, Liz. We've got to be loaded and at the rendezvous point in one hour," Tom said to his lead mule as he lashed the water-proofed load to her back.

After removing the grain pouches and letting them drink their limit at the water trough, he led the pair of mules to where his black gelding was waiting.

"Hi, old fella. Are you ready for a little trip? Here comes old Maggie and Liz to keep us company. Come on, you dumbyucks. Step lively or I'll use that two by four on you again."

Tom tied Maggie to the simple harness of Liz with a six-foot lead rope, then walked the animals to a little copse near the big timber.

The trail ahead of them was not marked since it had been abandoned by a now-bankrupt mining company who used it years ago. The trail was perfect for their purposes since not only was it seldom used, but many did not know of its existence. The only drawbacks were that it terminated at the border, and there was some rough going for several miles into the U.S., until it linked up with established trail rides through the park.

"Where the hell is Yellow Bird, my half-breed Indian nit-wit? Two bits he was drunk last night and will be late—again. I wish the boss in Whitehorse would give me a little better guide with a gun. The sonabitch is barely bilingual; half the time I'm not sure he understands what I say—unless I shout.

"Okay, girls, take a break. I'm going to catch some shut-eye while waiting for that dumb-ass Indian."

He held the lead rope of his horse and mules, checked to see if his gun was holstered, lay down on his butt, then leaned against the tree and, within seconds, was snoring.

Ten minutes later, he felt a kick in the ribs. He looked up, went for his gun, and stopped. It was Yellow Bird.

In mixed English and native tongue, Bird said, "We go now, Tom Tom."

"You sonabitch. If you kick me again like that, I'll blow your head off with this Glock, you half-assed, half-breed, dumb-ass."

Yellow Bird responded casually. "Glad you in good spirits. You sound like old bull of the woods. You in good shape, no? You ready to ride, no?"

"Yes, I'm ready, you dumb bastard."

Yellow Bird was dressed in dirty buckskin, topped off with a black fedora with several feathers of some unknown origin. His face was long and narrow with high cheek bones characteristic of Indians. His eyes were narrow slits framing an equine nose. The most interesting part of his dress was a large Bowie knife in a scabbard across his front as if protecting his crotch. More than six feet tall, he towered over Tom. In fact, his long braided black hair made him look even taller.

The Indian wasted no time in remounting his pinto Chico, grabbing the lead rope to the mules and heading to the primitive trail ahead.

Tom, still cussing, mounted the black gelding and followed.

The trail riders disappeared into the timber with their two bundles of drugs with a street value of more than one-million dollars.

*   *   *

Thirty miles to the south, just over the Canadian border, Ann and Rob were busy cooking breakfast after an enchanting night under the stars. Their clients, the Prestels, were enjoying themselves in the crisp morning air.

*   *   *

Fifty miles to the north, in Whitehorse, Canadian DEA agents were monitoring channel seven, as were U.S. agents, one-hundred miles to the southwest at DNR station Alpha, at Yakutat. They were all on a 24/7 schedule.

Chapter 18

"Bacon and eggs, raisin toast, and hot coffee—who could ask for a better breakfast?" Leigh said.

Bear added, "I think I'll have another cup, a cup with a little Jim Beam added. What say you, Leigh?"

"Heavens no. I've yet to share your cast-iron stomach. Make mine straight."

"It sounded like Ann straightened Rob out last night. I heard you love birds 'tweeting' at each other and the full moon. It must be true. The full moon brings out the best in us. I know Rob mooned Ann last night as they returned bare-assed from the stream."

"Aren't you the observant one? I thought you guys were long gone."

Bear chuckled. "We were, until we heard the splashing in the stream. Or maybe that was a spawning salmon . . . in either case: sexual."

Ann groaned, "Are you finished? You know, I could tell some stories about you two, like, ah, running naked through the clearing at the ranch. Should I continue?"

"I'd suggest you two call a truce before all our indiscretions are revealed," Leigh countered.

Rob finally spoke. "True."

It was Thursday morning. They had been on the trail since Tuesday evening. This was their second night camping out. They had seen no pack trains heading south across the area on Wednesday, but had come across a few student hikers from the University of Alaska—Juneau.

The hikers were on their semester break with plans to climb one of the higher peaks in the Takhinsha Mountains. They were invited to join them for lunch on Wednesday. The youthful animation added more flavor to their roast-beef sandwiches, raisins, grapes, and selected cheese wedges. Dessert was assorted fruit.

As students with limited income, Ron and Wendy set aside their peanut-butter-and-jelly biscuits and warm Coke as they enjoyed Ann's gourmand tastes served on a gingham table cloth. Ron whispered, "Wen, this is just too much."

Ann asked, "What? Did you wish for seconds?"

"No," Wendy answered. "He said this is wonderful and, yes, speaking for him he'll have seconds; but his mom—from the old school—has told him to never ask. It's impolite. I'm not of that school. He'd love seconds; he's always had a hollow leg. I rarely fill it."

After a few background questions dealing with why they were on the trail, wouldn't you know it, they knew of Big Wind. "We didn't know him well, but some of my friends were in the 101 Creative Writing class taught by a Gary . . . something. He was a stickler for grammar and POV."

"POV?" Leigh asked.

"Point of View. They say he was meticulous. The writer, he said, must get only into the head of his subject and tell what he or she is perceiving—not the author or other characters unless it's their turn to command the POV. Makes sense, doesn't it?"

"Yep. He's probably the one. My son was so grateful for him spending time with him and his writing needs."

"How's your son doing?" Ron asked.

"Fine. He's working in Juneau for the paper *The Juneau News*. He's on the police beat right now—you know, chasing sirens and the like."

"And the drug trade, no doubt," Ron said.

Ah ha, Leigh thought to herself, *he keyed on drug trade.*

Putting on her 'spy-hat' in an overzealous move, she cut short her conversation, thinking that this couple may be linked to the drug traffic from Canada, and just might be the advance party for the pack-train druggies headed their way.

"Well," Leigh stated rather abruptly, "have a good trip. We're going to load up and try for the foothills of those mountains over there ourselves."

Bear looked at her in a puzzled way and said, "Nice meeting you. Have a nice trip. If we bump into you again, join us."

Ann alertly spoke up, "Say, if you don't mind, let's snap a photo. Here, I'll set the camera on this rock. Come now, bunch together. I'll set the timer and join you."

They sat together on a large rock. Ann set the timer, jumped into the picture striking a goofy pose and an even goofier face.

Click-wink, light-flash, and the six Tongass Trekkers were on file to share with Big Wind.

As the pair got ready to leave, Rob gave Ron some fruit and a small bottle of Schnapps, saying, "It might be chilly up in the mountains; this will keep you warm if that cute little gal doesn't."

Wendy quickly responded, "He doesn't have to worry 'bout that."

Rob yelled, "Three cheers for the modern woman!"

Ann added, "I'm a modern woman, and I'm there for you at your beck and call."

Leigh added, "My, aren't we the romantic this morn?"

"No, last night," Ann said.

Ron giggled, and said, "You guys have been great. Give my best to Big Wind. See you. Bye."

When the couple was out of sight, Leigh spoke to Ann. "The photo was an excellent idea."

Ann looked at Rob, they both looked at Bear, and the three then looked at Leigh.

"What?" Ann said.

Bear giggled. "Leigh, that pair is not involved with any drug cartel. They're students on break, and probably in love with each other and the mountains. Now I understand why you abruptly cut off our conversations with them. Leigh, you're not a very good detective. I'll bet you will see several couples like that in this area, hiking and climbing on Mother Nature's breast."

Leigh paused. "Rob, Ann, what do you think?"

"Do you want the unvarnished truth?" Rob said.

"Why . . . of course."

"I think you've recalled too many Nancy Drew mysteries from your youth. That couple was the most innocent pair I could imagine. Didn't you note their expensive hiking boots, contrasted with their worn-out clothes? Probably from Goodwill Industries. Their ropes, and a dozen carabiners and pitons hooked on their belt validated their story to me. They're on their way to climb one of the peaks of Mount Takhinsha. Trust me, dear."

Silence.

"I feel like a fool. Did I mistreat them?"

Ann chimed in. "No, but it was obvious that you cut them off when they started talking about school, your son, and drugs."

"Damn, I hope we meet them again so I can apologize; I feel terrible."

"Leigh, it wasn't that bad. We just met them. Don't let it bother you."

Rob jumped into the conversation with a smile. "Well, I'm glad Leigh was so careful. I feared for my life. I may not even be here but for her vivid viva voce protectionism. I'm just glad to be alive. Ron could have been Brutus. I, Caesar . . ."

At that, Leigh picked up two large pine cones and threw one at Rob. He ducked, but the second one caught him on the noggin and knocked his hat off.

"Okay! Okay. I'll modify my comment. You didn't arrest them—yet." More pine cones flew.

Ann interceded. "Rob, stop. You know, she could be right."

"Yeah, and the pope smokes dope. Okay, I'll be good. Leigh, I'll be a good boy."

"Bear, make him stop."

"I'm rather enjoying it, my dear. Okay, come over here; you need a hug from Daddy."

After a hug, Leigh was finally able to laugh at herself as they packed up and continued the trek to the northeast along the foothills of the Takhinshas.

As he started to mount his horse to leave, she got in one more lick. Just as he was to put his foot in the stirrup, she gently slapped the flank of his horse. The results were satisfying as Rob plunged to the ground when the horse sidestepped.

Rob looked up. "Are you done now? Truce?"

"Truce," she said with a smile.

Ann hollered, "Bear, would you tell those children to stop?"

"I might as well save my breath, Ann, but I think it's over."

The four riders—two guides and two wealthy clients—and a lone pack horse headed out to explore the area and spot the druggies headed their way from Canada, druggies whose identities were unknown, their pack-train size unknown, the number of men and guns unknown, their route unknown. It was known that the men were desperate, dangerous, and heavily armed.

*   *   *

The two mules were led by Yellow Bird, with Tom following as the train crossed the border from Canada into the U.S. Riding through the tall timber all morning, they seemed to have slipped by the random flights of the spotter planes of the Canadian Border Patrol.

The next fifty miles would be in the open, but from the air they looked like any other hunting party in the foothills of the Takhinsha range.

They had changed horses from the earlier trip, and were using mules now instead of horses for pack animals. The only possible problem was the size of the two packs on the mules. A sharp border patrol officer or Mountie might surmise that there was far too much gear on the mules for a two-man hunting party. Tom's boss in Whitehorse also insisted that Yellow Bird dress at least in partial native clothes so officers or agents may be deterred from bothering the local natives. The Indians had a hard enough time making ends meet in the forest habitat.

"We stop here. Check horses' hooves. Take glasses when you dismount," Bird insisted.

"Why? None of the mules or horses are limping or lame."

"Dismount. Take glasses with you."

"You dumb bunny, okay."

After dismounting and checking the hooves of his pinto, Bird told Tom to check the ridge to the east.

"Why?"

"Do as I say."

*   *   *

Tom lay the glasses on the saddle horn, scanned the ridge, and focused on movement close to the skyline.

He spotted two people, a man and a woman. They were going through their rucksacks, pulling out various items. While continuing to look through the glasses, Tom talked to Yellow Bird. "Bird, it looks like a young couple getting ready to climb. They've got a lot of rope and . . . wait, a gun . . . oh, no, a small hammer, no problem. Now they're both putting on gloves. I thought we had a problem there for a moment. There's nothing there; let's get."

"Yes. Get back in saddle. We have forty miles to go before dark."

As they rode along in the open country, they'd periodically ride through a small copse and rest as well as hide. If anyone were searching for unusual activities, they'd at least be covered while eating and sucking a beer.

"Let's go!" Yellow Bird yelled.

"Shut uppp . . . wee bee gooen . . . in . . . minute," said Tom with a slur in his speech. He slipped and slid on the ground trying to mount the black gelding.

Finally the train left the copse with more noise than stealth as Tom sang some of his old favorites. "Don't bury me on the lone prairie . . . don't let my bones dry in the sun . . ."

Yellow Bird looked back at him with disgust as he weaved left and right on the trail behind the mules.

He yelled at Tom, "Shape up, you dumb drunk. We go many miles still."

*   *   *

Yellow Bird was getting impatient with Tom's singing and belligerence. They entered another swale along the trail to water the stock.

As The Bird led the mules back to the trail, he discovered Tom lying in the marsh grass by his horse. Spread-eagle and drunker than a skunk, he was singing, "Oh, my darling; oh, my darling . . . oh, my . . . darling . . . Clemmmeonnttine; we . . ."

"Shut up, Tom."

"She . . . gone . . . lost . . . ever . . . darling . . ."

Smack!

Blood spattered as Tom slumped over unconscious and bleeding from the temple.

"Uuuuggghhh."

Silence.

"You sing no more, dumb ugly. No sing. No call me dumb. No more."

As he lashed Tom's limp body over the saddle and tied his feet to one stirrup and his neck to the other, Tom was still breathing. He stepped back. "This not good. Tom look dead."

He took his rain slicker from the back of his saddle and covered Tom's body.

"Look good. Not perfect, but good. Got to go."

He had to keep moving no matter how bad the ride would be for Tom. He'd make it to the rendezvous point. He was certainly too drunk to ride. His breathing was irregular, but he thought all drunks had that problem.

They moved out of the copse looking pretty bad—one wrangler in the lead, two mules, and a saddle horse with something lying over the saddle covered by a rain slicker. It did not look right, but The Bird had to keep moving, and he only had ten miles to go.

He thought, *It's two o'clock. If we keep moving, we'll be there by eight. Gotta be there or the boss will give me hell. Gotta get to Haines before dark.*

"I wish Tom was still riding with me; he always had my back. Come on mules, I know it's tougher now dragging the black with Tom. I know, it's like dragging an anchor. Old black will soon get the idea. Gotta keep moving."

*   *   *

Ann and Rob led their clients into a swampy section of the trail for water. Just as they entered under the beautiful cedars casting a welcome shadow for their cooling shade, a herd of wapiti dashed ahead, stopped, looked, and continued to flee.

"Look, Bear," Leigh said, "a herd of elk just ran out. They're beautiful. Look, they've stopped again. Strange, they're now looking to the north, away from us. I wonder what they see? Look, Bear, it's kinda strange.

"Yeah. It's as though something is coming from the other direction. Look, they're not bolting to the west. Yep, that's strange. Maybe they're running from a predator of some sort."

Leigh added, "I'm going to take a look. I also would like to get a picture of those interesting white rumps."

"Take a photo of yours while you're at it. You've got a white rump, too. Dear, you're my wapiti."

"Stop, you horny old cowboy. I'll be back in a second."

*   *   *

"God damn elk, that's all I need. Damn, they're gonna draw attention," Yellow Bird swore. "This train is lookin' bad. The black looks like it is carrying a body wrapped in a slicker. That ain't foolin' no one. Damn. I go into this copse and see if Tom sober enough to ride."

Standing ramrod straight on the trail, the elk suddenly bolted away and disappeared over a hillock.

"It's about time I get out of way. Come on, pinto, let's get to that cover. Wait a minute, what's that? Christ! That's all I need."

Roaring above the horizon to the east, heard above the thundering hooves of the pack train below, was a bright yellow plane. As it got closer, it was clearly identified as one of the U.S. Border Patrol's spotter planes.

"Sonabitch. That damn herd caught the attention of the plane. Christ! Don't want to be caught in the open like this. Better head for the thicket. Git up, Nellie, Liz, let's get a move on. Come on, get your asses in gear."

As the plane banked and turned toward the elk herd, Yellow Bird dashed to the thicket, hoping not to be seen.

*   *   *

"What?" Leigh yelled, "What's this? It looks like a rider leading a couple mules an is headed this way, and he's in a hurry. Hold up, girl," she said to her horse. "Let's get back."

At the same time she reined in her horse to return to the copse, the galloping rider and pack train closed to within one-hundred yards; the plane also passed over them at one-hundred feet.

She looked up while riding at a gallop and saw the markings on the plane. "I've a feeling we're not going to need the radio to report the sighting of an unusual pack train. Trouble is, he's headed for the same place as I. Damn, this is going to be a problem. I'm riding toward friends and he's running away from the spotter plane. That's gonna cause problems."

*   *   *

Bear was waiting nervously for Leigh at the entrance, and he didn't like the scene that was developing to his front.

"Bear! Bear," Ann yelled, "do you hear me?"

"Yep."

"When Leigh arrives, bring her back here quickly."

"Will do. What's up?"

She told him the pack train was about ten miles north of Haines. "The patrol gave me the GPS lat/long and asked for ours. Bear, that's exactly where we are! Bear, that could be the drug train headed this way—right behind Leigh."

"Damn!" Bear replied. "I'll take care of things here. Thanks. I hear the plane now; it's circling the thicket."

The last transmission to Ann from Whitehorse was to urge her to leave the area.

Ann acknowledged the message and said they'd try to comply as soon as everyone got together. As Ann looked up the trail, she knew that would be difficult; the rider and train were about to enter the thicket.

Bear met Leigh at the edge of the tree line and gave her a quick briefing as they rode toward Ann and Rob, who were mounted and anxious to leave.

"Okay," Ann said. "Let's stay together and ride out as though nothing has happened."

As they turned to leave in trail order of Ann, Rob, Leigh, and Bear, the rider burst into the shelter of the trees and reined in his froth-covered gelding foaming at the mouth.

By plan, none of the riders turned around in their saddle to acknowledge the rider. So as not to cause too much alarm, they all urged their horses to a trot first, then a canter, and finally a gallop.

*   *   *

The rider yelled, "Hold on, folks. What's the hurry? Come back here. I'd like to meet you."

Being at the end of the line, Bear reined in his horse and turned around in the saddle to acknowledge the rider's wishes. He quickly spoke in a low voice to Rob. "Keep going. I'll handle it."

Much to his surprise, he faced an Indian with a desperate look on his face and a gun in his hand.

At thirty feet in the confined narrowness of the trail there was very little room for maneuver.

The Indian did not move, nor did he say a word. Then he looked past Bear to the riders riding away.

Tension filled the silent air as Bear stared at the Indian's gun barrel. The Indian finally spoke. "Tell your friends to come back. We need to talk."

Bear hesitated, delayed his response, hoping they could escape.

"Do it now," the Indian said as he pointed his automatic at Bear's chest. Reluctant to be a patsy for the deranged Indian, Bear did nothing. He stalled, then moved his horse toward the Indian.

Ka-Pow!

Bear took a slug in his side, then fell from his horse. It took off. "Uugghh . . .o-o-o," Bear groaned while lying on the trail.

Leigh screamed. Her horse reared and threw her off. She hit her head on the hard ground, and the horse bolted down the trail. She did not move . . . she was unconscious.

Rob's horse reared and ran with him hanging on while trying to stop.

Ann's horse jumped, kicked, and ran out of the thicket as she tried to rein in her frightened steed.

The Indian aimed above the riders and shot.

Ka-Pow.

The second shot echoed through the trees as his horse, too, capered.

"Settle down, you broken-down pinto. I could have them with you dancing. I just wanted to scare them into coming back. Damn, that didn't work."

In pain, Bear yelled, "Hold on, you fool. Whoever you are, I suggest you put down that gun."

"I'm in charge here. You're lucky slug only hit you in the side. Get up and see if that broad is okay. Be quick about it."

While holding his side to stop the bleeding, he stumbled over to Leigh. He slapped her face gently and whispered in her ear.

She sat up, and in a startled voice said, "Bear, are you okay? You were shot."

"It's nothing. How are you?"

"Fine. Just a little bruised and sore. Let me see that wound."

The bullet had passed through his 'love handle' on the left side. She put her handkerchief on the wound's entrance and held it in place with his belt.

"That's enough," the Indian yelled. "I'm very busy. Sit there, both of you. I have things to do. Do not move."

Bear and Leigh sat by the trail with Bear's horse. They looked down the trail's opening for signs of Rob and Ann. They were nowhere in sight.

The nervous Indian still had his gun in his hand as he ran back to check the entrance to the thicket. He scanned the horizon for the airplane he had seen earlier, but saw nothing.

"Good. I must have fooled them into thinkin' I was just hurryin' into the thicket to water the stock. Ha! I won again. Now, I've got to get goin'. I'll just tie up this couple and git. I'm only a few miles from the drop point near Haines. Ha! I got away."

He ran back to handle the problem of the couple nursing each other's wounds. Just about the time he reached Bear and Leigh, the familiar sound of a chopper filled the air. *Wop-Wop-Wop.*

"Christ! What the hell? I thought I'd slipped the bastards," Yellow Bird cried.

Apparently the spotter plane had called in a chopper.

The Indian quickly untied the pinto from the mule's lead rope. Then he ran over to Leigh, told her to stand up, tied her hands together. "Now, get up on the pinto. Do it quick. You're goin' with me. I need a hostage to get out of here."

Before Leigh moved to the horse, Bear leaped up despite the pain and attacked the Indian with a right hook to the temple.

Quicker than lightning, the Indian pistol-whipped Bear on the cheek, and he went down like a rock, holding his bloody face.

The Indian shot at the ground in front of him as a warning, saying, "Don't try anything again, or I'll shoot you."

As the chopper landed near the entrance to the thicket, the Indian grabbed Leigh, threw her on his horse, climbed up himself, and spurred on the pinto as he galloped down the trail toward the exit.

At the same time, two DEA agents entered the thicket from the opposite direction. Armed with automatic weapons and bullet-proof vests, they looked very lethal to anyone in their way.

*   *   *

Encumbered by Leigh, the Indian did not move as fast as he had hoped, but urged his pinto with his spurs as he galloped toward the exit.

Bear yelled at the agents coming his way. "Don't shoot! He has my wife as a hostage—don't shoot."

The agents acknowledged his cry as they moved past him in pursuit on foot. One of the agents paused when he saw all the blood on his face and side. "Do you need help?"

Bear cried, "No, go! I'm okay. Go! That Indian's desperate!"

*   *   *

"Here he comes; stay down," Rob whispered to Ann.

Rob and Ann had ridden out the exit, then came back when they heard a shot and ducked to the side of the trail by the exit. They saw the Indian tie Leigh's hands together and force her onto his horse.

Having no weapon, Rob fashioned a lariat from a rope tied to his saddle and waited at the edge of the trail.

Hoofbeats echoed from the copse.

"Here they come," he said. "Get ready to jump him whether or not I get the rope around his body."

"No problem. My karate lessons are about to be tested."

"For Christ's sake, be careful. Don't get too involved. Just neutralize him with a chop to the temple. He's armed and has an itchy trigger finger. It's hard telling what that second shot was about."

"I hope it didn't involve Bear. Then again, it could have been one of the agents."

"Stay down. Here they come."

Wop-Wop-Wop.

Another chopper approached from the exit side of the copse, the side where Rob and Ann were waiting.

"Christ!" Rob said. "Another one. Sonabitch. That could scare away our man . . ."

"No. Look. There they are."

The Indian had stopped momentarily after he saw the chopper. But, just before he made his next move, Rob stood and threw the lariat.

"What the hell!" the Indian yelled as he struggled against the tightening rope. It had encircled both him and Leigh. Rob pulled both off the saddle onto the ground.

Ann immediately jumped on the Indian, disarmed him with a chop to the wrist, and followed it with a chop to his temple. He collapsed like a sack of flour.

One of the agents joined her and helped as they removed the rope from Leigh's waist. The agent took the dazed Indian away in cuffs.

An agent appeared from the thicket and said, "Ma'am, you need to be with Bear. We'll take care of things here. I left an agent with him; he'll be okay."

"I'll go with you, Leigh," Ann said as both ran back into the thicket. Bear's wounds were being cleaned and field-dressed by an agent, and he turned Bear over to Leigh. She gave him a big hug for his work, got Bear up, and helped him walk to the chopper. He would not be riding home on a horse.

Tragically, the second pair of agents had found another man's lifeless body on the black horse, hidden under a yellow slicker. It was unknown, at that time, whether the extreme discomfort of the ride, alcohol, or both had taken his life. He smelled like a distillery.

The first team of agents loaded Bear in their chopper for evacuation. Leigh insisted on going with him.

The second team took the other man's stiff body, the Indian, and the load of drugs in their chopper.

Before the agents departed, they took a brief account of what happened, then called Director Geez, who was waiting anxiously for their report. He was gratified that Bear had survived the experience, but upset that he had been shot. He had hoped that there would be no bloodshed. He congratulated the agents and his team. He took the blame for putting them in harm's way.

*   *   *

Ann and Rob provided the remaining details to Agent Phillips's questions as the crew prepared to depart. Rob was concerned about the horses without riders as the choppers had the Indian and the body, plus drugs in one, Bear and Leigh in the other. That left only him and Ann to return the string of horses and two mules. He mentioned to the agent, "That's no fun on the trail. A couple horses, yes, but Bear's sorrel mare, Leigh's bay, the Indian's pinto, the dead man's black gelding—that's four horses and two mules . . . that's a bitch."

Agent Phillips said, "Well, son, I do believe we've a solution. Two of our student interns are just coming in after the smoke has cleared, which they are instructed to do, staying out of the line of fire, no matter what. They're criminal-justice students from the University of Alaska, involved for a couple of weeks now. They, too, reported the drug train."

"Who are you talking about?"

"Oh, here they come. Ron and Wendy, meet Rob."

"Well I'll be darned." Rob sighed.

Ron coyly said, "We've met. Mr. Phillips, I'll tell you about it later."

"Oh, okay. Anyway, here's your riders to help you return the livestock to Haines. It's only five more miles due south. We'll fly you back to Skagway, if you wish, and also deliver your horses later. It's up to you, by order of Director Geez."

"I'll check with Ann," Rob said as he mulled over the surprise of Ron and Wendy's participation. "Here's Ann now. Ann, meet our trail mates as we ride to Haines."

Ann smiled. "Welcome. I'll bet you've a story to tell. I'm anxious to hear it. Let's go."

Rob smiled at Wendy and said, "We may have the most amusing story to tell. It's a story of what role our friend Leigh thought you played in this little caper in the park. I'll tell you as soon as we hit the trail. Let's ride."

Chapter 19

Late Thursday night at Delta Station, Josie received a message from Geez informing her and all other stations of the apprehension of the drug runners. "We were lucky. Our personnel had been in harm's way."

Although serious, Bear's wounds were not life-threatening, and he was doing fine. Without a doubt he would want to return to work ASAP.

Geez signed off with a congratulatory comment on the continuing good work DNR personnel across the state were doing in support of other U.S. government agencies.

Several hours later the Delta Crew were discussing the message from Geez while having their last snack and drink of the day by the fire. Surprisingly, another message came in.

"That's strange," Josie said. "Did you hear that?"

She left the fire to see what could be so important at 2200 hours.

"I'll be right back—*ah, de bon qoust je bestes bruttes*; it's probably just a communications check or something like that."

*   *   *

Mark groaned. "Another French lesson, *on the fly*." He leafed through the *Berlitz* French/English reference manual and said, "Let's see, here it is—good eating, my brute beasts. How's that for a speedy look up?"

Matt added, "I think she threw that at us since you thanked her for the sandwiches and beer with a quick, *merci, mademoiselle*."

John opined, "Probably. Next time just say—thanks, or we'll be into French again."

Mark called Luke over, held him for a moment, and then whispered in his ear.

"What are you doing, Mark?" Matt asked.

"I've just talked to my partner here, and we've decided to show you our latest."

John said, "Partner? Latest? What?"

Mark asked Luke to sit. *"S'asseoir."*

He obeyed in smart fashion, knowing very well the reward that was in Mark's hand.

As Luke maintained a classic sitting position, Mark said, "Donne la Patte."

With a quick response, Luke lifted his paw and offered it to Mark.

Mark leaned forward, grabbed Luke's paw, and performed the obligatory shake. Then he said, "*Merci,* and Luke barked.

Luke leaped toward Mark for his treat, and the boys clapped in approval of Luke's performance.

Holding Luke while he licked Mark's fingers, Mark offered one last comment. "By the way, the bark was in French, too. His response: *de rien.*"

The boys groaned, and Matt added quickly, "But, can he read?"

At that, Mark threw Luke's chewed-up tennis ball at the pair.

*   *   *

By the time Josie got to the administrative yurt, the message was complete. As she scrolled down the screen she quickly determined that it was no routine message; it was specifically for Delta Station—from Geez.

She read the message again, printed two copies, and acknowledged receipt to DNR Headquarters.

As she walked back to the fire with the copies firmly in hand, she mulled over the assignment's impact on the station . . . and the boys. At least it was in their sector of operations and skill area versus fighting fires up north.

"What's up, Josie?" Matt asked. "Good news?"

"Yes and no. Geez just sent another message. We're about to get busier. Here, take a look."

The boys gathered around and read it with interest.

Alert

Attention: Josie St. Pierre, Manager, DNR Delta Station, Sitka

Friday, October 21, 1999, 2200 hours PST

A Native-American fishing trawler, *Ladybird,* is being towed by the USCG icebreaker *Woodbine* past Sitka Sound on/or about 0500 hours Saturday, October 22.

Ladybird, a 40-foot steel-hulled trawler, ran aground last night and damaged her rudder. Her aft fuel tank was also damaged, and may have lost its structural integrity. It may rupture while being towed to its home port in Juneau. She's a black cod and halibut long-line fisherman, the captain has indicated that the freezers are fully loaded with 35,000 pounds of fish worth $100,000. This weight has caused her to ride low in the water.

The ship belongs to the Tlingit Nation, and is captained by Phoenix Eagleshadow. Her first mate, Desert Flower, also a woman, is injured.

The captain of the *Woodbine* Commander L. Jones has asked for our assistance in the following priority:

1. Help in removing Desert Flower, whose arm requires immediate medical attention. She has other complications.
2. Follow the *Ladybird*, in support, to Pelican Island where we will turn east into Icy Strait.
3. Monitor the trawler's wake to determine if there is any leakage, and keep me informed. You may need additional support.

Contact Commander Jones and me when you are on station.

by W. Geez, Director, DNR, Juneau.

End of message.

Matthew spoke first. "Well, it looks like we've got ourselves a ballgame. We'll be humping tomorrow. It's fortunate that the twenty-four foot motor launch and eighteen-foot skiff are here now. We certainly could not have helped them out last week.

"True," Josie said. "Geez knows what's here, and I'm sure he volunteered us for just that reason."

Mark asked, "What if we have rough seas? That's fifty miles to Icy Strait. The launch can make it that far comfortably, but the skiff would be hard pressed to go that far."

"True," Josie agreed. "The way I look at our priorities, we first get the woman to the hospital by picking her up with the launch, then transferring her to the skiff at the station and taking her to Sitka in the smaller skiff.

Matt added, "That should work. Why don't you take her in the skiff, and we three tougher-than-nails-Wolvies can follow the trawler in the launch'?"

"Oh brother," Josie sighed. "Yes, that would work, but let's go over several options from each of you and we'll select the best—with my vote counting a little more."

They kicked around several options as the night wore on. With the preparation of the boats plus chow and talk by the fire, they decided at 0300 hours that they might as well skip sleep since they planned to be on station, waiting for the *Ladybird*, by 0400. They couldn't have slept anyway. The assignment was too exciting.

*   *   *

On rolling seas in the blackness of night, *Ladybird*'s captain, Psyche, short for Phoenix Eagleshadow, stood at the inoperable helm in the wheel house. Old habits of standing by the ship's wheel were hard to recast.

Psyche spoke to Desert Flower. "This is no way to run a railroad. I'll be damned. If Dad could see me now . . . he'd have kittens. Running aground and towed to port all in one day, now that's a bitch. Worse yet, he'll probably be at the dock to tell me so himself . . . Coast Guard and all. Yep, even after the DNR picks you up, they'll be trailing us, too. Damn."

The Ladybird trudged along in the blackness of the Pacific under a cloud-covered sky; not a star was in sight. The only moderate illumination was the fluorescence of the ship's wake. Her screws were turning at a low rpm to assist in the tow, her rudder was rendered useless in its jammed condition.

Flower chatted with her discouraged captain. "Don't be so hard on yourself. You have not lost your good sense like Captain Ahab. You saved your ship. If the long line hadn't been caught on that submerged wreck, you wouldn't have drifted over that shoal. You successfully retrieved the mile of hooked long line costing over a thousand bucks, and we're on our way to home port.

"Besides, our freezers are full of excellent black cod and halibut; you're bringing in the largest catch of the season. The crew will probably net about three grand each—not bad for four days' work. True?"

"True. You always seem to put things in perspective. But you're forgetting two—maybe three items, my dear: your broken arm and concussion while trying to clear the rudder's linkage below; the cost of repairing the rudder, maybe in dry-dock . . . uugghh; and worst of all, the chewing out by my dad Na-Nà-Ma-Kee, that ain't no picnic. Oh, add being towed in by the Coast Guard and followed by the DNR in case our aft fuel tank springs a leak. Sonubitch.

"I'm telling you, babe, when my dad's done with me, I'm gonna feel like I've been ridden hard all day and put away wet."

"Yes, I know," Flower replied, "but you're being too negative; lay off yourself. It was me who screwed up. The crew is with you. Look what you're doing for me. I wouldn't have to be dropped off at Sitka if I weren't a bleeder needing immediate attention. The crew sees what you're doing for me. Do you hear me?"

"Yes, I guess."

"By the way, our engineer, Red Cloud, will pull my watch after I leave."

"Good," Psyche answered. "He's a good man. I understand he's going to help in the transfer. He told me he's fixing a rig for you of some sort on our lifeboat davit—wait, there's a message coming in."

Being due west of Sitka Sound, she was expecting a call from the DNR boys at Delta Station.

Static . . . background noise . . . step tone . . . clear signal.

"*Ladybird*, this is Delta mobile. Over."

"This is *Ladybird*. I read you loud and clear. Over."

"Roger that; Matt here. We understand you will be lowering an injured person to our boat by your life-boat davit as we come aside."

"Affirmative," Psyche answered. "Come along our starboard at midships a ten feet off our beam and we'll make the transfer. We've already had a trial-run with a sack of ice. It should work. Our chief concern will be the sea swells; they're running about five feet—that—we could not measure accurately. It will be up to you to snatch her carefully at the peak of the swell. Over."

"Roger that. We'll do our best. We have two guys aboard ready to grab her at the right time. We'll treat your broken-winged cargo with tender loving care."

"Roger, I appreciate you DNR boys helping us so early in the morning. Dang, it's only four."

"Not a problem. This is late night to us. We never hit the sack after receiving the call at ten last night. Say, do you see our running lights yet?"

Silence.

"Negative. How far away are you?"

"About one-half mile. We see yours and the guard's lights. Ours are probably hidden in the swells. We'll start converging to your starboard. Should be alongside in about twenty minutes."

"Good. I'll inform Jones in the tow truck."

"Roger, you're closer. You could probably use two tin cans and a waxed string like we did in scouting. Thanks."

"Ughhhhh. Bad humor, Wolvie, I've heard of you guys."

"Don't believe those stories . . . lies, lies, all lies, they're not true."

Psyche chuckled. "We'll see. Standby."

Matt shared his conversation with John and Mark as they angled toward Ladybird's starboard beam.

Mark commented, "I suppose you guys realize this operation could not be done if we had larger breaking waves versus these rollers; I hope the weather holds up for us. Let's get this done fast; we're right on the edge of doability. We've got to grab that chick at just the right time or she'll crash into the launch."

"Everything you say is true, but we will do it, we will be successful, and you will grab her at the right time. We Delta boys will do it—understand?"

As Matt steered the launch toward the ship he thought he may have overreacted to Mark's comments, but at times Mark was a little too contrary.

The blackness of the sea and the sky isolated the two ships ahead as they motored over the rolling swells to help the injured Native woman. He thought, *Wouldn't it have been nicer to have done this in daylight? Darkness does add a dangerous dimension to an already difficult transfer maneuver. Mark's right; hope the weather holds. I wonder if the guys notice that I used some of Kicking Bird's motivational ideas. His worked on me, they just might work on my buddies, too.*

*   *   *

On the starboard deck of the *Ladybird*, the ship's crew was rigging a transfer chair with strong lines to the davit. The shadows of artificial light, sea spray, and a rolling deck exacerbated their task.

"Ouch! I'll be more careful, Red Cloud. I hit my arm on the lines holding your little chair. I'm okay. Your idea is just perfect."

Red Cloud had modified a normal wooden chair with a harness and lines to the davit. "Good thinking, Red," Flower said.

"Well, babe, you've got to use what's available; there's no Kmart at sea. Now, here's what we'll do in this order: I'll clip the quick release fastener from your chair to the davit line O-ring; make sure you're wearing a PFD; sit in the chair and fasten the quick release safety belt; Coyote Woman will activate the davit until the lines are taut; I'll swing you over the side when the launch is in position; and Coyote will slowly lower you to a height equal to the highest point of the sea swell. The rest is up to you and the DNR boys."

"That sounds like a winner, Red. Now all I've got to do is release at the right time and fall into the arms of those two hunks from Michigan . . . I can do that."

Red said with a wry smile, "I see you've been talking to Psych about the Wolvies at Delta Station."

"Oh . . . maybe."

"I'll say this, I like your attitude. I think we can pull this off. But please be careful. That splint on your arm is only temporary."

"One more item," Red said. "The boys have lined the bottom of the launch with foam and blankets for your controlled fall and ride to the hospital, but don't plan on falling—the boys are going to catch you in mid-air and let you fall on them. They say they can handle it. Let's hope so. Again—release only at the top of the swell, and you should have no problems."

"Yeah, is that why I have to wear your hard hat? Come on, Red Cloud, I may land like the boys of the 82nd airborne. All I can do is hope for the best."

Red Cloud noticed the ship's lights blink, a signal that the DNR boat was coming alongside. He told Flower and gave her a kiss. "Honey, we've done everything possible to get you to the hospital ASAP; now it's up to you. Let's get ready. I'll help you don your PFD. I'll be careful. Here, come on, they're ready for us."

Desert Flower sighed, "Calling me honey, giving me a kiss . . . I'll have to do this again—sometime.

"Come on, woman, let's boogie."

*   *   *

Matt signaled to the davit operator and Red Cloud that they were ready as their boat moved closer to the *Ladybird*.

"Okay, Wolvies, this is it. Tighten your PFDs; we're going in. Stand on that foam in the center if you can, or hold on to the gunnels or each other. We need to catch her in the center. I know, I've got the wheel for stability; just do the best you can," Matt yelled. "We'll be feeling the effects of the ship's wake soon—hold on."

Still unstable, John grabbed Mark and said, "Let's go to our knees until it's time to grab her."

Down they went, still holding on to each other. It was getting rough. "Shucks, John," Mark said, "I didn't know you cared."

"Straighten up, plebe; she's swinging out on the davit now," John yelled.

Matt yelled, "I see her. I'm headed in . . . here we go."

Matt maneuvered the launch closer to the ship's hull, then backed away a little and moved forward while looking up. He wiped the sting of the salt water spray from his eyes. Now all he could see was Red's face on the rail and the bottom of the chair with a pair of legs dangling. He eased the launch forward a little more . . . a little more . . . too much. He backed off . . . then angled closer. The sea swells tossed the launch in a vertical path, up and down and sideways. The swells were not even in duration or height causing many problems for alignment. He did the best he could.

The launch bobbed, weaved, and bounced as it moved in the ship's wake. Then a wave came rushing under the bow and raised the launch vertically to the top of the wave . . . "Now!" Matt yelled to Flower, and down she came with more force than they had planned. It was as if a piano had been dropped from a third-story window.

Standing now, John and Mark caught her when she triggered the quick-release snap from the O ring—and fell like a rock. Ungraciously, the boys grabbed on to anything sticking out, then lost their balance in the rocking boat, tilted sideways, and fell overboard into the sea. Flower struggled as they all went over, the boys holding on so she would not slip away into the ocean's blackness.

"Damn!"

"O-o-o-h-h . . . Christ!"

"Ow!" was all Matt could hear as he watched them all fall overboard and disappear below the blackness.

"G-l-u-u-b . . . bitch," echoed across the water as Matt spun the wheel around to do a 180.

The next sighting was better as he saw the trio pop up due to the air-filled PFD's. Mark still had a grip on the chair as they spit sea water. Matt arrived at their side in seconds, threw a life ring, and moved the launch toward them slowly. He killed the motor.

"Are you guys okay?" Matt yelled.

"Hell no," Mark barked. "Get us out of this frigid water, I'm about to swallow my cajones; it's damn . . . cold. Here, get Flower first. You pull the chair, not her, and I'll push. We'll keep her on the chair. She's probably hurting more now after that tumble."

Flower came around, spit, and croaked, "No. I'm okay. Somehow my arm did not take a hit—but I did kick one of you guys when I fell out of the boat." She was pulled and pushed over the gunnel. Finally with Flower aboard, Matt unstrapped her from the chair, and she wrapped herself in a blanket.

"Are you sure you're okay?" Matt asked again as they caught their breath.

"Absolutely. Let's get those boys. They saved my life."

"It's about time," Mark yelled as he pulled himself to the boat on the life line and slithered aboard over the gunnel.

He turned and said, "Here, John, grab this line; we'll pull you in," but there was no response.

All three looked at the bobbing body. Shocked, no one had noticed that John had not said anything after falling into the sea.

"John!" Mark yelled.

"John, do you hear me?" Matt yelled.

"Grab this ring!" Flower yelled as she tossed a ring to him.

"Christ," Matt said, "he's got to be knocked—out or something. You stay here; I'm going after him."

Matt jumped into the water, swam to his bobbing unresponsive friend who was face up in his PFD, and yelled, "John, do you hear me?"

Getting no response, he put his arms around him, searched for and found a good pulse. He was breathing. He presumed that John had been knocked out in the fall into the ocean . . . by the gunnel or something.

"Mark, we've got a cold-cocked Wolvie here; pull us in and we'll see how badly he's hurt."

Mark pulled the pair to the boat, lifted John over the gunnel while Matt pushed, and lay him down on the blankets. Flower rushed to his side as Matt got aboard and immediately joined her.

*   *   *

With her arm strapped to her side, Flower examined John's head. Sure enough, she quickly discovered the swelling and contusion on his right temple. She lifted him to a sitting position with her good arm, and threw several blankets over his body and head, asking for help.

She spoke in a firm manner. "Matt, before we head for shore, I want you and Mark to rub John's extremities vigorously to get his circulation going. Go ahead, you rub his legs, Matt; Mark, you rub his arms—hurry up."

As the trio continued to work on John, the launch drifted toward shore. Flower looked shoreward to see how far they had drifted. They were about 100 yards from the outer breakers. They'd be okay for the next couple minutes.

Their radio signaled an incoming call, but Flower quickly said, "Ignore it; it's just the *Ladybird* asking how we are. I can tell Psyche's voice. Stay with John; he needs us more."

The trio continued to work on John as the boat drifted near the breakers. Then . . . they noticed some reaction to their work.

"0-o-o-h-h . . . what the he-e-1-1. Ke-rist! Oh my damn head . . . hurts."

"Hey, guys, it worked; he's coming around. Let's back off the rub for a while. How are you, John? John, how are you?" Flower asked.

"Where the hell am I? What happened?" John groaned.

"Good morning, my dear. You're on the Pacific Ocean, just off Sitka Sound, and have just saved my life with your friend Mark. How 'bout that?" She leaned over and gave him a big kiss, "Here's your reward."

"Welcome back," Matt added.

"You'll do anything for a kiss," Mark said.

"Boys, give him a break. I'm probably the one that kicked him in the head when we fell overboard. Let's get off those wet clothes, dry him off, and let him rest awhile He's going to the hospital with me. A concussion is serious business. Let's haul ass, you land lubbers, we're almost to the breakers. Come on, Matt, let's get the hell out of here."

Flower definitely showed her colors as first mate of the Ladybird; she was used to being in charge. Without a doubt she took over command of the launch. While Matt headed for Sitka Sound, Desert Flower called Psyche and reported all was well. She relayed that they were almost at Delta Station where Josie was waiting to take her to the hospital; the launch would rejoin her soon.

She didn't bother Psyche with their concern for John's concussion, since he'd be going with her anyway—she had enough grief on her plate.

As they rounded the point into the harbor, Flower said, "Look at that. A raven is following us. That is good medicine."

"Indeed," Matt said.

"Yes, indeed," Mark echoed.

*   *   *

After Desert Flower and John transferred to the waiting skiff, Matt and Mark grabbed some food and coffee and dry clothes, then quickly departed the station to rendezvous with the *Ladybird*, now about one mile north of the station.

As the boys departed with their faces full of food, Josie hollered, "*De bon qoust.*"

"Ha," Matt said to Mark, "I got that one; it's something like *good eating.*"

Josie, with Luke looking forward from the boats bow, raced across the Sound with her injured crew, and deep feelings of the seriousness of John's head injury. She phoned ahead for an ambulance to meet them at the dock.

Although still tense about the results of the transfer problems, she was thankful for the first two priorities having been complete: the transfer and the DNR soon to be in position behind the *Ladybird*. She hoped the third item would never happen. Leaking fuel oil would be a major problem if it did not evaporate prior to reaching shore. Water sampling and testing along the coastline was a real possibility.

Ten minutes later, as she passed the halfway point to the city docks, she turned to see how her crew were doing. She caught the eyes of Flower, who smiled and winked as acknowledging her wholesome one-armed embrace of John. His head rested between her breasts. She smiled at Flower, turned, and thought, *I think John is fully aware of where his head lay; he knows where the best pillows are.*

Josie keyed the mic. "Sitka docks, this is Delta mobile. I'll be tying up in five minutes. Out."

Josie was unaware of the personnel who were waiting at the dock; nor the intrigue that would follow.

Chapter 20

It was a resplendent morning on Sitka Sound. Matt maneuvered the launch away from Delta Station around the point and headed north along the coast to rendezvous with the impaired *Ladybird* under tow.

The air was crisp and very clear. The sun's early-morning light gave the ocean a deep blue and sparkling look as if liquid sapphire. In contrast, on the steep shore, the forest climbing up the side of Mount Edgecumbe was ablaze with yellow birch, russet oaks, and golden tamaraks mixed in with the deep green of the dominant evergreens.

They motored into the long shadow cast on the sea by the eight-thousand foot mountain whose silhouette turned the deep blue of the Pacific to a translucent greenish-purple curtain. In the absence of sun glare, the shaded water was clear enough to reveal aquatic life in the rocky bottom up to four fathoms.

Mark scanned the horizon for a sign of the *Ladybird* as Matt guided the launch a little more to the north by northwest, away from the shore.

Matt was in a reflective mood with his concern for treatment of John's concussion and Flower's broken wing. They were a lucky pair; their injuries could have been worse. He was certain that the faithful would be thanking The Great Spirit for His protective involvement between man and nature.

As the launch moved away from the coast, he looked back to the point and the massive presence of the spectacular Mount Edgecumbe. Not wanting to bother Mark's concentration in scanning the expanse of the sea, he did not mention the stunning sight at Edgecumbe's peak. From about five-thousand feet to just short of the top, a cloud had formed. It looked like a doughnut encircling the crown. Matt had never witnessed such a beautiful sight from the closer Delta Station location. He had always thought the entire mountain was encased in low-lying clouds.

He thought, *oh, what the hell; Mark needs a break. I'll disturb him.* "Mark!" Matt hollered. "Take a look to the rear, to the eastern shore. Check out the top of Mount Edgecumbe."

Mark lowered his binoculars, turned from his position on the quarter deck, and looked to the top of the mountain.

"I'll be damned. That is beautiful. I wonder how often that little cloud parks on the peak?"

"Beats me, but it's sure pretty, or as Josie would say, *"Bonny."*

Matt laughed.

"I think I've spotted our ships. There's two black spots to the north by north-west. As soon as you get closer, I'll confirm the sighting, and you can give 'em a call."

"Okay, my man, I'll head that-a-way. Why don't you take a break and pour us some coffee and dig out some of Josie's buns?—or *un café, s'il vous plaît, Garcon.*"

Mark answered in his broken French, "*Oui. Tout de suite, monsieur,*" as he passed a hot cup from the thermos and said, "*Voilà, monsieur.*"

Matt thanked him for the good coffee, "*Quel bon café.*"

They relaxed a bit while heading for the two black dots. Matt looked over the stern again as they moved farther away from the shadowed shore.

Still a little pensive, he shared with Mark the impact of yet another experience as they motored from their home base—again.

"Just think, Mark, over two-hundred years ago Aleksandr Baranov, a Russian explorer, sailed across the Bering Strait, down the Aleutian Island chain, to Ya-kutat Bay, and cruised by this very spot before sailing into Sitka Sound. He viewed the same coast we're viewing now. The *same* beauty. I'll bet not a lick of timber has been cut from the island nor a mineral extracted—it's the same as he saw it in 1799. That's amazing to me. You?

"When we're writing our report on this Alaskan internship, we'll probably surprise our graduate advisors. I can hear them now. You did what? You jumped out of helicopters to fight forest fires, you swam with killer whales, you gave a humorous skit to the stoic Raven Clan Chief, you attended a Native American burial ceremony—what else did you do?

"The list could go on and on like that. Do you realize, Mark, this will be our first assignment where we're doing tasks we were trained to do? Add that we're already into the twelfth week of our twenty-four week stay at the Sound. Oh, well, no problem. It's been an enriching experience . . . whether in the biological/ma-rine sciences or not."

Mark laughed, "Tell that to John—just kidding, it's been a blast."

Matt continued, "You're right, he'd probably not want it any other way. I wouldn't either. But, all the historical writings we've read prior to the assignment have proven to be true. Don't you think that on the individual level—our level, the working level—the encounters we've had with the Tlingits must have been positive? Until the element of greed, the rape of the land, and the extraction of all their resources occurred, the Russian fur traders were driven from Sitka.

"Two-hundred years has not changed the basis for survival of man on this earth. We belong to the earth . . . the earth does not belong to us. The struggle is exactly the same today: it's man against nature, man against man, and man against animals. One thing is certain: nature, the earth, always wins."

Mark glanced at Matt, "My, but aren't you the historical and theological philosopher today? It must be either the sea or my good coffee."

"You, block head. I'm just explaining to you that in Alaska a lot of territory seen by early explorers has not changed, and in the struggle against nature, if we violate its fixed rules man always loses. We're seeing the same things Baranov saw two-hundred years ago, and we could make the same mistakes if we're not careful. He raped the coast of otters for personal gain. We may be doing the same with our need for oil."

"I'm taking notes, professor."

"That's it, you dummkopf. Since you're German, I'll bet John would appreciate my perspective."

Mark finally got serious. "Matt, you're right. I, too, think about this pristine land and how fortunate we are to experience its beauty, and I hope my children have the same opportunity before man ravages its magnificence. Your observations are on point. Ahhh . . . you may want to look in our wake. Our friends have returned."

"What?"

"Take a look. Big mama's brought her pod to us again; she probably wants to say a big Hello!"

"Damn, you're right. Let's just act like they're not there."

"Ah, yeah, like it would make any difference if they wanted to play *Tip the DNR boat*."

"We'll probably be okay. I told you, they eat fish, seal, and otter. They're not interested in humans. Wait, I forgot you look like an otter. You frequently lie on your back and eat anything palatable, including abalone or any other mollusk."

"Not funny, but you're right. Let's just go about our business and aim for the two spots on the horizon. Wait, it is them; I can see 'em now. They're about a mile away."

"Great, I'll call Psyche and Josie and let them know we'll probably be on station within the hour."

"Good," Mark said. "In the meantime, I'll put on a friendly mammalian face for our friends and thank them for the escort."

Just as the words left his lips, the pod came alongside, and the leader breached and flopped so close to the boat that both Wolvies were soaked.

"Christ!" Mark yelled. "Is that your way of saying hello, or is that a way of warning us you're our next meal?"

Drenched to the skin, Matt grabbed the mic and called, "*Ladybird, Ladybird,* this is Delta station mobile. Do you hear me? Over."

"This is *Ladybird,*" Psyche answered. "Have you guys decided to rejoin this slow-motion convoy? Over."

"Yes, wouldn't have it any other way. Now that your first mate and our John are on the way to the hospital, we're on station, as ordered—at your service. Josie should be giving us a call soon. We'll let you know how Desert Flower is doing.

"The transfer was a little rough, but other than John's hit in the head, we're all back in service to the grand State of Alaska. More specifically, at your service, Captain Eagleshadow."

After a little giggle, she answered, "My man, from what Red tells me, the transfer was anything but a *little* rough. Three in the drink, and one knocked out is *very* rough. I hope John's okay. Red tells me Flower thinks it's she who kicked him in the head. Whatever, you guys did a fine job under extremely difficult conditions. Our whole crew thanks you. Maybe you'll have a chance to meet them if you can get to our dockage in Juneau."

Matt quickly answered, "Let's plan on it. We'll bring the beer; you bring the girls."

"Whoa, big fella. Slow down, you midwestern Wolvie. What makes you think I've access to female consorts?"

"Ha. You forget I've been with Desert Flower for some time now. You do have an entire clan aboard—in fact, the Eagle Clan. I'm told there's two more, and when you process the catch, all four of you work below while Red takes the wheel."

She laughed, "Flower sure has given you guys the low-down on our operation. Yep, Red, our engineer, is the only man aboard. We wouldn't sail without him."

"Yep, I know that, too."

"Do you also know that the single women on board are cougars? That may change your mind, college boy."

"Yep, I know. No, it doesn't change our interest."

"We'll be talking to you periodically. No more traffic. Out."

*   *   *

Psyche looked at Red Cloud who was listening in on speaker to the conversation. He, too, had a grin on his face. It was much like hers. These boys were anxious for companionship—including cougars.

*   *   *

Red looked aft over the stern at the boys in the launch following about fifty yards behind, just beyond the screw-created turbulence. Then he looked forward over the bow at the icebreaker's twenty-five-yard towline.

He looked at Psyche and said, "You know, Captain, it's going to be at least four hours to the Icy Strait turn-off."

"Yeah, that's about right. What's on your mind?"

"That's a long time for those boys to be in that open cockpit launch, in sea swells, sea spray, and that biting wind coming off the water to the north.

"Where are you going with this, Red?"

"Well, I just came from down below, and I've removed the problem area where the linkage was rubbing against the fuel tank. The tank will no longer be in danger of losing its integrity. Good news, huh?

"So, I thought, if the Captain agrees, we could invite the boys aboard—for a while. They have been on station in that launch for an hour or so. They need not be out there. There will be no leak from our ship. Furthermore, we're the only ones who know. There would be no risk to the environment."

"Red, you're something else. I never would have thought of bringing them aboard. But, if you say there's no chance of a leak, I think it's a damn good idea. Let's do it, but on the q.t. No sense telling everyone. We need not use the radio. Their mission will only be altered a bit. Right?"

"Right," Red agreed. "I'll pass some harmless traffic for them to come alongside for a moment, and when there, if they agree, we'll tie up the launch and bring them aboard."

"Do it!" Psyche said. "It's better you than me. Do you dig?"

"I do."

"Wait, do you see any reason to inform Jones?"

"Absolutely not."

"Josie?"

"No, she's already got her hands full, and the boys already told her that they were on station and no leaks were observed."

"Let's do it!" she exclaimed.

Red radioed the boys, and they came alongside. Red briefed them on the good news on the fuel tank. He then made the offer to board for a couple of hours. It took the boys only a second to decide. They tied up the launch securely and ascended the boarding ladder.

As they cleared the gunnel and stepped on deck, they were met by three lovely ladies of the crew. Red introduced everyone and headed for the wheelhouse.

*   *   *

"Hi! I'm Psyche, your captain. This is Wind Song, and this is Morning Dove. Welcome aboard, Wolvies! Follow us gals below. The girls have a few things planned to make your ride a little more comfortable. Come on."

As Mark and Matt descended on the tight passageway ladder, Mark said, "Pinch me. Is this really happening?"

Matt answered, "We'll soon find out. Let's be cautious."

As they reached the main hallway below, Psyche led them into a small dining room with tables and chairs and a kitchen on one end. A stack of towels and change of clothes lay on the table in front of them. At the other end were several covered plates of food and a small tub with iced beer.

Psyche was first to speak. "We heard you stayed up all night, plus have been bathed in the salty Pacific several times, so we thought you'd like to shower and get into a change of clothes."

Mark and Matt looked at each other with an expression of disbelief, then at Psyche.

"I see you agree," Psyche said. "First things first. Mark, you'll be assisted by Morning Dove." Dove nodded and smiled as she approached. "Matt, you'll be helped by Wind Song." Song smiled as she went to Matt. "They'll show you the showers; the port one is Red's, the starboard ours. Go on now, get cleaned up so we can attack this brunch the gals have prepared."

The boys hesitated, not knowing their next move.

"Girls, they need a little help. Dove, take Mark to my cabin so he can get out of those wet clothes, and take him to the port shower. Song, take Matt to Red's cabin and do the same. Use the starboard shower. Now, git! Time's a-wasting."

"Neat cabin, Dove. I'll lay my clothes here," Mark said nervously.

"No, give them to me. We'll wash and dry them while we eat. Here, let me help you get those clothes off."

"Ah . . . okay . . . ah . . . thanks."

What happened next was beyond Mark's belief. Halfway through removing his clothes, Dove removed hers.

She looked at him with a smile. "I will shower with you. You'll need someone to wash your back," cooed Dove.

Surprised. That was a man's line. He agreed and said, "If you say so. Lead the way to the showers.

About 30 or 40 years old, Dove sported rich ebony hair hanging down over her huge rack. She showed no embarrassment. Her cute moon-like face had a special charm of candor, a frankness he enjoyed. There was no doubt to what she had planned in the shower. Her demeanor was alluring and accepting, a role he was unaccustomed to.

They skipped down the hall into the shower. She washed his back, and when he turned they embraced and she dropped the wash cloth. Her hands were busy elsewhere.

At a crucial time during their embrace, Mark asked, "Is it okay? Are you?"

"Yes," she added. "I've taken care of that. No worry . . . go ahead, my horny man."

Fifteen minutes later, the pair emerged with satisfied smiles, ran down the passageway, had another barenaked standup encounter in the cabin, got dressed, and rendezvoused with Psyche in the dining room.

Dove spoke first to Psyche. "Mark comes by his name naturally. This Wolverine's aggressive, like his namesake, and surfeit."

"Good. I'm glad you two enjoyed your shower. Have a beer, Mark."

"Don't mind if I do . . . I need an energy boost."

Dove smiled with pride as she opened one for her prize.

*   *   *

Wind Song lead Matt to Red's cabin and, without hesitating, started helping him off with his sea-soaked shirt.

As he started removing his pants, he stopped momentarily while she removed her shirt, too. Her firm breasts, even for a forty-year old required no brassiere. Her breasts looked like 75 mm cannon shells—ready to fire.

She looked willowy and thin, with slender hips and a very small butt. He assumed that nature had had a little help. As if a tease, her pigtails swung left and right over her nipples.

A tattoo on her back showed the silhouette of an eagle in flight—quite appropriate for the Eagle Clan.

Disrobing was quick.

Before he realized it, they were in the shower, washing each other's backs and erogenous areas.

She dropped the wash cloth and pursued him directly

He paused . . .

She said, "It's okay; go ahead, my dear."

In the middle of their peak activity, he hummed the melody from Ravel's Bolero: "dum-da-da-dum-dum-da . . ."

"You're certainly a musical one. Do all wolvies sing during love-making?"

"No. Only me." He giggled.

They embraced.

Matt thanked her for the experience.

She said, "The pleasure was mine. Let's boogie; I'm ready for a beer."

"Me, too. You've whet my appetite."

"Try one of these. They're here for you."

"Don't mind if I do."

She stood akimbo as he, and she, enjoyed an areolar moment . . . on both sides. "Is there anything else you'd like, my dear Wolvie?"

"Not a thing. You've made my day, my dear."

"No, you've made me—and mine, too."

Giggling, they ran back to Red's cabin, dressed, and hustled to the dining room.

*   *   *

Psyche was the first to speak. "Welcome, join us in a beer. Dove is heating up the seafood gumbo and crab legs. You guys look hungry."

Matt answered, "I could eat a horse. Wind Song gave me quite a workout, washing my back."

"Sure." Psyche laughed.

"She defines the word cougar. She's wonderful."

"Well, thank you, Matt. You didn't do so bad yourself."

Mark joined in as Dove returned with the food. "We've been treated so well by these Eagle Clan fisherwomen, I think we owe them a song."

"How 'bout, 'Hail to the Victors,' the Michigan fight song?"

"Absolutely. You girls sit over there, and we'll stand over here and serenade you."

The girls grabbed a beer and moved.

"Hail to the victors valiant/Hail to the conquering heroes . . ."

After singing a few songs to them, and together, they attacked the tasty delights of the sea. Later on, Psyche took a bowl of gumbo up to Red. As she left, the gang was singing, "Kumbaya, my Lord. Kumbaya . . ."

*   *   *

After she left, Matt asked Wind Song, "She and Red make a good team. Are they close?"

Wind Song smiled. "Yes, they share a shower, too; and since you're asking, Desert Flower shares the shower with all of us girls."

"Oh," Matt acknowledged with a smile.

During clean up, Matt leaned over to Mark and said, "Who would have believed the last twenty-four hours, Mark?"

Mark answered, "No one would. Let's keep this experience to ourselves."

"You're right."

Matt asked to leave a minute to chat with Red and see if there were any messages for the DNR launch following the Ladybird.

Alone, Matt followed the narrow passageway to the ladder and up to the deck, then found his way to the wheelhouse. Just before entering, he looked over the rail to see if the launch was still secure. Seeing no problems, he walked to the wheelhouse.

He opened the door. "Hi, Red. How the heck are you? Good gumbo, huh?"

Red answered, "I'm fine, and so is the gumbo. Those gals sure know their way around a kitchen . . . and men, too. Right?"

"What do you mean?"

"The entertainment wasn't just singing. Right?"

"I suppose you mean how friendly they are?"

"Ah . . . yeah. I'm sure they served you well."

"Damn, I guess there's no use. I should have known better. Yes, both Mark and I had a great time with the . . . women. I want to thank you and Psyche for your thoughts in making our mission enjoyable. I think they're all singing down there. They're quite a bunch."

"'Tis true."

"I do need to know if any of the DNR offices have called? Geez? Josie?"

"No, and I've been on station for the last two hours while you've been below. Nope, not a call, except from Coyote Woman."

"Dang. I'd forgotten about her. Where'd she go?"

"She's our liaison with the Coast guard. Psyche felt we needed one of ours aboard the *Woodbine* to keep things on an even keel. She's watching the tow line for us."

"I understand. Give her my best. I guess I'll take your advice and go below for another hour, but remember, when we get near Icy Strait, I want to be on station, too—behind, not in the *Ladybird*."

"Deal. I'll promise to call you on the IC if any calls come in."

"Deal. See you later."

*   *   *

Ten miles inland on Sitka Sound, Josie saw a crowd of people awaiting her arrival on the city dock. As she rounded the point and entered the no-wake zone, she throttled back and turned to rouse the sleeping couple in the stern. But, there seemed to be no need to wake them until they reached the docks. She cast her binoculars on the crowd on the docks, then gasped.

She thought to herself, *What in the world would Geez be doing here? Lynn, I under-stand. I hope there's no problem.*

"Come on, Luke, jump back here and wake up our sleeping beauties. You like to do that. Come on."

Luke jumped down from the bow, ran to the stern, and started licking faces.

Chapter 21

Day broke over Sitka as Josie's skiff coasted to the docks. The quaint fishing town's stunning landscape evoked the dawn of earth itself—its birth, its beginning. Mount Edgecumbe framed the town to the north, the seething ridges of the coastal range to the south. Mountains to the east emerged from their nightly respite. Such beauty was transcendent yet ruthless to man. Over the years, pilots learned to respect the easterly mountains and only approach Sitka Field from the west.

As Josie approached the dock, she thought about how family ties and long-lasting relationships continued regardless of the effects of time or spatial separation. This was indeed the situation that unfolded as she docked and old friends helped her unload her injured cargo into the waiting ambulance.

Why Geez was waiting remained a mystery. Was Lynn there to see one of her favorite Wolvie friends—or Luke? She certainly liked both with unbridled passion.

Much to her surprise, Big Bear and Joe emerged from the crowd. Then, Bear surprised her again by insisting on going to the hospital with the ambulance. He seemed to be paying special attention to Desert Flower. She didn't think too much of it; he'd always been very attentive to women. He had given Josie a big hug and kiss, too, but it was difficult to understand him coming to Sitka. Both he and Joe were working at Glacier Bay National Park area on the impact of the recent fire on logging interests.

She thought, *Oh, well, maybe it's the allure of a younger woman who had the responsible position as first mate on the* Ladybird.

Geez also seemed to be a little out of character. But he brought her a hot coffee and suggested they, and Joe, relax in the Pilot House Cafe after Bear left for the hospital.

As expected, Lynn's interest was primarily focused on Luke now, since it was obvious by their closeness in the boat that Desert Flower's interests were with John, too. Their embrace in the stern of the boat did not go unnoticed by her or the welcoming crowd. Lynn took Luke from Joe as she and Joe departed with Geez toward the cafe.

Josie said, "*Être bon*, Luke," as Lynn skipped away with her friend.

"Woof," was Luke's response as Lynn let him down to run the familiar docks of his past.

"He'll be good, Josie; he just wants to show the birds who's boss."

Several dock workers gave him a welcome back "hello" as he chased every seagull and duck from his domain. No one had ever told him that he possessed neither feather nor fin.

"Come on, Josie, I'm buying," Geez said as the threesome headed into the Pilot House.

It did not go unnoticed that Geez selected a table in the back portion of the room. It was in an area away from the early-morning fishermen who came to charge their batteries with coffee or the house special. Geez also had a more serious demeanor than usual. She was aware of management's pressures of personnel and financial problems—this was something different. He could not hide his feeling that lurked beneath his mien. Something was definitely bothering him.

*   *   *

The waitress took the order from Geez, who was used to being in charge. However, Josie had no interest in a fishermen's special of three eggs, a stack of pancakes, and bacon. Coffee and a roll would do just fine.

Geez got right down to business, saying, "Josie, I need to ask you, or for that matter Leigh, know anything about the relationship between Desert Flower and Big Bear? You saw him today. He has an intense interest in her."

Josie looked at Joe, then across the room and back to Geez.

Staring intently at Geez, she asked, "What has Joe told you?"

"Nothing."

Josie answered, "I know nothing of their relationship, either."

"Hmmm. I thought that might be your answer."

"Well, it's obvious that your friendship with Bear—and Leigh, too—is beyond probing. That's admirable. But, for reasons you may or may not know, I'll ask no more questions—unless you've changed your mind."

Not taking the bait, Joe and Josie remained unmoved by his indirect plea.

"Ah, here's our chow. Dig in, clam diggers."

"Sorry, Josie. He's still trying to be funny. He did have a good one while flying down here. How'd it go . . .? An agent looking for an appropriate epitaph for an actress he represented found it in: 'She sleeps alone at last.'"

Joe smiled.

Josie giggled. "Now that's funny."

"Thank you," Geez said. "My dear friends, I can break the ice here and tell you what I've learned from Bear in regard to my questions. Last night I received his call. He had heard through DNR channels of the Delta Station mission with the *Ladybird*.

"With an intensity I had not witnessed before," Geez continued, "he insisted on being at the Sitka dock. He pleaded . . . he wanted to be there when you came in with the injured gal and a Wolvie you had just picked up from the boys. I was hesitant to agree since there did not seem to be a pressing reason for him to be there. After all, you were there, Josie. That was good enough for me.

"But he persisted, and further pleas convinced me he was very serious. Finally he said he'd tell me why he had to be there on the way down in the chopper. It was important to him to be there at the docks—not later. So, for a guy like Bear, I agreed. He also wanted Joe to come with him to show their concern for Josie. They did not know at the time that she was not involved in the transfer at sea.

"We all know now of the assignment, the transfer, the dunking, the injury to John, the exchange with Josie, and the boys being back on station. Fortunately, no one drowned.

"As promised, on the flight down, Bear did share with me his relationship with Desert Flower."

He paused, thinking the pair would say something. Nothing. Nary a blink.

"My silent friends, you may know that Desert Flower is Bear and White Dove's child. She was born before Bear met Morning Star, who later gave birth to Big Wind known as Chinodin, also. He's a fine young man.

"After being raised by the women of the Raven Clan, Desert Flower left the clan in her teen years and has drifted into many experiences, finally landing with the Native fisheries and working her way up to first mate.

"She has kept in touch with Bear in a discrete way over the years. It became pretty obvious now why he asked to be here. He is very proud of her and her accomplishments. Her medical condition, as a bleeder, concerned him. A contusion or a serious cut could be fatal unless treated quickly and properly.

"My final question to you, Josie, concerns Leigh. Does she know that Desert Flower is Bear's daughter?"

"You'll have to ask Bear, or Leigh. It's not our or your concern. Is it?"

Her comment encased the three in silence.

Geez mumbled, "I just don't want to say the wrong thing around Leigh. Don't you understand? I'm asking for your help . . . your advice."

"Okay," Josie said. "Here's how I see it. You've done the right thing so far; you've helped your friend in need. Only now do I recall Joe mentioning, in passing, Bear's child."

Geez added, "But, I want to do more."

Josie continued, "Your job is finished. You did well. I'd suggest you do no more unless you're asked. No, I'd recommend you end this conversation here and resist getting involved. You see, if Bear wants to explain his trip here, it's up to him; and if you, Joe, or me need to tell a little white lie for cover, we will—but only if he asks us to do so. Enough said? If we don't back off, we may become Bear bait . . . and I know no one that would want to be on the wrong side of

Bear."

He looked at both of his friends with an appreciative smile and said, "Thanks for the admonishment, dear. I'm glad you two are on our team. Case closed."

The waitress came with a fill-up of coffee and the check. Geez grabbed it and said, "Now, the second reason I've asked two of DNR's best to meet with me is to tell them about the plan for an RTC in Glacier Bay National Park. However, it affects four others, all of whom live at Leigh's ranch. Yep, all six of you will be involved in the DNR's new Regional Training Center."

"What?" Joe said. "RTC?" he asked again. "What are you talking about?"

Geez answered, "You'll see. I want to talk to you all together. You're all flying with me this noon to the ranch. At that time I'll explain to all of you the structural changes being introduced to the educational arm of the DNR. My friends, you have been selected to launch the new program. Congratulations.

"More later. Let's go. I'd like to kick it with the dock workers a moment. Then, I've got to drag Bear away from Desert Flower in the hospital. I've called the doctor; she's going to be okay. John is in good shape, too. They're going to keep them overnight for observation purposes only. Come on, let's go."

*   *   *

As they left, Josie thought, *RTC? Was that it? What the hell does he mean we're launching a new program? How will it affect my boys? New structure? Key-reist!*

*   *   *

"What? This is hard to believe," Psyche said to Red.

Ladybird was just off Pelican Island and approaching the Icy Strait turn-off. A message had just come in from the DNR Headquarters, Juneau.

"Can you believe this? I have just been told that the boys are to stay with the convoy and report to headquarters for training. Goodness, what next?"

After giving the message to Matt, he returned the call and learned that he and Mark would be attending a two-week class on certain aspects of global warming and how to use new equipment to measure critical indicators in the environment. Apparently several members of the scientific community were scheduled to present papers and direct fieldwork and workshops.

The coordinator at Juneau indicated that John would join them within a day or two at the training session. He was a little puzzled that Josie's name was not mentioned.

Psyche was surprised and pleased with Matt's request for permission to stay aboard the *Ladybird*. He had gotten the okay from headquarters since there was no longer a problem with the fuel tank leaking.

Psyche went below with Matt to the crew to let them know the good news.

"My man," Matt said to Mark, "we're headed to Juneau for a couple weeks of training. John will be joining us tomorrow. Apparently, Desert Flower did not knock him nutty. I'm unsure about Josie. It looks like we'll be in the big city for at least a couple weeks—how'bout those marbles?"

The women smiled in silent approval.

Psyche's next comment spoke volumes as to the next few weeks' activities when she said, "It looks like you gals will finally get some sleep while aboard—if you choose the boys are going to be on shore for a bit. Maybe they can help you spend some of your money from this big catch—wisely—or frivolously. Then: again, maybe a little of both."

The gal's body language changed instantly with good news. One minute they were saying their good-byes, but the next the boys were staying aboard and on shore for a couple weeks. Wind Song giggled. "Have you guys any clothes other than what I threw in the dryer? If not, I've got news for you. You look like and are dressed like a couple homeless bums."

Morning Dove said, "You mean kinda garish?"

"No!" Song said. "It's true they look gaudy in our clothes; I'm talking about their torn and dirty work clothes. That's all they've got. We may have to borrow some of Red's street clothes."

"Not to worry," Mark added. "You gals can take us shopping. You're right. We'll need some clothes for class and doing the town."

Psyche interjected again. "Gals, you can solve dressing these boys later; as I said earlier, you can grab some sleep now if you wish."

"Good idea. I agree," said Dove. "Let's go, boys; our bunks will sleep two if we, as they say, tighten up. Let's go."

Both boys hesitated, looked at Psyche, and then the gals.

Sensing their concerns, Psyche spoke up. "Fellas, if any calls come in for you in the next hour or two, I'll get you up. I promise."

That did it. They paired up, entered the passageway, slid by the shower with an approving look, and slipped into the gals' cabins. Psyche was watching the high jinks of the two pairs as she followed them and ascended to the deck.

She checked the launch tie-up. Then upon entering the wheelhouse and grabbing Red's butt to let him know she cared, she called the hospital to check on Desert Flower and John. She shared the info with Coyote Woman on the Coast Guard ship, including that the boys were scheduled for a training session in Juneau. She immediately reminded Psyche that the girls would have to share them when they were on shore. Psyche's answer to Coyote was comforting; she explained that a third Wolvie was coming and she could have him all to herself—except, Desert Flower may be interested, too. Psyche added that they may all have to share.

Red reminded her that, after hearing all the chatter about the boys, it may be difficult to get the gals back to sea.

"You could be right, Red. But those cougars will get their fill soon enough. Money is still number one."

"Don't be so sure. This may be one of the last shots for these older . . . or should I say, middle-aged women. This may be their last chance to cast a line in the deep blue sea of love . . ."

"Believe me, Red, they'll be back. I believe in Malthusian's theory: survival requires food, water, and shelter first; reproduction—in the gals' case, sex—will come second in the hierarchical aspects of their life."

"You know, babe, you're probably right. You should know, you're one of the best."

"Keep it up . . . that talk will get you anything you'd like. Can you wait until after we dock?"

"I'll try. Look to the northeast; there's the entrance to Icy Strait. We'll soon be out of the Pacific and into the safety of the strait. We've made it, dear. Get your bank-deposit book out; our take's into six figures. Those numbers are almost as good as yours."

"Stop it, dear, or I'll be unable to stay away from you until we dock. Here, try this for a preview of coming attractions."

"Whew. You'd better stop that right now . . . I've got to stay alert."

She playfully answered, "Not necessarily, what I've got a hold of offers more action than that stationary wheel. I'll show you some real lively action. Hold still."

"We're turning, dear."

"Who cares?" Psyche groaned. "You'll soon forget the turn after I'm finished here."

*   *   *

Due north of the convoy as it sailed into Icy Strait from the Pacific, Geez headed his chopper onto the clearing at Leigh's ranch. Little did the residents below and the occupants in the chopper know, they were landing at the future home of the DNR's new Regional Training Center.

Geez had successfully dragged Bear from the hospital since Desert Flower received the requisite drugs to prevent hemorrhaging. Her concussion was minor. John, too, would be released after an overnighter.

As expected, the local Tlingit Chief, Golden Bear, had rallied his clan to stay with Flower and John until released.

Likewise, Bill at Sitka Field volunteered to fly both John and Flower to Juneau. Lynn would be flying copilot. She hoped John would notice her . . . but Geez thought not.

*   *   *

"Hi! Welcome, folks," Leigh yelled. "Good to see you again, Josie. I've been looking after your man while he's been working with Bear. How are the boys? Is John okay . . . ah, and a . . . gal, Flower, Desert Flower . . . an Indian gal off the *Ladybird?* That was quite a rescue you and the boys pulled off."

"Everyone's fine, Leigh. It was nice of Bear to come down with Joe in case we needed more help. Luckily, things worked out better than we thought, but thanks for lending us your man."

"No problem. I'm glad you boys are okay. Come on, let's go inside and grab a cup of coffee, beer, or booze . . . whatever you'd like."

*   *   *

Bear overheard part of Josie's story as the three men approached. Leigh did not see Bear wink at Josie as he grabbed Leigh and gave her a kiss. Her story was quick, factual, and to the point, without details that triggered more questions. Leigh seemed satisfied with Bear's reasons for traveling to Sitka—to help Josie and her boys.

*   *   *

Geez heard Leigh's invitation to Josie and asked, "Can the boys and I get in on that invite? We've buttoned up the chopper for the night and, in doing so, have triggered a thirst for fine women and aged wine. Notice, I didn't mix the order of the two."

"You sure can; come on," Leigh said. "Oh, look. Here come Raven and Windy. They've been busy in the barn."

"Hi, Geez!" Raven Maiden yelled. "Welcome to the ranch. Watcha doin' here?" Looking for a job? We've a lot of manure in the barn to spread on Leigh's garden. Have you ever spread roadside chestnuts? I'll bet not."

"Ha, says you, you cute little whimp. I've shoveled more in a day than they have shoveled in the legislature in a week—wait, that was from a bull."

He grinned, hoping his joke had come off to their critical ears.

"Hi, Windy. Now that we're all here, let's get together either by the fire-pit or the dining table. I've a proposal for the six of you. You're going to like it."

"Oh brother," Leigh mumbled to herself. "What's he up to now?"

"Did you say something, Leigh?"

"No, just wondering if there was enough beer."

"I'll get it, Leigh. I'll bring it to the fire-pit. They're cooling down in the buried crate next to the river." Raven grabbed seven water-cooled beers and headed for the pit.

Geez noticed the cooling crate next to the river and said, "There's an example of a project that one of your students could build to conserve energy."

"What students?" Raven asked.

After the first swig of beer, Geez presented the state's proposal for the RTC to be developed in the Glacier Bay National Park and the preferred location on the Bitterroot River near the clearing where Leigh held her temporary camping permit.

Geez said, "The ranch location was perfect. Access would still be by chopper until the need for a road was warranted. Water access would be from the northwest arm of Glacier Bay. Its terminus was only twenty miles from the ranch. An overland trail was planned, with hopes of avoiding the need for anything more than a simple two-track.

"A large two story lodge-type instructional building would be built on the east side of the clearing. It would be made of local cedar logs. In addition, four, six-person yurts would be built next to the river to house up to twenty-four attendees.

"The Training Center will present a broad range of subjects to satisfy the training needs of current and new managers and new hires, with refresher courses for existing DNR employees.

"A few of the suggested subjects included, but were not limited to:

• Forest Management	• Game Management	• Native American Culture
• Marine Biology	• Fire-fighting	• Animal husbandry
• Enforcement	• Plant ID & Treatment	• Fisheries Management
• Survival/summer&winter	• Surveying/maps	• Environmental measures for CO_2, methane, etc.

"Local management would be handled by Joe Bloom and Josie St. Pierre. Instructors, in residence would be the four of you: Bear, Leigh, Windy, and Raven. I cannot think of a more competent staff.

"There will be visiting lecturers. These could include Ann and Rob for pack-train preparation and routing since they have a wealth of experience of how to move safely over terrain. Milt and Dave could present a briefing on the use of aviation in supply, survey, and enforcement. They could also give flight instruction.

"Finally, on a rotating basis, each of the DNR research stations along the coast—Alpha, Bravo, Charlie, and Delta—would present a summary of their activities and results from sampling and management of marine resources.

"What do you think? Before you answer, I have to address Josie. My dear, you will be relieved of your duty as supervisor of Delta Station when the Wolvies finish their tour in next month. They are richer for their experience with you.

"I hope *you* all choose to accept your new assignments and embrace the plans for the RTC. Let me tell you why it is proposed. It's because of you. Yes, you. Over the months and years of our operations from the southeast region of Alaska, the Juneau office has presented to Washington a reporting system second to none; you have been timely, accurate, and clear. You have made recommendations that have been implemented to improve in industrial, citizen, and Native use of our precious national treasures—yes, the Tongass itself. Top management wants you to share your positive experiences with others coming online with the DNR. Congratulations . . . Later, we will determine how long each session should be, and what time of year would be the best. Well, that's about it. What say you, Joe, Josie?"

Silence.

Joe looked at Josie, then at Geez. "Damn, you don't waste time in putting an idea and staff together. I love the idea. I have been out in the woods long enough . . . it's about time to share. Geez, your jokes are corny, but this idea with this staff at this location is brilliant. Josie, what do you think? Is this doable?"

"Honey, I have never been so pleased. I'm finally going to be able to work with the person I love, doing the work I love. I'm blessed."

Bear spoke next. Looking at Leigh, he said, "Peering into your eyes, I see a look of contentment, of happiness and satisfaction, of a woman who wants to embrace this project wholeheartedly. Do I see correctly, my dear?"

"Geez, Bear sees well. I know, by Bear's eyes, he is ready to share his experiences; he, too, has had enough of sleeping overnight in the forest.

"My plans are similar. This opportunity will be the third book of my trilogy, the final chapter of my life. It started beautifully in Ann Arbor, Michigan, with love gained and love lost; then I found and lost love here . . but Bear came to my rescue. Now we can share our lives here with this outstanding assignment to the RTC. I, too, Josie, am blessed."

Wind Spirit spoke last. "Raven and I have been talking while our mentors and parents have given reasons for embracing this project. We're pleased to be considered and proud to be able to serve with the team you've selected. We, too, are ready to share our experiences at the RTC."

Raven spoke. "I have little to say. I am overwhelmed with this chance to serve and be with my partner, friend, lover, and protector. My spirit of the wind— Wind Spirit."

Silence followed.

Each person seemed to be reflecting on the future in a quiet way.

A "croak" echoed across the clearing as a raven circled and perched on one of the twin pines.

Silence.

Geez spoke. "That, my friends, is good medicine. I feel Manitou, has spoken. Thank you for accepting our proposal. I'm looking forward to working with you."

The six started to discuss the many questions they had concerning schedule, subjects, and costs. Geez put a halt to the confusion with a short statement. "Folks, get a good night's sleep. We're all flying to Juneau tomorrow morning. I'll be able to go over all your concerns there. When we're finished, I'll buy dinner. Girls, bring a good dress . . . we're going first class tomorrow night.

"Again, don't worry about details; I'm paid to do that. In fact, I'm good at it. I plan to have a build schedule, subject outline, syllabus for a few key courses, and a cost estimate—all by tomorrow night. It will be done. Remember, that's what I'm paid to do, and I do it pretty well. Leigh, could you lead us in a prayer of thanks in honor of the Great Spirit?"

Of course. Shall we all join hands? Let us give thanks.

> "Greetings, all my relations
> and the Great Spirit.
> Have pity on us, help us
> to walk the straight path
> with our new challenge
> here on earth.
> We thank you
> for your guidance and blessing."

While walking to the hut, the DNR Director had a gratifying chat with his newly enlightened Training Center supervisors and instructors. He had a feeling they would all have a tranquil night's sleep.

Chapter 22

It was another captivating morning in the park as the giant cedars cast their shadow across the clearing.

Leigh's feeling of contentment was richer than ever before as she strolled along the Bitterroot. It was here, right on this spot, right here on this small gravel bar, that she and her dog, Boy, were dropped by air to start her journey, a journey of discovery of who she really was, an introspective look at what she wanted to be. She reflected on her comments to Bear and Geez that the RTC opportunity would indeed be the closing experience in her life's trilogy.

Time had not changed the river's crystal glow as it rushed to the sea. The little plovers still raced along the bank of the river looking for food. Their animation pantomimed Charlie Chaplin's movements:

Step, step, step, tilt head—listen—peck . . . and repeat.

Yes, she was wiser and more experienced as to the ways of the denizens of the forest and mankind who shared it. She had learned a lot; the experience had taught her that when man goes against nature, nature always wins.

Three frolicking wolves preceded her now where her wonderful dog, Boy, once pranced and danced on shore with her, in and out of the cool flow of ice-melt water from the glaciers upstream.

Looking back at the clearing, she thought of those first days assembling the octagon hut with Boy at her side. *Now look at it*, she thought. *It has a nice addition for the lovely couple who are my adopted children.* They also built a small barn, a smoke house, a sweat lodge—all unplanned—they just happened through need. Also, she had cherished an unplanned relationship, a spiritual marriage to a wonderful man, a man with whom she would spend the rest of her life.

She asked herself if their common goals and agreement for future plans in the RTC were an accidental happening or the result of having similar life experiences. They had both loved and lost. They had both stared death in the face—and won. They both lived on the edge, by choice, and had lived life to its fullest because of that decision.

The wolves suddenly ran downstream and disappeared into a small copse at the edge of the river. The howling started. Running, she arrived at the edge; and as expected, Tough, The White, and Jet had treed the neighborhood black bear sow. She was harmless, and the wolves knew it. They were simply showing off their skills and giving Jet a little training session on treeing bruins. They should be ashamed; they knew the difference between the local black bear and a new-comer. Of course, if it were a grizzly, they may chase it; but if it turned to fight, they would not stay unless protected by a hunter with a gun.

Leigh yelled, "Okay, you've proved your point! Come back here, all of you. Come on! Let that old sow go about her business. You've shown her that she's in your special place in the park. Leave her alone and she'll go away. Come on. Tough, get back here."

They soon returned to her side in a reluctant swagger that involved a turn and howl—just to let the sow know one last time who was really in charge of the clearing. Jet, being the youngest, mimicked the older wolves—with just as much saunter in his walk. Finally they continued their peaceful walk along the river.

"There you are," Bear said as he followed her along the river. "I heard the wolves howling. I thought there may be a problem."

Leigh gave him a big hug. With visitors, they had not slept together. She said, "No, just a little show-time for the pack. They're so predictable; they'd do the same if it were a coyote, stray wolf, or cougar from the hills."

"Yep," Bear said, "half the time it relates to their breeding territory."

"Speaking of cougars . . . and breeding, Josie tells me the boys have become seriously involved with the women on the *Ladybird*. What do you think? Is that going to cause a problem?"

Bear answered with a contorted look. "Why? Did one of the women pick an apple from a tree?"

"You're not being serious. This is not about Genesis . . . it's more like Revelation . . . could they get in trouble with their advisor at school in Ann Arbor? With the women in Juneau? They'll be there, in the city, where they live? Don't you think they could get in trouble?"

"Why? Did one of the women take a bite from the apple? Was there a talking serpent in the tree?"

"If you won't get serious, I'll take a bite out of you. I'm just wondering if these older women might take advantage of the boys. They're a good fifteen years older. You know what I mean."

"Dear, if the boys have something they want, and vice versa, they're going to get it. They've been on an island for a month now. I hope they get some pleasure from their relationship.

"Having said that," Bear answered, "just where did you plan to bite me? My stomach? My back? My neck? Let me know so I can bare the flesh. But, please give me a warning; and remember, I bite back."

"Men. I might as well be talking to that tree. You men also have that pack instinct, sticking together and covering up for each other."

"Leigh," Bear replied with a sardonic look, "are the boys and the cougars old enough to be consenting adults if something is going on under the sheets?"

"Yes, but . . ."

"No buts. I've heard they're all single, and the boys will only be in town a couple weeks, and the gals will be back at sea in a few days, Geez tells me. Now, rather than biting me, how 'bout a BNR here in this dry swamp grass before we have to leave? You know, this place is going to get busier when school is in session. Hard telling when a guy will be alone with his gal."

"Poor baby."

"Wait. We haven't been alone for a long time."

"Try three days, you jerk. Of course, a Bare Naked Roll Around sounds great. I'll race you to bare. Wait. Tell the wolves to git!"

Bear got rid of the wolves, won the contest—again took care of business with his amorous lady-of-the-clearing, and was startled by the next sound.

"Leigh," Geez yelled across the clearing. "Bear. Where are you? We're getting ready to leave for Juneau."

Bear gave her one more kiss and said, "Let's go; let's not keep the RTC awaitin' for us. Over here, Bill, we're coming."

*   *   *

The meeting in the executive conference room on the fifth floor of DNR Headquarters went very well. The crew was a little surprised that Bill's boss was a woman. Ms. Wilson was tall, shapely, and pretty. She had a confident air about her in her body language and speech. However, when she talked, her serious demeanor changed to a sensitive woman with a rich sense of humor. She loved to poke fun at Geez. Everyone liked that. She looked like the kind of woman who liked to work hard and play hard, too.

She was more than satisfied with the work the crew had done that morning in suggesting the type of classes to be presented at the RTC. Bill had also put together a sample syllabus for Forestry Management instruction that the other courses would have, too. She liked the format.

Bill's assistant, Carol, had helped them block course-work times; suggested potential teachers, created certificates, and designed fabric patches with DNR identity.

A building schedule with accompanying costs was submitted without comment, along with a planned start date of January third for the first class, to which Wilson agreed.

The prefab building plan for the Instructional Lodge and four yurts would be awarded immediately, as would any other support buildings. All of the buildings were of existing designs used successfully in the National Park Service.

Wilson did ask Geez to add a series of high-school-level classes/seminars for weekend presentation. She also asked Geez to design a few weekend presentations for VIPs and governmental attendees, both from the state and federal level.

*   *   *

Carol finally lay down her pen and looked at Wilson as if to say, Is there any more?

"Geez," Wilson said with a matching smile, "Carol's pondering if there's any more plans for the RTC. Tell her." She beamed with satisfaction.

"We're done," Geez said with a smile on his face. "We're done here, but we've just begun at the clearing. We'll be celebrating in our new buildings on New Year's Eve—I know we can do it. That gives us three months. Can you guys do it? Yes, I know you can. What do you say, Carol?"

She smiled, looked at Wilson, looked at the crew, looked at Geez and said, "Absolutely!"

Wilson said, "Good. This part of the RTC planning meeting is over. I have the pleasure of announcing that we're all going to dinner tonight with a few guests, and Geez is picking up the tab."

Geez said, "I'm bringing my wife; Wilson's bringing her beau; Carol her boyfriend; and the Gospel Boys, who are in town, are bringing their dates from the *Ladybird*. That should please you, Josie."

Wilson added, "If there's nothing else, I'll see you all tonight at seven in the Harbor House lobby; my fellow employees. Did you notice that term, Leigh and Raven Maiden? Yes, you two are now on the DNR payroll, too. Congratulations, new employees, welcome aboard. And you, my friend, Wind Spirit, you are no longer an intern. You are a full-time employee as of today. Welcome."

Silence enveloped the room as Raven Maiden and Leigh's cheeks glistened with tears, and Wind Spirit shook hands with Joe and Bear.

Josie thought, *My boys with dates off the Ladybird. Ohmygod, I hope they know how to, act . . . ohmygod.*

*   *   *

When the crew entered the Harbor House, the boys and their dates were waiting at the bar. After Josie found them and made a few casual comments, she asked Matt to make introductions. Dressed to the nines, the gals from the ship looked stunning. She sensed an air of sexual chemistry radiating between the couples. It was obvious to her; with others, time would tell.

"I'd like to present Wind Song, who is with me. Morning Dove is with Mark. This is Coyote Woman; she's with John. Finally, this is Phoenix Eagleshadow the ship's captain; she's with Red Cloud, the ship's engineer. Desert Flower sends her regrets; the broken wing needs a little bit more tender-loving care. She sends her best wishes to all of you."

While ordering drinks, Josie took a long studious look at the cougars. Wind Song had fixed her hair in a formal-looking bun pulled tightly back with accents of small forget-me-not flowers that complemented her white dress, a Native faux bone necklace, and off-white pumps. Her plunging neckline and thin dress left little to the imagination—a bra was not a part of her ensemble.

Morning Dove wore her hair in a pony tail tied with a blue scarf that matched the color of her empire-style floor-length dress. It had a stunning red waistband with Native symbols in navy blue.

Coyote woman was in a trim print dress, with perfectly coifed blond hair, looking a picture of commanding cool—all svelte and charming. A yellow scarf with Native designs was tied around her waist.

Psyche, short for Phoenix Eagleshadow, looked striking in a classy tan dress with tasteful accessories of red and gold. Her hair was in a single braid that flowed to her waist. Her earrings and bracelets were of Native origin. Her demeanor was that of a leader. She was the captain, the leader, the one the gals respected.

The boys were another story. They looked like they had all gone to the same haberdashery and bought practically the same set of clothes. They wore identical loafers, navy-blue corduroy pants, white button-down-collared shirts, and light brown sports jackets—definitely preppy . . . and expected. Clothes had never been their forte. Josie guessed that, if the truth be told, they had bought everything on sale . . . from last year's stock, no less.

Josie smiled and said to the attractive coterie of women, "You all look very nice; it's a real pleasure to meet you. I'm so glad we could help you and Desert Flower. Give her my regards and wish for a quick recovery. Are my boys behaving?"

Psyche answered, "Very well. We thank the DNR for your assistance. Fortunately, the transfer was all we needed. The boys—or shouldn't we call them the men?—performed very well."

Josie answered, "You're welcome. Yes, they are men. That's obvious, but we gave 'em that 'handle' to separate them from Joe, Bear, and Windy . . . and it stuck."

Psyche laughed. "It's no problem. The boys does have a certain ring to it. Many refer to my ship as being 'manned' by 'gals.' What's in a name? They've proven themselves as men and, more importantly, scientists who may help us by figuring out what's happening to our fisheries along the coast. Yep, they're real men, doing real work, for all of us. I kinda like the Wolvie name, short for Wolverines, they tell me."

"True; I like Wolvie, too. I'm certainly going to miss them when they leave and I go to my new assignment with Joe. You'll hear, in a bit, from Geez, that Joe and I will be the managers of the new Regional Training Center in the park. Nevertheless, I'll still be with them as they finish their last couple weeks at Delta Station."

Psyche said, "I'd sure like to hear more about this series of stations along the coast. Is a visit possible?"

Josie gave a nod, and looked at the entrance. Sure enough the Skagway crowd had just arrived. Rob, Ann, Star, Milt, Janet, and Dave had flown in earlier in the day. The women were also dressed in an electrifying fashion.

After introductions were complete, all twenty-six dined on Alaskan king crab and side dishes that had the state's name incorporated on the menu. Of course, dessert was Baked Alaska. Bear did require a little look of disdain by Leigh as he addressed the young, slim, and comely waitress with "This wine, my dear, is like my first wife: robust and full-bodied . . . she'd make two of you." He drained his glass.

Surprisingly, everyone seemed on the same page with interests or concerns about Alaska's economy, environmental challenges, and the role the DNR played in managing the state's resources—especially fisheries. The *Ladybird* crew was especially interested in the boys' role at Delta Station, so all five of the ship's crew cornered them to determine just how they were measuring the dramatic increases in carbon dioxide concentrations along the shoreline. Their interests were real, since their livelihood depended on healthy fisheries. They were interested in marine health all the way from the Beaufort Sea in the north, through the Bering Strait, and to the Gulf of Alaska to the south. The DNR crowd was surprised to learn that Psyche had fished along the entire Alaskan coast. She asked what remedial actions the DNR would be taking to improve fisheries. She said she did not like the quota system, timed fishing, and sector limits. All those conditions affected her income and caused trouble among competing boats. It got nasty at times during the salmon season.

*   *   *

Geez answered, "I, too, do not like the rules for the salmon harvest, but I'm also convinced it had to be done. That's where the boys, the Wolvies, play a key role. They'll soon determine, with the aid of the other three stations, by sampling and testing, to determine what chemical or food chain problems are affecting our fisheries. It could be too much carbon dioxide, a break in the food chain/feeder fish depletion, or other natural or manmade problems—some yet to be determined. Our office will present our findings from their research in December.

"That, my dear, is in part why we're establishing the RTC. It will provide a forum for you, and others, to present the facts of your work at sea, for some on land, and others in the air. You are one of our resource persons. You are important to us, Psyche. Your whole crew is important to us. We'll have you attend one of our scheduled sessions—soon. I wouldn't be surprised to see you at one of the sessions that the boys present."

"That's cool," Psyche chimed in. "The RTC sounds like a great idea."

Sensing the evening activities had run their course, Geez got their attention. "Folks, all twenty-six of us have had an excellent night of good drinks, good food, and outstanding fraternity. I'm impressed with some of the exchanges that have taken place here tonight. It makes me even more sure that the RTC is just what the doctor ordered to evaluate future directions in habitat, be it wet or dry. We may not have all the answers, but we'll certainly try our best to get 'em—before they get us. I'm impressed with the talent in this room, including our hostess, Ms. Wilson. She has some comments for you."

"Here's the good news. I do not talk as long as Bill. Yet, I have some important things to say.

"I'm saying them on behalf of the governor, who on our recommendation, has agreed to honor one of our group as the keystone, the basis for many of our group's successes. This person has been steadfast when others would have moved on. This person has an open-arms policy to those who need help. No one is cast aside. Ask yourself. Where do folks go, whether Washichu or Native? Where do we congregate? Where? I'll tell you. It's on the edge of a clearing in the middle of Glacier Bay National Park. It's where a woman established herself several years ago. She went there to discover who she is and who she wanted to be—to explore the Alaskan frontier as a way to find herself. She was intended to record her observations in her journal.

"Look what we've done to her." Wilson laughed. "She entered little in her journal. Rather than being alone to reflect on her life . . . she's married—to an Indian, no less. She has adopted two teenagers from the Tlingit Nation. Now that takes guts! Her small little hut has become the focal point for many a meeting or rendezvous for fighting fires, criminal apprehension, or soothing Native unrest. She has touched the hearts of everyone in this room, if not earlier, tonight. She works fast.

"In honor of her contributions to the Park, Native Americans, the state and yes, the federal government, I'm proud to announce the new name of our RTC. As of tonight it will be called the Leigh West Regional Training Center.

"Can you think of a better way to end this beautiful evening? I can't. Thank you all for coming tonight and helping Geez today, and finally, Thank you, Leigh West."

*   *   *

Silence followed as Wilson sat down and looked at the stunned woman across the table.

Bear leaned over and kissed Leigh's damp cheek, whispering, "How 'bout them apples? I told you to put on your best face tonight. See?"

Over the applause, Leigh said, "You jerk. You knew, didn't you?"

"I know nothing. Don't you think you should stand and acknowledge the applause?"

"You know I can't speak in a crowd. What can I say?"

"My dear, you have no option. You must say something."

"You jerk. You knew . . ."

He whispered, "Get off your butt, woman. Talk to them like you talk to me. Like the day I asked to stay with you."

"You jerk. You never asked. You just moved in."

"I did?"

The applause subsided as Leigh stood to address the crowd of twenty-five celebrating denizens from southeast Alaska.

She wiped her cheek with Bear's handkerchief, then leaned over and kissed him on the forehead. She stared at Geez, looked at Wilson with an approving nod, sought and found Raven Maiden and Wind Spirit's eyes, winked and finally spoke.

"My friends, I have little to say and do not have the eloquence of Wilson. It's true, as she has summarized, the reasons for my stay in the park. However, I have been fortunate to have many fine people join me in the pursuit of common goals. What are they? It's no mystery. It's preservation. Preservation of our forest, our waters . . . our planet. It's a rich life in the wilderness with plants, animals, and man. I have been blessed to have found all three. Yes, I have loved and lost, that's true; but as I stand humbly before you tonight I can say that your love has made me whole again. I came to Alaska, viewing the world through dubious eyes; now, I view the world through eyes filled with love. You all have had a part in that change of vision. I thank you and the Great Spirit, Manitou, for my rebirth. I love you all.

"Please hear my favorite poem that I always carry with me. It speaks to my hope of the future for you, for Bear and me, and for the Training Center. I'll read it, bear with me . . . you'll love it as I do. It's by Ardis Whitman.

> "Hope for the moment. There are times when it is hard to be-
> lieve in the future, when we are temporarily just not brave
> enough. When this happens, concentrate on the present. Culti-
> vate *le petit bonheur*, the little happiness, until courage returns.
> Look forward to the beauty of the next moment, the next

hour . . . the likelihood that tonight the stars will shine. Sink roots into the present until the strength grows to think about tomorrow."

*   *   *

It was a clear, cool night with the moon illuminating the clearing and the path of the Bitterroot through the trees. Leigh, Bear, Windy, and Raven sat around the fire in the moon's purple glow. Leigh was just about talked out of her comments on the night's activities, the cougars, the boys, and picking on Bear, as usual. Raven loved to hear her chat about others. She was kind, but also a little devilish. She still thought Bear was a jerk for not warning her of the honor that was coming her way. Then again, she'd learned earlier that a people rarely have any control of the events in their lives—and never will. They just happen.

Fortunately Geez had not been drinking, so he dropped them off with the chopper flight to Gustavus, a small village at the entrance to Glacier Bay. He had a meeting scheduled there with the Tlingit Nation's Eagle Clan in the morning. He was unsure what they wanted, but told Carol he'd be there.

Raven commented, "He is always on the go, isn't he? I hope he likes his job. He's gone from Juneau frequently."

"Yes," Bear answered. "He loves his job. He lives and breathes DNR business, much to the chagrin of his lovely wife, Gay Lynn. For all I know he may be flying back here tomorrow. We've a meeting with Big Tree, the Tlingit Chief of the Raven Clan, about some concern of his. If he doesn't show, I'll cover for Bill. I have a feeling it's about the RTC, or should I say, more correctly, LWRTC." He offered with a big smile. "I think the plans are to meet here, and have you sit in also, Leigh.

"Now, my lady friend, the honored one, don't you think it's time for you to turn in for the night? Come on, you've analyzed the cougars, the boys, and Wilson's beau, and caught them kissing, you say. Maybe he was just whispering in her mouth."

"See, Raven? See how corny his jokes are? He is king of corny. Quit laughing, Raven; you'll encourage him to tell more."

"Disregard her. She does not understand men. You do.

"Come on, you've had a busy night. I'll even carry you to bed."

"Watch your back," Windy warned Bear. "It's not her weight . . . it's her shape!"

"What? What did you say?" Leigh yelled at Windy.

"Believe me, you women do not have any good place to grab—or you think we're getting fresh. Been there, done that. Raven's hit me a couple times—for no reason at all."

Raven spoke quickly. "Liar."

"Windy," Bear said as he started to walk away with Leigh over his shoulder, "you may not recover from this with logic. Give it a rest."

"True . . . but watch your back."

"Bugger. Bear, make him stop."

"Stop what?"

As they all walked toward the hut, Raven said, "I hope Josie and Joe survive the night on the town with the boys and those women, the cougars. Those gals look like they could party all night. I hope the boys know what they're getting into. Do you think they'll go to their own rooms . . . or the boys'? They could certainly afford to pick up the tab after the big check they got from *Ladybird*'s catch."

Windy stared at her and said, "Aren't we being a little too judgmental?"

"Dear, there is no charge for their erotic interests . . . except, maybe, 'Thanks, I needed that.'"

"Hussies."

"M-E-0-W . . . that sounds just a little catty," Windy groaned.

"Read it as you like."

"Sorry, dear, I disagree. I think they were cool, proper, well dressed, and well mannered."

"Well, maybe you ought to get *aboard*, too."

"Naw, I've hooked one of the best already."

"That's nice. Okay, you're right. What the boys do on their own time, in Alaska . . . stays in Alaska. Reel me in."

As the moon maneuvered across the sky, the four two-legged and three four-legged denizens of the clearing moved toward the hut, winding up an exciting evening with the peacefulness of fireside fellowship of kinfolk. It had been a re-warding day for all . . . especially Leigh.

*   *   *

The meetings with the Tlingit Nation's Eagle Clan had always been an enjoy-able experience for Geez. The members had a few complaints about logging reg-ulations, fisheries management, and tourism, but he was surprised when he saw the RTC on their agenda when he arrived in their chambers.

He thought, *How the hell did they know about it? Is this the first conflict in planning for the RTC? I'll soon find out.*

After responding to their questions about the goals and objectives of the RTC, they asked him to return to one particular item, the twenty-mile access trail. It started on the shore of Glacier Bay's western finger and passed through the park due west to the clearing most called Leigh's ranch.

Again, Geez explained that it was planned for those who could not, or would not, fly by chopper to the RTC. It would always remain an unimproved foot path.

Silence followed as each member whispered to each other and to the council's chairman, Wind Walker. He asked, "Mr. Geez, how often do you plan to use this trail through the park property?"

Geez answered as best he could. "Infrequently, but many will arrive by boat from Icy Strait and prefer to hike to the clearing. A four- or five-hour hike, it too satisfies one aspect of the training: forestry, habitat, and topographical instruction. An instructor will meet them and guide them while tutoring to the clearing. The hike is an integral part of the instructional program. Those who fly in will have to take a similar hike to satisfy course needs."

"How many people are in the hiking group?"

"No more than six or seven, including the instructor."

"Would you mind drawing the suggested route on this map?"

"Of course."

With a SWAG—Some Wild-Ass guess—he drew the route. Of course, the ground would prescribe the exact route due to the lay of the land and items the teacher chose to explore along the way. Nevertheless, he gave the map to Wind Walker.

Wind Walker gasped, then passed the map to other members—who also whispered breathlessly.

Geez was puzzled. "May I ask, what is your concern?"

Silence returned to the council.

Finally, after conferring with the others, Wind Walker spoke. "My friend, what I'm about to say must stay with you and no one else. Do I have your agreement?"

"You do. We've known each other for years. I keep my word as you have to me. I have earned your respect, and you mine."

"Agreed. My friend, we are concerned that the traffic over the route you've sketched will disturb our sacred burial mounds. The mounds look innocent enough to the untrained eye, and may not be defiled by your hiker . . . but, your route passes directly over the mounds . . . and by accident, they may be desecrated. Do you understand our concern?"

"I do, and I will promise you this: I will personally propose a trail that does not come anywhere near your sacred mounds. I will carefully mark the trail with signage that ensures that our instructors and their students will be routed around the mounds."

The council discussed his proposal by whispering back and forth to each other and reviewing the map of the area.

Wind Walker spoke. "My friend, thank you. The council has asked that I personally go with you and guide you to the best route to miss the mounds with your foot path. Is that agreeable?"

"It is. I can go with you today. I have trail markers in my chopper. Let's go."

"My, you are an eager one. I've heard so from others. My friend, we will have lunch together and depart this afternoon. Thank you for being so understanding."

"It's my pleasure. Since I'm buying, why don't you bring all your members? I'd like to go to Blackhawk's Brazier if it's still open."

"Indeed, it is."

"Good, let's hit the road."

As Geez left the council room, he thought, *I sure wish old Wind Walker got to the point quicker. I couldn't let on that I already knew where the mounds were; it was smarter in the long run to handle his concerns the way I did. Now, he'll be at my side when the path is marked.*

*   *   *

At the edge of the clearing, Bear and Leigh were walking over the area where Geez said the Instructional Lodge-type building would be built. Hearing a noise, they turned to see a delegation from the Raven Clan ride into the clearing from the east.

"This must be the council that requested a meeting. Why don't you join us, since Geez is not going to make it? I may need your help."

"Sure."

Bear welcomed the riders and gave the chief, Big Tree the traditional native greeting. Left arms interlocked at the wrist, right arm around each other's shoulders, and a whispered personal greeting completed the process.

"Welcome, Big Tree. You are always welcome at our lodge to share a meal and to warm your spirit by the fire."

"Thank you, Chi Mukwa. May I introduce you to the Raven Clan council?"

After introductions, and a move to the benches around the fire pit, Leigh joined the group with refreshments. Introductions followed, for they had heard of the lady of the clearing, Runs with Wolves.

"Chief, it's your meeting—what's up?"

"To the point, the council has embraced the RTC idea in total. However, we have one minor concern. It's the foot path from Glacier Bay, about twenty miles to the clearing. It appears to pass near our sacred burial mounds. Would you please make sure that your path is routed around the mounds? I know you understand. Our brave warriors, chiefs, and fine woman must not be disturbed. That would be bad medicine."

"You're absolutely right. I will make sure their path is marked to avoid the mounds; as you know, I know their location."

"Thank you, my friend. I know it will be done."

Bear thought, *I hope if Geez was also called to address the path's location that is was cleared up as easily as I just did. It may have been harder for Washichu to do so . . . we'll soon see.*

*   *   *

Leigh, feeling the timing was right, said, "My friends, will you join us for a bowl of my famous seafood gumbo? I've just finished making it."

Big Tree answered for the group. "Runs with Wolves, we'd be delighted. Please sit with me and share your plans for the RTC. I can be with Bear any old time, but you are special."

"Hold it, Chief. She's mine," Bear said with a smile.

Leigh added, "Keep it up, Chief. Bear needs to know other men are around."

"True . . . I'm one of them. Seriously, Leigh, would you mind sharing with an elder, an old warrior, a brother of Manitou, and an admirer of beautiful women, your plans for the RTC? Bill has already asked me to make a presentation on North American Indian culture and traditions. He said you'd help—you and Chi Mukwa. I'd rather work with you."

"What a way to start the day. Two men fighting over my attention, and one asking me for help . . . or is it my chowder, Chief?"

"I assure you, it's both," the chief said with a grin.

"I'm so excited. One thing impresses me about this brief beginning: the Natives and the Washichu can work together in harmony, as the French would say, tout à fait."

Sitting with the men, Leigh explained key aspects of the RTC's objectives that involved their skills. It was indeed a blending of various skills, a blending of humanity to address the toxic substances that were making critical inroads into the earth's crust and waters. Her charge was for them to effect change in the attitude of the students, managers, or technicians who would be attending the training sessions.

"I'd like you to impress on them that the earth is fragile and frail. Its forest are the lungs of the planet; they sequester our excessive carbon. What's important is for you and the scientists to tell your students that they are the force. It may be a charming phrase from Jedi wisdom to say, 'May the force be with you,' but remember, you are the force. We all are the force, the force to protect our environment for us and especially our children."

She got off her soap box with one last comment. "John Muir, co-founder of the Sierra Club in the early 1900s, said, 'Any fool can destroy trees. They can't run away.'"

Leigh looked around the fire at the men to see if she had their attention, their interest in conservation, their strength to be the force. With one look she was satisfied they did. She was an expert on men's needs and wishes. The men embraced a change in the way they would look at their environment.

"I trust you understand," Leigh said, "that I will be here to help you and your people, Big Tree. Certain 'uniformed people' may call me a tree hugger because I'm so intense on saving this forest and this planet. If so, I'm flattered. I want to spend the rest of my life protecting the plants and animals that live on the land or in the water of this beautiful earth. I'm going to do my part, at least in the state I love, Alaska. Care to join me?"

In a surprising move, Leigh gave each of the Tlingit men a hug and thanked them for their attention.

"I've used great writers lately to express ideas that I cannot. Bear with me as I read a saying from one of my favorite 16th-century French authors, Montaigne, whose work has dramatically affected my life.

> "And if you have lived a day, you have seen everything. One
> day is equal to all days, there is no other light, no other night.
> This sun, this moon, these stars, the way they are arranged, all
> is the same your ancestors enjoyed, and that will entertain your
> grandchildren."

"Gentlemen, have a good day. Take care of my man, Chi Mukwa. He is the foundation from where I stand firm in spirit. I'm going to join the other love of my life, my children, Wind Spirit and Raven Maiden, who will be continuing the work for their generation."

As she walked to the river to be with them . . . the new generation of Tlingits, she heard the pulsating pattern of drums as a white owl flew silently by and perched above. As Manitou had said, she was in The Place We Go To Listen—to listen to the songs of the earth, where the spirits show their pleasure with man's fulfillment.

Feeling His presence, she knelt to thank The Great Spirit, Manitou, for the privilege of serving Him in His Kin(g)dom.

Tears of happiness flooded her eyes.

Epilogue

The instructional lodge and housing yurts were built in time for a New Year's celebration and dedication.

All the coastal stations attended, along with many people from headquarters in Juneau. Special guests included personnel from Ford Flight Service (FFS) and Sitka Field. Several Indians attended, including Chief Golden Bear, Chief Wind Walker, Chief Big Tree, and the Holy Man Wind In Hair.

Of special importance, the first class of DNR employees attended. They would be the primal class, the starting point of a rich future in learning the latest techniques in managing the environment.

Over time, scores of DNR new hires and existing employees cycled through the Leigh West Regional Training Center, LWRTC, as the team that Geez assembled shared their knowledge and experiences learned in Alaska's mysterious wilderness.

Josie and Joe had a nice apartment in the lodge; Leigh, Bear, Windy, and Raven remained in the geometric twelve-sided hut. At the New Year's celebration, Geez gave Leigh a certificate of ownership to the land around the hut with riparian rights to the river.

Leigh felt blessed in helping to raise her granddaughter, Evening Star, whose parents Windy and Raven were frequently in the field with workshop/seminar attendees.

Bear had earned his helicopter license, built a landing pad on the edge of the clearing, and frequently flew missions of transport to and from the RTC and on assignments in the bush.

Joe, Windy, and Bear still answered the need for emergency field assignments directed by Geez in Juneau. As the population increased, along with fishing and hunting pressure, they answered many calls to resolve disputes among greedy people.

Given the informal title of Queen of the Training Center, Leigh acted as a goodwill ambassador for the DNR for visiting VIPs.

Her legacy spread across the Tongass and continued over the years as she moved on to another life with her wolves. When Leigh, Bear, Joe, and Josie all passed, Wind Spirit and Raven Maiden, and their daughter Evening Star, took their place as the guardians of the environmental movement.

Leigh's last words charged the next generation to pass on to their children what they had done in their behalf, and to seek the courage to fight the good fight to save our planet earth:

"The present generation is in your hands. I know you will not fail, as we did not fail you."

The Fresh Ink Group

Publishing
Memberships
Share & Read Free Stories, Essays, Articles
Free-Story Newsletter
Writing Contests

Books
E-books
Amazon Bookstore

Authors
Editors
Artists
Professionals
Publishing Services
Publisher Resources

Members' Websites
Members' Blogs
Social Media

www.FreshInkGroup.com

Email: info@FreshInkGroup.com

Twitter: @FreshInkGroup

Google+: Fresh Ink Group

Facebook.com/FreshInkGroup

LinkedIn: Fresh Ink Group

About.me/FreshInkGroup

COURAGEOUS LADY:

A Woman's Alaskan Quest for Native American Spirituality

By Mark Allen North

In the first novel of *The Lady Trilogy*, auburn-haired Leigh West travels to Alaska's majestic and mysterious Tongass National Forest in search of self-discovery and harmony with nature. In her journal, she chronicles all she learns from native Tlingit tribesmen and nature: the cunning wolves, belligerent brown bears, and those transforming seasons of the region's glorious landscape. It is through Native American spirituality that she sparks new passion within herself, a new appreciation for the physical world, and a life filled with love.

www.FreshInkGroup.com
ISBN: 978-1-936442-12-6

INTREPID LADY:

A Woman's Alaskan Quest for

Native American Spirituality

By Mark Allen North

In the second novel of *The Lady Trilogy*, auburn-haired Leigh West continues her adventures in Alaska's majestic and mysterious Tongass National Forest in search of self-discovery and harmony with nature. In her journal, she chronicles becoming the Spiritual wife of Chi Mukwa (Big Bear) and guardian of two Tlingit teens. It is through Native American spirituality that she sparks new passion within herself, a new appreciation for others, and a life filled with love.

www.FreshInkGroup.com
ISBN: 978-1-936442-13-3

PAPALA SKIES

By Stephen Geez

Chicago native Rochelle DuFortier likes to imagine the future, her world a series of picture postcards so vivid they sometimes seem real. When a foolish mistake at thirteen causes her mother's death, she's sent to a secluded Hawaiian valley, an outsider "haole-girl" among pidgin-speaking boys who hurl flaming papala spears under the full moon to summon her mother's spirit. After boarding school and a prestigious university back east, the ambitious young woman is torn between chasing new career opportunities, discovering her mother's heritage in a remote French village, and meeting obligations pulling her back to Hawaii.

On this island steeped in ancient mythology and modern superstition, Rochelle tests the possibility of sharing pieces of her life with those whose beliefs she barely understands and never intends to embrace. She dives the depths of a pristine coral lagoon, conceals bodies in a subterranean lava tube, and challenges the eruptions of a living volcano, even as she deciphers the truth about her mother's death and struggles to satisfy new debts born of old betrayals.

Papala Skies is the story of a young woman who makes all the right choices, only to find herself living an unexpected life. It is about the need to belong, and seeking one's own version of truth amid such differing cultures' responses to wrenching loss and abiding grief. It is about yearning for a sense of place, yet having to confront new ways to honor the love of family and friends.

Will Rochelle lose what matters most, or might she learn what the smart octopus already knows?

www.FreshInkGroup.com

ISBN: 978-1-936442-07-2

JAZZ BABY

By Beem Weeks

While all Mississippi bakes in the scorching summer of 1925, a sudden orphanhood casts its icy shadow across Emily Ann Teegarten, a pretty young teen.

Taken in by an aunt bent on ridding herself of this unexpected burden, "Baby" Teegarten plots her escape using the only means at her disposal: a voice that makes church ladies cry and angels take notice. "I'm gonna sing jazz up to New York City," she brags to anybody who'll listen. 'Cept that Big Apple—well, it's an awful long way from that dry patch of earth she used to call home.

So when the smoky stages of New Orleans speakeasies give a whistle, offering all kinda shortcuts, Emily soon learns it's the whorehouses and drug joints promising to tickle more than just a young girl's fancy that can dim a spotlight . . . and knowing the wrong people can snuff it out.

Jazz Baby just wants to sing—not fight to stay alive.

www.FreshInkGroup.com
ISBN: 978-1-936442-10-2

BEEN THERE, NOTED THAT:

Essays In Tribute To Life

Observations, Inspiration, Remembrance, & Noteworthies To Share

By Stephen Geez

The simple lives of everyday people in a mundane world prove extraordinary in this collection of 54 personal-experience essays by novelist Stephen Geez. The eclectic mix of memoir, commentary, humor, and appreciation covers a wide range of topics, each beautifully illustrated by artists and photographers from the Fresh Ink Group. Geez catches what many of us miss, then considers how we might all share the most poignant of lessons. *Been There, Noted That* aims to reveal who we are, examine where we've been, and discover what we dare strive to become.

www.FreshInkGroup.com
ISBN: 978-1-936442-05-8

www.ingramcontent.com/pod-product-compliance
Lightning Source LLC
Chambersburg PA
CBHW020110180626
46812CB00006B/2554